First there was dust, rising in a swirling curtain around them. Kormak approached, his hulking figure a dark shadow in the sandy mist. He hurled something toward them—a knife? a bomb? it was too dark to tell—but the object was caught in the unnatural wind. The force churned up the earth, gouging out rocks, scrub plants, and hunks of the desert floor and adding them to the expanding maelstrom. The noise became monstrous: Jaya was shouting, and Skiver was shouting back, but Alaeron just crouched over his relic in the small circle of safety, watching as Kormak's feet left the ground and he, too, began to spin.

The ring of destructive force got wider and wider as the Kellid tumbled end over end around them. Kormak was not giving in to the wind: he was trying to *swim* in the vortex, doing his best to claw his way toward Alaeron and the others. But even his ferocious dedication couldn't overcome the power of the artifact. He rose up in the wall of dust, which was now at least twenty feet high.

Skiver and Jaya were both shouting in Alaeron's ear now, but he was watching, trying to time his moment to stop the artifact and send Kormak flying—ideally back to the east, or at any rate *not* to the west, where they'd have to step over his broken body on their journey later. But the Kellid was now just one dark shape among many, spinning by faster than the eye could follow.

Jaya grabbed him by the shoulders and shook him, and Skiver screamed in his ear: "The obelisks! The elementals!"

Alaeron froze, remembering the view through Ernst's spyglass: a thousand lights, each a bound elemental, held in place by the sigils inscribed on weathered obelisks. And he was sending an expanding circle of destructive force toward those artifacts . . .

# The Pathfinder Tales Library

*Winter Witch* by Elaine Cunningham
*Prince of Wolves* by Dave Gross
*Master of Devils* by Dave Gross
*Plague of Shadows* by Howard Andrew Jones
*The Worldwound Gambit* by Robin D. Laws
*Song of the Serpent* by Hugh Matthews
*Nightglass* by Liane Merciel
*City of the Fallen Sky* by Tim Pratt
*Death's Heretic* by James L. Sutter

# City of the Fallen Sky

## Tim Pratt

paizo

Cover art by J. P. Targete.
Cover design by Andrew Vallas.
Map by Robert Lazzaretti.

Paizo Publishing, LLC
7120 185th Ave NE, Ste 120
Redmond, WA 98052
paizo.com

ISBN 978-1-60125-418-4 (mass market paperback)
ISBN 978-1-60125-419-1 (ebook)

Publisher's Cataloging-In-Publication Data
(Prepared by The Donohue Group, Inc.)

Pratt, Tim, 1976-
  City of the Fallen Sky / Tim Pratt.

    p. ; cm. -- (Pathfinder tales)

  Set in the world of the role-playing game, Pathfinder.
  Issued also as an ebook.
  ISBN: 978-1-60125-418-4 (mass market paperback)

    1. Alchemists--Fiction. 2. Good and evil--Fiction. 3. Imaginary places--Fiction. 4. Fantasy fiction. 5. Adventure fiction. I. Title. II. Title: Pathfinder adventure path. III. Series: Pathfinder tales library.

PS3616.R385 C58 2012
813/.6

First printing April 2012.

Printed in the United States of America.

For Ginger, who never stops fighting for me.

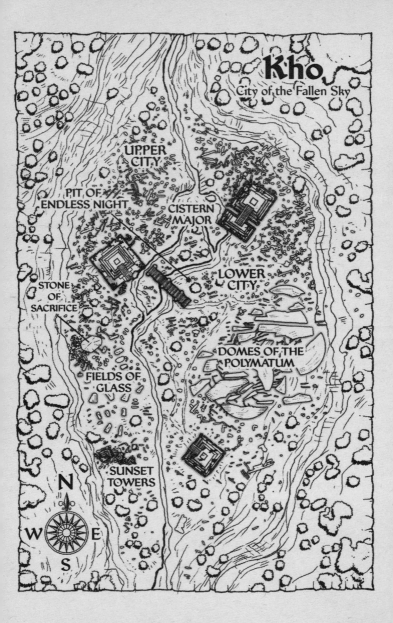

# Chapter One
## No Good Deed Goes Unpunished

No one who knew Alaeron—alchemist, arcanist, artificer—would call him a coward. He was never one to let the possibility of explosion, corrosion, or permanent nerve damage stop him from mixing together exotic chemicals just to see what might happen. He never missed the chance to crawl into the booby-trapped ruins of fallen civilizations in the hope of discovering some fragment of forgotten wisdom. He'd even been known to sneak into the well-guarded libraries of wealthy idiots to steal precious texts from the less deserving. When it came to seeking knowledge without pausing to calculate the cost, Alaeron was one of the most courageous souls north of the Inner Sea.

But his courage was not the sort that leapt at the opportunity to start a fight with a couple of well-armed thugs, and so he hesitated at the mouth of a certain alleyway located between a weaponsmith's shop and his own modest laboratory in an unfashionable section of Almas, capital city of Andoran. He'd intended to use the alley as a shortcut home, and thus avoid walking past the tannery, because the stink of rendered animals tended to overwhelm his sensitive nose—and, in his lab, the sense of smell was sometimes all that stood between him and accidentally poisoning himself and half the neighborhood.

Today, alas, the narrow pathway was occupied by two men of a curiously disreputable sort: dressed well enough to pass for clerks, but with scarred faces that suggested rougher work. They were engaged in such work as Alaeron stepped into the alley. One, who wore a mangy fur cap despite the day's warmth, had a woman pressed against the wall, an unnecessarily long knife pressed to her throat. The other, whose tattered left ear lent him some resemblance to a violent tomcat, slapped a cudgel against his open palm.

The part of Alaeron that had survived by his wits in hostile territory was tempted to just step back out of the alleyway again and take the long way home, stink of rendered animal fat and all. But he'd seen too much casual cruelty visited on the weak in recent months, usually when he could do nothing to help. In this case, he could easily intervene.

Unfortunately, his hesitation made things difficult. If he'd walked away, there'd have been no harm done—to him, anyway. And if he'd launched himself into the alley without a moment's thought, pulling a few of the prepared vials he always kept on his person from his coat and tossing them at the attackers, he might have neutralized them before they even realized he was there. But his hesitation made things complicated, because Tattered-ear caught a glimpse of him and turned around. His eyes were the yellow of an alcoholic who'd nearly used up his liver—Alaeron's father had a similar piss-colored gaze, near the end—and his lips were as shredded as his ear, as if they'd been sewn up once, and the stitches torn out by hand.

"Move along," he growled, gesturing with his club.

Alaeron sighed. "No."

The man cocked his head, eyes widening in surprise, and then a sly smile crept across his face. "You hear that?" he called over his shoulder to his compatriot with the furry hat. "He says 'no.'"

The other thug just grunted, not taking his eyes off the woman. Who could blame him? She was something to see: great masses of black hair, eyes dark and deep, skin the dark brown of the glass bottles Alaeron used to store silver sulfide—she must hail from the south, somewhere in Garund. What brought her to Almas, and more particularly to this alley, with these men? Alaeron's curiosity was the source of all his troubles—but then, it was also the source of all his delights, and now he wanted to know her story.

Only one way to find out: save her, then ask.

"Are these men bothering you, miss?" Alaeron called.

"Fool," she said. "Run away!"

"See?" Tattered-ear said. "We're all in agreement. Now, do you want to leave this alley right now on your own two feet, or in an hour or so in a corpse wagon?"

"Have you ever been to Numeria?" Alaeron said.

Tattered-ear scowled. "What? What are you talking about?"

"Noo-mare-ee-uh." Alaeron enunciated each syllable clearly, gesturing widely with his right hand while his left slipped into one of his coat's innumerable pockets. "Far to the north. A harsh land, where the dread Black Sovereign rules from his decadent throne. Where the dark arcanists known as the Technic League pick over the ruins of ancient fallen stars for anything they can use to terrorize, or cozen, or otherwise profit by."

"Cozen?" the man said, bewildered. The woman and the man with the knife were both staring at

Alaeron. He recognized the look. They thought he was a madman. Ah, well. Genius is so seldom understood in its own time.

"I have been there," Alaeron said. "I have searched the ruins, cracking the seals on chambers no man of this world has ever entered before, and do you know what I found there? Besides strangely glowing fungi and a lot of broken glass and corrosive pink slime, that is?" He drew his left hand from his pocket. "I found . . . this!"

Tattered-ear stepped back, raising his club defensively, then lowered it. "What's that, then?" he said.

"I honestly have no idea." Alaeron gazed at the metal object in his hand. It was the size of a hen's egg, a dull non-reflective sort of silver in color, etched with dark blue lines in a seemingly random zig-zag pattern. There was a depression at the top—or the bottom, or on one side, who could say?—just big enough for him to slip the tip of his index finger into. "I wish I knew what it was," Alaeron continued. "But I know what it *does*. It does . . . this."

He pressed his fingertip into the divot. The object grew warm in his hand. The light in the alley took on a subtle, blue tinge, and the man with the torn ear gaped at him, unmoving. His fellow thug was also frozen, as was the woman he menaced—and everything else.

Well, everything else in the vicinity. Alaeron wasn't sure how far the relic's field of slowed time extended—it seemed to move with him, so he'd never found the edge—but it couldn't possibly extend to the whole world, or even the whole city. It extended far enough, though.

Alaeron slipped the relic back into his pocket, reached out, and plucked the club from the man's hand, placing it behind a broken crate, out of sight. He took the other man's knife, jammed the blade into a crack in the stone wall on one side of the alley, and leaned all his weight into the hilt, grunting, until the blade snapped off.

He was counting in his head all the while—"one hundred twenty, one hundred nineteen, one hundred eighteen," and so on—and he judged that he had time to kneel and bind the ankles of the thugs with a couple of lengths of twine. He always had various things in his many pockets. Twine was among the least dangerous. He found the remnants of some torn sacks among the refuse on the ground and used more twine to bind them around the thugs as makeshift blindfolds. That should slow them down. Of course, he *could* be using this time to flee and put distance between himself and the dangerous men, instead of devising small obstacles and humiliations . . . but this was more fun.

At the last moment he thought to check their coats for money—after all, reagents weren't free. While he was all right financially for the moment, that wouldn't last forever. Alas, neither man had more than a few copper coins. Alaeron took them anyway.

By the time he took the woman's hand and placed it against the still-warm relic, his mental count had gotten to "thirty," so when she stumbled forward a step, gaping, pulled into his own accelerated timestream, he didn't take time to explain, just grabbed her elbow and propelled her out of the alley and along the next street, where various citizens stood frozen in mid-stride, -argument, -barter, -banter, or -flirtation.

"You're a wizard?" she said, and her accent was disappointingly non-exotic. Her ancestors clearly hailed from distant lands, perhaps even the depths of the Mwangi Expanse, but she sounded like any other woman Alaeron might encounter here in Andoran.

She was rather more pleasant to look upon than usual, though.

"Not a wizard, no, no," he said. "Just a tinkerer, that's all. Though I didn't make this device. I found it, and I'm trying to understand its purpose."

"Seems obvious," she said, nodding toward the frozen people, the bluish air, the whole frozen world.

"No, I don't think so. I believe the slowing of time is just a side effect, not what the relic is *meant* for." She frowned, and, as always, Alaeron attempted to fill the silence with something he found fascinating, without giving much thought to whether others would agree with that opinion.

"It's impossible to *know*, of course, but I think . . . well, look at it this way: Say you'd never seen a tea kettle before. You see one sitting on a stove, and it suddenly begins venting steam and emitting a piercing whistle. You'd have no idea *what* the point of the shrieking thing was—an alarm system? Some sort of terrible local musical instrument? An inefficient method for steaming vegetables? It would almost certainly never occur to you to pour the boiling liquid inside over some leaves, wait a bit, and then drink the resulting concoction. So it is with many relics—we can observe what they do, but we can't always tell *why* they do it, or why anyone would want them to do such a thing in the first place."

By the time he finished his little speech, normal time had caught up with them, and if anyone found the sudden appearance of a pale man and a dark woman striding along at a good clip peculiar, no one let on. Almas was a tolerant city. If people wanted to go appearing out of nowhere, that was their business, as long as they didn't bother anyone.

"We'd better get off the street," he murmured. "Care to come into my workshop?"

She glanced around, then nodded. "Yes, is it—"

"Just here." He steered her toward a low stone building, fitting his key into a lock of his own devising, twisting it once right, then once left, then once right again, then counting very slowly to five—better safe than asphyxiated by a gas trap—before turning the knob and easing the door open. He gestured, and the woman slipped inside. Alaeron came after her, taking a moment to rearm the trap above the door, and turning to smile at his guest.

The smile was wasted on her. She was staring at Alaeron's lab. He tried to see it as a stranger would, but immediately gave up. Everything was too well-known to him—every beaker, every retort, every length of tubing, every rack of neatly stoppered vials, tops daubed with colored wax so he could tell which was which at a glance. Alaeron lifted a pile of books from a bench and gestured for her to sit, then bustled around one of the worktables. "Something to drink, ah . . . what's your name?" he asked.

"Jaya." She looked around at the potions and philtres and tinctures and shook her head slowly. "As for the drink, no, thank you." She paused. "But I *should* thank you for trying to help me back there."

"I'm Alaeron. And just *trying* to help? I'd say I succeeded, wouldn't you?" He poured the last of his wine into a leather-wrapped cup and took a sip. Thin stuff, and sour, but better than water.

She sighed. "Those men weren't muggers. They work for someone who believes I owe him money. He'll simply send more people after me."

"Ah," Alaeron said. "Moneylenders of the less reputable variety. I may have need of such a man myself, but I don't suppose I'll ask you for a recommendation. Their methods of collection seem a bit harsh." Andoran was famed for the honesty of its banks—bankers who charged excessive interest could be charged with extortion and exiled—but despite the famously liberal policies of the legitimate financial institutions, there were still a few men willing to loan money to people the banks couldn't—or wouldn't—deal with: new immigrants without means, criminals trying to finance their endeavors, desperate gamblers with a history of defaulting on loans, and the like. He wondered which Jaya was. Perhaps all three.

Jaya looked down at her hands. "I'm afraid I've made trouble for you. If my, ah, business associate finds out who you are, he might send someone to teach you not to interfere with his dealings."

Alaeron waved that away. "I've been pursued by scarier men, believe me. If your situation has reached the point where people with knives are attacking you in alleys, perhaps you should consider leaving town? I've bought you enough time for that, anyway. I just advise you not to go north. At least, not too far." He shuddered.

"Were you serious, about Numeria? I've never known anyone who came from there, but of course I've heard the stories. So outlandish . . ."

"Outlandish? Perhaps, but Numeria *is* the outlands, or near enough. Home to a thousand impossible things. I'm not *from* there—I'm a child of Andoran, actually—but I spent some time there not long ago, pursuing my studies."

"What studies are those?"

She seemed genuinely interested—rare, in Alaeron's experience, so perhaps she was just being polite because he'd saved her from being killed or at least cut up a bit by way of motivating her to pay her debts. He wasn't one to pass up a sympathetic audience, but the true details of his time in Numeria were complex, just this side of unbelievable, and painful to recollect, so he simply smiled widely and said, "Oh, this and that. Alchemy, mainly. Relics. Really any knowledge that's been forgotten, or has yet to be discovered. The study of why things are the way they are, and how they might be changed."

She frowned, and he supposed such abstractions must sound ridiculous to a woman dealing with practical issues like needing money and trying to keep angry men from killing her. But in his experience, such lofty abstractions were the only things worth living for. Wasn't the history of Andoran founded on men willing to kill and die for abstract principles like freedom and equality and opportunity? He'd grown up believing anything was possible, and he still believed that—though in recent years he'd come to realize that meant all sorts of truly terrible things were possible, too.

"I should go." She rose, then took his hand, her grip firm and warm, dark eyes gazing directly into his. "Thank you again. If I'm ever in a position to do you a good turn, I will. Though I may take your advice about leaving the city, at least for a while."

"The world is full of interesting things," he said. "Travel broadens the mind." He was babbling—a woman hadn't touched him in a long time—and he forced himself to stop talking. "Good luck, Jaya."

"And to you." She leaned in and kissed his cheek, then hurried to the door, opening it a crack—it was safe to open from the inside—to survey the street beyond before slipping out and away.

"Mmm," Alaeron said, then shook his head sharply. Women were lovely, but even the most dangerous relics were more predictable. He sat down at his work table, adjusted the lenses and mirrors that focused a beam of concentrated light on the work surface, and placed the oblong relic—he thought of it as the "time egg" and hated himself for the imprecision of the term—in the circle of brightness.

A number of new lines had appeared on its surface, thin as hairs and faintly blue. New markings appeared every time he used the egg, and he had no idea what that *meant*—was he using up charges? Were they cracks, and if so, merely cracks in the surface of the relic, or cracks in time itself? Was the time-slowing even relevant, or was it just a side effect, a sort of endochronic reaction unrelated to its true purpose? He'd used it often when he first discovered its powers—there were never enough hours in the day, after all, and the egg gave him more— but he resolved to use it only in emergencies from now on. He'd hate to use it up or have it crack into pieces before he'd figured out its true purpose.

As he sketched out the new lines on a blank sheet of parchment, looking for patterns, he fell into the work, and the hours flew by, as they always did when he was deep into his studies: time flowing like water around him, without the necessity of magic at all.

# Chapter Two
## The Runaway Apprentice

Alaeron took most of his meals at home—smoked river fish and apples could be stored in a dry cool place indefinitely—but he was relatively rich off the proceeds from selling the last of the skymetal he'd smuggled out of Starfall, so the night after he saved Jaya he decided to splurge. Of course, by his standards, a meal of luxurious excess involved little more than stopping by the common room of the Golden Eagle tavern, taking one of the small tables in a corner of the room, and calling for ale and bread and lamb.

One of the most wonderful things about Andoran's capital city was the wild mix of cultures and classes there. The nation was founded on tolerance and equality, where no one was a slave—the polar opposite of Numeria, where essentially *everyone* was a slave, and could be murdered or tormented at the whim of its rulers.

The Golden Eagle was one of the city's most famous taverns, its owner the proud descendant of one of the patriots who'd plotted the People's Revolt. The tavern was popular among radicals, merchants, soldiers, and citizen representatives, and its proximity to the docks and the size of its vast stone-and-timber common room made it attractive to passing trade as well. At all hours of the day and night it bustled with variety, the noise of shouted conversations in half a dozen languages vying against drunken songs, the scents of cooking food and spilled alcohol and fragrant smoke filling the air, and all sorts of people from all sorts of cultures making deals or making merry.

Almas, where everything was tolerated except intolerance, and where men were free to be anything they liked, except slaves or slaveholders.

Glancing around as he tucked into his tender cut of lamb, Alaeron saw a uniformed Eagle Knight arguing with a man in scholar's robes; a dwarf with a braided beard draining a tankard the size of his own head; an elf chatting with a sullen-looking man who had an obvious touch of orc blood; a fat merchant with a golden necklace bellowing for more wine; a ghost-pale Chelaxian playing a game involving a checkered board and small stones against a smirking Taldan; an Ulfen sailor with long, luxurious yellow hair and silver rings on every finger; a hulking Kellid in the doorway . . .

Alaeron swallowed hard. Kellids were rare even in a place as aggressively multicultural as this, and most people wouldn't even recognize this man as a member of that ostensibly barbaric race of savage northmen. Kellids by and large were lean, hard folk, not tall and broad like this one, and as portrayed on stage Kellids usually wore rough furs and leathers, while this one was dressed in a long black coat and quite fine boots, and even wore small round-rimmed spectacles.

But his scarred face, and long dark hair, and hard black eyes, and the way he carried himself through the doorway—graceful, but a grace in service of potential violence—revealed his nature unmistakably to Alaeron.

The alchemist had spent a year among such people in Numeria, and his gut ached like he'd swallowed a stone. Had he seen *this* man, in particular, in the capital of Starfall? Perhaps during the one banquet where Alaeron had met the addled and vicious Black Sovereign himself? Had this brute been among the Kellid bodyguards arrayed throughout the hall, perhaps?

Surely not. Almas was a large city, and there must be many Kellids in the area, families who'd been here for *generations*. Alaeron was just being paranoid, and while paranoia had been the only sensible survival strategy while working for the Technic League, it was hardly necessary here, back home—

The Kellid looked directly at Alaeron, bared his teeth in something that was not quite a smile, and picked his way through the crowded common room. Alaeron considered running away, but it was possible he was still mistaken. Alaeron's table had another chair, and the room was quite crowded, so perhaps the man just wanted to share the space.

The Kellid lowered himself into the chair across from Alaeron, his clothes making a curious clanking sound— like metal clicking and clattering against metal—as if he had a jumble of silverware in his pockets. "Hello," he said, nodding seriously, and Alaeron made a noncommittal "Mmm" sound and took another bite of spiced lamb.

"My name is Kormak," the Kellid said. "I believe we have some mutual friends." He chuckled, though it was rather grating and harsh for a laugh. "Well. My *employers*, really, and your enemies, but we might as well say friends."

"I think you are mistaken," Alaeron said, as apologetically as possible. "I don't believe we've met before."

"We weren't introduced." Kormak crossed one leg over the other and picked at a piece of lint on his knee. "But I saw you, at a certain dinner party for a certain king. I remembered you, because you were new, and I wondered if you might be trouble. Turns out you were, though not in the way I'd imagined. Anyway, Alaeron, I recognize you, so no use pretending you're anything but a runaway apprentice to the League, and a scheming thief besides. I've been sent to retrieve you—ideally alive—though more importantly to retrieve the things you stole from the Silver Mount."

"I was more a consultant than an apprentice," Alaeron muttered, thinking furiously. There had to be a way out of this.

"Here's what we'll do. We'll leave quietly, pick up the devices you stole from wherever you've hidden them, and then take the long journey up the Sellen River back to Starfall, where you'll face whatever justice the League sees fit to dispense."

Alaeron snorted. "Justice? They'll kill me. If I'm *lucky*. More likely they'll experiment on me. You can't expect me to go quietly."

Kormak shifted in his chair, making that clanking sound again. This time the noise struck Alaeron as significantly more ominous. "The League wasn't entirely sure what the relics you stole could do, so they sent me with a few of their favorite devices, just to make *sure* you'd be outmatched. You really don't want to see what I've got hidden inside this coat, boy. Some of these artifacts do such terrible things, even *I* don't like carrying them."

Probably true, Alaeron thought, but he doubted Kormak would actually unleash any weapons of the

Technic League here, in a crowded tavern, in the middle of a city. The members of the League were obsessively secretive, guarding their discoveries even from one another, and they wouldn't want their agent calling attention to himself. Alaeron wished he hadn't used the time egg yesterday—it would be days before it was sufficiently rested or recharged to work again, and he'd left it secreted away with the other relics he'd stolen from the Silver Mount in the meantime. The others were too dangerous or unpredictable to carry in his day-to-day business. He was armed with a few vials, of course, as always, but splashing acid or tossing bombs around wouldn't help this situation—at best it would bring guardsmen, and at worst, it might prompt Kormak to make good on his threats to unleash the esoteric technologies of the Technic League. "I don't have the relics anymore," Alaeron said. "I sold them. Surely you know the wealthiest Andorens are fanatics when it comes to relics from distant lands."

Kormak sighed. "Must we do this? If you'd sold those relics, you'd be rich enough to live in a mansion, not your father's dusty old workshop, and you'd be eating somewhere finer than *this*, and dressed rather better, too, I'd imagine. You still have them. And you will give them to me."

Kormak leaned forward, putting his elbows on the table, and resting his chin in his hands in a surprisingly disarming and boyish way. Boyish except for all the scars and his oft-broken nose, anyway. "All right. I've had a long journey, and I don't relish the prospect of a fight, even against someone as obviously easy to crush as *you*. I want to get back to court, where when I'm not standing against a wall watching for assassins I can relax with women and wine and other pleasures. I've no great love for the Technic League. I served the Black Sovereign when he was still known only as Kevoth-Kul, when he sought to ally the warring tribes into one great empire. I don't like the influence those twisted little men in the League have over him. So let me make you a proposal: give me the relics you stole, and I'll return to the League with those, and tell them you died while I was torturing you for information. All right?" He lowered his hands and leaned closer, his face inches from Alaeron's own. "The alternative, of course, is to *actually* die while I'm torturing you for information."

Alaeron chewed his lower lip. He didn't believe Kormak—perhaps he'd been one of the Black Sovereign's bosom companions before the warlord became a drug-addicted puppet of the Technic League, and perhaps not. But there was no way the League would have given weapons of power to someone who was not entirely in their control.

But even if Kormak had been sincere in his offer, it wouldn't matter. Alaeron had endured unspeakable hardships to win that handful of relics from a certain unexplored chamber in the Silver Mount, and he'd barely begun to uncover their secrets. If he simply gave them up now, he'd never be able to live with himself. Alaeron was more likely to drink acid or take a bath in quicksilver than to let such secrets slip from his grasp without doing everything in his power to retain them.

So he rose suddenly to his feet, knocking his chair over in the process, and pointed an accusing finger at Kormak. He shouted, loud enough to overwhelm the other conversations in the tavern: "You dare say such things *here*, in Andoran, the cradle of freedom?"

Kormak narrowed his eyes and slid one hand inside his coat, and Alaeron shouted even louder. "How can you pledge fealty to the Black Sovereign, you Kellid dog? Are you a spy sent down the Sellen to measure this city for barbarian conquest?"

"Here now, what's this?" The owner, a man Alaeron had known since he was a boy, came from behind the bar, slapping a length of wood sheathed in iron against his palm. "I want no trouble here—"

"This man offered to sell me a slave." Alaeron was no longer shouting—but in the sudden silence of the tavern, he didn't need to. "A 'Numerian wench,' he said, trained in the brothels of the savage capital of Starfall to give pleasure. He said I could buy her and pretend she was my *daughter*." Alaeron spat, but not on the floor: he spat down on the top of Kormak's head. Perhaps that was excessive, he thought, as the Kellid rose slowly to his feet, like an avalanche in reverse.

"You little—" he began, but the owner growled low and shouted, "Slaver! Out of my tavern, you scum, before I set the guards on you!"

"Step aside," Kormak rumbled

But now the Eagle Knight Alaeron had spotted earlier stepped forward, blue and white regalia spotless, golden epaulets gleaming, with a hand on his sword. "A loyal son of Andoran has made serious charges against you, stranger," he said. "You will come with me and answer them." The Eagle Knights were devoted to upholding the ideals of Andoren culture, especially the self-evident truth that slavery was an unmitigated evil, and they were revered with good reason in the nation as a whole and the capital in particular. They were seen as shining paragons of everything good and true in the country.

Which was why Alaeron couldn't help but smile when Kormak made the colossal mistake of putting one of his huge hands on the Eagle Knight's chest and shoving him back, making him stumble into a table and then fall onto the floor.

The Andorens in the inn roared with a single voice, while the foreigners who'd just stopped in for a drink gaped in astonishment. The tavern's owner brought his cudgel down on the back of Kormak's neck with all his strength, making the Kellid drop to one knee, though failing to knock him out. A woman in long skirts took the opportunity to kick him in the face, knocking his spectacles askew, one lens dangling over his cheek. Kormak struggled to his feet, and a man sturdy as a dock worker seized him and lifted him bodily off the ground. The Kellid roared, but the crowd moved as one—oh, the patriots of Andoran, united in single purpose!—and carried him to the door, cheered by onlookers. They hurled him into the street, then made way for the furious Eagle Knight, who stalked out, followed by the tavern owner, presumably to deal with Kormak in some more official way.

Alaeron didn't expect them to keep the Kellid busy for long, especially if he unleashed any of his borrowed devices, but he wouldn't need long. He went around the bar and through the kitchen—the cooks were out front, watching the drama in the street—and toward the back door. He could cut through a few alleys, climb over a low roof, and drop down behind his own workshop. He would grab what he thought of as his "panic bag"—a pack filled with essential traveling gear and enough specialized equipment to qualify as a mobile laboratory—and the relics from the Silver Mount, and try to lose himself. He hated to leave Almas again, but it seemed wise to make himself scarce. He could find a place to work in Absalom, probably, or even the once-gilded city of Oppara in neighboring Taldor. Money was a problem, as he didn't have *that* much, but he might find work teaching or working as a lab assistant in a university in Oppara, though Taldan intellectuals tended to disdain scholars from other countries. Neither Absalom nor Oppara were *home*, of course, but after his time in Numeria, being in any of the civilized cities of the Inner Sea would be like a vacation—

Alaeron was so busy planning the next hours and days and weeks that he didn't pay sufficient attention to the here and now. Which was why he barely noticed the figures lurking in the shadows behind the tavern, and was completely unprepared when one of them clubbed him over the head.

Kormak had basically shrugged off a blow like that a few minutes before. Alaeron's constitution was not so strong, however, and he hit the ground like a fallen tree. The Kellid must have hired someone to watch the back door and prevent Alaeron from escaping that way. Smart of him, though surprising, too—Kormak had seemed so confident in his own powers and so contemptuous of Alaeron that it was remarkable he'd bothered with a backup plan.

"I'll cozen you, you tricksy bastard," growled a familiar voice, and in the moment before the next blow knocked him unconscious, Alareon's final muddled thought was: How strange that Kormak should hire the same thugs who threatened Jaya.

# Chapter Three
## An Offer You Shouldn't Refuse

Alaeron had been knocked unconscious twice before—once on the journey to Numeria, and again as part of his initiation into the very lowest rung of hangers-on to the Technic League—and waking up this time was much the same as his previous experiences: grogginess, painful light when he opened his eyes, a thudding ache that felt strangely wet (even if it wasn't bleeding) at the back of his head, a sense that his ears had been muffled by cotton, and a profound temporal disorientation, with no idea if it was day or night or how much time he'd spent in the blackness.

Three data points hardly constituted a sufficient sample size to draw any definite conclusions, but he would be comfortable stating that being clubbed unconscious was among his least favorite things. Who knew what such trauma was doing to his *brain*, and without that, what good was he?

Once the blur of light and shapes resolved into recognizable objects, he took stock of his situation: he was tied to a chair in an extremely cluttered room, sitting across from Jaya, who was also tied to a chair, and had a rather nasty black eye, the flesh swollen and purplish. Alaeron winced. At least they hadn't hit him in the face, there was that—

Wait. Jaya was here. Which meant Kormak hadn't coincidentally hired the same thugs Alaeron had time-frozen in an alley. Of course not. He would have realized right away if he hadn't been so disoriented. This situation was totally unrelated to the Technic League.

Oh, good—a whole *new* set of problems. He really should have walked past that alleyway without interfering. Saving Jaya had made him feel good about himself and gotten him a kiss on the cheek, but now it was threatening to hamper his work.

"I'm sorry," Jaya said softly. "I was afraid this might happen."

"I should have been more afraid myself, it seems." His tongue felt thick in his mouth, but his words seemed to emerge clearly enough. "Where are we, exactly?" He looked around. "Apart from in a storeroom, I mean." The narrow space was cluttered with stacked crates, and the shelves on the walls held innumerable pieces of artwork and small relics—some quite interesting, actually. "Apart from a *rich man's* storeroom," he amended.

"His name is Ralen Vadim," Jaya said.

Alareon whistled. "*The* Ralen Vadim?"

"Unless there are two," she said.

That seemed unlikely. Alaeron didn't know much about Vadim. He was the sort of man about whom people said, "Well, he's not *really* a criminal," and it was basically true. He was a former adventurer who'd brought great wealth to the city, currently a collector of and trader in relics from distant lands and fallen empires. There were rumors that he didn't much care how those relics were acquired, but so what if he took stolen goods? They hadn't been stolen from *Andorens*, after all, and anything from elsewhere was better off here anyway. Vadim was a tireless promoter of Andoren ideals . . . though he was, by all accounts, more interested in the mercantile aspects than the philosophical ones. Alaeron's father had done some work for him once, crafting alchemical lights for his mansion—Alaeron had been his father's apprentice at the time, and he remembered Vadim as a dashing, flamboyant man with a black pointed beard and a mischievous twinkle in his eyes.

The door to the storeroom swung open silently, and the man who stepped in had rather more white than black in his beard, and his eyes were anything but mischievously twinkling, but he was unmistakably the man Alaeron had met as a boy. "Hello," he said, voice smooth and cold as fine marble. He stood in front of Alaeron, hands on his hips, looking down his noble nose at the bound alchemist. "We haven't been introduced. I'm Ralen Vadim."

"You knew my father." Alaeron tried not to babble. Might the reminder of some personal connection save him here? He didn't see how it hurt. "The alchemist, Edmondus? He did some work for you."

If the news stirred Vadim's emotions one way or another, he didn't show it. "He did good work. Some of his lamps still light one of my houses. I was sorry to hear he'd passed away."

"Thank you," Alaeron said. "I—"

"I'd be sad to hear *you'd* passed away, too," Vadim continued, as if Alaeron hadn't spoken. "Perhaps we can avoid that outcome, hmm?" He turned on his heel and stared at Jaya for a moment, then clucked his tongue. "Alaeron," he said, "do you know this young woman? I know you've *met*—she gave us your name—but do you *know* her?"

"Ah, no. Sir. I happened upon her, and she seemed to be in some trouble, so I tried to help. We have no prior relationship."

Vadim *hmmed*. "Understandable. Even admirable, though I'm afraid your kindness was misplaced. You see, *I* am the injured party here. Jaya and her brother presented themselves to me, claiming to be explorers and adventurers in possession of rare artifacts from the deeps of Osirion and the Mwangi Expanse. We struck an agreement to make a trade—a certain sum of gold in exchange for some few artifacts. I am a cautious man, of course, and so I gave them a small amount of gold in exchange for a sample of their wares, with the promise that, if the artifact proved valuable, we would complete the exchange. They gave me a very fine piece indeed, a death-mask from Osirion cracked only slightly by the passage of time."

He paused. "But one of my employees noticed that some of the paint on the mask was a color not in common usage until some several hundred years after the mask's supposed provenance. When I sought out Jaya and her brother to . . . make inquiries . . . they were nowhere to be found."

Jaya stared fixedly at the floor during the man's speech. Vadim turned to Alaeron and spread his hands. "A more ambitious thief would have given me a *real* artifact, and only subsequently traded me a crate full of worthless fakes in exchange for a chest of gold. That would have angered me, but I would have respected the audacity. Jaya contented herself with stealing a mere jingling pouch. Why, I spend more money than that on wine at dinner most days."

"That was the idea," Jaya said. She lifted her eyes, and though they brimmed with tears, that only increased their luster. "We thought, for such a paltry sum, you would not bother to pursue us."

"Ah, foreigners." Vadim gave Alaeron a broad, toothy smile. "They don't understand the importance of honor and integrity to Andorens! I spent far more on tracking down Jaya than she stole from me, because it is a matter of principle. No one may cheat me and escape the consequences." He waved his hand at her as if shooing a fly. "No matter. She is dead; she is the past—"

"Please!" Jaya cried, face a mask of anguish. "I will repay what we stole, I'm sorry, I had no choice. My brother, he is very ill, and we needed money to pay the healer, but we will—"

Offhandedly, without even looking at her, Vadim cuffed the side of Jaya's head, rocking her in her chair. She gasped. "Dead women shouldn't speak," Vadim said. He crouched, looking into Alaeron's face. "You, however, still live. And you said some very interesting things in that alley, according to my men. About Numeria, and the Silver Mount, and artifacts."

"Ah." Alaeron cleared his throat. "Yes, about that . . . ."

Vadim's bushy eyebrows went up. "They tell me you had a device in your hand, they saw a flash of silver, and then, moments later, they were tied up, and you were gone. Was it some relic taken from the Silver Mount?"

"No, merely a potion, sir. When I spoke of Numeria, I confess, I was just hoping to distract them long enough to allow me to imbibe one of my extracts. Your men must have seen the glass vial twinkling in the light. The potion gave me a brief burst of speed, you see, allowing me to move with such haste that I became effectively invisible."

The old adventurer frowned. "So you have no artifacts?"

Alaeron sensed that he could trade his relics for his life . . . but he wasn't ready to make that deal unless no other alternative presented itself. "I assume your men searched me, sir. Did they find any such devices?"

"They did not," Vadim admitted. "I suppose your mention of the Silver Mount was a lie as well?"

"No, sir. I went to Numeria, in hopes of learning some of the secrets of that place, and I did indeed see an inner chamber of the Silver Mount, in exchange for services to the arcanists who claim it as their own."

Now Vadim smiled. "Do you think you could go *back*, and enter the Mount again, and bring out some beautiful things for me?"

Alaeron closed his eyes. Numeria had been a hell—a fascinating hell, full of strange wonders, but he had no desire to return. "I . . . did not leave on good terms, sir. I did some work for the Technic League, but I found their methods vile, and my opinions are known to them. I do not think I would be welcomed back, and the Silver Mount is so well guarded that no man may enter without leave of the League."

"I've heard tales of steel men who serve that League. Nonsense, I trust?"

"Gearsmen," Alaeron whispered. "I have seen them, sir, and they are not men—more like metal devils in the shape of men. Relentless, and deadly, and incapable of feeling pain. They are the ones who guard the Mount."

"A pity." Vadim stood up. "If you can't offer me relics, then you are useless to me, and I'm afraid I'll have to turn you over to the men you fought off in that alleyway. They are divided over whether the best course of action is to kill you or merely to cut off your thumbs—death is more permanent, but an alchemist with no thumbs is like a cart without wheels, and they think it might be amusing to make you suffer." The old adventurer shrugged. "I think it's an overreaction, myself, but I try to give my employees a certain amount of latitude to deal with minor problems as they see fit. Good day."

He started toward the door, and Alaeron opened his mouth, on the point of saying "I have relics! Take them!" He could always try to steal them back, after all, but if he lost his life—or, worse, his thumbs—he would suffer a marked reduction in opportunities.

But Jaya spoke first. "I can give you relics," she said.

Vadim snorted. "You have, in fact, proven that you can *not*."

"No lies this time," she said, her tears dried up, her voice calm. "I can take you to the ruins of Kho."

# Chapter Four
## The Wrong Circumstances

Vadim hesitated a step from the door. Alaeron admired Jaya's audacity. As far as gambits and delaying tactics went, this one didn't suffer from a lack of ambition. The Silver Mount was one of the most famous sites of shattered antiquity in the world, but the ruins of Kho were just as legendary—and almost certainly less well guarded and previously plundered, since no one seemed to know quite where they were.

"My mother originally came from an Uomoto village," Jaya went on. Vadim tilted his head toward her a fraction, not turning around, but not turning away, either. "Just to the west of Osirion, not far from the Kho-Rarne Pass. She left to seek her fortune in the wider world, but I still have family there . . . and my people know the location of the ruins. 'The City of the Fallen Sky,' they call it. My mother saw it with her own eyes, standing on a ridge above the valley."

"If that's even true," Vadim said, "which I doubt, then I'm sure your *people* have emptied the ruins of every item of value by now."

"Not so." Jaya sounded completely sincere and most convincing—but then, believability was probably a crucial quality in a professional liar. "There is a strong taboo against entering the ruins, and rumors of terrible things lurking within. But they will guide *me*, my lord—" She winced, probably remembering the anti-aristocratic stance of Andorens, though Alaeron wondered if even *that* lapse was studied and intentional, to give Vadim a sense of superiority over her. "I'm sorry, *sir*. My family in the village will show me how to enter the ruins. I will bring back anything I find." She inclined her head toward Alaeron. "He should come, too. If he has experience delving into such ruins, then his expertise would help the expedition."

Alaeron said, "I, uh . . ." then fell silent. She was trying to save his life, he realized. He cleared his throat. "I would of course be happy to lend my meager skills to such an endeavor."

Vadim didn't speak. He drummed his fingertips against his leg.

"You win no matter what," Jaya said. "If we fail, and die in the ruins, we've saved you the trouble of killing us yourself. And if we succeed, and bring you treasures, surely you can forgive our minor transgressions?"

"I will consider your offer," Vadim said abruptly, and left the room.

They sat in silence for a while, Alaeron straining to hear anything beyond the confines of the room—nothing much, apart from muffled footsteps—while Jaya stared up at the ceiling, apparently lost in thought. After a while she said, "I don't suppose your ropes are loose?"

Alaeron strained his wrists against the rough ropes binding his arms to the chair frame, then shook his head. "Alas, no."

"Perhaps he'll take us up on my offer," she said, but without much hope.

"I doubt you're likely to fool him twice," Alaeron said. "But it was a good effort. I appreciate you attempting to save my skin along with your own."

"I got you into this trouble, so I should do what I can to get you out. The sad thing is, I'm not even lying—this time. My mother really *did* come from a village a half-day's walk from the ruins of Kho. And I do still have family there. I've never *been*, but I know the way, more or less—my mother often talked of visiting, but the time was never right before she passed away."

Alaeron began to get interested despite himself. "What do you know about the ruins?" Once upon a time he'd considered going in search of Kho, before deciding to go to Numeria instead, simply because it was more *known*, and practically speaking it was far easier to catch a boat up the Sellen River and travel with caravans of crusaders bound north for the Worldwound than to cross the Inner Sea and somehow make his way beyond the desert of Osirion to . . . most likely wander in the mountains and die, assuming he made it that far. But while the Silver Mount was under the tight control of the Technic League, the ruins of Kho were, presumably, largely undiscovered by the wider world.

Jaya shrugged. "A great sky-city from the days of the Shory Empire, brought down by accident or treachery, and crashed into the mountains. My people still tell stories of that time—the Night of Fire, they call it. When I was younger I thought it was . . . what's the word? A fable. A story to teach us a lesson about the dangers of being too prideful, too ambitious, without heeding the cost. To tear a city from the earth and place it in the clouds—how could such a thing last? But my mother convinced me it was truth. There really were cities in the sky, once upon a time."

"All fallen now," Alaeron murmured.

"So you believe in them?"

"Oh, yes. In my researches I've seen documents from the time of the Shory, about the cities. Some believe the tales of flying metropolises were nothing but propaganda to frighten the enemies of the empire, perhaps propped up with a few illusions to strike fear into the hearts of the credulous. But some of the documents I've seen were prosaic things about provisioning flying cities, inventory lists, plans for dealing with sewage and traffic—the sort of dull documents no one would *bother* to fake, you see? Cargo manifests make poor propaganda tools. On the off chance that Vadim does take you up on your offer, it could be interesting." He looked at Jaya thoughtfully for a moment. "Of course, I suppose if he lets you out of this room, you'll do your best to disappear completely. Actually *going* to the ruins of Kho isn't your intention, is it?"

Jaya shrugged. "I do what I must to stay alive, and protect my family."

"Yes, your brother, of course."

"The same. He, at least, is long outside the city by now, waiting for me to meet him, assuming I can get out of this room alive." She looked around. "I doubt Vadim would kill us *here*, because he'd hate to get blood all over his artifacts, and if we're taken elsewhere, there's always a chance we can escape. I've been in dangerous situations before."

"As have I," Alaeron admitted. "Though I've usually had my hands free. I can't say I like this variation."

"Oh, I don't know." Jaya tossed her hair. "In the right circumstances, being tied up can actually be very liberating."

Before Alaeron could begin to think of a response to *that,* the door opened again. Vadim entered, followed by the single most disreputable-looking man Alaeron had ever seen. He *insinuated* himself into the room, not so much walking through the door as sidling through it. He was dressed in clothes tinted the indefinable brownish-gray that came from long wear between washings, and his frame was so thin it seemed he might vanish if he turned sideways. His nose was long and pointed, his dark hair slicked back either with pomade or by natural grease, and his eyes darted around like a watchful rat's—indeed, his whole affect was decidedly rodentlike. But most disturbing of all was his smile, exposing a great number of off-white teeth.

Alaeron had seen hard men smile in frightening ways, but usually, their eyes were cold, or angry, or cynically amused, giving lie to their mirth. This man's eyes gave away no such secrets, and seemed as merry as his grin—you'd think seeing two people bound and ready for murder was the most delightful thing he'd encountered all year. He leaned against the doorframe, removed a long knife with a thin blade from his pocket, and began examining the edge minutely, occasionally pressing his callused thumb to the blade, apparently engrossed in the task.

"Jaya," Vadim said in kindly, almost grandfatherly tones. "Did you really think I'd just let you go with a promise to hurry to far-off Kho and bring back treasures for me? Simply open the door and wish you good luck?"

"Of course not. I'd hoped you'd also pay my traveling expenses."

Her tone was so dry that Alaeron almost laughed, and the man by the doorway did snort in an amused way. "Funny," he said, gesturing at Jaya with the knife.

Vadim nodded. "Yes. One of her many . . . qualities." He picked up a few rolls of cloth, set them aside, and sat down on a crate. "All right, Skiver, go ahead."

The man by the door grunted and stepped forward, knife in hand. Jaya made a low moan and closed her eyes as he stood behind her chair. Alaeron opened his mouth, once again planning to offer his relics for his life—and for Jaya's life, too, why not?

But Skiver didn't move to slash Jaya's throat. Instead, he cut through the ropes binding her. Jaya looked at Vadim, her eyes narrowed, and rubbed at sore wrists. Skiver winked at Alaeron—just being *winked* at by the man was enough to make you want a hot bath with some good strong lye soap—and then came over to cut him free as well. Skiver returned to his spot by the door while Vadim beamed at his now slightly less captive prisoners. "There now," the old man said. "It doesn't do to talk business with people who are tied up—we should at least have the pretense of fair dealings in our negotiations, wouldn't you say?"

"What are we negotiating?" Alaeron asked.

Vadim laughed. "Why, your upcoming expedition to the ruins of Kho, of course! It's true, I was initially doubtful, but I happen to have a source who could corroborate Jaya's story—or portions of it, anyway, and at least he didn't contradict anything."

Jaya's eyes widened. "What do you mean?"

"I think you know what I mean. Or, rather, *who* I mean. Did you think I just had men looking for you, Jaya? Of course I captured your brother. He's tied up elsewhere. I asked him about your mother's history, about the ruins of Kho, and his version agreed with yours on all the relevant points."

Jaya started to stand up, but Skiver immediately slid forward a step, and she sat back down. Trying for icy dignity, and just missing the mark, Jaya said, "If you harm my brother—"

Vadim rolled his eyes. "I'd say that's entirely up to *you*. As generous as it is for you to offer to die on this mission, I'd much rather you succeed and return with treasures, and I find that my employees work best when there's strong motivation. So: if you aren't back by next spring, your brother won't live to see next summer. Do you understand me?"

Jaya gritted her teeth and nodded.

"Fine!" Vadim boomed. "How about you, Alaeron? I have no such leverage over you—your family's dead, near as I can tell. I suppose I could threaten to sell you to the Technic League, but frankly I have no agents that far north, and the thought of making inquiries seems terribly tedious. But at the very *least* you'll have to leave town, because otherwise it's death or the loss of your thumbs, as we discussed previously." He squinted at Alaeron, like a jeweler inspecting a gem for flaws. "I'm guessing that a man who braved the terrors of the Silver Mount for the chance to catch a glimpse of relics from the stars might be tempted by the chance to explore the ruins of the great city of Kho, though. Do I have your measure?"

Alaeron bowed his head. "That you do, sir." Having Ralen Vadim as an enemy meant Almas could no longer be Alaeron's home, so he'd have to go *somewhere*—he might as well agree to undertake this mad expedition, especially since such acquiescence seemed like his best chance to leave this room alive and in possession of all his digits.

"Excellent," Vadim said. "Now, there's just the small matter of a company man to provide oversight. I can't risk the chance you'll decide brotherly love isn't so important after all, Jaya, and decide to run off to live on a beach somewhere. I'm sending along one of my best lieutenants to make sure you remain focused on the work at hand."

"Cheers," Skiver said, still smiling. He never stopped. Alaeron found it profoundly unnerving.

"Skiver isn't much of a world traveler," Vadim went on, "but he's resourceful, dependable in his way, and he needs to leave town for a while anyway. Some unpleasant people want to have a word with him—just a misunderstanding, of course, but it's best he's out of the city for a few months while things work themselves out. I'll make arrangements. You'll depart in a day or two, depending on when I can find a ship with a discreet captain headed south. In the meantime, I trust you'll enjoy the hospitality of my house?"

"My brother—" Jaya began, and Vadim sighed heavily.

"Yes, of course. I'll permit you to say goodbye—I have to prove to you that I have him, anyway—but my household guards will be present, so don't think you'll have an opportunity for escape." Vadim leaned over to Alaeron. "I have him locked up in my basement, in the cage where I keep some of my most valuable relics and works of art. I thought it quite amusing to lock a thief in a cage with a bunch of valuables, all too large to hide on his person. Like sewing a glutton's mouth shut and throwing him into a candy store, eh?" He elbowed Alaeron in the ribs.

"The height of hilarity, sir," the alchemist said.

Vadim sniffed. "You Taldans," he said. "You have no sense of humor."

"I'm not Taldan," Alaeron objected. "That is, my father's family was, but my mother's people were from Cheliax, mostly—I claim to be nothing more than an Andoren."

"Oh," Vadim said. "Please accept my most abject apologies. You just seemed Taldan to me, because you obviously think you're smarter and better than everyone else, even though you're just the son of a pissant alchemist with a workshop that stinks of sulfur." Vadim leaned in close. "You may be smart, but I'm smarter. You may have seen amazing things up north, but I've *done* amazing things, all over the Inner Sea and beyond. Remember who you're dealing with. And don't fail me, or you'll have to settle for being the smartest dead man in an unmarked grave, understood?"

Alaeron swallowed. "Perfectly, sir."

"Good." Vadim glanced at Jaya. "You, I don't need to use harsh words with. We understand each other, don't we?"

"We do."

"Marvelous. Skiver will show you to your rooms. I'll—"

"Wait," Alaeron said, holding up his hand. "I will only agree to this arrangement on one condition."

Vadim looked to his lieutenant. "He wants to dictate terms to me, Skiver. What do you think of *that*?"

"Not funny," Skiver said, though his smile didn't slip.

# Chapter Five
## A Vote of No Confidence

It's necessary if I'm to do the best possible work for you," Alaeron said, speaking quickly enough, he hoped, to stave off violence. "I just need to return to my workshop and get some of my supplies. An alchemist without his tools is nothing more—as you've so recently pointed out—than a man who stinks of sulfur."

"I can have whatever supplies you need brought here," Vadim said. "Just make a list and give it to Skiver."

"No—no, sir, I'm afraid that won't work, I need my formula book at the very least. It holds all the recipes for my potions and . . . other items . . . and that's something no alchemist would sell. An alchemist's formulas are highly personal and individual, as important to my work as a wizard's spellbooks, and—"

"I can take him," Skiver said. "It would shut him up, at least."

"Are you sure you want to be out on the street, given your current situation?" Vadim said.

Skiver laughed. "No one's looking for me yet. I've got a few days before I need to worry about showing my face. I can babysit the scholar a bit."

"Fine, fine," Vadim said, "I've spent too much time on this already, just deal with it." He pressed the heels of his hands against his temples, and Alaeron felt a brief and ultimately ridiculous stab of sympathy—the old man looked tired now, and clearly had larger problems than this on his mind. "A speculative venture to the ruins of Kho!" Vadim boomed. "What can I be thinking?"

"It's a gamble, right enough," Skiver said. "Most likely it'll come to nothing. But it could pay off big, and the buy-in's right: all it costs you is leaving three shallow graves empty for a while longer. Seems like a decent gamble. And I've always wanted to see the world."

"I'm hardly likely to take gambling advice from you, old friend," Vadim said, clapping Skiver on the shoulder. "Given your current circumstances. Eh?"

Skiver's smile slipped, just slightly, and his eyes narrowed, but only for a moment. "I can slit their throats and dump them by the docks if you're having second thoughts, boss," he said.

"No, no, by all means, set off on your journey, have your adventure. Just bring me back a souvenir. Say, a chest full of treasures." He jerked his thumb at Alaeron and Jaya. "Or else their heads in a sack."

"The perfect gift for the man who has everything," Skiver said, grin at full breadth again.

"Come on, Jaya," Vadim said. "One of my men will show you your brother." She cast a worried glance at Alaeron, and an even more worried one at Skiver, and then followed Vadim out of the room.

When they were gone, Skiver turned his attention to Alaeron. "All right, scholar. Let's go." He led the way out of the storeroom, through a number of narrow hallways paneled in dark wood. Alaeron considered trying to hit his guide over the head and run away. After all, *he* didn't have a brother locked up in a cage—there was nothing holding him here but a gentleman's agreement, and Vadim had already proven he was no gentleman. But the fact was, he had to go back to his workshop before he could flee more permanently, and Vadim knew where that workshop was, so giving Skiver the slip now wouldn't help him much: there might very well be armed men waiting for him when he arrived home. But once he was at his lab, in possession of his tools, then the equation would change. It should be trivial to incapacitate Skiver and make a run for it.

Certainly, the possibility of seeing the ruins of Kho was tantalizing, and the chance to spend more time with Jaya had its own temptations. She was treacherous and untrustworthy, certainly, but there was much about her Alaeron couldn't begin to understand . . . and he loved nothing so much as the chance to strip a mystery bare. So to speak.

But he had to be practical. Such an expedition would be treacherous, necessitating a voyage across the Inner Sea, a trek across the burning sands of Osirion, and then on into the mountains, and once they got there, they were likely to be slaughtered by monsters in the high passes, or murdered by Jaya's savage relatives— assuming they even existed. If their team beat the odds and actually found the ruins of Kho, who knew what sort of horrors would lurk inside? All that knowledge . . . but, no, Alaeron had already *had* his adventure, and returned with his hard-won prizes. He should settle down for a quiet chance at study. He just had to escape from his current predicament first.

Skiver unlocked a heavy wooden door that led outside to a stable smelling of fresh hay and old manure.

Judging by the sky, it was late afternoon. Alaeron felt adrift in both time and space.

"Thinking of trying to escape?" Skiver said conversationally. "Can't say I blame you. There's never been a fish on a hook that didn't do its damndest to wriggle free. But even if you did get away from me—which you won't—Vadim's got connections everywhere. He's not a man you want to cross, at least not unless you're in a position to make sure he can't cross you *back*."

"I will take your words under advisement." Alaeron put all the snobbery and superiority at his disposal into his tone.

"No, you won't," Skiver said, almost mournfully. "But that's all right. No one ever does." They passed through another gate—locked, but unguarded—and into a cobbled side street, and Alaeron's mental map oriented itself: they were in the old part of the city, where some of the great houses of the deposed aristocracy had become private residences for wealthy merchants, or else been chopped up into dozens of apartments for poorer sorts. His workshop was off to the east, not an impossible distance, but a longish walk. "I don't suppose Vadim has a carriage we could use," he said. "Only I'm a bit sore from being beaten over the head and tied to a chair."

"Good for you to walk and work the kinks out, then," Skiver said cheerfully, strolling along the gently curving street past the gates of once-stately residences. "You'd best get used to it, anyway. I'd bet we're going places sensible animals like horses won't go near, so we'll be doing a lot of walking. Your soft little feet will have to get toughened up."

"I think you misunderstand me, sir," Alaeron said with icy dignity. "Perhaps Vadim didn't tell you, but I've traveled to Numeria in the far north, and talked my way into the Technic League, and seen the terrible secrets of the Silver Mount—"

"Oh, Vadim mentioned," Skiver interrupted. "I know what you *say* you did. But people say all sorts of things. I know a man says he went to Absalom and saw that great cathedral there and someone bet he wouldn't go inside. Now that man, he likes a bit of a gamble, so he couldn't resist. He says he made his way to the center of the cathedral and looked upon the Starstone with his own eyes, that he could have reached out and touched it—but then he decided he didn't *want* to be a god after all, sounded too much like hard work, so he walked on out again, collected his winnings, and lost it all betting on a pit fight the next day." He gave Alaeron a sly sidelong look. "He *says* all that. Don't mean it happened. My old mother had a saying for people like him, and for anybody who puts on airs and claims more than they have a right to—'He's all pointy hat and no magic,' she'd say."

"If you're implying—" Alaeron began.

"Can't say as I blame you. Your back was up against it back there, and no mistake. I'd have said just about anything to keep my thumbs. You just did what you had to do."

"Ah," Alaeron said, hope stirring. "Then would you mind if I, hmm, slipped away? I promise I'd never come within a day's travel of the city—"

Skiver spat on the cobbles. "I said I understood, scholar. I didn't say it was worth my life to get you out of the trouble you got yourself into. No, you'll come along with us. If you're really an alchemist maybe you can at least pour me the occasional drink. Let's get to this laboratory of yours."

They continued walking in silence. Skiver never asked the way to the laboratory, but he kept taking all the right turnings, which meant Vadim and his people were entirely too familiar with the details of Alaeron's life. As they walked, Alaeron looked around the city, trying to memorize every brick and board of its buildings, every twist of its streets, every drifting scent in the air. There was a good chance he'd never see Almas again, and that thought left a hollowness in his chest as echoing as the great chamber he'd discovered in the depths of the Silver Mount.

"Here we are," Skiver said, rapping on the door to Alaeron's workshop. "Guess you'd better open it up."

Alaeron opened the lock, but didn't perform the necessary steps to deactivate the gas trap. It wouldn't kill Skiver, but it would knock him out, and give Alaeron time to gather his things and make his escape before the alarm was raised. "After you," he said, stepping back.

Skiver snorted and drew his long, thin knife. "I don't think so, scholar. Never go through an unknown door first if you can help it. After you." He gestured with his knife.

Alaeron cleared his throat. "Of course. Just, ah, I think I forgot to . . ." He hurriedly twisted the lock again, deactivating the trap, while Skiver chuckled behind him.

"What was it?" the man asked. "Crossbow tied to a string?"

"Of course not. Nothing *lethal*. I don't want dead men in my doorway. Just a trap to release a chemical composition of my own devising."

Skiver shrugged. "Nice try, anyway. But you can still go in first."

Alaeron opened the door and ducked inside. Skiver followed a moment later, eyes taking in every corner of the room, knife in his hand. He slammed the door all the way open, hard, presumably to break the nose of anyone hiding behind it. Satisfied there was no immediate danger, he tucked his knife away, hooked a stool with his foot, dragged it over to one of the dirty windows, and sat down. He licked his thumb and cleared away a little patch of grime on the glass so he could see outside, and alternated between watching Alaeron and watching the street.

The alchemist's travel pack was already prepared. It was just a matter of tucking in the formula books he'd been using most recently, checking the multitude of pockets in his coat to make sure all the appropriate items were in their proper places—it wouldn't do to reach for a flash-bomb and get a stink-bomb instead—and making sure he hadn't left any overly volatile chemicals sitting too close to their reagents. He might never come back here again, but that didn't mean he wanted his father's laboratory to explode.

There was only one little problem. He needed to get his relics from the Silver Mount. And he didn't especially want Skiver to know he had them. He was well armed with weapons now—better armed than Skiver could imagine, Alaeron was sure—but they didn't do him much good in such enclosed quarters. The laboratory was essentially one large room, and tossing a bomb here would hurt him as much as it would Skiver. Damn it, if only the man had walked into the gas trap—

"Who's this?" Skiver said. "There's a big man in the street, he's walked past three times now. You have an appointment today? Somebody come to buy one of your love potions?"

Alaeron closed his eyes. The Technic League enforcer, Kormak. Almost certainly. "I, ah—"

"He's coming to the door," Skiver said, stepping back from his stool. "You got that trap you laid for me all ready to go?"

Alaeron swore and hurried to the door, attaching delicate wires to carefully placed hooks on the door frame, glancing up at the apparatus bolted to a roof beam. "Get away from the door," Alaeron whispered. "The gas is fairly dense, almost a mist, so it shouldn't drift too far, but we don't want to be close to it." Alaeron scurried to the far corner. Skiver gave him a thoughtful look, then went to the other corner, where Alaeron had hung a curtain to separate his sleeping pallet from the workshop proper. Skiver ducked behind the curtain and out of sight.

Alaeron did a rapid calculation of risk. Skiver was probably watching the door and not Alaeron, who was partially screened from view by a battered wooden cupboard full of reagents anyway. The timing hardly seemed ideal, but when would he have another unobserved moment? Alaeron knelt and lifted up a floorboard near the wall. His father had kept an emergency sack of coin in the little space underneath, once upon a time, but Alaeron used it for more precious things. The hole appeared to be empty, but that was a minor illusion purchased from a wizard, so he reached in anyway and drew out a drawstring bag, no bigger than a wineskin, that clinked gently when it moved. Alaeron took the cloth-wrapped items from inside the bag and secreted them in various pockets of his traveling coat before replacing the board.

The door rattled ominously a few times while Alaeron was retrieving his stolen relics, and then there was a horrible squeal as Kormak broke in, prying the door away from the frame. The door popped open and a shadow loomed, filling the entryway.

The canister attached to the roof beam hissed as one of the pulled wires activated it, spraying a dense greenish mist toward the intruder's face. Kormak reached up with one huge hand and wiped at his cheek, grunted, and then fell forward as suddenly and solidly as a chopped-down tree. Alaeron smiled—he'd never actually seen the trap work before, and it was gratifying to know it behaved as designed. He waited a moment for the mist to dissipate, then stepped toward the Kellid. The gas should render Kormak unconscious for a few hours, at least, which was ample time to go through that clanking coat of his and see what kind of devices the Technic League had armed him with. Why, with luck, Alaeron could find items valuable enough to buy himself out of this problem with Ralen Vadim—or even to overwhelm the old adventurer by force, rescue Jaya, and earn her no doubt plentiful gratitude.

He knelt, reached out for Kormak's coat—

And the Kellid lifted his head, gave Alaeron a smirk full of contempt, and seized the alchemist by the throat. As Alaeron choked and scrabbled hopelessly at the man's fingers—how could mere flesh grip tight as iron?—he noticed flashes of silver, like tiny metal corks, in each of Kormak's nostrils. The Technic League used such filters to traverse some of the more poisonous rooms in the Silver Mount—they allowed the wearer to breathe, more or less, while preventing more noxious substances from entering the body.

"Greetings, runaway," Kormak said, and despite sounding nasal and strange from the nose plugs, there was no mistaking the satisfaction in his voice.

# Chapter Six
## A Grateful Woman

Kormak rose, never letting go of Alaeron's throat. He walked into the room, kicking the door shut behind him and slamming the alchemist against a cupboard. Alaeron clutched uselessly at the man's hands, sure death was upon him.

Then the Kellid grunted, his eyes sagged half-shut, and he released his grip. Skiver was there, behind the man, holding a chunk of brick in one hand. He slammed it down on the man's head again while Alaeron scurried away. The Technic League had provided Kormak with formidable protections, but apparently they hadn't been prepared for an attack from behind with a blunt object. Skiver tossed the brick aside. "This a friend of yours?" he said.

"No," Alaeron croaked. "I've never seen him before. Perhaps a rival alchemist hoping to steal my—"

Skiver grunted. "Then you won't mind if I do this." He drew his knife and plunged it straight into Kormak's back.

At least, that was clearly the idea. In actual fact, the blade snapped off cleanly near the hilt, the broken shard of metal bouncing on the floorboards. "What in the nine layers of Hell?" Skiver said. "That was my third-best blade! It didn't even tear this big bastard's coat!" He kicked Kormak in the ribs, and the Kellid groaned and started trying to lever himself up.

"None of that," Skiver said, and stomped down on the back of Kormak's head. The big man growled and kept trying to get up. Skiver looked at Alaeron, and for once, he wasn't smiling. "He's got a thick head for an alchemist. Let's go."

Alaeron just nodded and snatched up his pack. Skiver darted out the door, and Alaeron pursued him as the man ducked into alleys Alaeron had never even noticed, quickly taking him deep into a world that ran between and behind the city's buildings, past heaps of refuse tossed from rear windows, starving dogs gnawing at their own matted fur, and puddles of black, stinking water. Some of the passages were so narrow Alaeron had to take off his pack and hold it in his hand as he squeezed through sideways. Annoying, but there was no way the larger Kormak could follow them without knocking down the buildings first.

Of course, depending on what weapons the Technic League had given him, that might be in his power.

They were almost back to Vadim's house when it occurred to Alaeron that, with Skiver so focused on the path ahead, he might slip away unnoticed. But Kormak was out there, and doubtless even more unhappy with Alaeron than before. Suddenly the idea of returning to Vadim's fortified mansion didn't seem so unappealing.

They approached the house from a different direction than the one they'd departed from, coming to a door that was guarded by a pair of men. They recognized Skiver and gave him a lazy nod, then looked Alaeron up and down scornfully before opening the door.

Once they were safely inside, Alaeron slipped the heavy pack off his back and let it rest on the floor. Skiver exhaled heavily as if he'd been holding his breath all along. He leaned against the wall of the entryway and crossed his arms. "That fella. If he's an alchemist, I'm an Eagle Knight. Care to tell me who he really was?"

Alaeron thought about that. "No," he said.

Skiver sighed. "Do you owe someone money? I know what that's like. I figure alchemy has to be an expensive business, with all the . . ." He waved his hands vaguely. "Bottles and fluids and such. Did you take out a loan you couldn't pay back?"

"Something like that." Alaeron kept his eyes downcast.

Skiver sighed. "Vadim wants you on this trip. He thinks you're worth the trouble, who knows why. I'd much rather make the journey with just the lady and myself, but I don't make the decisions around here. We'll be out of the city tomorrow, and when we get back—if we get back—you can settle your debts then."

Alaeron swallowed. "Are you going to tell Vadim what happened?" If the old adventurer heard about the attack and got curious, he could make inquiries, and find out Alaeron didn't owe any of the shady dealers in the city money. He might realize someone from the Technic League had come looking for Alaeron, and decide to sell the alchemist for a sure profit instead of funding this speculative expedition. It was a long chain of "ifs" and "maybes," but just plausible enough to make a knot of fear twist up in Alaeron's belly.

Skiver shrugged. "If I told Vadim every time I hit a man over the head with a brick, we'd never have time to talk about anything else. As far as I'm concerned, it's your business, and since we're leaving the city, it shouldn't affect Vadim." Skiver grinned his terrifying grin again. "But just remember, scholar, that you *owe* me now. And I don't let debts go uncollected." He shouted, and a servant girl hurried in from a side door. "Show the alchemist to his room." He plucked Alaeron's pack from the floor with one hand as if it weighed nothing, and gave a wink. "I'll hold onto this until it's time for our journey."

Alaeron was very glad he'd hidden the relics in his coat instead. "Just be careful with that. There are volatile compounds, and my books—"

"I wasn't planning to mix up all your little bottles of perfume," Skiver said, "and I ain't much of a reader. I just don't want you making a batch of knockout gas and trying to run away."

Alaeron had ample components in his coat pockets to make any number of powerful concoctions, but he didn't bother correcting Skiver. The average person thought alchemy and potion-making required a laboratory full of retorts and beakers and glass tubing, and while those were all helpful and even necessary for some processes, once you made your initial preparations, you could produce remarkable effects with no more equipment than you could carry on your person. "I wouldn't mind a change of clothes," Alaeron said.

Skiver snorted. "Save the fresh clothes for after you fall in the ocean or some quicksand or get goblin blood all over you, not after a night spent in one of Ralen Vadim's feather beds." He clucked his tongue. "Soft, scholar, soft." He strolled off into the house with all of Alaeron's least-prized possessions in his hand.

The servant beckoned Alaeron forward and led him down a hall and then up a staircase, without even a trace of obsequiousness. Even the maids in Almas knew themselves to be the equal of any other person—at least in some intangible essential sense, if not in terms of power, wealth, or influence.

The man with the tattered ear stood waiting by the door at the top of the stairs. He looked at Alaeron, turned his head and pursed his lips as if to spit, then clearly thought better of sullying the landing in Vadim's house, because he swallowed it instead. "If you try to escape, Vadim says I can beat you with a shovel until the shovel breaks."

"I'll keep that in mind," Alaeron said.

"Your room's the first one on the right. The windows are barred, and we've got people watching 'em anyway. Sleep well, you tricksy shit." Tattered-ear opened the door with a show of over-the-top graciousness, sketching out a little bow, and stepped aside just far enough to let Alaeron through. As the alchemist passed through the doorway, Tattered-ear stuck out his foot to trip him. Alaeron saw it coming, and could have avoided falling, but why antagonize the man further? He let himself stumble, falling to his hands and knees and groaning while Tattered-ear and the servant tittered. (The servant laughing at him too—that hurt a bit.)

The door slammed shut behind him, locking with a sound of great finality, and Alaeron got to his feet . . . and saw Jaya standing at the end of the short corridor, watching him with a look that was equal parts pity and amusement. "They're letting the prisoners congregate?" he said, brushing himself off. "How kind of them."

She shook her head. "Not all of us. My brother is in a cage in the basement, like an animal!" She took a step toward him. "I'm sorry, again, for getting you into this."

He shrugged. "I got myself into this. You were merely the vector. Think nothing of it." Alaeron was beginning to resign himself to the reality of the coming journey. In a way, it was to his advantage—Ralen would pay for his passage and Skiver would act as an armed guard, and that would help him escape Kormak and the Technic League. Once they reached the southern continent, he could slip away. Rumors said the ruler of Osirion often allowed outsiders to access the ruins in the desert for study. Surely a man of Alaeron's experience could find work enough there to keep a roof over his head and continue his researches.

Jaya came even closer. The hallway wasn't long: an afterthought sort of passage, with two doors on the left, presumably leading to two guest rooms, hers and his, and an ugly old antique dresser at the end of the hall, probably because taking it all the way up to the attic was too much trouble. Jaya had a certain way of filling the available space more than an ordinary person should, the pleasant scent of her seeming to permeate the air. Alaeron had been the subject of seductions before—the Technic League believed in using any method necessary to ensure loyalty—but when Jaya looked at him with her big, dark eyes, and placed her hand against his cheek, it didn't feel like seduction. It didn't feel like anything she was doing at all; it felt like something she *was*.

"No," she said. "It's my fault. And despite that, you're going on this trip with me, to *save* me . . . and to save my family. I cannot tell you how grateful I am. You have made a friend in me, Alaeron."

He started to say, "I was hardly given a *choice*," but a beautiful woman murmuring sweet words of gratitude was a pleasure rare enough that he didn't want to spoil it. "Ah, anything I can do to help, of course, I'd be delighted . . ."

She stepped back, and the sudden absence of her warmth and proximity was like a shadow falling over him, or a cloud passing over the sun. "There's a tray of food in your room," she said. "Cold, by now, but it wasn't very good when it was hot, so I doubt it's suffered much. Would you like some company while you eat?"

Alaeron glanced at the door. "They don't mind if the prisoners, ah, fraternize?"

She shrugged. "I don't think they care what we do, so long as we do it locked in here. We're going to be traveling together—we may as well get to know each other a bit, don't you think?"

"Of course." He opened the door to his room and let her enter first. The guest room was comfortable enough, if a bit devoid of personality—a sturdy wooden bedframe, an only slightly threadbare armchair, an empty chest of drawers. A tray of cold meat and whole fruit rested on the bedside table next to a pitcher of water and a cup. Alaeron removed his clattering coat and hung it on a hook in the corner, then perched on the edge of the bed and selected the least-mushy-looking apple.

Jaya lounged in the chair, her obvious exhaustion barely making a dent in her beauty. "I never should have tried to trick Ralen Vadim. I let my brother talk me into it—his ambition has always gone beyond the boundaries of good sense, but I have such a hard time saying no to him. And we were desperate." She sighed. "And now we're even *more* desperate. To stake my life, and my brother's, on a trip into the ruins of Kho? It seems like madness, but when the only other choice is death, madness can seem quite attractive. And this man Vadim is sending with us, Skiver—you were with him this afternoon, weren't you? What's he like?"

Alaeron thought for a moment. "Cunning, if not exactly intelligent. Not averse to violence. I get the sense he likes gambling, and that gambling may have gotten him into some trouble. A bit rude, but handy with a blade, I think, and that can be a good quality in a traveling companion, especially in the wild places."

"Loyal to Vadim, I suppose. He'd hardly send the man otherwise."

"Loyal to himself, over all, I suspect," Alaeron said carefully. "But he certainly respects Vadim, and I doubt he'd take our side over his."

She nodded briskly. "Then we'll have to play it straight. You have experience searching through ruins for relics, Alaeron. How do you rate our chances?"

He swallowed a chunk of apple. "The sky cities of the Shory are not my area of expertise. I've read a bit of speculation about how their cities flew—we call it Aeromantic Infandibulum, but just because it has a name doesn't mean it's understood. Some combination of aeromancy and the electro-thaumaturgy of the ancients, we assume, but who can say for sure? There's no denying it was powerful magic, though . . . and powerful magic leaves traces."

He shifted on the bed, leaning against the hard headboard. "The Silver Mount fell from the sky, too—from *beyond* the sky, from the depths of the stars—and when it crashed, it broke apart, though not entirely. Terrible forces were released on impact, nevertheless. Magic is a method of containing forces so powerful they can obliterate the world. When the containment fails, the results can be unpredictable. I wouldn't dare to guess what we might find in whatever remains of Kho. Mad elemental beings?

Toxic magic twisting the local wildlife into monsters? Devastation that extends beyond the merely physical and into the nature of time and space itself? Any of those. But also items of great power and antiquity, certainly, if the site hasn't been picked over by adventurers already."

"Few who go to Kho return, or so my mother said," Jaya told him. "And those who do return seldom carry anything with them, except terrible, contradictory stories. Most die in a few years, either from drink, or carelessness, or suicide, or strange diseases, or the bad luck that clings to them like a stink." She sighed. "Obviously, I was desperate to suggest going there, even assuming my mother exaggerated. Still, I think whatever treasures the city held are still there in the ruins."

"Mmm. Then the question will be getting them out again. I can't say for sure until I've been there, until I've seen it for myself, but . . . I rate our chances of getting out of Kho successfully rather better than those of most adventurers. As you say, I have experience in these matters."

A smile just touched her lips. "No false modesty in you, is there?"

"To my knowledge, I went deeper underground in the Silver Mount than anyone else ever has," he said simply. "And I came out sane, with all my limbs, without any terrible addictions, and bearing artifacts of power. I do not claim to be a man of many talents. But what few talents I have are considerable, and well developed."

"I think I can say the same about myself." Did she lick her lips, just then, a flicker of pink tongue? Did she take a deeper breath than usual and thrust out her chest provocatively? Alaeron couldn't be sure. "I am quite good with a bow, for example," she said, voice entirely deadpan.

Before Alaeron could respond, she yawned widely, covering her mouth with her hand. "Forgive me. The day has been more exhausting than I realized. I should get some sleep—there's no telling when Vadim will roust us out of bed in the morning." She rose with fluid grace—if that was how she moved when she was exhausted, she must be *exquisite* when fresh— and paused in the doorway. "You are in the process of saving my life," she said. "I owe you a debt I can never repay—but I'll spend the rest of that life doing my best to make it up to you." She gave a little wave, and departed, closing the door after her.

Alaeron put the remains of his apple aside and stretched out on the rather comfortable bed, staring up at the ceiling for a while. "Damn it," he said at last, but softly, because who knew how thin the walls were? "It looks like I'm going to Kho after all."

It took him a long time to sleep, but when he did, he dreamed of Jaya, and they were exactly the sort of dreams one might expect.

# Chapter Seven
## Setting Sail

The windows were still dark when someone jabbed Alaeron in the side, making him bolt up in bed, gasping. Skiver stood holding a lantern that illuminated his grin. That was all the reminder Alaeron needed that he was a prisoner, and not a guest—if he'd been a guest, the maniac sent to rouse him would have knocked politely at the door first.

"Up, up!" Skiver shouted with good cheer.

Alaeron groaned. "You're one of that loathsome species that loves mornings, aren't you?"

"Any moment I'm drawing breath is a good one, scholar. Rise and get your boots on. We sail with the tide." He paused. "Actually, I've no idea if we're really sailing with the tide, but it sounds like a good reason to get up while it's still dark outside, doesn't it?" He went out in the hallway, and by the time Alaeron had gulped a glass of water, splashed more water on his face, and put on his coat and boots, Jaya was in the hall waiting too.

"Let's go, children." Skiver whistled as he descended the stairs, then led them deeper into the house, and eventually out to the stables. There wasn't even a hint of dawn in the sky, and it was cold. Jaya's bow case and a pair of traveler's packs waited alongside Alaeron's far bulkier baggage. "You get your weapons back now, you two," Skiver said. "Don't go trying to use them on me, though, eh? Mr. Vadim has agents almost all the way along the route, and I'll be sending messages back with them as we proceed. If he doesn't hear from me right regular, he'll send nastier men than me out to find you. Letting you escape would be an insult to his pride, and if there's one thing he can't abide, it's looking the fool. Fair warning." He grinned and put one arm around Jaya's shoulders, and the other around Alaeron's. "But never mind, I'm sure I've nothing to worry about. We'll soon be the best of friends. Off on an adventure! I always wanted to go on one of those. I only ever get invited to heists and massacres."

He led them to a closed carriage, where a bored-looking driver sat waiting. Skiver and the driver piled the luggage on top and secured it—Alaeron winced as they manhandled his pack, even though everything breakable inside was fairly well wrapped, and he hadn't put any chemicals that combined explosively close to one another. "Inside, my darlings," Skiver said, and they climbed in.

The carriage was marvelously padded and comfortable inside, though it was as dark as the backside of the moon. Skiver sat next to Alaeron, and Jaya across from him, and they rode in silence as the carriage rattled down the largely deserted streets. Gradually light filled the carriage's windows, and Alaeron took a final look at the city he loved.

They reached the docks at the mouth of the Andoshen River, and Skiver hopped out promptly, with Alaeron and Jaya following with considerably less enthusiasm. The wharves stank of tar and salt, and the docks were bustling with activity even at this early hour, with sailors doing inscrutable things involving coils of ropes and heaps of crates and stacks of barrels. Alaeron knew little about boats—or were the big ones ships?—and cared even less. Boats, like horses, carts, and carriages, were all just a means of covering the regrettable distance between places that actually interested him. He glanced back for one last look at the city . . . and saw a pall of smoke rising above the buildings to the north. Jaya was a little distance away, staring at the ships, so he looked over to Skiver, who was adjusting the straps on his pack. "Fire there," he remarked, pointing.

Skiver glanced up, and for once his grin faded. "Ah. About that. I heard from Vadim that an alchemist's workshop burned down in the night. Terrible thing, he said. But they're dangerous places, with all those chemicals and such. So Vadim said."

Alaeron closed his eyes. His workshop. His *father's* workshop. Alaeron had grown up there, essentially— oh, they'd had a house, of course, but the laboratory had always felt like *home*, and now it was a smoking crater in the ground. "Did Vadim have it burned down? To, I don't know, teach me a lesson in respect?"

Skiver shrugged. "I couldn't say for sure. He didn't tell me he'd done it, and it's not much of a lesson about respecting him if you don't *know* he's the one who burned it down. Could have been your other friend, I guess, the legbreaker who got sent around to collect your debts. Not sure if that's any better, though. I never asked, who do you owe? I know most of the enforcers working hereabouts, and that Kellid looked like somebody brought in special from out of town to make a point, and there are only a few fellas who go in for that kind of flashy display."

"I'd rather keep my business to myself," Alaeron said stiffly.

Skiver shrugged. "Suit yourself. Nobody ever lost anything by keeping a secret. You must owe a heap, though, if they imported that kind of talent to go after you. Probably ought to get on board before he comes looking for you again, hadn't we?" Skiver shouted at Jaya to come on and set off along the dock, dodging passing sailors and heaps of what Alaeron could only think of as "boat junk" with alacrity.

Jaya fell into step beside Alaeron. "Have you done much sailing?"

"On river barges," he said. "Seldom on seagoing vessels. Yourself?"

"Oh, yes. I've been all over the Inner Sea region. My parents traveled a great deal. Always chasing the next opportunity—or running away from the *last* one, after it went wrong. My youth did not lack excitement."

Alaeron would have been very much surprised to find out she was older than nineteen or twenty, and so she still had a bit of youth ahead of her yet. But then, he was a bit short of his thirtieth year himself, and sometimes thought he'd experienced enough for two reasonably full lifetimes, so who was he to say? "What sort of boat are we being saddled with, then?" He gestured to the vessel floating at the end of the pier where Skiver had stopped and started talking intently to a man who was so obviously a sailor he might as well have been made of tar and old rope.

"Ship, not boat."

"What's the difference?"

"Basically? Ships are *bigger*. Call a ship a boat and you might offend the crew—just like if you called the crew themselves 'boys' instead of 'men.' This one isn't too exciting. Three-masted merchant ship, square-rigged on the mainmast and the foremast, lateen-rigged on the mizzenmast."

"Hmm. Now I know how people feel when I start talking about retorts and alembics and crucibles, at the moment when their eyes glaze over."

She laughed. "It's not the fastest ship, but it's fast enough, and roomy. I think Vadim just bought us passage on the first ship he could find running cargo to Absalom."

"As long as we don't have to travel belowdecks with the crates and barrels," Alaeron said, just as Skiver beckoned them over.

The ship was called the *Pride of Azlant*—rather an overblown name for a trading vessel, Alaeron thought—and while they weren't to be stowed in the cargo hold, Alaeron was dismayed to learn he'd be sharing a tiny room with Skiver. There was a bed, of sorts—Alaeron had seen more comfortable sleeping arrangements in prisons—and a hammock hanging over it, so one of them would have the other swinging in a net above him all night. Alaeron couldn't decide which berth would be more unpleasant. He suspected it would be whichever one he happened to be using at the time.

"Jaya gets her own room, of course," Skiver said. "With a good strong lock on the door."

Alareon put his bag down in the corner of the room. "Do you think she's in danger from the crew?"

Skiver shrugged. "Sailors aren't always the most savory characters, scholar, and there are about fifty of them on this ship, so the odds are, we've got a few of the nasty type. Someone might try to visit her at night, just to try their luck. Not that I'm worried about Jaya, but it would make things tense with the crew if she put a knife in the eye of a deckhand, don't you think?"

"How long will we be on this oversized bath toy?" Alaeron sat on the edge of the bed, though he had to hunch forward so his head didn't brush the hammock above.

"You'd have to ask the navigator. Except he's an important man, so don't bother him. We have to head around the western side of the Isle of Kortos, then swing eastward to dock at Absalom. A week, or perhaps nine days? From there we'll get another ship going to Osirion, dunno how long that will take, maybe a week or so if all goes well. I'm sure you can keep yourself out of trouble. Mixing up your medicines and what have you."

"A man of learning is never bored, for his mind can always be engaged," Alaeron said.

"Must be nice. I'd rather be engaged with dice or a deck of harrow cards. I'm going up on deck. Never been on an ocean voyage before. I feel like one of those great explorers—practically a Pathfinder, ain't I?" He dropped a wink—Skiver could have made prayers look dishonest, so his wink practically radiated disrepute. He ducked through the low doorway and away.

The Inner Sea hardly counted as a real ocean— oh, it was wide, but nearly every bit of it was known and well traveled, nothing like the vast and trackless expanse of waters to the far west. They'd follow a standard shipping lane to the Isle of Kortos, and to the legendary great city of Absalom. (Alaeron had been there twice, once as a child and once as a teenager, and preferred Almas for reasons he assured himself weren't entirely patriotic and sentimental.) From there they'd head to the southern continent, which was, admittedly, approaching the edge of the known world as far as Alaeron was concerned, but Almas had something like diplomatic relations with Osirion, and they weren't exactly savages there, even if they were overly preoccupied with tombs and the dead and had an inordinate fondness for beetle-related artwork. Hardly undiscovered country. But for someone as steeped in city life as Skiver, a canoe trip across a lake would probably count as a major aquatic undertaking.

Once they headed into the mountains, though, to the edge of the Mwangi Expanse—a place so wild there weren't even *nations* there, just scattered tribes who seemed perfectly content ruling themselves—well, then Skiver might have a point. That would be territory largely unexplored by any but brave adventurers and Pathfinders. (And all the people who lived in the area, of course, but walking around the place you'd been born wasn't the same as exploring; it only counted if you came from the outside, and took news of what you'd discovered back home.)

Alaeron decided to go up on deck himself. He might never see Almas again—watching the city disappear into the distance would suit his melancholy mood, especially with that plume of smoke rising over it. He went up, finding a spot by the railing that seemed reasonably out of the way as sailors bustled past him doing inscrutable things with ropes and pulleys. After a moment Jaya appeared by his side, leaning forward with a mournful expression on her face. Alaeron was feeling fairly mournful himself. "You see that smoke?" he said.

She nodded.

"That was my father's workshop. Well, mine, really, but it started out as my father's." He shook his head. "I think Vadim had it burned down, as a sort of threat. Or comment. Or something."

"I'm sorry," she said. "Was it worth a lot of money?"

He frowned. He hadn't though of it in *those* terms. "A building on a bit of land near the center of Almas? I suppose, not that I'd sell it. But that's not the point, it's more . . . it was my *father's*."

Now she nodded. "Ah. And you loved him, then? You were close?"

"Hah. I can see why you'd think that. But most of the time we couldn't stand each other." Some of the sailors jumped down to the dock and untied some ropes as thick as their own forearms, then climbed back on deck. The ship lurched, and then began slowly sliding away from the pier. "My father and I were very different people," Alaeron said. "He was . . . methodical, even plodding, but he was very *precise*. I can be precise when I need to, but my father would never, oh, break into a burial tomb because he heard there was an interesting bit of parchment rolled up in a tube down there. He was smart, but he wasn't *clever*, or curious, except in a very narrow way."

Jaya turned her back on the city—there was a touch of drama to the gesture. She leaned back with her elbows propped on the rail and squinted at Alaeron. "It must have been quite a trial for him, having you as a son."

Alaeron gave a small smile. "Yes, I'm sure it was. I never appreciated that until it was too late to tell him so. But I owe him, you know. His discipline gave me the foundation I needed. I didn't *want* to study his formula books, or learn descriptive chemistry, or study stoichiometry. But it was the family business, and I was an apprentice, and so I learned to make alchemical lanterns and alchemical torches and industrial solvents, all the things we sold. Without learning all that, though, I wouldn't have learned to make . . . more interesting things. Potions. Explosives. Rare extracts. My father gave me the bedrock I needed to build the castles of my own ambition."

Alaeron glanced over to see if his turn of phrase had impressed her; if it had, she was doing a remarkably good job of keeping her admiration to herself. "But by the time I figured out what I owed him, he was gone. Still, I think maybe he knew. I hope so. While he was alive we argued constantly, about everything from philosophy to what we should eat for dinner—except in the workshop. There, we worked together like two gears in a greater machine, and for a long time after he died, when I'd be working alone, I'd sort of forget he was gone. I'd hold out my hand, you know, and say, 'Number two pipette please,' and expect him to hand it over. Always a bit of a shock, until I got used to it. Part of why I set out to explore, and learn about forbidden things, and eventually ended up in Numeria, was to get away from all those memories. I've spent more time away from the workshop than *in* it these past few years, but I always knew it was there—it was *home*. And now it's ashes." He gestured at the thread of smoke, which was getting thinner with distance as the ship made its stately way out of the crowded harbor and toward the open sea. "No more home."

Jaya put her hand on his arm. "You are a very sensitive man," she said.

"Why, thank you, I—"

"I am also sensitive and sentimental," she said. "About my brother. It is a shame, really, that we are so weak, you and I. Sentimental adventurers are more likely to die. It is better to have nothing to lose. Then you have no fear, no hesitation. If the time comes to run and leave everything behind, and start fresh somewhere else, they can run. But I cannot. A terrible weakness."

"I'd . . . never quite thought of it that way," Alaeron said.

She shrugged. "We sentimental adventurers just have to be more dangerous in other ways."

Skiver strolled by, leered at them in what he probably thought was a friendly way, then strolled toward the raised bit at the front of the ship where some sailors were congregating. "I don't think *he* has any sentiment," Alaeron said.

"No," Jaya said, turning back to face the water. "We are fortunate he is on our side, then."

They watched silently as Almas disappeared over the horizon, and their journey began.

"No luck?" Skiver said the next morning, leaning in the doorway to their cabin and chewing on an apple.

Alaeron frowned. He'd just come back downstairs after his third failed attempt to casually run into Jaya up on deck. "I can't imagine what you mean."

Skiver snorted. "I've seen you go all doe-eyed and dewy-eyed and cow-eyed at Jaya, gazing after her longingly when she walks away—and not just staring at her rear end, either. Nice enough for those that like such as her, I reckon. But she's not my type."

Alaeron stared at him. "Strong, smart, gorgeous, a smile that could set the world on fire—what *is* your type, if it's not her?"

Skiver laughed. "I like something a little less feminine."

"She carries a bow and arrow *everywhere*—"

"Let me rephrase: I like something a *lot* less feminine. Entirely less feminine. Which is to say, not female."

Alaeron blinked. "Oh. I didn't realize you, ah . . . that is, that you were . . ."

Skiver crunched into the apple core and then spat a seed onto the floor at Alaeron's feet. "And why should you have? *You're* not my type either, scholar. So don't worry about having me as competition for her affection."

I wasn't worried, Alaeron thought.

"But I'd be careful around her if I was you," Skiver went on. "She's a beautiful woman, and she *knows* it, and lest you forget, she's the one who got you into this mess with her thieving ways."

"Her brother was sick—" Alaeron began.

Skiver rolled his eyes, then stepped out of the doorway. "I've seen her brother, and you haven't. Nothing sick about him. They were sick of having no *gold*, I'll believe that. Besides, I don't fault 'em for stealing. I like stealing. Truth is, I've found nothing livens up a long sea voyage more than stealing something."

Alaeron paused before entering their room. "I think stealing something on a boat is technically piracy," he said. "It's the sort of thing that might get you thrown overboard."

"Might do," Skiver agreed, "if I'd stolen something from the ship or the crew." He grinned and sauntered around Alaeron, toward the short set of stairs that led up to the central deck.

"No," Alaeron murmured. "No, no, no." He went into the tiny cabin, where his pack rested, apparently unmoved, shoved into the space under his bunk. Alaeron gently slid the bag out, pulling by the one safe strap, then knelt beside the satchel and checked the various trick clasps and trapped buckles. Anyone who tried to open the bag without knowing how to disarm it first would get a face full of memory-erasing poison if he were lucky, and lose a fingertip if he weren't. At the very *least* anyone who breached the inner compartment without taking the proper precautions would be sprayed with a deep orange dye that wouldn't wash off, ever. Everything seemed to be in order, every trap poised and every potential countermeasure primed. It was the work of seconds for Alaeron to disconnect the proper threads and twist the appropriate buttons—all indistinguishable from the *normal* loose threads and buttons in the bag—and make the satchel safe for him to open, but only because he knew *exactly* what he was doing.

He moved aside the padded vials, the thick ceramic jars with their lids sealed with wax, and finally uncovered the inner compartment, where six smaller bundles all waited, wrapped in cloth. After glancing around to make sure the door was firmly shut, he laid out the bundles and opened them. The silver teardrop of the time egg was there, and the coil of golden chain, and a red metal ring. When he touched the chain it slithered around his wrist like an amorous serpent, and he shook it off impatiently—that was the most active of the artifacts, lengthening and shortening at the least provocation, and trying to twine around any warm flesh that touched it. He hurried to open the other three bundles, but inside those . . . there were rocks.

Alaeron closed his eyes. He stood, and opened the door—

And Skiver was standing there in the entryway, grinning and juggling three objects. They whirled past in a silvery circle, but Alaeron recognized them: a little dull gray disc, no bigger than a human ear but heavier than it should be. A shiny black gearwheel about a hand's width across. And a pearly white and gold device the size of a plum that could be spun like a child's top (albeit with more dramatic results).

Alaeron gritted his teeth. Just *moving* some of those devices was dangerous, especially the top, though fortunately this looping juggling motion didn't have the same result that spinning it on its point did. "Those are mine," Alaeron said. "Give them back."

"Sure," Skiver said, but didn't stop juggling. "I'm a reasonable man. Come on, though. Admit you're impressed I got into the bag."

Anything to make him hand over the relics. "I am impressed." And he was, almost as much as he was enraged. "And surprised."

"I am more than a simple cutthroat and cutpurse," Skiver said, winking. "I'm a *complicated* cutthroat and cutpurse." He took a step forward, still juggling, and Alaeron retreated into the cabin. Once Skiver was fully inside, he kicked the door shut, then stopped juggling, catching the relics as they fell and making them disappear—up sleeves, into hidden pockets, who knew?

Alaeron glanced at his bag, which still yawned open on the floor. Quarters were too close for a bomb, but if he grabbed the golden chain—

"No need to get rough," Skiver said mildly. "I *said* I'd give them back. But first, let me say—hell of a bunch of traps there. I've never seen better. Really tested my ingenuity. Vadim asked around and said he thought you were the real thing after all, but I had my doubts. Consider my doubts put to rest then. You know your business. Of course, I know mine *better*, but I'm older than you, it's only to be expected, I've been at it longer." He leaned against the door and crossed his arms. "And now you know I know *my* business. There's not a door I can't get past—barring those sealed up by magic, but you can often get around those, too, with a little thinking. You've got no idea how many fools put a bunch of magical wards and barriers on a door, but the door's just set in an ordinary wall of wood or stone, something you can get through with a sledgehammer and enough time. You and me are professionals, all right, is what I'm trying to say. It's good if we can respect each other, and trust one another to do whatever falls into our, what would you call it, area of expertise."

"So your attempt to foster a sense of group cohesion involves stealing some of my most prized possessions?" Alaeron said.

Skiver shrugged. "I had to make a point, didn't I? Besides, I was curious. To go to *that* much trouble to seal up a traveling pack, I thought you'd have gold or jewels or something in there. Not weird bits of metal and enamel. I'm sure they're all very interesting and technical and all that, but if you didn't make it so obvious they were valuable, nobody'd *bother* to steal them, they'd think they were just bits of tinkerer's junk." He took out the top and held it forward on his palm. Alaeron reached for it, but Skiver closed his fist and pulled it away. "Ah, ah, ah. Not yet, scholar." Skiver squatted down on his heels, his back leaning against the door. "Turns out sea voyages are boring. I've not seen a single sea monster, the captain doesn't let his crewmen gamble, and one mile of water looks much like another. So let's make an arrangement: Tell me a story, and I'll give you back your trinkets. One story, one trinket. Only true stories, mind." He tapped the side of his long nose. "I can smell a lie."

"This is ridiculous. You've *stolen* from me, and I demand—"

"Oh, did you make these, then?" Skiver said. "You didn't steal them *yourself*, from some dirty hole in the ground or rich fella's collection? Stealing something that's already been stolen once is a time-honored tradition among thieves."

"I am a seeker after knowledge, not a *thief*—"

Skiver made a placating gesture. "Please, scholar, no offense meant, I *am* a thief, and it's an honest living, more or less. I don't mean any insult. Humor me—play along. What else do you have to do today? Pace around on deck hoping the beauty from the south will decide to come out of her room? Why not tell me a story? Like, say, where you stole—sorry, *discovered*—these little things? Do that, and I'll give you back this one that looks like a rich child's toy."

Alaeron hesitated. He was more than willing to go to war over the relics, but if there were an easier way . . . "How do I know you'll honor our agreement?"

Skiver laughed. "I saw what you've got in your bag. All manner of acids and potions and such. I have to sleep *some*time, and I'd rather not have you pouring acid into my eyes while I'm doing it, all right? I'll be honorable. I just want a game to keep things interesting. You can't tell me *you* don't hate being bored. And you must want to tell about your exploits. I've hardly ever met an adventurer who didn't."

The man was ridiculous, his logic profoundly illogical, but telling a story was a small price to pay to get his relics back. "Fine." Alaeron sat down stiffly on the bunk.

"I found them near the end of my time in Numeria. They were the *reason* for the end of my time in Numeria . . ."

# Chapter Eight
## The Silver Mount

Alaeron hated the Technic League. They weren't interested in knowledge, only in *power*. The majority of them were utterly incurious about the origin of the Silver Mount—they just wanted to plunder it for weapons they could use to enforce their control of the country, or drugs to maintain their power over their figurehead, the Black Sovereign. Of course, Alaeron wanted to plunder the Silver Mount too, but that was because he needed to *understand*.

The least objectionable member of the Technic League was a woman named Zernebeth, who claimed to hail from the ice-locked and witch-haunted land of Irrisen, where the heirs of Baba Yaga ruled. Zernebeth had hair the color of snow and skin with a faint undertone of blue, and there were whispers that she possessed no small measure of fey blood. She certainly had an intellect that was vast and cold and analytic. Alaeron felt some small affinity for her because she'd left a land of dark magic, ruled by fear and superstition, in order to pursue her own voracious hunger to understand the world, a passion Alaeron shared.

As two of the more obvious outsiders in Numeria, the two were naturally pushed together by other members of the Technic League, who assigned Alaeron to be her assistant. He was not a true member of the Technic League, and wasn't inclined to try and become one—the proofs of loyalty they required were monstrous—but he'd proven himself knowledgeable and resourceful enough that they were happy to use him as a sort of half-apprentice. The ruling members of that cabal were fundamentally lazy and decadent, bored even by the atrocities they organized for their amusement, but Zernebeth was different: she wanted nothing more than to wander the plains of Numeria, picking over the wreckage of the Silver Mount, and after months of him assisting her in collecting, cataloguing, and researching relics found in the smaller crash sites, she turned to him one morning and said, "You are ready to see the Silver Mount."

Alaeron grinned at her like a fool across the breakfast table. She had never invited him into her bed, which was just as well—her skin was so cold it made his flesh go numb if she happened to touch his hand, and if she'd shown any romantic interest in him, he would have had a hard time coming up with a delicate way to refuse— but she let him sleep in a storage room attached to her apartments in the palace at Starfall, the better to wake him at three in the morning to ask his opinion on some esoteric point that had been worrying at her mind and keeping her awake. "Thank you." He paused. "When can we go?"

She squinted into the middle distance, then nodded slowly. "Noon. It's the best time to see the Mount up close for the first time."

Zernebeth could never be hurried, so Alaeron had to endure the remainder of the meal as she slowly ate and drank, then told him to clear the dishes away. They had servants for that, of course, but she didn't like letting anyone else into her rooms, so Alaeron was general housekeeper as well as apprentice. He'd barely slept in recent months, and he'd never been happier in his life.

Finally she declared herself ready to set out, and strode from her rooms. Alareon engaged the complex lock on her door and hurried along after her. The palace at Starfall was a brutalist hunk of rock dressed up with bad imitations of the sort of tapestries and other art objects the Sovereign assumed royals enjoyed in the south. They passed a servant girl in a torn dress who scrubbed at a bloodstain on the stone floor while openly weeping, and Alaeron hesitated a moment. He did his best to lose himself in his work, but it was impossible to entirely forget that he was in a country that not only had a monarch, but a puppet monarch who cared nothing at all for his people, ruled by advisors who cared even less. Numeria was a malevolent dictatorship, and even more abhorrent to Alaeron given his Andoren upbringing.

But Zernebeth didn't break stride, so Alaeron tore his eyes away from the weeping servant and hurried after her. He had vague dreams of finding some weapon in the Silver Mount, something so powerful he could use it to destroy the Black Sovereign and the Technic League both and liberate the oppressed people of Numeria, but he knew such notions were impossible from a practical standpoint. The Technic League had already *found* an ultimate weapon in the Mount—the Gearsmen—and that was firmly in their control.

Outside the palace, Zernebeth led the way to her personal conveyance, which she called the "Yaga-walker." The vehicle had been a black carriage, once upon a time, but the wheels had been ripped off and replaced by four legs with multiple articulated joints, each one equipped with a vicious-looking three-toed claw. The top of the carriage had been torn off as well, and the entire seating area was now filled by a gray metal dome that housed whatever strange machineries and power source drove those legs. The only seat left was the high bench where the driver had once perched. At rest, the Yaga-walker resembled a crouching beast. Zernebeth had been inspired by the legendary chicken-legged hut of the witch queen Baba Yaga, though Alaeron secretly doubted that Baba Yaga's hut provided such a rough and bouncy ride.

"Activate the engine," Zernebeth said, seating herself on the padded bench at the front.

Alaeron sighed. He clambered into the interior of the Yaga-walker, stepping over the thick pipes and twisted wires and settling onto the decidedly unpadded remains of one of the passenger seats. He grasped the handle of the hand-crank, which Zernebeth had "requisitioned" from a blacksmith who'd used it to turn a small grinding wheel for fine work on blades. Now the crank was connected to some mechanism beneath the beaten metal dome—Zernebeth wouldn't let him look inside, as it was a device of her own invention that she didn't want copied—and after a few turns he felt tension in the handle, and something under the dome began to hum and rattle. Alaeron hurried up a short ladder and then onto the main bench (that strange engine got *hot*) as the four legs straightened, raising the whole carriage six or so feet off the ground. A pair of levers allowed control over the front and back legs respectively, and another lever acted as the brake, but it took a lot of practice to operate the thing without getting the legs tangled up together.

It all seemed like a lot more trouble than just harnessing a horse to a cart, but then, horses tended to shy away from the Silver Mount, and some of the more exotic riding animals favored by the League—rare giant geckos, desert spiders grown to impossible size by strange radiations—would occasionally go into killing frenzies or mating heats once they got within a few dozen yards of the wreckage, or so Alaeron had heard.

Zernebeth sat rigidly upright in her black cloak threaded with bits of silver wire, looking at the peons in the courtyard with disdain as they scrambled out of the Yaga-walker's path. Alaeron was already sweating in his own coat, and he couldn't understand how the brutal Numerian summer didn't seem to affect Zernebeth— being a creature of the cold, it seemed she should be *more* susceptible to the heat, but no.

Alaeron steered the walker through the courtyard and out the gates, toward one of the roads that radiated from Starfall like the arms of—well, a star. The guards on the gate paid them no mind, and the walker picked up speed as it hit the hard-packed road, and soon they were racing along the flat plains, bouncing alarmingly as they went. Alaeron pulled a rope that set off a horrific high-pitched squeal to warn anyone on the path out of the way. The warning signal had been his idea. Zernebeth didn't seem to *enjoy* the idea of running down peasants with the walker, but she didn't seem especially bothered by it, either. He'd convinced her to implement the safety measure by pointing out that such a collision could damage the armatures of the legs.

The Mount loomed before them. It was the dominant feature in the landscape, so huge it cast a giant shadow for much of the day. Alaeron had no idea how high it was, but it was taller by far than the highest spire in

Almas, literally the size of a mountain, rising from a relatively rounded base to fragmented peaks, all craggy with jagged spires. It *was* silver, in the main, though dark liquid streaks ran down the walls, some of them as broad as rivers, many of them collected by servants of the League. Some of those liquids were terrible poisons or deadly corrosives, but others were potent and addictive drugs. Or, rather, they had the *effect* of potent or addictive drugs; that obviously wasn't what they *were*, but simply a side effect. That was the difference between Alaeron and the arcanists of the League: they only cared what the mysteries of the Mount could *do*, while Alaeron wanted to know what they were *meant* to do.

The skalds of Numeria told of the Silver Mount's arrival in the deep and distant past: a great screaming falling star that looked bigger than the moon and broke apart high in the sky, dropping fragments that exploded on impact, destroying farms and villages. No one knew where the ship (if it was a ship, and not a palace, or even, as some believed, a living thing) came from—were there other worlds in the sky? Had it come from *outside*, some other plane, and encountered an unexpected obstacle in the form of Golarion itself? Whatever its origin, the Mount had fed the livelihood of countless adventurers and plunderers—and been the death of many more. For decades it had been in the complete control of the League, and as the walker drew near, they passed checkpoints manned at first mostly by human servants and, as they reached the inner ring of barricades, by the terrible Gearsmen who made League control absolute.

The name was a misnomer, Alaeron thought as one of the Gearsmen beckoned the walker toward a spot just off the road. He had seen clockwork automata, and these were nothing like those—the Gearsmen were humanoid, but their bodies seemed made of smooth metal, like cooled quicksilver, but with the color of burnished steel. Some of them seemed like mobile suits of armor—without the joints—while others had the sort of faces children would make in clay dolls with their fingertips: indentations for eyes, a slash for a mouth, noses without nostrils or nostrils without noses. They looked like sculptures of humans created by a beginning artist who didn't entirely understand anatomy or fundamental physical proportions—something about the length of legs, or the torsos, or perhaps the position of the elbows or knees, simply seemed *off*.

But that very alien-ness made them even more menacing. They seldom spoke, and Alaeron had never heard their voices—from what he'd been told about the ear-ringing qualities of their vocal harmonics, he was glad. They served the League as unkillable enforcers, immune to the thrusts of swords, indifferent to the fall of clubs. There were stories about one being crushed by a boulder, only to crawl out from underneath—*in pieces*—and put itself back together again. They were the bedrock of the League's dominance, and the greatest treasure ever found in the Mount.

And yet, Zernebeth did not like them, and avoided sending them on errands. When Alaeron had asked why, she'd looked around, lowered her voice, and said, "Because sometimes they do not *listen*. Ninety-nine orders out of a hundred, they will obey unhesitatingly, but sometimes, they refuse, or do the opposite of what they're asked. They do not question, and they certainly do not *explain*—they just *act*. And in those moments, the League has no recourse. How do you punish an invincible metal man? So all we can do is . . . accept their disobedience. If the Gearsmen decided, for their own incomprehensible reasons, to murder us all in our beds, they could do so without trouble. They are our guard dogs, and our pack animals, but they could turn on us in a moment. And yet, without them, how could we rule?" She shrugged. "I care not for League politics. I am only interested in the work. But without the League's dominance, I could not *do* that work. Sometimes I think the decision to use the Gearsmen was the greatest mistake the League ever made, as dangerously stupid as the bargain the Chelaxians struck with the devils who gave *them* an empire."

The Gearsman guarding their chosen entrance to the Mount showed no inclination to murder them. It simply showed them where to put the walker, then led them toward the Mount.

"A moment," Zernebeth said, pausing some distance away from the base of the great ship. "The sun is nearly at its peak. Look."

Alaeron looked, just as the sun emerged from behind the highest peak of the Silver Mount and poured its light down upon the structure. He gasped, averted his gaze, then looked back through slit eyes.

The mountain caught the sunlight the way a faceted gem catches lamplight: throwing sparkles. But these were sparkles on a monumental scale, great flashes of silver light so bright they outdazzled the sun that spawned them, and the whole mountain seemed to coruscate with light—it was, Alaeron thought, like looking into the blazing heart of discovery itself, so beautiful it was overwhelming, so powerful it might strike you blind. And there were colors in the lights, too, a full prismatic dispersion, including hues he couldn't even put a name to.

The perfect confluence of sun and Silver Mount lasted only a minute or so. Then the sun moved on ever so minutely, and while the mountain still gleamed, it no longer seemed to radiate light from every curved and jagged inch of its surface. "Beautiful," Alaeron murmured.

"Yes," Zernebeth said matter-of-factly. "There are colors there, shades of blue, that I have only seen in the heart of glaciers. Sometimes birds fly over at just the wrong moment, get dazzled, and fall dead to the ground." She patted the side of the Mount in a friendly way, as if greeting a family pet. "Inside, it is much darker, but there is beauty there, too."

The patient Gearsman decided they were ready and hauled open a ragged hatch that had been cut into the surface of the Silver Mount—using tools forged from even more durable substances found *inside* the Silver Mount, no doubt, as most tools didn't even make a mark on the mountain's skin. "We will be the first ones through," Zernebeth said. "This is new as of a few days ago, and leads to a passageway no one else has explored."

Alaeron couldn't help it: he grinned, widely and unselfconsciously. "I can't wait."

His mistress passed him an alchemical lantern that glowed greenly, but brightly, and checked her own supplies—enchanted knives, ropes, a prybar, mesh sacks that could block the dangerous emanations produced by some relics—and pronounced herself ready. "You first," she said, and nodded toward the dark opening.

That made sense. Send the expendable apprentice. He ducked through the opening, lantern held aloft.

The opening led to a gently curving corridor of metal, smooth and polished as a surgeon's instrument, just tall enough to stand upright—if he'd gone up on tiptoes, he would have hit his head. "Left or right?" he said, as Zernebeth entered behind him.

"Left, to start." She marked the wall with a blob of paint that fluoresced in his lantern's glow. At his questioning look, she shrugged. "Always mark your path in the Mount. Sometimes things . . . shift. It's easy to become lost."

As he moved along the slightly convex floor, he tried to mentally orient himself: if the Silver Mount was a ship, and it had crashed nose-down, then this hallway was sideways and perpendicular to . . . but his spatial skills failed him, partly because the passage itself changed, narrowing and widening at irregular intervals, sometimes so tight he had to turn sideways to pass, other times so wide a battalion of Gearsmen could have marched down it in formation. "Is it all like this?" he said, whispering despite himself.

"No," she said. "Some passages are more . . . organic. Others seem to be stone. Some are made of a substance clear as glass, but infinitely more durable. *Those* are frustrating—we can actually *see* things on the other side of those clear walls, relics beyond counting, but we have yet to find a weapon or tool that can so much as scratch the surface of the walls, and there are no doors."

"No doors here, either," he said, a bit glumly. The passageway slanted downward at a sharp angle, so steep he wasn't sure they'd be able to climb back *up* if they went down it—they'd practically have to slide instead of walking to descend."

Zernebeth grunted. "Adhesive?" she said.

"Ah, right." Alaeron reached into his coat, his fingers finding the right vial by the markings incised on the lid, and passed over a substance of his own devising. You might call it "glue," but only in the same way you might call a broadsword a potato peeler. Zernebeth carefully tipped over the vial, dropping a blob of the pale pink adhesive onto the floor, then pressing the end of a climbing rope into the substance before it could dry. They waited a few seconds, then she tugged on the rope experimentally—the adhesive held it fast. The rope was stuck there permanently, probably—the glue was the strongest Alaeron could make, and it would hold the weight of a war mammoth.

Alaeron descended first, slowly easing his way down the slope—he *could* slide down, except there was no telling what he might slide into. The ramp went down for what felt like miles but was really probably only a few hundred yards, based on counting his steps. Zernebeth came after, and finally the passage flattened out again . . . and dead-ended in a door of sorts, a circular hatch with no visible hinges.

"We must be deep underground," Zernebeth said. "Few passages go so far below. Here—take a breathing apparatus." She passed him a pair of small filters for his nostrils. He slipped them in, though he hated the discomfort. Better than being killed from inhaling some ancient gas from the stars, though. Of course, a corrosive mist could still melt their flesh, or a horror that only existed halfway in this dimension might emerge and eat their souls, but those things happened relatively rarely, so the odds were in their favor. Such were the risks you took when you explored the Mount. Most chambers the League unsealed were entirely empty, or full of nothing but dust and bones that crumbled into similar dust when touched.

Zernebeth examined the crack that ran around the outside of the hatch, then chose a long prybar from her pack. She slotted the flattened end of the bar into the gap and heaved, putting all her weight into it. The door creaked and squealed but didn't open. "We need more force," she said. "You brought your mutagen?"

Alaeron sighed. That was one of the ways he'd bought his way into the Technic League, and they'd even forced him to demonstrate the effects of his mutagenic potion for the Black Sovereign himself, not that the barbarian had seemed to pay any attention. But Alaeron hated the way the mutagen made him feel, dulling his mind as the cost of enhancing other capabilities. "Yes." He fished out the vial, then took off his coat and handed it to Zernebeth—no reason to burst that at the seams. He uncorked the vial and tossed back the slimy contents in a single gulp, the better to avoid tasting it. A mixture of hormones, chemicals, extracts from fell monsters, and other secret ingredients, the mutagen gave Alaeron himself certain properties of a beast.

The change came over him quickly, and he shivered, coarse hairs sprouting from his skin with pinprick sensations, fingernails elongating and hardening, spine curving and hunching him over, muscles gaining mass and definition, teeth growing longer and more crowded in his mouth as his face lengthened, almost forming a snout. His vision constricted and grew dimmer, but the acuity of his nose increased hugely in compensation, smell his most powerful sense even with the nostril filters in. He took in Zernebeth's icy scent, with its odd floral undertones; the alien metal of the Mount itself; and, beyond the hatch, wisping through the tiny crack Zernebeth had made, the scent of dust and ancient death.

"Go on, before it wears off," Zernebeth said.

Alaeron bared his fangs—who was she to tell him what to do, she was *little*, he could tear her arms off without effort—but he wasn't entirely bestial, and his conscious mind overrode his instinctive rage. He moved closer to the hatch, feeling constricted by the narrowness of the passageway and eager to open up more space. He seized the prybar in his clawed hands and *shoved*, pushing with so much force it would have snapped his bones if they hadn't been strengthened by the mutagen.

The hatch howled, metal grinding against metal, and Alaeron growled and pushed harder. The barrier popped open, not swinging on hinges but simply falling to the floor with a huge *clang*. Like it wasn't meant to open at all, but merely set in place to seal something in. No gases emerged—not visibly, anyway. Alaeron dropped the prybar and picked up the lantern in one of his clumsy clawed hands, then stepped through the hole into the space beyond, swiveling his head around in search of lurking dangers. Sometimes members of the League went into the Mount and never came out again. Even in this massive tomb, things yet lived, and some of them were hungry.

The room was spherical, as round as the inside of an eyeball, the size of a decent inn's common room. The walls were mostly the same silver as the corridor, except for a wide rectangular panel of black glass, so smooth it made a shadowy mirror.

There was nothing else, except the bones.

"Safe," he said, voice still half a growl, though his teeth were getting smaller, his muscles bulging less, his spine straightening. The mutagen didn't last long, though he'd been working on refinements to make it more powerful. He'd rather be smart than strong just now, though.

Zernebeth came after him, grunting as she scanned the room.

Alaeron crouched on the curved floor, examining the mess piled in the center of the room. At first he thought it was a jumble of bones from several people, piled together, until his perception oriented itself sufficiently for him to realize it was the remains of a *single* life form. The skeleton—which seemed at least as much stone and metal as bone, and had a few joints that appeared made of steel—had no fewer than nine limbs, some ending in a profusion of smaller bones that might have been fingers, others ending in fused lumps of metal that could have been decorative or prosthetic or something else entirely. Alaeron crab-walked in a circle around the skeleton, pointing out its flattened skull, which sported a single ocular cavity and no fewer than three jaws. "Amazing," he murmured. "Is this one of the creatures that piloted the Silver Mount through the heavens?"

Zernebeth's silence was very loud. Alaeron glanced over at her. She stood with her arms crossed, staring critically not at the dead creature, but at *him*. He winced. "Of course, a fallacy of assumptions. Because it is *on* the ship does not mean the ship *belongs* to it. It could be a servant, or a slave, or a prisoner, or a stowaway."

"Good," Zernebeth said, finally stepping into the room. "Though not good enough. You're still making assumptions. This creature could be *vermin*, the equivalent of a wharf rat. Or it could be livestock. For that matter, who says the Silver Mount is a ship? We simply have no idea." She squinted. "Look at these. Relics. Devices."

Alaeron nodded. Scattered among the bones were six small objects: one gray and disc-shaped; another like an egg; a short length of golden chain; something like a child's toy top made of porcelain and gold; a circle of dark red metal that might have been a child's bracelet;

and a toothed black gear-wheel the size of a saucer. "Do you think this creature had them in its clothes, and then the clothes rotted away? Or that it somehow wore them like jewelry, or kept them to hand as tools—"

"All fascinating questions," she said, "but I'm more interested in seeing what they *do*." She reached out, touching the spindly golden chain—and it reacted almost as if alive, drawing its segments inward and curling into a ball, like a pill-bug rolling up to protect itself. "Hmm," Zernebeth said, but then all the *other* pieces started moving too: the top began to rotate slowly, not quite picking up enough speed to stand on its point; the egg jumped as if something inside it wanted to hatch; the disc hummed and *levitated*, floating a few inches off the ground; and the gear-wheel turned with a horrendous grinding sound, even though it wasn't turning *against* anything at all. The relics began moving toward one another in a shuddering, slow, inefficient way, with the terrible sounds of broken machinery trying to work despite catastrophic failure.

Zernebeth hissed and drew back her hand. "Separate them. Who knows what will happen if they combine? I want to *know*, of course, but in a contained environment."

Alaeron nodded, and hurriedly drew out one of the mesh bags they used for carrying dangerous relics— basically a chainmail shirt of skymetal made into a sack. He pulled on thick leather gloves, then reached out tentatively for the gear wheel, which continued turning, but slowly, as if it were sticking on something. He plucked it from the bones, and it stopped moving. All the other relics did, too, falling inert to the floor. He put three in one bag and three in another, unwilling to let them all touch, just in case. "All right," he said. "Do we take some of the skeleton with us, or—"

There was a *click*, loud as a snapping twig in a silent forest, and Zernebeth swore, softly. Alaeron looked up and saw her staring down. There was a discolored patch on the floor beneath her boot, as if the metal were tarnished . . . or just worn from being touched many, many times. "I think I just activated something," she said, in the same tone one might use to say, "I think it's incurable."

"Should we run, or . . ."

She shook her head. "If it's a trap of some kind, and I remove my foot, it could do anything: explode, crush us, suck all the air out of the room—" She frowned. "Look."

Alaeron turned his head. The black glass panel on the wall was changing, shapes flickering across it in clear white lines, diagrams and drawings like blueprints or maps or schematics, flickering past too quickly for comprehension. Beams of light shone forth from the corners of the screen, and when Alaeron traced their paths, he saw the beams converged directly on Zernebeth's face—shining right into her eyes. Her expression was glassy, and her breathing became ragged. "So much," she murmured. "I see, I see, it's so much, it's . . ."

Then she screamed. Smoke began to rise from her eye sockets, and as Alaeron watched, blood poured from her nose, ears, and mouth. Still she screamed, but she seemed rooted where she stood, unable to step away, and now the black screen was alive with colors, more colors than a rainbow, than a slick of oil on water, than the Silver Mount at noon. Alaeron scrambled backward, averting his eyes from the screen. The twist of colors made his stomach churn. The relics in their sacks buzzed and jerked and twisted, and Alaeron nearly dropped them—but he was arcanist enough to hold on. Zernebeth began to jerk and shiver as if being jolted by lightning, and Alaeron's hair all stood on end. Something was happening in the room; some sort of charge was building. "I'm sorry," he said, though Zernebeth was beyond hearing, and he bolted from the room. He snatched up his coat, shoved the relics into the wide pockets, and seized the rope with both hands, climbing as fast as he could, the lantern left behind on the floor. As he ascended through the darkness, away from the puddle of light below, he heard a great crash, as of glass shattering, and the whole passageway hummed and vibrated, a resonance that made his teeth ache.

He made it to the top, down the hallway, through the gash in the skin of the Mount, and into the light. The Gearsman still stood guard. "Zernebeth," Alaeron said, gasping. "Of the Technic League, she's inside, I—I think she died."

The Gearsman regarded him impassively for a moment, then picked up the metal sheet cut from the Mount and slid it back into place, closing up the opening and hammering on the metal to bang it firmly back into place. Then it returned to its position, standing and waiting for who knew what.

"Are you going to . . . to retrieve her body, or . . ."

The Gearsman said nothing, and Alaeron backed away until he reached the walker. Then he cranked it up and awkwardly guided it back to Starfall, shaken by what he'd seen and trying to think of what he would tell the members of the League.

Deciding, early on, that he *wouldn't* be telling them about the relics he'd recovered. Zernebeth was the closest thing in this place he'd had to a friend, and she'd given her life to get those relics out of the Mount. He owed it to her to find out what they were.

# Chapter Nine
## Confusion Bombs

Hmm," Skiver said when Alaeron finished speaking. "Not bad, but next time you tell it, make it so you and Zernebeth were in love. Makes a better story, and there's a whole added bit of heartstring-pulling when she dies that way. Makes you more mysterious and all scarred by loss and such too. Makes you seem more *deep*. People love that."

Alaeron shook his head, and almost laughed. "You said you wanted the truth."

"Well, sure," Skiver said. "But the truth shouldn't get in the way of a good story." He tossed the relic shaped like a child's top toward Alaeron, who snatched it from the air and slipped it into his pocket. Gods, what if Skiver had decided to set it *spinning*? Here, on a boat, at sea, the consequences would have been disastrous.

He'd never told that story before, and though it was sad to think of Zernebeth's death again—even if she had been, looking at it objectively, nearly as bad as everyone else in the League—it was also nice to let it all out, and Skiver was an attentive and appreciative audience.

"Want to play again for another of your toys?" Skiver said. "I wouldn't mind hearing how you made it out of Numeria, assuming you didn't just give them a week's notice and say you'd had a better job offer someone else."

Alaeron nodded. "I suppose I could—"

The door rattled, and Skiver rose as it opened. Jaya was there, eyes wide, hair wild, with a bow in her hand and a quiver of arrows slung over her shoulder. "Come on!" she shouted. "Up on deck, right away!"

"What's the trouble?" Skiver said, more serious than Alaeron had ever seen him before.

"Pirates," Jaya said grimly. "Following us, and getting closer."

Skiver began to grin. "Oh, good. There's killing to be done, then."

But all Alaeron could think was: What if it's not pirates?

What if it was his past, trying to catch up with him again?

The captain was standing on the deck at the back of the ship—Alaeron didn't know what it was called, stern or bow or mizzen or something—peering through a spyglass. He claimed to be of nearly pure Azlanti descent, and Alaeron had *just* managed to keep from rolling his eyes at such pretentious twaddle. The captain at least had the old Azlanti look, more or less, except for the bushy oversized sideburns he grew in apparent compensation for his receding hairline. The sailors were all working busily as usual, but they were casting lots of looks behind them to where a ship approached, growing visibly larger with each passing moment.

The captain snapped his spyglass closed and looked around. "You two!" he shouted. "The archer says you might be of use. Can you fight?"

Skiver produced a knife from somewhere and twirled it around his fingers a few times, grinning lazily. The captain nodded, then squinted at Alaeron. "You?"

Alaeron coughed. "I have . . . certain items, and expertise . . . which could be useful in a battle."

The captain stroked his beardless chin. "I've heard of alchemists who experiment on themselves—growing extra arms, tentacles. Gills like a fish. Wings. Great long claws and teeth. Are you that sort?" Jaya looked at Alaeron wide-eyed, and even Skiver lifted an eyebrow.

Alaeron did have a vial of mutagen in his coat, and he'd improved the formula since his time in Numeria, but he'd never actually used it in a fight. Having teeth and claws and a terrible temper didn't actually make one a competent warrior. (As for tentacles, wings, and gills—not to mention mobile attack tumors, the power to vomit swarms of spiders, or spawning fully functional duplicates of his own body—he hadn't invested the time or considerable gold necessary to master such effects, his interests lying mostly elsewhere.) So he decided to mention something he thought they might like just as much: "Well . . . I can make bombs."

"What, alchemist's fire? Could be some use, I daresay—"

"No," Alaeron said. "I mean, yes, I have alchemist's fire, but I also have rather . . . more exotic items that could be of greater use once the pirates are in range."

"Mmm," the captain said. "At the rate they're gaining, that'll be sooner rather than later. Just be sure you don't drop any of your bombs on my deck. Best get ready, everyone, to repel boarders."

Skiver wandered over to a group of sailors snatching up swords from a barrel—mostly a battered bunch of secondhand weapons by the look of them. Alaeron went to Jaya's side, then knelt by his bag, mixing catalyst into prepared flasks, measuring out ingredients by hand. He'd had a lot of practice making bombs. The Technic League loved them. But he was making some bombs here that he'd *never* shown the masters of Numeria.

"All those little bottles and things," she said. "They'll make explosions? Put a hole in that ship?"

"Among other things," Alaeron said. "Are we sure they're pirates? I thought the shipping lanes in the Inner Sea were safe."

Jaya shook her head. "They're flying no flag, and bearing down on us fast, but ignoring the captain's attempts to communicate with flags or signal mirrors. If they're not pirates, they're lunatics. But, yes, it's rare to see piracy so close to the Isle of Kortos—it's not as if we're in The Shackles. Absalom punishes pirates gravely. When they do strike here, they usually go after high-value targets, ships known to carry gold or treasures. We're carrying cloth, mostly. It's a routine trip . . . the captain doesn't understand it. The pirates must be truly desperate to risk their lives attacking us. At least they don't have yellow sails—those are the trademark of the Okeno slavers, and they're merciless. With ordinary pirates it's possible to negotiate, though the captain seems determined to fight it out." She shook her head.

Alaeron tried to weigh the possibilities. If this sort of piracy was rare . . . What were the odds that Kormak would hire a ship to come after him? How would he even *find* Alaeron? Vadim was hardly the sort of man to let word of his business spread. Probably just coincidence, he decided. Corsairs, not Kormak.

Once his bombs were prepared and arrayed in the belt of pouches he slung over his shoulder, he stood up—and was shocked to see how close the ship had come. Not within range of his bombs yet, but close enough to make out the individual figures on deck. The pirate vessel was smaller than their ship, and riding higher in the water, but Alaeron's lack of maritime knowledge prevented him from making any other determinations about it. The ship was fast, anyway, and the deck was swarming with figures. A few of them were practicing swinging ropes with grappling hooks on the end, the hooks splashing down into the water only to be reeled in and thrown again.

"Archers!" the captain bellowed. Jaya stepped forward, along with a couple of sailors holding crossbows, and readied their weapons. "We'd better take out the men with the hooks, hadn't we?" he said.

The crossbowmen fired, but their bolts fell short. The pirates returned fire, with similar results. Jaya clucked her tongue. "Crossbows. They're toys. Anyone can use them—but what good are they? Even the best of them is nothing compared to a real bow." She lifted her weapon, selected an arrow, nocked it, pulled back, and released. Without pausing to watch the arrow's flight, she slotted another, drew, and loosed that too. A pair of the men with the grappling hooks tumbled into the water before the rest scampered back.

Alaeron didn't know much about archery, but Jaya looked sufficiently pleased with herself that he assumed her work was impressive. The captain confirmed that when he whistled. "Fair shooting, archer!"

"Here, don't kill them all," Skiver said. "Save a few for the rest of us. Especially me."

"Plenty to go around," the captain said. He glanced at Alaeron. "Well? Shouldn't you be hurling pots at them?"

"Ah. Well, I'd need to be quite close to throw them. Ideally no more than about twenty feet—"

The captain went red. "Twenty *feet*? If they're that close they'll be *boarding* us, locked in hand-to-hand combat with my men! I won't have you tossing firepots into a melee, man!"

"I have a sling," Jaya said, drawing and loosing another arrow. "Can you use one?"

Alaeron smiled. "Oh, yes. Not as well as you, I'm sure, but with these weapons, precision strikes are not necessary—as long as they fall in the general vicinity of the pirates, they will be most effective."

Jaya crouched, reached into her bag, withdrew a leather sling, flung it at Alaeron, and nocked another arrow.

Alaeron untangled the sling. He'd used such weapons often as a boy, hurling pebbles at rats and such, but not lately.

"Mind you don't set my ship on fire!" the captain growled.

"Fear not. I do have explosives, of course." Alaeron watched the gap between the ships narrow as the pirate ship sped on, weighing the bomb in his sling. Better to let them get a *bit* closer. "But I don't propose to begin with those. I was recently in Numeria, where I obtained certain rare substances. The decadent aristocrats of the city of Starfall are known to imbibe all manner of mysterious fluids collected from the great wreck known as the Silver Mount." He hefted a round-bottomed flask in his hand, the dark purple fluid inside sloshing and fizzing. "These fluids have myriad effects, often hallucinatory, from providing a sense of peace and well-being to making the drinker feel trapped in a realm of living nightmare. I have carefully mixed a number of the most potent drugs to create this concoction. I call it a confusion bomb." He smiled at the captain. "Any alchemist can make a bomb that burns wood," he said. "But I have crafted weapons that sear *minds*."

There was a moment of silence as the crew, Skiver, and Jaya regarded him. Then the captain said, "Do you always give flowery speeches when you're about to be attacked by pirates? Go on and throw it then!"

Alaeron sighed. No one appreciated his genius. He judged the pirate ship was close enough now, just. He fitted the bottle into the sling's pouch and set the weapon whirling over his head, then loosed the projectile. It sailed in an arc up and over the deck of the pirate ship, where it splashed down on the deck, spraying purplish fluid in all directions, and producing a great haze of mist that shimmered with the colors of the Silver Mount at noon. He slung another confusion bomb—that one missed the ship by a few feet and sank, damn it—but his third struck a different part of the deck. He slung his fourth and final bomb as far toward the rear of the ship as he could, where most of the pirates had gathered to avoid bombs and arrows.

"Better ready another volley, archers," the captain said. "It doesn't look like the alchemist's bottle of purple juice has done anything—"

Then one of the pirates leapt off the deck, clawing at his clothes and shrieking, and tried to swim frantically toward the *Pride of Azlant* before sinking under the waves. Other pirates started climbing into the rigging, only to fall off, or become entangled and hang upside down, or leap from a greater height into the sea. Some were fighting one another, or writhing on deck, or trying to set fire to the sails, while those who'd been outside the range of the bomb did their best to restrain their fellows. The ship began to veer just slightly off course.

"By Gozreh's trident," the captain said. "I've never seen the like."

"You are a master of terrible magics," Jaya said gravely, but not without admiration.

"That's proper monstrous, all right," Skiver said. "Are they mad forever, then?"

Alareon shook his head. "The effects should wear off soon." He handed Jaya back her sling, which she handled gingerly, as if afraid the bombs might have left some residue behind.

"We don't need to kill the pirates, then," Jaya said. "We can just get away."

"Hmm," the captain said. "Isn't it pretty to think so? But no. If they caught us, they'd put us all to the sword, or take us as slaves, or throw us into the sea to drown. I don't see any reason to show them mercy just because their plan to murder us all failed." He paused, watching as one pirate successfully set his own hair on fire and began capering around the deck. "Not that this looks all that merciful, really. When the alchemist's madness *does* wear off, I don't imagine they'll decide to leave us alone. We could try to board their ship, take the ones left as prisoners to the authorities in Absalom . . . but I don't fancy that. We're behind schedule already." He clapped Alaeron on the shoulder. "So. About that alchemical fire?"

"You would burn them all?" Jaya said. "As they go mad, and claw at themselves?"

"They knew the business they were getting into," Skiver said, almost gently. "If you break into a man's house to steal his gold and he catches you and skewers you with a sword, you've got no business complaining— that's the risk that comes with the job."

"I'm afraid I agree with Jaya," Alaeron said. "I'm . . . not comfortable burning them out like this." In truth, he didn't care one way or another whether the pirates burned or drowned—they were scum, and murderers, no doubt—but he thought standing with Jaya might earn him her admiration, and she did give him a grateful look.

The captain shrugged. "I could throw you off the deck for disobeying me—it's my ship, and my word is law—but your patron paid me good money to deliver you safely, and that was a good trick with the bombs. So, fine, don't give me any of your fire. Tar bombs it is!"

"Wait—" Jaya said, but the captain was already calling orders to the sailors, who produced lumps of sticky tar hanging from short lengths of rope. Once the blobs were lit, the sailors whirled them around on their ropes—much like Alaeron had just done with the sling—and released, sending a barrage of flame arcing toward the pursuing ship. Several missiles slammed into sails and decking and stuck fast. The crossbowmen sent off a few flaming arrows as well, adding to the conflagration.

The captain strode back toward Jaya. "I'm not without mercy," he said. "I won't shoot the ones who abandon ship. They can grab a bit of flotsam, and if the gods decide to save them, so be it."

"I'm going belowdecks," Jaya said. "I've seen enough fires in my life, I don't need to see another."

"I'll go with—" Alaeron started to say, but stopped. He'd seen something, on the pirate ship. Could it be? No, certainly not . . .

"What?" Jaya said.

"I, ah . . . I'll see you later, then," he said, leaning over the railing and peering at the other ship, which was rapidly becoming engulfed in smoke and flame, with sailors mad and sane alike leaping into the water to escape the certain death on board.

"Don't suppose I could buy a few of those bombs off you?" the captain said. "Could be useful."

"They don't work for anyone else," Alaeron said absently, squinting into the smoke. "They're attuned to my personal magical field."

"Shame," the captain said. "They're just the thing to break up a riot—or start one." He walked off, bellowing at his crew, leaving Alaeron to stare, and to look for . . .

There. A man, stepping out of the smoke toward the front of the ship. He was a huge figure, bigger by far than the other pirates. The ship was listing to one side now, sails completely aflame, with the body of the vessel not faring much better, and the distance between the ships was growing ever larger, but even at this distance, Alaeron could recognize the man: Kormak, the Kellid enforcer sent by the Technic League. The man stood on the burning, sinking ship as calmly as if he were on a street corner, and he extended his arm, straight out, pointing at Alaeron across the gulf of water between them. As if to say: *You. I'm coming for you.*

Alaeron took a step back instinctively, even though there was no way the Kellid could reach them . . . unless the Technic League had given him equipment enabling him to fly, or leap great distances. Alaeron's mouth went dry. Were those men even really pirates? Or just sailors the Kellid had hired—or threatened?—into pursuing his quarry? Was Alaeron to blame for the madness and death of innocent men?

A horrible thought. The sort of thought that made him want to retire to a laboratory in the country, where he'd never have to see or speak to another person, but just lose himself in his researches.

Fortunately, the Kellid apparently lacked the power to fly. The ship slowly sank, with Kormak never moving from his position on the foredeck, until he was obscured entirely by smoke.

Too much to hope that Kormak would drown. But being adrift in the Inner Sea might, at least, slow him down. Surely he wouldn't be able to pursue Alaeron forever? Not once their party got to Osirion, and on into the mountains on the eastern edge of the Mwangi Expanse—even *Alaeron* didn't know exactly where they were going, so how could Kormak possibly follow?

Initially Alaeron had counted himself lucky that the League had sent a human after him, instead of dispatching one of the tireless Gearsmen to bring him back. But what if Kormak was even more relentless than a metal man from the stars? After all, Kormak had the capacity to take things *personally*. What if the Kellid never stopped his pursuit?

I hope the savage lands of the south suit me, Alaeron thought, for I may never be able to return to civilized lands again.

# Chapter Ten
## The City at the Center of the World

The remaining days of their voyage to the Isle of Kortos were rather pleasant, since the captain invited Jaya, Alaeron, and Skiver to dine with him each night in thanks for their service in repelling the pirates. Skiver hadn't actually done anything, but no one doubted he would have enthusiastically stabbed anyone who managed to board, and Jaya had apparently forgiven the captain for his harsh treatment of the pirates, though she may just have been playing nice for the pleasure of his table.

The food was quite a bit better than they'd enjoyed previously on the journey, and the captain was the most educated person Alaeron had spoken to in some time. They were both adept at ignoring Jaya's boredom as they discussed their conflicting interpretations of world philosophy over their meals, though Alaeron had his chance to be bored when Jaya and the captain began comparing experiences in the various far-flung cities of the Inner Sea, trying to one-up one another regarding visits to the most outlandish ports of call—the captain had been to Halgrim in the far-off Lands of the Linnorm Kings, so Jaya conceded defeat. (Though if they actually made it to the ruins of Kho and back, she'd never lose a "most exotic destination" argument ever again, Alaeron reflected.) Skiver never seemed bored by anything, though he did perk up a bit whenever talk turned to killing pirates, putting down mutinies, sea monster attacks, and the fine points of scuttling ships infected with the plague.

The only problem with the trip was the fact that Skiver still had two of Alaeron's artifacts, and didn't seem inclined to give them back. Alaeron had offered several times to trade him more stories for the relics, but Skiver refused: "I found a secret floating dice game belowdecks," he said happily, "and there's nobody on this boat who can throw worth a damn. I'm keeping plenty entertained, thanks. I'll just hold onto your trinkets a while longer. I figure if nothing else they're insurance for your good behavior, eh? If Ralen Vadim had known you had something you cared so much about, he'd have kept them locked in a box in Andoran against your safe return. All I'm doing is borrowing them for a while. That's a kindness by comparison. I'll keep them safe, don't you worry."

Alaeron had considered drugging the man and stealing his possessions back, but he and Skiver were trapped on a ship together, and unless Alaeron was willing to actually murder the man and throw him overboard, any sort of conflict would just lead to more problems. Besides, Ralen Vadim had paid the captain of this ship—who knew what their relationship was, or what instructions the captain had regarding Alaeron? He didn't dare make a move.

Which meant his studies were interrupted. He'd been testing the relics methodically to see how they interacted with one another. He'd never seen all of them begin to buzz and move and draw together as they had in the Silver Mount, but they *did* affect one another— sometimes sticking together almost magnetically, or growing warm in proximity, or setting up a strange resonating hum like two lute strings vibrating in sympathy. It took time to work through every possible set of combinations, and he had a journal filled with notes no one else would be able to decipher, but Skiver had torn away one-third of his data set, and why? Because it amused him. What a peculiar and infuriating man.

On the good side, Jaya seemed to have a new respect for Alaeron, either because she'd seen his alchemy at work, or because he'd spoken up to agree when she'd opposed burning the pirate ship. They'd begun spending more time together, walking up on deck, enjoying the generally fine weather and the sea breeze, and talking: Alaeron telling her for free stories Skiver was forced to extort from him (albeit casting himself in a somewhat more heroic light, for her benefit), while Jaya was a fount of hilarious and harrowing stories about her travels with her family throughout the Inner Sea region. Alaeron had always told himself he had no time for romance, but as he grew more fond of Jaya, he began to suspect he'd actually had no real *opportunity* before. Not that romance blossomed between them, precisely, but there was certainly friendship, and the way Jaya occasionally put her hand on his, or took his arm as they strolled around the foredeck, gave him hope for future intimacy.

"Look!" she said, on what the captain assured them would be the last day of their voyage. She pointed toward the eastern horizon, where a smudge of brown and green was visible.

"Land, finally," Alaeron said. "I haven't been to Absalom since I was a young man. They do a wonderful sort of spiced cake there. I wonder—"

"No, not that," Jaya interrupted. "There, in the water."

Alaeron squinted, seeing nothing but rippling water and the dazzle of sunshine on the waves—ah! Something was moving in the water. It looked like a man swimming, but here, this far from land, with no craft in sight? Alaeron gripped the railing so hard it made his knuckles ache, and his throat began to close up with fear. Was it Kormak, swimming tirelessly, fueled by the strange tinctures of the Technic League, ready to clamber up the side of the ship and seize Alaeron by the throat again?

"Gillmen move so gracefully," Jaya said.

Alaeron closed his eyes for a moment, taking a deep breath, then opened them again. With his eyes unclouded by panic, he could see the figure in the water wasn't big enough to be Kormak anyway. Looking closer, Alaeron saw the gillman had the pale skin and dark hair—and, presumably, purple eyes—of the old Azlanti people. "Ah. Yes. I don't think I've ever seen one."

Jaya nodded. "I haven't, often, and only around Absalom. They have an embassy at Escadar, you know, and worship at some old Azlanti ruins there."

"Looks just like a human," Alaeron said.

"So they once were," Jaya said. "Or so the stories say. They have gill slits, in their necks, and they don't do well if they stay out of water for long, but otherwise, yes, they are very like men. In every . . . relevant detail." There was a small smile on her lips that Alaeron found both intriguing and horrifying. Was she suggesting that she'd . . . been *intimate* with one of them? If so, what was the attraction? Just the exoticism?

And was, say, an alchemist exotic enough to catch her fancy too? Maybe he should have spent more time studying bodily mutation. If she liked men with gills, he could learn to grow them, given some time and a decent laboratory . . .

The captain approached. "Archer, alchemist, you'd best pack up your things." He'd never called them by their names once, and for that matter, Alaeron's group never called him anything but "captain." "We'll dock within the hour, and I need you off my ship and on your way."

"Of course," Alaeron said. "Thank you for your hospitality."

The captain waved it away. "No thanks necessary. It was nice to take a few meals with people who talk about something other than shipping lanes and import tariffs. You're a decent foredeck philosopher, Alaeron, even if you are dead wrong about the implications of the Prophecies of Kalistrade for international commerce. I might bring an educated civilian along on every trip in the future, just for conversation." He bowed formally to Jaya. "My lady of the bow, you are as charming as you are deadly, and as deadly as you are beautiful, and I'll be sure to try that fish house you recommended next time I'm on the far side of the Arch of Aroden. If you ever need passage anywhere my ship goes, you need only write, care of my address in Absalom."

Jaya kissed the captain just to the left of one of his muttonchop sideburns, which gave Alaeron the new and ridiculous experience of being jealous of another man's cheek.

Alaeron followed Skiver down the gangplank, with Jaya at his back. Stepping onto the solid ground of the dock after so long at sea was profoundly disorienting—he had to lower his head and take deep breaths and walk very carefully to keep the world from seeming to roll and tilt beneath him.

"Absalom," Skiver said, stopping on the dock and gazing at what little they could see of the city. "It's as grand as they say, innit?"

"Your first time here?" Jaya said.

Skiver grinned. "The world I come from, dearie, if you stray more than a dozen blocks from where you were born, they say you're getting above your station and putting on airs. My clan is not known for their worldly ways. No, I've never been anywhere. Happy for the opportunity to see the world. Why, there must be dozens of kinds of people I've never beaten at cards or kicked in the unmentionables or cadged a drink off of. About time I expanded my horizons."

No denying the city was impressive. Even the ships in the harbor were a wondrous and varied bunch, from cogs, caravels, and carracks to longships that must hail from the Lands of Linnorm Kings and junks with ribbed sails like the fins of swordfish. (Dining with the captain had forced rather a lot of knowledge about ships into Alaeron's brain, which always had room for one more bit of trivia anyway.) There were also any number of wrecked warships in the harbor, tilting masts sticking up from the waves, forming a sort of unnatural reef or maze. The government of Absalom left the ruins of would-be invaders in the water for the same reason savage kings mounted the heads of their enemies on spikes at their gates: as a warning to other potentially hostile visitors. It was also a source of revenue, since an accredited harbormaster from the city had to guide any ship of size through the wreckage for a fee.

From the docks, you could see enough of the city itself to have your breath taken away: golden domes topped with statues; towering spires beyond counting, including one so high it seemed to literally brush the clouds; even the small buildings crowded together close to the water must be exotic to eyes that had only seen Andoran, with tiled roofs and baroque decorative touches. Even the poor here were a house-proud bunch, and why not? They heard every single day that Absalom was the center of the world, and had no reason to doubt it.

"We're going to see a bit of the city," Skiver said firmly. "We don't leave on our next ship until tomorrow morning, so we've got all day, hey?"

Alaeron groaned, and Jaya elbowed him in the ribs. "Come on. Humor him. He hasn't seen the world like we have. Don't you remember your first time here? You didn't go gawk at the cathedral in the Ascendant Court, or drop a note with a wish written on it into the chasm?"

Alaeron had of course done both things—but then, he'd been a boy when he last visited. But seeing Skiver enthusiastic about something other than knives, gambling, or causing annoyance was at least a change from the ordinary.

"So what should we see first?" Skiver said. "You two've been here before."

"The Petal District is very beautiful," Alaeron said. "Views of the whole city from up there, and lovely palaces, and of course the flowers."

"If you're interested in seeing people from all over Golarion, we might visit the Foreign Quarter," Jaya said. "They have food from all over the Inner Sea, too. Chelish spice beef, candied eels in Drenchport style, Katapeshi almonds." Skiver didn't look impressed. Jaya said, "Well, and there's an arena there, too, we could take in a fight . . ."

Skiver grunted. "Better, but how about getting *into* a fight? A city this big, there must be places to eat and drink and gamble, where I can see all sorts of interesting foreigners and take their money away."

"Ah," Jaya said. "You don't want to see the Precipice Quarter, or the Azlanti Keep, or—"

"I want to see the bottom of a tankard of ale," Skiver said. "I'd like to see it several times in a row, if you get me. That watered rum they had on the ship didn't agree with me. And then I might like to see a different sort of bottom, or two." He winked. "So what do you say?"

Jaya and Alaeron exchanged a glance. "Well, then," Alaeron said. "I guess we should go to . . . the Coins?"

Jaya nodded. "The Coins."

"Sounds grand," Skiver said. "The Coins. A rich place, is it? Streets paved with silver and gold?"

"Not exactly," Alaeron said.

Skiver took to the Coins like he'd been born to it, though in point of fact, very few were *born* to the Coins. It was the chief trading district, mainly, but it was also where sailors just off the boat went to spend their money, where cutpurses lurked to work the crowd, and where women and men of negotiable virtue could be negotiated with. There were more or less respectable sections where the serious merchants went to make their deals, but the rest of it was given over to a transient population of various peoples looking to make money by any means necessary, or spend it on any vice imaginable.

"Oh, this'll do fine," Skiver said, gawking around like the newcomer he was and leaning against a statue of a two-headed monster that Alaeron dearly hoped was entirely imaginary. "A man could find lots to keep him occupied—Here now!" Skiver's voice was filled with delight, and he lifted up a dirty-faced boy by the wrist, letting the child dangle and twist in his grip. "This little bastard tried to pick my pocket! Me! Why, back home none of the little dips would dare. Does you good to go new places, doesn't it, opens you up to new experiences."

"Don't hurt him," Jaya said, and Alaeron was again touched by her sympathy. He belatedly joined in, saying, "Yes, he's just a boy."

The child was spitting, cursing, and trying to bite. Skiver grinned. "Settle down, little man, we're all of the same fraternity. I'll give you a coin, and a second if you tell your friends that me and my companions here are off limits." He leaned in closer. "And if you think to come back with some friends to empty my purse by force, well, then I'll have to take those coins *back*, and maybe an ear with them, so you'll remember you should have listened to me. Understand?"

The boy stopped fighting, and just nodded. Skiver put him back on his feet and tossed him a couple of coins. Alaeron had expected him to toss copper, but the metal had the glint of gold. Must be nice, having Ralen Vadim's money to spend. The boy snatched the money out of the air and scampered off.

"Ah, youth," Skiver said. "I wasn't so different from that boy in my time. We'd better walk on. If I was him I'd go find the biggest fellas I knew and start following us with an eye to coshing us over the head and robbing us hollow." He set off whistling into the throng of sailors and shouting street vendors. Alaeron trudged after, his pack growing heavier with every step, avoiding the puddles of piss, ale, and piss that could probably double as ale. If anyone tried to pick *his* coat pockets they'd lose a finger—he'd improved his security overall after Skiver's act of larceny—and Jaya moved with an easy grace that looked dangerous enough to keep people from trying their luck with her.

Skiver finally settled on a tavern—called the Dagger and the Coin—though what differentiated it from the other dozen smoky, noisy bars on the block was a mystery to Alaeron. Skiver tracked down the tavern's owner and haggled for a while, securing a pair of rooms for them— apparently two of the whores had killed each other in a knife fight the night before, so there was space to spare. Alaeron resolved to sleep on the floor, and let Skiver brave whatever passed for bedding in the room. He and Jaya settled into a small table in a corner of the room with mugs of ale before them, where they could both keep an eye on the door. Absalom was a city of some three hundred thousand people, not counting the huge number of sailors and traders and adventurers just passing through, so the odds that Kormak would appear in this particular doorway seemed infinitesimal . . . but the last time Alaeron had been in a tavern was the first time he'd seen the Kellid, so he was automatically nervous.

Skiver found a card game and wheedled or bought his way in, and looked settled in for the night. He was playing with a disreputable-looking pair of sailors and one hellspawn woman in a bright red robe. Purple hair was gathered in a knot atop her head, and short, sharp horns jutted from her pale red brow. Alaeron didn't think he'd care to gamble with a devil-spawn, but perhaps Skiver considered such individuals kindred spirits. Jaya clucked her tongue disapprovingly. "Look, they're playing with a harrow deck."

"Ah," Alaeron said. "They're usually used for fortune-telling, yes?"

Jaya narrowed her eyes. "They are used for great and sacred magic. In the right hands, they are a powerful tool of divination, and can show what the future holds. They're not meant for gambling and playing towers."

"Mmm," Alaeron said. "I don't dispute that fate and destiny exist—for some. Certainly those who, oh, brave the test of the Starstone and emerge victorious as gods. Those may be acting out a part in some preordained plan. But for most of us, I don't believe we have any particular fixed future. We're too small for the universe to take any notice. We have to seize our own futures, not wait for destiny to sweep us along."

Jaya laughed. "Perhaps. Is it nice to think we're free to live or die on our own, or sad to think that the gods don't care if we live or die?"

"The former, if you ask me," Alaeron said. "My preference is to leave the gods alone, and hope they do the same for me."

"Ah," Jaya said. "So you've never been tempted to go to the heart of this city and try for a chance to touch the Starstone yourself? See if you can *be* a god?"

Alaeron shook his head. "The odds don't favor it, do they? How many hundreds—thousands!—have tried their luck since the Starstone fell from the sky and gouged this great sea into the earth? Only four people have touched the stone and come back alive. And one of *them* is dead anyway. No, I won't be crossing the chasm anytime soon, though I'm sure it's fascinating inside—they say the interior of the cathedral is never the same for any two people who venture in. Of course, I'd love to have a few scrapings from the Starstone to analyze in my lab, see how they react with various substances, see if I can synthesize its effects—how wonderful would it be to have a potion that turned you into a god for, say, an hour or so, then let you go back to being peacefully mortal?" Jaya laughed, and touched his hand, and Alaeron grinned.

After a moment, her face became serious. "Kho, though—it might be just as dangerous. The empire of the Shory is not as old as the Starstone, I know, but it *is* old, and from the tales my mother told me, it has its share of dangers."

Alaeron nodded. "It might be wise for you to tell me what you know, or suspect, or have heard of the city. Before I went to Numeria, I mastered the language of the Kellids, learned about the way they dress, learned all I could about the Technic League and the Black Sovereign, interviewed people who'd been there—and even so, I was ill-prepared for the reality. If I'd been given more time to prepare for this journey, I would have found books, and sought out historians and experts, to piece together whatever information *does* exist about Kho—though I gather it's not much. But instead I find myself woefully lacking in knowledge."

She shrugged. "Before we get to Kho, we must pass through Osirion. Shouldn't we worry about that, first?"

Alaeron waved it away. "Osirion is *known*. There are maps of the place, histories, diplomats, embassies. I've never been there, I admit, but I've met people who have, even people who hail from there. I'm not worried about Osirion. I'm worried about the great mystery beyond its southwestern border."

Jaya nodded. "Fair enough. I'll tell you what I can of Kho, but remember, this is all secondhand—worse, thirdhand, fourthhand. First, it's wrong to think of it as a ruined *city*. I'm sure that's what Vadim envisions— buildings covered with vines, crumbling statues, roads with trees growing up between the paving stones. But I don't believe it's like that."

Alaeron nodded. "It was a city that fell from the sky— it must have *shattered*."

"So I understand. My mother said the tribesmen do not approach closely, but that from a distance you can see a sparkling plain of glass. Thousands upon thousands of shards, from the hundreds of windows that broke when the city fell. The ruins fill a valley of sorts, but it's a *high* valley, a *cloud* valley. Filled with mists and waterfalls, which is why no one can describe it well, even though many have tried to look down on it from the safe distance of a far-off ridge. There is a taboo among my mother's people about going to the city. Adventurers come, hoping to buy relics from the villagers instead of going in after their own, but the Uomoto do not trade in such things. They don't stop adventurers from going into the ruins, and might even guide them partway, if the fools pay for the privilege. But there's no need to stop them. Very few of them ever come out again, you see, and those that do usually turn back before they even make it across the Fields of Glass, not even entering the ruins themselves." She looked around, then leaned forward, lowering her voice. "Mother did not like to talk about it, but of course my brother and I adored the scariest stories, so we made her. There is a stone—called the Stone of Sacrifice. It is a fallen monolith, thrown from the city when it crashed. Those who break oaths, or rape, or do murder, are taken and bound there . . . and when the morning comes, they are gone, taken by things that live in the ruins."

Alaeron groaned. "What things, exactly?"

Jaya shrugged. "My mother did not know. She said it was a dark bargain, struck long ago—generations ago—by tribal elders. The monsters stay in their valley, as long as they are sometimes appeased. There are creatures who fear light that stray from the ruins— *tuitele*, they're called, "light-haters"—but as for what they *are*, I cannot say, and I gather they are more nuisance than true danger."

"Ruins like this can be . . . unpredictable," Alaeron said. "All the Shory are dead thousands of years, but their legacy remains, broken magic spilling out. Magic like that is a beacon for certain creatures. They feed on it, or hope to profit by it, or just want to bask in its strange light. Such ruins attract all manner of things. I suppose we won't know what we're dealing with until we get there. Perhaps we can filch a few artifacts from the outskirts, enough to satisfy Vadim, and find our way out."

"And perhaps my relatives can tell me a better way to approach the city," she said, sipping her ale. "I assume they just send adventurers through the Fields of Glass the same way a crooked boatman directs newcomers to an inn where he knows they'll be robbed. It's just what you *do* with people who don't know any better, when there's profit in it."

"Ha," Alaeron says. "That reminds me of when I first went to Numeria. They've made an *industry* of fleecing the crusaders on their way to fight in the Worldwound—"

Suddenly, Skiver's voice cut through the crowd noise. *"Bugger!"*

Alaeron and Jaya looked over, but there was no obvious ruckus. "What's happening?" Alaeron said.

"I believe," Jaya said. "That the man who holds all the funds for our journey has just lost badly at cards."

Alaeron and Jaya walked over to the table. "Everything all right?" Jaya asked, laying a hand on Skiver's shoulder. The hellspawn holding the deck gave them a lazy smile and puffed at a foul black pipe.

"Ah," Skiver said, slumping in the chair. "Just a bit of bad luck. Spot me a bit, maybe, to win it back?"

"Can we speak to you for a moment?" Alaeron said. "Privately?"

"Won't hold the chair forever," the hellspawn woman drawled. Alaeron had expected a Chelish accent, but her voice was more lilting and southern. "We'll play a three-handed round now, but find money quick, or someone else will buy in."

Skiver got up from the chair shakily and followed Alaeron and Jaya back to their table. "Did you lose *everything*?" Jaya said, voice low.

Skiver rubbed the back of his head, then shrugged, his grin distinctly sheepish. "Everything? That's about the size of it."

"A crooked game," Jaya said, but Skiver shook his head.

"No, no, I talked to the boys on the ship, they said this was the place to come for a straight game, and I know enough about cheating to know they weren't. It's just . . . towers isn't my game. I'm a dice man. I had a bad run, that's all. I wouldn't worry about it, I can always find more *funds*, but . . ." He glanced at Alaeron. "You have to understand, I had the best cards I've ever seen in my *life*, I thought there was no chance I'd lose, and I was down to nothing, my pockets empty, otherwise I never would have bet it—"

"Bet what?" Alaeron said, his body going terribly still.

"Just a little gray disc," Skiver said. "One of your trinkets."

# Chapter Eleven
## Cards and Coins

Alaeron closed his eyes. He turned and marched back to the table where the card players laughed and drank. He cleared his throat until they all looked at him. "My friend inadvertently bet something that belonged to me."

The hellspawn lifted up the gray disc—the relic from the Mount that had levitated, though Alaeron had yet to discover what *else* it could do, and it had never floated again, either. "This?"

"The very same. Could I buy it off you? I have . . ." He looked through this money pouch. He'd recently sold his last bit of skymetal from Numeria, so he wasn't as poor as usual, but he was poor enough. Still, the relic was worth everything he had and worlds more. He held the coins out in his hand. "All of this."

The hellspawn puffed at her pipe, then shook her head. "No. Not enough. We valued it at three or four times that in the bet."

Alaeron nodded. "Very well. My friend has had enough of the game. But I'd be grateful if you'd deal me in."

The devilborn raised her eyebrow.

Jaya, behind him, gripped his shoulder. "Do you even know how to play towers?"

He shook his head. "But I'm a fast learner. And it can hardly go any worse for me than it did for Skiver."

"Just don't ask to borrow any money from me," Jaya said. She paused. "Mostly because I don't have any, and I'm not about to bet my *boots*."

Skiver perked up. "Say," he said. "Would you be willing to stake me something in exchange for my boots?"

The hellspawn snorted. "I admire your dedication to giving me all your possessions, but I think I'll let the man with a little gold sit at the table for now." She gestured, and Alaeron sat. The hellspawn briefly explained the rules. Towers essentially involved arranging the cards together so that certain symbols were adjacent to one another, with each player placing cards in turn, trying to use up all his cards, and owing a debt at the end of the game for each card he *didn't* use. A matter, then, of patterns and permutations; it was possible Alaeron might be able to excel at the game, with a little time.

But since he didn't have a little time, and couldn't afford the losses any learning curve, however shallow, would require, he slipped the red circle of metal he'd found in the Silver Mount around his thumb. The circle squeezed around his flesh, shrinking from the size of a bracelet to the size of a ring. It began to warm up, and once he was sure it wasn't *visibly* moving, he took his hand from his pocket. Alaeron wasn't even remotely sure how the ring worked—if it was magic, or simply some technology indistinguishable from magic—but he knew what it could *do*. In a way, it was the most disturbing of the effects he'd discovered—he had no idea what its limits were, if any—but it was worth the risk to win his trinket back.

"Let's play," the devil-woman said, and grinned, showing pointed teeth. She dealt out several cards on the tables—the "foundations" of the towers they would build by arranging their cards as the hand progressed. Then she dealt around to Alaeron, the two sailors, and herself. The others went first, giving Alaeron an opportunity to see how the game was played, and when the time came for his turn, Alaeron laid down three cards with deliberate slowness. If he was correct, he had essentially a perfect hand, but even with the best imaginable draw, it would take a few rounds to win. He tried not to pay attention to the names and lurid illustrations of the cards—The Betrayal, The Tyrant, and so on—as play continued around the table. He made a great show of dithering over the cards, leaning forward to peer at the existing towers, and *hmming* to himself before each move. He put the cards down carefully, as if afraid they might explode.

Alaeron put down his final card, paused for a moment, frowned at the others around the table, and said, "Is that . . . did I win, then?"

The hellspawn puffed on her pipe a moment before nodding. "Lucky," she said at last. She pushed over his winnings . . . but the pile didn't include the gray disc.

"Really," he said. "All I want is the disc." He gestured at the coins. "You can have all this if you'll just give me that. It was a gift from my father, and has great sentimental value."

"Shouldn't have let him get his hands on it, then," she said, nodding at Skiver. "Because it looks like the sort of thing that might be worth more than *sentiment* to the right collector."

Alaeron gritted his teeth. He couldn't play an endless number of hands. They'd realize he was cheating, and quickly. The problem was, there was no way to moderate the ring's effects. The glib explanation would be to say the ring gave the wearer "good luck," but "luck" was an inexact term. The ring seemed to like *order*, though. Throw the fragments of a broken pot onto the floor while wearing the ring, and the shards would spontaneously fall back into their original shape. Jump from a rooftop with the ring on, and your bones wouldn't shatter; instead, you'd land in just exactly the right way to avoid doing harm to yourself, standing up whole. Throw dice, and they would end six pips up, every single time. But if your situation would be improved by chaos, entropy, disaster . . . well, as far as his experiments had been able to determine, the ring was no help then. It was ideal for a game of towers, where orderly patterns were the way to win, but it meant he would have exactly the right cards to complete the towers. Every. Single. Time. And the only way *that* happened was by cheating. He needed to finish this game quickly.

"Then let me make another suggestion." He drew the porcelain-and-gold top from his pocket. "I will wager you this, against the disc, on this next hand. If you win, you get both. If I win, you get neither. Fair?"

"Hmm." She puffed thoughtfully, then glanced at the sailors. "Seems fair. You gentlemen mind sitting this out? Letting us play one-on-one?"

"Could do with another drink anyway," one said, and the other grunted, and they both pushed back. Jaya and Skiver took their seats, the better to watch the action. The sailors returned holding mugs, and stood around the table watching, too.

The hellspawn put down the six towers, each corresponding to one of the principle virtues admired by the Varisians. This time Alaeron went first. With only two players, the odds of having good cards to fit on each tower were much improved, but Alaeron still had vastly better luck than his adversary. He continued his ruse of being slow and hesitant and in over his head, and even made the careful calculation to let a few moments when he could have seized the advantage go by. Those displays of inexperience would make his inevitable win less rapid, and thus, he hoped, less suspicious.

When he laid down his last card, the hellspawn looked at him hard, blew a long stream of smoke out of her nostrils, then flicked the gray disc toward him. "Fine," she said. "Enjoy your sentimental value."

"Thank you for the game," Alaeron said politely. He reached out for the gray disc and the top . . .

But, unfortunately, he reached out with the hand wearing the red ring. He'd never tested these three relics together before, especially not with the red ring in its active state. To his dismay, the disc glowed blue and levitated an inch off the table, and the ring around his finger began to pulse a rich, bright red, flashing in a regular if inscrutable pattern. The golden top started to turn, and he had to put a stop to *that* before it got going fast enough to spin balanced on its tip; if that happened, the whole tavern would be destroyed. He snatched the top and the disc and shoved them into his coat pocket. The red ring was getting hot, so he swore and tried to twist it off his thumb, burning his fingertips in the process

"Magic ring," the hellspawn said, one eyebrow raised. She looked at the sailors. "See that? He's got a magic ring. What's your magic ring do? Help you win at cards? Is that what it does?" The sailors growled menacingly.

"You cheated?" Skiver said, eyes wide. Then he grinned. "I didn't know you had it in you!" He shoved his chair back, slamming hard into the gut of the sailor standing behind him, then stood straight up, fast. The top of Skiver's head collided with the bottom of the sailor's chin with a terrific *crack*, and the man stumbled backward with a bloody mouth. Jaya coolly kicked the table over, smashing it into the hellspawn before standing up and drawing a knife from her belt, waving it casually to encourage the crowd to part.

The last remaining sailor looked at Alaeron.

Oh, the alchemist thought. Am I meant to deal with this one?

Alaeron kicked the man in the shin, snatched up his pack, and ran for the door. He was followed by Jaya, and by Skiver, who hooted, "Ha, great warrior! Mighty fighter!" Jaya darted around Alaeron, calling, "This way!" and leading him toward one of the alleyways twisting through the maze of market stalls. One of the local guards watched them go by, but didn't call out or try to stop them, even though they were obviously fleeing some kind of trouble. The constabulary in the Coins were known as the "Token Guard" and were notoriously lax, unless someone paid them to be zealous, in which case, Alaeron understood, they could be very handy with a truncheon.

After running long enough and hard enough for Alaeron to develop a painful stitch in his side, Jaya paused in the doorway of a derelict building and looked behind them. "I think we're clear," she said after a moment.

"Is that what you think?" The hellspawn emerged from the shadows across the street, blowing smoke from her nostrils, her eyes glowing red. She held a wand of black wood in her left hand, and the tip of it sparked with silver light and made a strange low humming sound. "You aren't the first bunch of fools to try and cheat me." She snapped her teeth at them like an animal. "I know a man who's always looking for slaves. The girl will fetch a good price. The other two, maybe you can be chopped into dog food."

"Sorry for the misunderstanding," Skiver said. "We'll give you back the money, call it evens?"

"Too late for playing nice," she said.

"Oh, we can play it any way you like, then." Skiver twisted his wrist, and a knife fell from his sleeve into his hand.

The hellspawn lifted the wand, and the end glowed more brightly. "Pleasant dreams," she said.

"Bugger," Skiver said, then closed his eyes and fell, slumping against the wall and sliding down, his knife clattering to the stones.

A magic wand, Alaeron thought. He hoped it only put its victims to sleep, instead of doing some more permanent damage. Could he reach one of his weapons before she put him to sleep too? Could Jaya do something?

"Pardon me," a voice boomed from another doorway. A tall, broad-shouldered man with a vast dark beard and merry eyes stepped out, thumbs hooked into his belt. He wore a stained traveler's coat and a disreputable-looking straw hat, and had a rucksack dangling from one shoulder, but he wasn't obviously armed, apart from a crooked walking stick bound onto his pack. "It's not polite to waylay travelers. And did I hear you say you were planning to sell them into slavery?" He clucked his tongue. "Is that the hospitality that's made Absalom famous the world over? These strangers will think ill of us."

"Away," the hellspawn said. "This is our business, not yours. Or do you want to join them in the slave pits?"

"No need to be rude," he said. "I can't abide rudeness. What harm in being pleasant? I'll show you how: that's a lovely wand. See? I just paid you a compliment. Now, the truth is, I hate wands. They make magic too easy. Anyone can pick up a wand and cast a spell, but that's not how magic should work—you should have to *work* for it."

"I was just saying the same thing about crossbows a few days ago," Jaya said.

"Exactly!" the stranger boomed. "Try to make a device that any idiot can use, and who's going to use it? Idiots! And do we *really* want to arm idiots? With wands *or* crossbows?"

"Enough," the hellspawn said, and lifted the wand again.

The stranger twisted his left hand in an odd motion, as if delicately plucking a flower that wasn't there, and said something that sounded like "Air moh eblis" in a ringing, clear voice.

The wand's light fizzled, and the hellspawn's eyes widened. She shook the wand vigorously, but nothing happened.

"Won't work for a while, alas. By tomorrow, maybe, for all the good it will do you. That's the sort of thing *real* wizards can do, hellchild. Render little toys like this useless." The stranger took a step toward her and plucked the wand from her unresisting hands. "Better for me to keep it, so it doesn't fall into the wrong hands. Run, now?" He used the same tone of voice one might employ to ask if a guest wanted a cup of tea.

The hellspawn recovered from her momentary shock. She hissed and drew a wickedly curved dagger that was nearly long enough to qualify as a sword. "Wizards bleed like anyone else," she said, and lunged forward, slashing.

Alaeron reached into his pocket and touched one of his bombs, but the wizard was too close to the hellspawn for him to risk throwing it.

But the bomb wasn't necessary. The wizard danced backward away from the attack, moving both hands in a series of strangely delicate motions, and spoke a harsh, barking syllable. The devil-woman paused, frowning, and put one hand to her horned head.

The wizard spoke again, this time in a voice of command. "Go. *Now*."

She began to run, racing right past the wizard, along the street, and away, the sound of her pounding feet gradually diminishing.

The wizard winced. "I hate dominating the minds of hellspawn. You have to make a psychic link, you see, and—well, basically, my mouth is going to taste like sulfur for days." He shuddered, then smiled, and prodded Skiver with his foot. "Wake up!" he shouted.

Skiver leapt up, looking around in alarm, and another knife appeared in his hand. "What? Who? Where?"

"There, you're all squared away," the wizard said. "Probably best you move on, though. She won't run forever, and when she's done, she may run *back*."

"Wait," Jaya said. "Why did you help us?"

He shrugged. "Sticking my nose into the troubles of others is a weakness of mine. Glad you're all right."

"I'm Jaya," she said. "This is Alaeron, and Skiver. Thank you for helping us."

"What?" Skiver said again, rubbing the back of his head. "This fella helped us?"

"He helped Jaya," Alaeron said, a bit sourly. "Helping us was just a side effect."

The wizard winked at Alaeron. "Can you blame me? She's surely worthy of assistance. My name's Ernst."

Jaya stepped forward and kissed Ernst on his bristly cheek. Alaeron watched with narrowed eyes. It wasn't so long ago that *Alaeron* had been the one saving her from thugs in an alley, and he hadn't gotten a kiss—he'd gotten kidnapped and press-ganged into an expedition that was very likely to kill him. Some men had all the luck.

Then again, he'd be traveling with Jaya for a long time to come, so he would have other chances to impress her. Maybe he'd have a chance to save her life again. He could always hope.

Skiver stepped forward and offered his hand for Ernst to shake. "Much obliged." He looked the man up and down. "I always thought wizards were bookish types. You look like you could wrestle a bear."

Ernst laughed. "I wouldn't want to try. But I'll take that as a compliment. I'm a . . . practical sort of wizard. I've studied at some of the finest magic schools in Absalom, but by the gods, I learned to access all this power, so why should I sit in a library somewhere just *thinking* about it? Might as well go out and *use* it, that's what I think."

"A battle mage," Alaeron said. "Off to find a war, then?"

"More seeking my fortune," Ernst said. "But if I happen upon a good war, I'll make the best of it."

"Good luck on your journey," Jaya said formally. "If our paths cross again, I hope we can repay the kindness."

"If I'm lucky enough to see you again, Jaya, I'll consider that repayment enough." He bowed low, sweeping off his hat in an exaggeratedly courtly gesture. "Enjoy your own travels, friends. And try not to annoy any more devilspawn, all right?" He strode off in the direction of the docks, whistling as he went.

Jaya watched him go, and sighed a little when he was out of sight.

Skiver nodded. "I know. I don't usually go for the burly-and-bearded types, but there's something about him. Wouldn't mind taking him for a roll. Wonder if he leans my way or yours?"

Jaya laughed and shook her head. "We're just lucky he happened by."

"We could have dealt with the devilborn woman ourselves," Alaeron said. "It's not like we're *helpless*."

"No," Jaya said, "but this way there was no bloodshed, and Skiver even got a nap, which I'm sure he found quite refreshing."

"Magical sleep's not as refreshing as you'd think," Skiver said, and started walking. "A magic wand! Hell of a thing to spring on a man in a fight, too. Hardly fair at all. Don't get me wrong, magic's got its place, but I don't much like it being turned on *me*." He bumped his shoulder against Alaeron's as they walked. "And you! All this time you had a magic luck-ring! You couldn't have loaned it to me while I played dice on the ship? I should have taken *that* toy from your bag, but it just looked like a bit of old metal. Shows what I know. Guess there's a reason I'm not an arcanist."

"You'd roll nothing but double sixes every time with this ring," Alaeron said. "It doesn't help you cheat *well*. The sailors would have stabbed you."

"I suppose," Skiver said. "But I would have died a rich man."

"What toys?" Jaya said. "You have other things, besides the ring? Oh, and the egg you used, the first day we met. There are others?"

"What do you care? They're just *toys*, used by *idiots*, aren't they? As if it doesn't take study and knowledge and care to unlock the secrets of an artifact, as if anyone can just pick them up and—"

"Oh, don't be that way," Jaya said. "Ernst wasn't trying to insult you. He doesn't even *know* you. Besides, wands you can buy or steal from some wizard are different from ancient artifacts, everyone knows *that*."

"All right," Alaeron said, somewhat mollified. "The ring and the egg are just two of the relics I discovered during my time in Numeria. I'm studying their properties. The ring—well, it's a circle of metal, I doubt it was meant to be worn on a finger, but it serves as a ring—alters likelihoods. Flip a coin while wearing it, and it might come up heads a thousand times in a row. Things like that."

"I didn't realize you had so many of these artifacts. What do they do?"

He shrugged. "I have half a dozen." No use lying; Skiver knew that much. "You've seen what the egg does, Jaya, and you've both seen what the ring does, more or less. The others . . . I'm still studying their capabilities." He didn't want them to know what the top did, and he honestly had no clue about the disc or the gear wheel or the golden chain. It was possible they didn't do anything useful on their own at all. "I don't like using them, honestly—their powers are too unpredictable. I'm still in the midst of my researches. And I certainly don't go around using them to cheat at *cards*." He glared at Skiver. "But he didn't give me much choice."

"You could have traded those artifacts to Vadim," Jaya said. "For your own freedom. Why didn't you?"

Alaeron shook his head. "I went through . . . well. I won't say Hell; I've never been to Hell. But I've been to Numeria, which must be almost as bad. I did terrible things, and had terrible things done to me, to get those relics, and I have no intention of giving them up for any reason until I divine their secrets. So you can imagine I was upset when *he* gambled one of them away."

"I already told you 'sorry,'" Skiver said. "Which is more than I've ever said to, oh, anybody else ever at all. And look at it this way—you got your disc back, and you didn't even have to tell me a secret to earn it." He grinned. "Now how about you hand over that gold you won?"

Alaeron barked a laugh. "Why should I?"

Skiver shrugged. "Vadim arranged for us to take passage on a ship heading to Osirion tomorrow, but the captain still needs to be paid. What you won won't even cover that, let alone a place for us to sleep tonight, since I imagine we aren't welcome in the rooms I took for us back at the Dagger and the Coin. Now, we can wander the streets all night, since you say this district never sleeps and has lights blazing all through the dark hours, but paying for passage is a bigger problem. Give me what you've got, though, and I'll use it to make more money."

"What, by gambling?" Alaeron said. "That worked well last time."

"Nah, gambling's for fun," Skiver said. "This is business. I know ten thousand ways to empty a mark's pockets, but it works best if you've got a bit of gold to splash around first. Nobody expects you to trick them out of their money if you look like you've got plenty to spread around—they'll take all kinds of bets." He held up his hand before Alaeron could speak. "I don't mean *straight* bets. I mean the sort of bets you make with new friends in a bar . . . or people who think they're your new friends. Sucker bets, trick bets, ones you can't lose."

"I was in a tavern once," Alaeron said slowly. "A man bet me a drink he could balance an egg on its end and I couldn't. The bartender kindly provided each of us an egg. I tried and failed to make mine stand up. The man who bet against me took his egg, shook it violently, and set it on its end without a bit of difficulty."

"A classic," Skiver said. He glanced at Jaya. "See, you shake the egg hard enough, it breaks the yolk inside, and all the heavy bits drift to the bottom, so it stands up easy as you please."

"I believe I've seen it done," she said.

"I just bet you have." Skiver grinned wider. "Anyway, yeah, that's the sort of thing I mean. There's a game you can play with toothpicks, too, you can't lose if you know what you're doing. So give me the gold—save a bit out for yourselves if you must—and meet me at the Golden Pearl tavern down by the docks in a few hours. I'll buy us all a nice meal with my winnings."

"If you lose money and strand us here," Jaya said, "And my brother pays the price for your mistake—"

"Oh, don't worry," Skiver said. "Worst case, we steal a boat and make for Osirion on our own." He winked and sauntered away.

"Does he even realize how far away Osirion *is*?" Alaeron said. "Or realize that none of us are sailors?"

"I think he was joking," Jaya said. She paused. "I *hope* he was joking."

# Chapter Twelve
## The Following Fire

Jaya and Alaeron nursed drinks at the Golden Pearl, where they sat deep in shadow in a corner, hoping the hellspawn gambler wouldn't appear in the doorway. Alaeron wished one of his relics could make them invisible, or that he had a potion handy that could do the same—he knew how to make a potion that would render himself invisible, but it wouldn't help Jaya, and anyway he didn't have the right ingredients—though then they'd have people constantly attempting to sit on them, thinking their chairs were empty. Better to be visible but inconspicuous.

The Pearl was almost exclusively a place for short-term visitors: sailors making a brief stop before setting sail again, or travelers waiting to move from one ship to another. They rented rooms by the hour here, and not for the usual lascivious reasons; it was just more practical for people hoping to grab a meal and a nap before setting off on another sea voyage.

Skiver sauntered in long after dinner, while Jaya methodically ate her way through their fourth bowl of complimentary nuts—highly salted to encourage more ale purchases, not that they could afford more. Skiver saw them, dragged a chair over to their table, and dropped down. "This is the jolly corner, innit?" He dropped a clinking bag (rather lovely purple velvet) in front of Alaeron. "There's your card winnings back, scholar, never say I don't repay my debts." He paused. "Well. Never say I don't repay my debts as long as they're debts of modest size. Not paying back *big* debts is part of why I'm off on this grand adventure with you lot, but if I come back successful, Vadim will open his purse and make things square with the people I owe." Alaeron didn't answer, just opened the pouch and counted the coins. Triple what he'd started with, not that he cared about money for its own sake, but it *could* be useful, no denying it. He'd passed a market stall in the Coins that sold herbs from the Mana Wastes, things he'd only ever read about, and he had some interesting ideas for possible applications. He'd grown sick of the sea, and was preemptively bored with the sea voyage still before them, and had been thinking increasingly that it might be nice to *fly* . . .

Skiver scowled. "I'm trying to foster a sense of camaraderie here, you lot. See? We're all in this together. Vadim's holding something over *all* our heads."

"Yes," Alaeron said, "But *you're* the thing he's holding over *my* head—the promise that you'll try to kill me if I leave, remember? He doesn't have any hold over me otherwise."

Skiver shrugged. "I was gone for hours winning friends and making bets. Why didn't you bugger off then?"

Alaeron just looked down and mumbled "Well, you still have one of my relics . . . ."

Skiver snorted. "Ha. Yeah, fair enough." He jerked his thumb at Jaya. "But also because *she* wouldn't have liked it if you ran off, right? She knows we need you. I can't tell a valuable relic from the innards of a broken water clock, and while she's probably got a better eye than me, you're the one who'll be able to separate the magic rings from the bits of old metal." He slid Alaeron's mug over to himself and drained the remaining puddle of ale inside.

Jaya put her hand on Alaeron's. "I do need you," she said, and when he looked up, she was staring at him with those deep, dark eyes, an expression of open pleading on her face. This was a woman who might make him forget all about science, perhaps for hours at a time.

"Between my knives and her eyes, I'd say you've got plenty of good reasons to stay with us," Skiver said. "Besides—adventure, eh? Off to the land of sand and mummies and tombs the size of palaces, sailing at first light. In the meantime I'm going to order a great giant platter of fish, the more fried the better. Who's with me?"

"It's hard to be angry at you," Jaya said, "when you're the one buying dinner."

They spent the next several hours together, drinking and talking and speculating about what they might encounter on the road ahead. "I've been to Osirion once," Jaya said. "But only briefly, to the port city of Totra. I can't say much about it, except that it's *hot*. I've never been to the capital or the interior."

"So we're bound for Sothis," Alaeron said. "Where the Ruby Prince rules. I've never been, either—never set foot on the continent of Garund at all, truth be told. I know a smattering of the Osiriani tongue, though. They're one of the oldest civilizations on Golarion, and there are a great many ancient scrolls in that language. It was necessary for me to learn enough to muddle through a few of them during some of my researches. Their mummification process is *fascinating*."

Skiver grunted, dipping another chunk of battered fish into a pool of slimy white sauce. "No doubt. All I know about the place is the things you hear in stories— great fanged lizards and tombs shaped like triangles and god-kings. I hope we can find someone there who speaks a *normal* language, though, if all you've got is a smattering. Though I s'pose steel blades and shiny coins are a universal language. Vadim sent a letter ahead to a man he knows there, a dealer in relics, who's supposed to help us get on a ship down that big river they've got, but for all I know we'll get there before Vadim's message does. We may have to make our own arrangements."

"It shouldn't be a problem," Jaya said. "The Ruby Prince welcomes foreign explorers—for a price. Pay a fee on whatever you find, and you can pillage to your heart's content, they say. Anytime foreigners are invited to come spend money, there will be people who can speak any language you care to name. I'm sure there are treasure hunters and Pathfinders swarming over the place. I don't suppose we could join up with a group of them, and find some relics for Vadim without going all the way to Kho . . ."

Alaeron shook his head. "Vadim knows relics. He'd be able to tell a bit of old Osirian pottery from something more exotic, I'd wager. He'll want something he's never seen before, some unmistakable item of ancient arcane technology." Which is why he'd love the artifacts Alaeron had looted from the Silver Mount, if he ever found out they existed.

"The market's flooded with death masks and statues of beetles anyway," Skiver said. "We see heaps of 'em, and Vadim's got a storeroom full. Osirian artifacts are popular now, because their prince is letting people cart them off. Vadim wants something *nobody* else has."

Skiver's bar bets had been successful enough that he splashed out to buy them each a room for a solid five hours at the end of the evening. Alaeron sat in the privacy of his room—though it was more a tiny stall, just big enough to hold a bed—and considered taking out the relics and his journal to continue his studies. The implications of the way those three artifacts had interacted earlier tonight were fascinating. Were they more powerful when more were used at once? Did the order in which they were activated affect the nature of their behavior? But he was too exhausted (and, frankly, filled with alcohol) to actually deactivate the traps on his bag, get out the objects, and start working. Better to sleep now and hope he could get some work done on the journey to Osirion.

Skiver pounded on his door in the morning, and Alaeron was ready to go in moments, since he hadn't done any unpacking beyond removing his boots and coat. Jaya, naturally, looked fresh and well-rested in the hallway, and they trooped down the stairs, pausing to grab fresh(ish) fruit to eat on the walk to their next ship.

Despite the fact that it was still essentially night to Alaeron's eyes, the docks were full of activity. "Our ship's called the, ah, *Blue Beetle*," Skiver said as they walked along the quay. "I think that's it. Ha, beetle, right, it's like it's got a lot of little legs."

Alaeron stopped on the bustling dock, scowling. The ship was single-masted with a great rectangular sail, but there were dozens of oars poking out along its considerable length—the "little legs" Skiver had referred to. "Driven by slave labor, no doubt," he said flatly.

Skiver shrugged. "Doesn't sit right with me, either, but the whole world doesn't see things the Andoren way—not yet, anyhow."

Jaya laughed. "You Andorens. Slavery is unpleasant, yes, but natural. The strong use the weak. Even ants enslave aphids. And aren't you yourselves slaves to Ralen Vadim, though you lack chains? I hope you won't pitch a fit about riding on a boat rowed by other slaves. There are many more where we're going."

"Slaves? We're not *slaves*," Skiver said sharply. "We are under an *obligation*. But we are still free men, and when our obligation is finished, we will be even *more* free, get it? The poor buggers who get chained to those oars can't do anything to better their lot."

Alaeron felt his heart swell with affection for the treacherous light-fingered rogue. Different as he and Skiver were, they were both Andorens. "There were many slaves in Numeria," Alaeron said. "I did not like it, but I did not try to strike off their chains, either. I will not make a scene here. The enlightened ideals of Andoran will spread across the world in time."

"I suppose it is a beautiful dream," Jaya said, shrugging. "It's not that I disagree with you—but freedom is more precious than gold, and I don't imagine the rich will begin handing either one out for free."

"Ideas are powerful," Alaeron said. "And Andoran's ideas are righteous."

"Ideas aren't all," Skiver said. "Blades too. Our Eagle Knights can make it cost more to *keep* slaves."

"Ideas *and* swords," Jaya said. "Well, maybe you have something there, after all. Shall we find the captain?"

Skiver went, but he came back a bit later, shaking his head. "They're behind schedule. The first mate got hit over the head with a cosh in a whorehouse and his trousers were stolen, and some of the rowers ate some bad mollusks and got the runs. Or something. Taldane's not the captain's first language. Anyway, they're leaving in three hours, so we get to enjoy the pleasures of Absalom for a bit longer." He took a deep breath. "Ah, smell that salt air. I'm right sick of it, aren't you two?"

After a brief consultation, Skiver agreed to let them split up, but told them to meet up again well before their departure time, "Just in case these southern bastards don't know how long a proper hour is." Jaya asked if she could borrow some coin—she wanted to buy more arrows, having left a few sticking out of pirates earlier—and Alaeron obliged, feeling richer than usual, especially with Skiver buying meals and passage.

Alaeron set off for the Coins again, pausing only to buy a ridiculous floppy broad-brimmed hat that he hoped would disguise him if he did happen to run into the hellspawn or the sailors from the night before, though in truth, he wasn't sure he'd recognize the latter—they'd been dirty, greasy-haired humans, and hadn't made much impression beyond that. But it was worth the risk: that herb stall had been most intriguing, and he had some ideas about new mutagens that could do more interesting things than make him hairy and give him claws. He'd experienced a couple of alchemical epiphanies in his time: discovering the right mix for the feral mutagen, and realizing the hallucinogenic fluids from the Silver Mount could be used to make bombs, and he felt himself on the cusp of something new. His alchemical studies had been slowed by his devotion to the relics from Numeria, but he'd never entirely stopped dabbling and pondering, and some of those Mana Wastes plants, with their infusions of wild magic, could open up all new avenues of—

He stopped. This street was familiar, but something was wrong. Something . . .

The Dagger and the Coin was gone. Blackened timbers leaned against one another, and gray ashes and chunks of unidentifiable char covered the ground. Nothing recognizable remained. The buildings on either side were utterly untouched, which implied an astonishingly controlled fire: this was clearly arson of a magical sort. A group of the Token Guard stood around the wreckage, prodding at ashes with the ends of their pikes. Alaeron sidled over to a group of robed merchants chattering and pointing at the flames, close enough to eavesdrop.

"He was over seven feet tall, I tell you!" one bearded man said in the heated tones of one who expects to be disbelieved. "A half-orc, I'm sure!"

"Looked like a Kellid to me," said another merchant, rather more calmly. "Bigger and wider than most, but there's no mistaking that long black hair and the scars on his face."

A lady merchant sniffed. "Nonsense. Kellids wear *furs*. He was dressed like a banker. Besides, when have you ever heard of a Kellid who could work that kind of magic? To conjure such intense fire! From what I've heard, those northern savages think wearing *shoes* is magic—"

Alaeron stepped away, finding a wall to put against his back, and scanned the street. Kormak had been here, to the very inn where Alaeron and his friends had dined and gambled the night before. And when the Kellid was done looking around, or maybe even asking questions, he'd burned the place to the ground. Perhaps Ralen Vadim wasn't to blame for the destruction of Alaeron's workshop after all; fire seemed to be the Kellid's signature. But *how*? How had the Technic League lackey tracked Alaeron *here*, to this particular tavern in a city full of them? All right, it was easy enough to guess that Alaeron's ship was likely to dock in Absalom, but in a city of three hundred thousand that hardly narrowed things down. So how—

Alaeron closed his eyes and swore softly under his breath. The relics. He'd activated one in the Dagger and the Coin, and Kormak had arrived some hours later. And earlier: he'd brushed against the golden chain on the *Pride of Azlant,* and soon afterward, Kormak had tracked that ship. Alaeron had used all the artifacts often in his workshop, and Kormak had found him there. He hadn't actually used them in the common room where Kormak first located him, but Alaeron dined there regularly, so finding the right neighborhood would be enough to track him down further. Alaeron *hadn't* used the relics in Ralen Vadim's house, and Kormak hadn't appeared there.

The Kellid must have a way of tracking the relics, at least when they were actually used. If the League had investigated the chamber where Zernebeth died, they could have found some other fragment—a scraping from the metal floor, or a bone fragment from the old skeleton, or a shard of glass from the shattered black mirror—to create a sympathetic link between Alaeron's relics and the room where they'd rested for so long. Kormak might have a compass that spun and pointed when the relics were active, or an enchanted map that showed their location, or perhaps his spectacles were charmed to glow when he looked in the right direction—whatever the mechanism, *that* was most likely the way he stayed on Alaeron's trail.

Which meant the alchemist didn't dare activate the relics again.

Except that wasn't acceptable. He *needed* to study them.

So he'd have to choose the right moment to activate them, knowing Kormak would come. And when he came, Alaeron needed to be ready.

He made sure his hat was pulled down low, then hurried through the market stalls until he found the vendor he'd noticed the day before. Kormak was huge, strong, violent, and armed with an unknowable quantity of arcane Technic League artifacts.

Which meant Alaeron had some work to do if he was going to be a match for him.

"We sleep on deck like the sailors do," Skiver said. "Apparently the bit with a roof there is just for the captain and the first mate."

Alaeron groaned. "Lovely." At least with no private space to himself he wouldn't be tempted to use any of the relics, but it did complicate things in terms of his mutagenic researches. He'd acquired various interesting components at the market stall, but couldn't quite figure out what they might amount to. He found a place for his bag and sat down, near the back of the ship.

Skiver joined him, and Jaya sat as well, smiling. "Don't be gloomy. The weather should be nice this time of year, and your silly hat will keep the sun off your head. I've slept on dozens of decks, and it's never done me any harm."

"I just wish we'd push off already," Alaeron grumbled. Kormak was doubtless out there, searching the city, probably searching the *docks*, and even without the relics to guide him, he might track Alaeron down.

"Then you're in luck," Skiver said as the ship lurched. The harbormaster stood up front, shouting orders to the captain—a big, bald man with tattoos on his scalp—who relayed them to his first mate, and from there down to the men rowing belowdecks. The motion was jerky to start with, but soon became smooth as the ship easily navigated the forest of broken masts from dead warships. They paused near the little island in the mouth of the harbor to let the harbormaster disembark, then continued on into the open sea. A few gillmen swam alongside the ship for a while, almost like an escort, before diving down and out of sight. The sun was still fairly low in the east when they set out, and before it had risen to the zenith of the pale blue sky, they were miles along, nothing but open sea on all sides, and nothing of interest to watch, either.

The companions sat together in what scraps of shade they could find, and after their first few desultory attempts at conversation fizzled, Skiver said, "All right, then, scholar, let's have another story. I'll trade you that black wheel of yours for a tale to stir my blood. And pass a few of the bloody hours stretching out before us."

"What's this?" Jaya said. "A wheel?"

"Skiver stole one of my . . . items," Alaeron said. "Something I'm studying. Just like he stole that disc he tried to gamble away at the tavern last night. He won't give *this* one back unless I tell him a story about my time in Numeria."

"Did you ever consider just asking him about his adventures, Skiver?" Jaya sounded more amused than outraged, which was disappointing. "Without the element of extortion?"

"Where's the fun in that?" Skiver said. "I'm a betting man, and this way, even a conversation has stakes."

"What's to stop you just stealing them again, then?" Jaya said. "And keeping poor Alaeron on the hook forevermore?"

*Poor Alaeron.* Well, that was something. Alaeron would have preferred her admiration over her pity, but pity would do in a pinch.

"Oh, he didn't like it when I pilfered his toys," Skiver said. "He took steps, you see. He's got his bag so tricked out with traps even I wouldn't mess with it now. Anyone tries to pry in there without permission is apt to lose his hand, if not his sanity."

"True," Alaeron said. He sighed. "Get me one of those water skins. If I'm going to be talking, I'll need it."

Skiver fetched the water, and when he came back, he said to Jaya, "So here's what you missed, from the first story he told me—he went into this Silver Mount place with a friend of his, looking for treasures . . ." Skiver recited the barest details of how Alaeron came by the relics from the Mount, but at least he didn't add any embellishments, or say Alaeron had been desperately in love with Zernebeth, or anything of the sort. Though having Jaya think of Alaeron as a romantic sort, perhaps one with a tragic loss in his past, might not be *so* bad. Since he couldn't study his relics anyway without risking Kormak's wrath, and he didn't have so much as a work table at his disposal to develop further mutagens, why not turn his mind toward more . . . *social* interactions?

"Well?" Skiver said, elbowing Alaeron in the ribs. "Let's hear it. How'd you come to leave Numeria with a satchel full of treasures, then?"

"After I escaped the Mount . . ." Alaeron began.

# Chapter Thirteen
## Escape from Numeria

He piloted Zernebeth's walker back the way he'd come, racing up the roads toward the palace, making the whistle shriek and sending peasants diving out of the way. About halfway home, he began to wonder what he was in such a hurry *for*. He'd have to find some member of the League, he supposed, and let them know one of their number had perished in the Mount. And what would happen after that? Another member of the Technic League had died during Alaeron's time in Numeria. In attempting to fashion a weapon from some parts scavenged from the Mount, the arcanist had managed to melt the flesh off his bones, but lived on as little more than a screaming skeleton for fully half an hour. None of the League members, including Zernebeth, had bothered to put him out of his misery: instead, they'd taken notes on his condition, and once he was dead, they'd fallen upon his workshop like locusts sweeping over a field, squabbling over the various half-finished projects in his rooms. Zernebeth had come away with a metal staff topped by a copper ball at the end that shot bolts of red lightning, fusing whatever they struck—be it animal, vegetable, or mineral—into lumps of black glass.

Alaeron doubted Zernebeth's fellows would mourn her death any more than they had the original owner of that staff. And what would happen to Alaeron? Zernebeth had been the closest thing he had to a friend, and she'd grudgingly let him help in her researches, but if another League member took responsibility for him, Alaeron might find himself tasked to make explosives all day and all night again, as he'd done to prove his worth in the first place, or even used as a pawn in some complex stratagem, if he ended up in the care of one of the more politically-minded members of the League.

And then what would happen to the relics Zernebeth had died for?

Back at the palace, Alaeron did his best to act normally, hurrying down the broad and filthy corridors with an expression of intense distraction on his face, as if he were contemplating vast and weighty subjects. (Which he was. Like how to keep his hands on the relics.) He unlocked the door to Zernebeth's rooms and slipped inside, pulling the door shut behind him. He hurried to Zernebeth's workshop—

Where a captain of the Technic League named Gannix was waiting, flipping through a sheaf of his dead colleague's notes. Gannix's head was shaved bald, and rumor had it chunks of his skull had been replaced by metal plates. Half his face was covered by a chrome-rimmed prosthetic lens that replaced an eye he'd lost in an accident—though rumor had it the lens didn't give him sight, exactly, but some other, stranger sense. His missing left hand had been replaced by a seven-fingered claw made of skymetal and decorated with pulsing red gems. He wore the leather and fur popular at court that year (and, Alaeron assumed, all years), and had a chain whip coiled on the belt at his waist. Alaeron had seen the whip in action once. At the push of a button, the links of chain would stiffen into an unbreakable staff, crackling with white sparks that left burns on anyone who fell under the weapon's onslaught. Gannix was considered overly impulsive and sadistic even by the standards of the League, but he'd braved the depths of the Silver Mount and survived many times, so his standing was high.

He grunted when Alaeron entered. "You. Zernebeth's boy. You were there when she died?"

Alaeron swallowed. "Ah, yes, sir, I was assisting her . . . "

Gannix laughed, a sound like clashing gears. "Remind me never to let you assist *me*, then. We'd assumed you were dead too." He shook his head, mouth twisted in distaste. "Now we'll have to figure out what to *do* with you."

"How did you know about Zernebeth?" Alaeron said, then belatedly added, "Sir?"

"I keep track of my people," Gannix said sternly, eyes narrowed. Alaeron bowed his head. He wondered what that meant, exactly. Some device implanted in Zernebeth's body? A little vial of living tissue scraped from the inside of her cheek, kept on Gannix's shelf, that curled up and turned black when she died? It could be anything. Alaeron was reasonably sure they didn't have any way to track him—Zernebeth's opinion of him had been reasonably high, but for the most part he was considered barely a step above a servant, just a useful outsider from whom the League might wring some work. Hardly worth the effort of surveillance. "Was anything recovered from the Mount on this ill-advised expedition?"

This was the moment of truth; or, more accurately, the moment of lies. "No, sir. We unsealed a chamber, full of bones and black glass, and were just beginning to investigate when . . . it was lightning, of a sort, that took her. I think she triggered some device."

Gannix grunted. "Very well. We'll have someone go in and recover her, and investigate this device. Anything that can kill someone as well-warded as Zernebeth could be a useful tool." He rolled up the notes and tucked them into his sleeve, then stepped around the table.

I got away with it, Alaeron thought.

The captain started toward the door, then paused. "Oh," he said. "Strip."

"Sir?"

Gannix's hand strayed to his coiled whip. Alaeron didn't ask another question, just shrugged out of his coat and handed it to Gannix. The captain rifled through his pockets, lining up the various bottles and vials on the table. He didn't take any of them, but Alaeron assumed that was only because he knew they'd be worthless to him—except in rare cases, an alchemist's potions wouldn't work on anyone other than the alchemist himself, as they were specially attuned to their creator's aura and drew a certain degree of power from the alchemist's own life force.

Alaeron stripped off the rest of his clothes, and Gannix sorted through those, too, emptying Alaeron's coin pouch into his hand and then slipping that money up his sleeve, too. It wouldn't quite leave Alaeron penniless—he had some funds hidden in his bedroom/closet—but the casual, open theft was a humiliation. As one of the richest men in Numeria, Gannix had no reason to steal from Alaeron, except for the captain's own amusement.

When Alaeron was completely naked, Gannix slipped on a pair of thin black gloves and subjected him to a body search as horrifying as it was thorough, then tossed the soiled gloves onto the stone floor.

"Fine," the captain said. "Shame you didn't try to pilfer something. I like a little ambition in my lickspittles." Alaeron was silent; he knew if he'd been found with a relic from the Mount, the captain would have given him over to some of the League researchers as experimental fodder—he'd done the same with a slave suspected of stealing a teacup.

There was a pounding at the door, and Gannix opened it to let in a number of slaves while Alaeron hurriedly dressed. "Help these scum clear out Zernebeth's rooms, boy," Gannix said. "Report to me when you're done and we'll see about a new assignment for you."

"Of course," Alaeron said. "I'm happy to serve any way I can."

After Gannix was gone, Alaeron gathered up his few possessions into his pack. He stopped in Zernebeth's workshop and filled his pockets with the most valuable (and portable) items he could find: samples of rare alchemical ingredients, vials of hallucinogenic fluids from the Mount, coils of skymetal wire—anything small and not too heavy. The slaves wouldn't say anything about his pilfering, or his departure; Alaeron's status at court was below that of the Technic League, but miles above that of a slave, and they wouldn't dare risk his ire, even though he'd shown them nothing but kindness. Or, to be more accurate, indifference—slavery as an institution was abhorrent, of course, but some of these individual slaves were subliterate savages.

Alaeron walked as brazenly as he could out of the room and through the castle. It was early afternoon, but most of the court was still slumbering—Starfall was a nightlife sort of place—so apart from slaves, he had the place to himself. He stepped through the door to the courtyard where he'd left Zernebeth's walker—and where he'd left the relics, secreted beneath a trapped hidden panel near the machine's engine, where none of the superstitious slaves would dare to snoop.

But the walker was a ruin: legs pried off, seat smashed to splinters, body reduced to boards, engine disassembled . . . and relics gone. Alaeron stared at the wreckage, then grabbed a passing slave by the sleeve. "What happened here?"

"The League, sir," she said, cringing away from him. "They came and took it apart. I had no hand in it!"

Alaeron nodded and let her go. "Of course. Sorry," he muttered, but from the look on her face, he might as well have been speaking a foreign tongue. She scurried off, and Alaeron considered his options. Gannix's people had taken the walker's treasures as spoils, of course, but there was no reason to think Alaeron had been involved with hiding the artifacts—more likely they'd assume Zernebeth had been the one to secret the relics in the vehicle. The League guarded their projects jealously, from one another as much as from the outside world. Alaeron could simply return to his old mentor's rooms, cart off her possessions to Gannix's workshop, and then accept whatever new position they gave him. But how long before he'd be allowed near the Mount again? The League should have been men of science, but they were horribly superstitious and naturally suspicious, so treacherous themselves that they saw treachery everywhere. Many would probably assume Alaeron had murdered Zernebeth, and others would fear he was bad luck, or that the Silver

Mount had taken a dislike to him. Realistically, he'd be stuck making bombs or scavenging around lesser dig sites in the Numerian hinterlands until someone casually murdered him for some imagined or actual slight. He'd been inside the Silver Mount once, and he didn't imagine he'd ever make it there again, unless he underwent the terrible tests of loyalty required to become a full-fledged member of the League.

For a terrible moment, he considered it.

But that would just mean becoming a monster, and working for worse monsters. Besides, he wanted *those* relics, the ones Zernebeth had died for. Those broken pieces had tried to join together. They were part of some shattered whole. The League would break them up, trade them for power and favors, find uses for them or simply destroy them in the testing process. They were only interested in the power the relics could give them—they didn't have Alaeron's burning need to *understand*, to see what they were *for*, not just what they could *do*.

Which meant Alaeron had to steal them back.

He returned to Zernebeth's quarters. The slaves were nearly done carting things off, but he grabbed a retort and an alembic so he'd have something to carry to Gannix's workshop. The captain was not the head of the Technic League—his superiors spent their time feasting and whoring and whispering in the Black Sovereign's ears—but he was in charge of several League members who went on expeditions to ruins, and he had apartments appropriate to his standing. Alaeron joined a group of slaves as they carried his dead mentor's treasures across a courtyard containing a fountain filled with poisonous quicksilver and on through a high archway that led to Gannix's rooms.

The high-ceilinged, spacious suite would have been lavish if it hadn't been so cluttered and filthy, with huge glazed pots holding the bare stems of dead flowers, looted tapestries stained dark by decades of chemical fogs, and filthy furniture that would be impossible to clean with anything short of fire. Everywhere shelves and long worktables held broken bits of relics, along with scrolls, ledgers, tools, and dirty glassware.

A disorderly laboratory, Alaeron thought, was the sign of a weak mind. Too bad Gannix wasn't weak in any *other* discernible way.

The captain himself wasn't in evidence, so Alaeron followed the slaves carrying some of Zernebeth's more valuable items to the small room—really a closet, but larger than Alaeron's quarters—where Gannix kept his most prized items. Normally it was impregnable: the door was enchanted iron, the lock keyed specifically to Gannix's aura, the hinges recessed and inaccessible, and the inner walls covered in steel, so it wasn't possible to easily cut in through an adjoining wall. But Gannix had opened it so the slaves could do their work. Why not? None of them would dare steal from him—he would discover any theft, and the consequences would be considerably more unpleasant than mere torture and death. He probably assumed Alaeron would be similarly cowed.

But when it came to the things that fascinated him— that obsessed him—Alaeron was rarely cautious. During a lull in the flow of slaves, he darted into the room, eyes scanning the shelves. There were treasures aplenty, to be sure: a transparent globe full of crackling orange light, a great hammer with its head wrapped in silver wire, a gauntlet with a glowing bulb at the end of each finger, a helm covered in glass hemispheres bulging like the eyes of a spider, a serrated blade chained to the wall and straining against its bonds—but Alaeron wasn't here to plunder. (Besides, those had been here for a while, probably, and might be booby-trapped.) He just wanted the relics he'd carried with his own hands from the Silver Mount.

And there they were, piled together haphazardly, not even separated in their protective mesh sacks. Sloppy, and dangerous besides. It was a wonder Gannix had survived this long; or, alternately, no wonder at all that he'd lost an eye and a hand in the course of his researches. In the Technic League, boldness was rewarded, but the distance between bold and dead was a narrow one. Alaeron plucked the relics from the shelf and secreted them in the pockets of his coat, moving a few of Zernebeth's newly relocated items around a bit to cover the gap.

He stepped out of the strongroom . . . and there was Gannix, ten feet away, cuffing a young male slave on the side of the head. Alaeron backed into the workshop quickly. What were the chances that Gannix would leave without looking in here first? Probably not good. Alaeron felt in his pockets for the extracts he'd prepared that morning before setting out with Zernebeth. Ah, yes, the sigil of a closed eye etched into a vial's stopper: that would do. He swallowed the extract, shivered at the slimy cold taste, then waited a moment. Alaeron held up his hands in front of his eyes. He couldn't see them. Invisibility. Wonderful stuff for an adventurer who wasn't that particular about who owned the relics he wanted to investigate.

Alaeron stepped out of the room, taking a long route around Gannix—being invisible wouldn't make his footfalls silent, after all, or stop him from disturbing the air around him with his movements. But to his dismay, Gannix barked a last order at the slave and started for the door just as Alaeron was approaching the same exit. Alaeron paused . . . and Gannix moved, quick as a mongoose, and seized Alaeron by the throat.

"I *see* you," Gannix said in a singsong voice, and grinned. Half his teeth had been swapped for jeweled or metal replacements. "This artificial eye of mine isn't troubled by invisibility, boy."

Gannix was squeezing hard enough to make black spots bloom in Alaeron's vision . . . but the alchemist still had his hands free. He reached into his pocket and pulled out a simple folding pocket knife, teasing out the blade. He tried to jam it into Gannix's remaining human eye, but the captain turned his face away, so the blade scored his forehead, scraping against one of the metal plates in Gannix's skull and merely slashing across the eyeball rather than jamming in straight to his brain. Gannix screamed and dropped Alaeron, howling probably as much in outrage as in pain. He'd realize now that Alaeron had a certain fundamental difference from the slaves: the slaves didn't hit back.

Gannix crouched, cupping his wounded eye, and shouting at the slaves to "Seize him, seize him!" But the slaves couldn't detect invisible people, so it was trivial to dash out of the room and into the palace itself.

Time was very important now. Gannix would be coming for Alaeron soon, and even blinded, he had his more esoteric eye to hunt with. Worse, he'd mobilize the other members of the League—and the Gearsmen. Alaeron had to get out, and now.

Fortunately, he'd considered the possibility that he might have to flee quickly, and with angry people in pursuit. Alaeron wasn't always cautious, but he wasn't entirely reckless, either, and the idea that the Technic League might turn on him had hardly been unforeseeable. He made his way out of the palace via several seldom-used passageways—shortcuts Zernebeth had shown him, cutting through old wine cellars and the hallway outside a sealed-off suite haunted by a noisy ghost. He shoved open a rusty door and emerged into the sun just as his invisibility spell faded, but fortunately, there was no one around to see him.

The Black Sovereign's court had a passion for exotic mounts, from tame cave spiders to riding lizards, and they were stabled together (though far enough apart to keep from killing each other) on the other side of the palace. The League preferred arcane vehicles, including sedan chairs that traveled on countless spindly tentacles and thrones that hovered on cushions of poisonous yellow light, along with more practical items like Zernebeth's walker with its strange engine.

But no kingdom can run without horses, so there was a sizable stable, too, and that's where Alaeron emerged. The League didn't have much use for horses—the animals tended to shy away from the more interesting wrecks in the landscape, and what status was there in using the same mount a slave might harness to pull a cart? Alaeron was no great horseman, but he knew how to ride, and he'd spent the past few months here making friends with the stable slaves—amazing what a few small gifts of food could do—and getting to know the stock. One horse in particular, a black gelding named Shuri, was lean, fit, and responsive. None of the stable-slaves were around at the moment, so Alaeron fetched his own saddle and bridle and got Shuri ready to ride.

A Gearsman stepped into the stable. It stopped and stared at Alaeron, its alien face unreadable. Shuri shied away, tugging the bridle lead out of the alchemist's hands.

"Ah," Alaeron said, fingering the vials in his pockets. Would ice or flame even hurt something like this? "Can I help you?"

The Gearsman abruptly turned and walked away, and Alaeron sagged against Shuri in relief. "It's all right, boy," he murmured. The metal men came and went at will, often with no apparent purpose. But its appearance was a good reminder that he needed to move, and quickly.

He mounted, clucked his tongue, tugged the reins, and set out along a track leading north, away from the palace and out of the city. The League would expect him to flee south or east, he thought, so he'd head in the direction of the Worldwound first for a while before cutting east to meet the Sellen River. The route along the river was long and heavily traveled, and he'd be able to lose himself in the traffic there. The Silver Mount loomed on his right as he rode, and he shuddered, recalling Zernebeth's death. The road dipped down into a valley, and he slowed Shuri for a safer descent. The horse stepping in a hole and breaking a leg was the worst thing that could happen to him just now.

Or so he thought until he emerged from the valley, crested the hill, and found a dozen Gearsmen spread out across the road in a line, with Gannix in the middle, his crackling whip squirming in his hand like a live thing. The captain had a bulky bandage over his damaged eye, but his gaze fixed on Alaeron nonetheless, the prosthetic lens glittering. "Capture him!" Gannix shouted.

The Gearsmen looked at one another, their odd heads swiveling soundlessly. Maybe they won't, Alaeron thought. Zernebeth had said the Gearsmen sometimes disobeyed, following their own whims, and the one in the stable had let him leave—

The Gearsmen advanced, armed with nothing but their own hands, which would be more than sufficient to their task.

Alaeron slid down off Shuri, putting the horse's body between him and the metal men. He only had seconds. He had a few bombs, but not enough for all of them, if they even had an effect. A mutagen might make him tougher and stronger, but even in beastly form he'd be no match for the Gearsmen. He was out of invisibility extract, and none of the other vials he'd prepared seemed likely to help him—being able to scale a wall like a spider was no good on the cracked plain, and the power to detect hidden doors or breathe water were likewise useless.

But he had other things. The most powerful items in Numeria were relics salvaged from the Silver Mount and the other wrecks littering the region. He had no idea what the things he'd taken from the Mount might do . . . but that didn't mean they wouldn't do *anything*.

He pulled them out of his pockets and put them on the ground, picking them up one after another. The golden chain? It squirmed around his wrist, but had no obvious martial application. The strange egg? Showed no sign of hatching into anything useful. The red loop of metal, not quite big enough to be a bracelet, likewise gave no indication of being anything other than metal. Nothing here looked like a *sword*, or a crossbow, or even a cannon-in-miniature. Nothing screamed its destructive potential, or any potential at all—

He picked up the white-and-gold relic, the one that looked like a toy spinning top. Something to twirl for a child's amusement. It seemed unlikely that spinning the top would do him any good, but it *had* tried to spin of its own accord, it seemed, back in the Mount, and short of throwing his relics at the Gearsmen and hoping one of them would turn out to be a high explosive, he didn't have any better ideas.

So Alaeron set the top on the hard-packed dirt of the road and gave it a spin, making it turn swiftly, balanced on its point.

The world began to turn with it. Or so it seemed to Alaeron. Chunks of soil lifted up from the ground and began to first roll, then lift up in the air and fly, all hurtling in the same direction the top was spinning, forming a dusty vortex around Alaeron. At first the Gearsmen kept stepping gamely forward, but then they started to list and bump into one another, until they too lost their feet.

Alaeron gaped. The movement was like water swirling around a drain, but instead of water, it was *everything*. The air filled with clouds of black dust torn from the ground, and the Gearsmen spun and twirled in midair, round and round. The force the spinning top produced picked up Gannix, too, and slammed him howling into one of the Gearsmen with tremendous force. It didn't hurt the metal man, but Gannix stopped screaming, and a mist of blood and bone joined the rest of the debris in the whirling field.

Shuri was spooked, but didn't try to dart out of the charmed circle where Alaeron crouched by the top. The movement of the cloud of death encircling Alaeron got faster and faster until a wall of metal, rock, and dead Technic League captain spun around Alaeron in a blur, the tornado towering easily twenty feet into the air. Alaeron realized his mouth had been hanging open, and he closed it with a snap. The top itself showed no sign of slowing down. This must be what it was like at the center of the great permanent hurricane called the Eye of Abendego: a circle of calm surrounded by impassable destruction. No one could penetrate that barrier of wind—and anyone who lived in the eye of that hurricane would be there forever, unable to escape.

Alaeron feared he might be in a similar situation. The Dust Devil of Abendego, they could call it, a tornado on the Numerian plain, where Alaeron could perish in the calm, still center of the devastation.

Well. That was unacceptable. And if you're trying to figure out what to do, why not begin with the direct approach?

He touched the tip of his index finger to the upper point of the spinning top.

The friction of his finger stopped it spinning instantly. Whatever titanic forces it might produce, the relic acted like any ordinary toy.

The affect on the whirling maelstrom was equally instantaneous, but more dramatic. Instead of continuing to spin around, everything spun *out*. Chunks of dirt and dust sprayed outward with tremendous force, then pattered down. The Gearsmen and Gannix's remains hurled through the air in all directions, landing so far away Alaeron couldn't even see the metal men glint in the distance. They would be standing up soon, though. Maybe with Gannix dead, they wouldn't bother to pursue him. Or maybe they *would*.

Alaeron cooed at Shuri for a few moments until the horse calmed enough for Alaeron to mount again. They made their way over the broken ground until they reached an unmarred stretch of road. The top's winds seemed to have made a perfect circle, perhaps fifty feet across. The offensive potential was obvious. Sneak an unassuming agent with this relic into, say, the heart of the Great Andoran Fair, and hundreds or thousands could be killed, along with incalculable property damage. The League couldn't be allowed to have a weapon like this.

Especially, Alaeron thought as he sped east toward the Sellen and freedom, since it's probably not meant to be a weapon at all. He wondered if the relic might in fact be part of some gyroscopic balancing system, or a device to produce the sort of unimaginable torque you'd need to power an engine that might send a ship the size of a city through the depths between the stars. Those were *much* more interesting possibilities than just having some weapon to level the castles of your enemies.

# Chapter Fourteen
## The Land of Sand and Scorpions

I had *that* in my hands?" Skiver said, appalled. "What if I'd taken it into my head to give it a spin?"

"Then we probably wouldn't be having this conversation," Alaeron said, "though it depends on where and when you decided to give it a spin. This is why you shouldn't play with my *toys*, as you call them."

Skiver took the gearwheel from a pocket and looked at it as if it were a live asp. "And what in Hell does this thing do, then?"

Alaeron shrugged. "Nothing, as far as I can tell, except turn, sometimes, by itself. No hurricanes then, though. Just a grinding noise." He took the gearwheel when Skiver offered it, and sighed in relief. All six relics, together again. It felt like having a lost limb restored.

"Such power," Jaya said. "And you didn't think to use it for your own profit? Something like that spinning top you could sell to any number of warlords or rebels. Even your own Eagle Knights of Andoran could find a use for such a thing. Take it into the heart of a slave market—"

"It would kill all the slaves," Alaeron said dryly. "Not exactly what we're trying to accomplish."

She waved her hand. "Fine, to some government building in Cheliax, then. Level the place."

"Places like that are protected," Alaeron said. Though he didn't know if they *would* stand against the relic, despite their magical safeguards—who knew how spells would react to artifacts from the Silver Mount? "And, anyway, I don't *care* about weapons, I care about truth, and secrets."

"I can't decide if you're a wonderful man or a very foolish one," Jaya said, her beauty not at all impaired by the frown line marring her forehead.

"Too much weapon for me," Skiver said. "Give me a couple of knives and I can get most jobs done. Knives are *manageable*." He scratched his chin. "Funny, though. After all that, killing a captain and such, flinging their metal men all hither-and-yonder, you'd think the Technic League would have come after you. Hard to believe you got away clean."

Alaeron shrugged, trying not to let his discomfort show. "Numeria is very far away. And getting farther with every passing moment." He stood up and stretched. "I've been sitting too long. I think I'll take a walk around the deck."

"You go right ahead," Skiver said, voice cheerful. "And I'll just tell Jaya about the great big bastard of a Kellid who tried to kill us back in Almas. You know, the one I'm dead sure the Technic League sent to drag you back."

Alaeron paused for a moment, looking at the ocean. Jumping into the water and drowning suddenly seemed like a fairly good idea. Instead, he sat back down. "All right," he said. "I admit, I wasn't completely forthcoming, but it's my business, and nothing to do with either of you."

"What are you two talking about?" Jaya demanded.

"Big bastard of a Kellid," Skiver said. "Tried to kill Alaeron, or at least catch hold of him, in our scholar's workshop back in Almas. I tried to stab the bastard and broke my knife on his coat. He weren't wearing plate or mail underneath, either. Just looked like an ordinary coat. Sort of thing the Technic League might have, seems to me now. And then someone blowed up the scholar's lab. I half thought it might be Ralen Vadim making a point, but it's not Vadim's style to do something like that without letting you *know* he did it. And Alaeron's just been talking about how the League likes their bombs and explosions. Now, Alaeron told me the fella I fought was there to collect a nasty debt, but I know all the enforcers who work roundabout the city, so that never rang quite true to me. Should've put it together before now, maybe. The question is, are we clear of this Kellid, or is he going to make trouble for us again?"

Alaeron put his face in his hands for a moment. "Kormak," he said, looking up. "The man's name is Kormak. If I ever met him at Starfall, I don't remember, but there were always great big savage men around, the Black Sovereign's old friends and warriors from the days when he was a fighter instead of an addict. Kormak works for the League now, anyway. He confronted me the same day Vadim's men kidnapped me. I escaped him, just in time to run into Vadim's thugs."

"So that's why you agreed to this expedition," Jaya said. "You had a reason to flee Almas too." She smiled suddenly, like lightning in a blue sky. "And here I thought you just wanted to spend more time in my company."

"Both were factors."

"All right," Skiver said. "But is this Kormak *still* after us? And don't say 'he's after me,' scholar. We're all together, and I doubt he'd scruple overmuch at killing Jaya and me to get at you."

Alaeron considered. He didn't trust Skiver at all, and though he was growing fond of Jaya, he had precious little reason to trust her, either. But it was unfair to leave them ignorant of their danger, even if, as he devoutly hoped, that danger was past. "The pirates," he said. "I thought I saw Kormak on the deck of the ship when it sank."

"That's him done for then," Jaya said. "I don't imagine Kellids have much cause for learning to swim."

Alaeron shook his head. "The Dagger and the Coin, the tavern where Skiver gambled away my artifact? I went back that way before we left Absalom, and there was nothing left but ashes, and people said a Kellid had come in and called down some fiery magic to destroy the place . . . " He shook his head. "I'm sure it's Kormak."

"Wonderful," Skiver said. "A mad bastard from the north who likes burning things down, chasing us across the whole Inner Sea."

Alaeron lifted his hands. "Wait. I figured out how he was tracking me. He only went to places where I used the artifacts, so I think he has some way to sense them when they're activated. I haven't used them since last night, and I *won't* use them again. At least, not until I'm ready to lure Kormak into a trap even his Technic League weapons won't enable him to escape."

"You should have told us," Jaya said. "You've put us all in danger."

Alaeron nodded. "I know. I'm sorry. But I think we're safe now."

"Good we cleared the air," Skiver said. "Now we all know where we stand. If the ruins of Kho don't kill us, Alaeron's Kellid friend will. I like to have options." He pulled his filthy hat down over his eyes and went to sleep leaning against the rail.

"He'll be snoring in a minute," Alaeron said. "You don't want to be here for that."

Jaya shook her head. "I don't much want to be around *either* of you right now. Shame this ship is so small." She rose gracefully and strode away.

Alaeron sighed. "That went well."

"Still hoping for a love match, then?" Skiver said, voice muffled by the hat over his face.

"I suppose so."

"Infatuation's a terrible thing," Skiver said. "I probably shouldn't say, but . . . she tried to seduce me, you know, back at Vadim's. Wanted me to free her brother and help her escape. Promised me rewards of various sorts. One sort, mostly, truth to tell. You can imagine what I mean. Turned her down, of course. She's got nothing to offer me along those lines. Her brother, on the other hand . . . I still wouldn't have done it, but I might've been *tempted*. She was ready to do whatever she needed to in order to get away, though. Not what you expected from your not-so-fair lady, is it? She does like to play at being good."

Alaeron shifted uncomfortably on the deck. "Well. She was desperate."

"Oh, I don't think less of her for making the effort. Use any tool you've got to get the job done, I say. But don't forget she got herself into this mess. She's no victim. She tried to cheat Vadim, and now she's paying the fine. And you're here helping her pay it."

"What are you saying?" Alaeron asked, though he knew it was nothing Skiver hadn't tried to tell him before: *don't trust her*. Which should have been funny, coming from someone as obviously untrustworthy as Skiver himself. But somehow, it wasn't funny.

Skiver didn't answer. A moment later, he started to snore.

The rest of the voyage was a hell of boredom, though no one seemed to mind but Alaeron. Skiver and Jaya both largely ignored him as he brooded over the artifacts he couldn't test, or even dare to touch. His alchemical researches were likewise difficult to pursue—he did what was necessary to keep his extracts, mutagens, and bombs prepared using his little field kit, but without at least a *room*, and a *table*, he couldn't work on anything more complex, or experiment. He could feel himself on the verge of some great epiphany—perhaps related to the artifacts, perhaps not—but whenever he attempted to turn his attention to it, it skittered out of his mind.

Skiver taught Jaya some game involving little stones and a board marked with stripes, but when Alaeron asked if he could play, Jaya coldly told him it was a game for two, and they were enjoying themselves just fine without him. So Alaeron was left with only his thoughts. Normally that wasn't a problem—the mind was a cathedral—but his attention returned relentlessly to all the things he *couldn't* do.

Finally, after too many long days and warm nights, the ship arrived in sight of land, and the three stood near the front of the ship, watching the southern continent approach. "A bit *beige*, innit?" Skiver said.

"The heart of Osirion is a desert so vast it can swallow armies," Jaya said. "The remnants of one of the oldest kingdoms in the world."

Skiver grunted. "Big beach, most with no ocean. Lovely."

The ship eventually moved into the harbor, a bay connected by a series of canals to the River Sphinx, one of the great waterways of the world, and the lifeblood of

Osirion. Most of the country's major settlements were spaced out along that river, and they'd be traveling its full length upriver, into the tributary called the Crook, and then on to that river's source in the east, something like five hundred miles in all if the maps were to be believed. Which meant more ships. Alaeron was extremely tired of ships.

The great city of Sothis, capital of Osirion, drew into sight late in the afternoon. The buildings were sand-colored stone, with their many golden minarets catching sunlight, but there was something else towering over those minarets, something *dark*. Skiver squinted. "What's that?"

"The molted shell of Ulunat, child of the dark god Rovagug," Alaeron said. "I've read about it, but it's . . . bigger than I thought."

"Wait," Skiver said. "The Rough Beast? That Rovagug? The god who has no use for people at all and wants us all dead?"

"The very same. You haven't heard of Ulunat?"

"Maybe," Skiver said dubiously. "I didn't go to school like you, scholar."

"The god Rovagug spawned many monsters," Alaeron said. "The Tarrasque, you may have heard of?"

"There's a drink called Tarrasque's Blood," Skiver said. "Mate of mine invented it. Mostly grain alcohol. Knocks you right out."

Alaeron laughed. "Well. Ulunat is even older, perhaps the first of Rovagug's spawn. It was a great beetle who came crawling out of a dark hole in the earth thousands of years ago. It laid waste to civilizations." Alaeron nodded toward the great monster's shell. "It died in Osirion. The stories about *how* it died are conflicting, but it probably took the combined power of the old god-kings of Osirion to defeat it."

"They built their capital around the husk of a big dead *bug*?" Skiver said. "Foreigners are so bloody *odd*."

"If it's really dead," Jaya said. "When I was in Osirion, I heard stories—some think the wizards who fought Ulunat merely knocked it unconscious, or paralyzed it, or drove it deep into sleep. Some say it may wake again."

"Grand idea to build their capital around its body, then," Skiver said. "How long's it been sleeping?"

Jaya shrugged. Alaeron cleared his throat. "Going on . . . nine thousand years?"

Skiver blinked. "Oh. All right. Probably not likely to wake up while we're in the city, then. That's something."

"That husk is just the beast's discarded shell, anyway," Alaeron said. "Not its actual corpse. It's not likely to come back to life any more than an empty suit of armor is apt to start walking around."

"That sort of thing happens," Skiver muttered. "I blame magic."

Alaeron ignored him. "The locals call it the Black Dome. It's supposed to be full of palaces and important government buildings and the like."

"Guess it explains all the little beetle statues Vadim's been offered by treasure hunters lately," Skiver said. "Something like that looming over you makes an impression, I reckon."

The port of Sothis was tightly regulated, and though the waterway was crowded with ships from various ports of the Inner Sea, there was none of the chaotic jostling common in other harbors Alaeron had seen; everything was orderly and measured, with Osirian harbormasters directing all movement. The great Crimson Canal connected the capital to the River Sphinx in the west, and its multiple locks branched around the Eye of Sothis, an island where all traffic coming and going was directed. The banks on all sides of the canal were green with growing things. Arable land was rare and precious in this desert country.

The captain, who hadn't spoken to them once on the entire voyage, appeared and scowled at Skiver. "You pay now," he said. "Then go."

"Ah," Skiver said. "Right." He paid out a handful of heavy gold coins, and the captain directed them to a small rowboat manned by a slave, who took them and their packs to the island, which was connected to Sothis proper by a network of bridges arcing gracefully across the canals. Skiver seemed to have some idea where he was going, so Alaeron and Jaya followed after him as he walked confidently through the throngs of sailors toward the island's center, a vast plaza given over to merchants, food vendors, and a dozen other methods of parting new arrivals from their money. The plaza's bustle made the Coins look tame, and after days of quiet on the sea, Alaeron found the press of people overwhelming.

Skiver seemed to be affected as well, stopping to gaze up at the tall obelisk in the center of the plaza, and the great curvature of the bridges over the canals, each tall enough to allow the passage of a ship underneath. The golden minarets and the mirror-smooth Black Dome all glittered in the late afternoon sun.

"Beautiful," Jaya said, and Skiver nodded.

"Yeah," he said, shaking himself. "I mean, Absalom was something, but it wasn't so different from Almas really, and this . . . they just took a great ugly lot of desert and a big dead bug's shell and they made *this*? Carved their own rivers into the ground and built those bridges and towers and all?" He shook his head.

"I knew the world was a big place, but I don't think I ever quite understood how big and wide and different, until now. And this is just the very tip-top of a whole *continent*, extending on down right off the edge of all the maps I've ever seen . . . Makes me think maybe the place I grew up isn't the center of everything after all."

"You see?" Jaya said, smiling at Alaeron for the first time in days. "Travel *does* broaden the mind. Even Skiver's."

"Watch it, you," Skiver said, but he ginned. "My mind's broader than you'd like to imagine. All right then. Vadim said we should go to an inn called . . . well, something foreign, but it's supposed to have a picture of a red beetle on the sign, so let's get over into the city and see if we can find it."

Alaeron knew only a smattering of Osiriani, and even that wasn't much use—he could puzzle out simple words in writing, but was almost useless with the spoken tongue. (There were certainly Garundi people in Absalom, but he hadn't spent much time with them.) Fortunately Sothis was where the rest of the world met Osirion, and almost everyone they met spoke Taldane, the common trade language, at least well enough to try and sell them something, so they found directions to the inn called the Ruby Scarab without much difficulty. It was made of blindingly white stone, with a sign depicting the golden scarab of Osirion, but in bright red instead of gold—Alaeron wondered if it were an homage to the reigning Ruby Prince.

The inn was a bit deeper into the city than some others, and while there were a few people inside who obviously came from the northern side of the Inner Sea, the majority seemed more southern—Garundi, Keleshites, and Vudrani. There was also a giggling gnome in one corner piling up small circular stones into an impossibly high tower, but as far as Alaeron was concerned, the less said about gnomes, the better. The alchemist had quite enough chaos in his life without adding one of *those* to the mix.

Skiver slipped through the small round tables and went straight to the bar. "Ale?" he said hopefully, and the young, dark-eyed bartender shook his head sadly.

"A thousand apologies, but we serve only wine here, though we have a hundred varieties. We cater to a specialized clientele who appreciate—"

Skiver wrinkled his nose. "Water for me, then. Wine for them." He gestured at Alaeron and Jaya.

The bartender bobbed his head. "And what sort of wine—"

"It's questions like that that make me hate wine," Skiver muttered. He put a coin on the polished bar top. "Never mind, we'll have three waters, and we'll pay well for them. Oh, and for the answer to a question. I'm looking for Chuma."

The bartender shrugged. "A common name, sir."

Skiver nodded. "They call him Chuma the Scorpion."

The bartender looked down at the coin. Skiver added another coin, and after a moment, a third. The bartender swept them into his hand. "He's there, in the far corner. But he . . . does not enjoy having his time wasted."

"Who does?" Skiver said, glancing over. "Farthest corner away from the gnome. That's just good sense."

"Don't speak against the gnome," the bartender said. "He's been here two days, and says he has to drink a bottle of every sort of wine I can bring him. He may well provide my daughter's entire dowry."

"Wonder if he plays cards?" Skiver said. He picked up an earthenware cup and took a sip. His eyebrows went up. "Say, this water . . . it's good."

"From one of the famed oases of Sothis," the bartender said. "Sweeter and more refreshing than any wine."

"You should charge for this and give the wine away, there was any sense in the world," Skiver said. He strolled toward the corner the bartender had indicated, and Alaeron and Jaya followed.

"Chuma the Scorpion?" Alaeron said. "Doesn't sound like a friendly sort."

"The name means nothing to me," Jaya said. "But then, my involvement with the criminal classes is more haphazard than Skiver's. If he is an associate of Ralen Vadim, I think we can assume he is only friendly when it benefits him."

Skiver stopped in front of Chuma's table. The man was Keleshite, big and possibly fat, though it was hard to tell, as he was dressed in flowing robes of linen. His long beard was more dark than white, and he stroked it as he looked over a pile of parchment sheets. He had a tiny silver teapot and a small ceramic cup on the table before him, and nothing else.

He didn't look up, so Skiver kicked the table, jostling the teapot.

Without looking up, Chuma said, "I have had men killed for less than splashing tea on my papers."

"I've killed men *personally* for less than ignoring me when I'm standing right in front of them," Skiver said.

"Is that a dog barking?" Chuma called to the bartender. "I hear the barking of a dog. You let filthy dogs into your place of business now?"

"I'm a dog all right," Skiver said, grinning. "And my master's name is *Ralen Vadim*."

Chuma sipped from his teacup, then looked up at them for the first time. His eyes were gold. "Mmm. That name is known to me. But anyone may say a name."

Skiver hooked a wooden chair with his ankle, pulled it over, and sat down. He glanced back at Alaeron and Jaya. "You two, sit, drink your oasis water." Then, to Chuma, "Vadim was supposed to send you a letter."

Chuma spread his hands. "I have received no letter."

"Good thing he sent me with another copy, then." Skiver reached into his jacket and drew out an envelope sealed with a fat blob of wax. He sailed it across the table, and Chuma picked it up, broke the seal, scanned the words, and then flung the letter back.

"That appears to be Vadim's hand. He urges me to extend to you all possible courtesies. Well. All possible courtesies extend no farther than my asking you to leave, politely, before having you thrown out. I do business with Vadim, from time to time, but that does not mean I am obliged to take care of his *pets*."

"Ralen Vadim is a powerful man," Skiver said, frowning.

Chuma shrugged. "On the other side of the Inner Sea, certainly." He leaned forward. "But *I* am the Ralen Vadim of the southern lands, dog. Would he take kindly to one of my . . . employees . . . demanding his personal attention?"

Skiver nodded. "I see your point. I do. But maybe I'm a *useful* dog, eh? Or even a dog you shouldn't bother?"

"The desert is large," Chuma said. "It is easy to lose bodies there. I have lost *many* bodies there."

"Do you know a man named Omari? Some people called him 'the Spider,' or at least, he liked to tell people he was called 'the Spider.'"

For the first time, Chuma looked interested. "Yes. I know of this man.

"Spider, scorpion," Skiver said. "Reckon I'll meet the beetle next. Or the camel! What is it you know about this man, then?"

Chuma stroked his beard. "Omari. Yes. He disappeared."

"Oh?" Skiver sipped his water, then grinned. "Nobody ever found him? Not even recently?"

"I understand *parts* of him were found," Chuma said slowly.

Skiver nodded. "His head. And his hands. Still wearing those great big rings, right, with the emeralds and diamonds and rubies, wasn't he? Turned up in an alley around the corner from your, what do you call it, import/export business in Almas."

"Omari was a treacherous man," Chuma said. "He stole from me. I wanted him punished. It was not so much that my men could not *find* him—they could find him—it was just that none of them returned from finding him alive."

"Dangerous fellow." Skiver leaned forward. "The reason I left the rings on his fingers was so you'd know it wasn't some robbery for money. Any ordinary thief and killer would have taken the rings, you see."

Alaeron and Jaya listened in rapt (and for Alaeron's part, horrified) silence.

"Why cut off his head and hands?" Chuma said, his voice low.

"Cutting off the head was the way I killed him," Skiver said. "I find it's usually very effective. As for the rest, isn't that what they do with thieves down here? Cut off their hands? Or is that just one of those, what do you call them, myths? Thought you might appreciate the gesture. Anyway, hauling his whole body over to the alley by your warehouse would have been a right pain in my ass. Head and hands are much lighter, and make just as good an impression. Seems maybe I did a favor for you, doesn't it?"

Chuma lowered his head for a moment, drumming his fingers on the table. "All right," he said after a moment. "The letter said you wish to travel east, all the way to the Slave Trenches of Hakotep, and from there, you desire a guide through the mountain passes to the Mwangi Expanse."

Skiver nodded. "That's what we need, right enough."

"What business do you have on the far side of the mountains?" Chuma said. "What is Vadim looking for? There are many rumors about lost cities, great fortunes to be made, but why send a man of your, ah, talents into the jungle?"

"I fancied seeing the world," Skiver said. "But really I'm just here to keep the experts motivated. The woman's a tracker and explorer, knows the Mwangi Expanse like I know the back alleys of Almas, and the man's a scholar, can tell you more about artifacts than a butcher can about cuts of meat."

"What do you seek?" Chuma leaned forward eagerly, his great belly pressing into the table. "Where are you going?"

"I don't imagine we're supposed to say," Skiver said, then looked left, and right, and left again. "But let's just say Vadim heard of something in a place called the Screaming Jungle, something the right buyer will pay a king's treasury for. That's where my archer here hails from. The Screaming Jungle. Sounds like a shit place, but go where the money is, I always say."

Chuma stroked his beard, nodding. "Indeed, indeed . . . Well. Yes. I own a felucca, a sailboat, with a crew of three. Room enough for ten or twelve passengers, but I'm happy to let you have it—"

"Is that the kind of ship where you have to sleep on the deck?" Skiver said.

Chuma nodded. "Yes, indeed, there is no better blanket than the stars—"

"We need a boat that's got rooms with *roofs*," Skiver said. "We've been sleeping on a deck for too many days already. We could all use a bit of privacy. I haven't had a moment alone with just my thoughts and my hand in *ages*."

The Keleshite crime lord roared laughter, pounding his fist on the table. "Fair enough, my dangerous friend. All right. I will give you use of my personal pleasure barge. It has enough cabins for all three of you, and a fine cook, and comely servants."

"Will you be joining us?" Jaya said.

Chuma shook his head. "Though I would love the opportunity to accompany such a beautiful woman on a journey into the wild places, pressing business keeps me here. When do you wish to depart?"

"Soonest," Skiver said.

Chuma nodded. "Give me a day or so to prepare. Do you have lodgings for the evening?"

"This'll do," Skiver said, glancing around the Ruby Scarab.

"I insist you stay in my home," Chuma said. "It would be my honor."

"You're too kind," Skiver said. "But we wouldn't want to impose."

"It is no imposition. For the man who slew the Spider? I would give you my own bed."

"No, no, we couldn't, but thank you," Skiver said. "Truly."

Chuma spread his hands and gave a little shrug as if to say he'd tried. "Very well. At least let me pay for your stay here tonight?"

Skiver nodded. "That would be most gracious."

Who is this polite person, Alaeron wondered, and what has he done with Skiver? How had he gone from calmly talking about beheading a person to extending verbal courtesies in the space of mere moments?

"I'll see to it." Chuma pushed back from the table, sweeping the papers into a pile and tucking them into a satchel. "If you'll excuse me, my friends, please enjoy your time in the city, be it all too brief." He paused on the way out to speak to the innkeeper, pointing to Skiver and the others, then bustled out the door and away.

Skiver took his chair and grinned. "That went all right, even if I am the one saying so."

"Why didn't you agree to stay at his house?" Jaya said. "Were you afraid he meant us harm?"

"Nah, nah." Skiver waved a fly away. "Vadim told me the Scorpion's a peculiar fella. If he offers something, you've got to refuse him three times. If he offers a fourth time, it means the offer was sincere. If he accepts your refusal, then he *wanted* you to refuse. Dunno if that's a Keleshite thing, or just Chuma. You notice he only let me say no twice? Guess he didn't want to risk me losing count and saying yes too soon, heh."

"While points of etiquette are indeed fascinating," Alaeron said, "I'm more curious about this 'Spider.' You really killed him?"

Skiver snorted. "Nah, he'd have cut me into ribbons if I'd tried. He was a right nasty piece of work. Couldn't hold his liquor, though. Got drunk one night, fell off the steps of a tavern, and cracked his head open. Looked pretty much like the same wound you'd get from being hit over the head with a cudgel, though, so Vadim paid the corpse-collectors to give us the body so we could claim it as our own, thinking we could use it to buy a little influence with Chuma. No, I didn't kill the Spider." Skiver sipped his water and looked at the ceiling meditatively. "I've killed whole cartloads of other people, though, if that makes you feel any better. Or worse."

"And what was all that about the Screaming Jungle?" Alaeron said.

"Basic misinformation," Jaya said.

Skiver nodded. "I was lying, he knew I was lying, I knew he knew, he knew I knew he knew, and so on. But we had to go through the motions for, you know, the look of the thing."

"It seems I have a lot to learn about being a criminal operator," Alaeron said.

"What," Skiver said, "did you think just *stealing* things was all it took? Anyone can steal stuff. Being a good criminal means getting *away* with it."

# Chapter Fifteen
## The Journey on the Sphinx

A slender, bald, obsequious man in voluminous white pantaloons and no shirt at all met them in the inn's common room the following morning. He was Chuma's associate, and his duty, he said, was to make sure they were appropriately outfitted and provisioned for their journey. They spent the morning among market stalls, where Chuma's wealth bought them linen and cotton clothes in the loose-flowing, cool native style, and where Alaeron had to be torn away from a few stalls selling rare artifacts and even the occasional newly unearthed scroll, some still sealed in their copper tubes and unseen by human eyes in centuries. He couldn't afford those anyway, but he spent a few coins on alchemical supplies and some insect and animal parts he thought might make ingredients for the extract of flight he'd been mulling over. Finally they were led to a dock abutting the broad, shimmering canal.

"That's a *boat*?" Skiver said. "Looks like a lord's country house!"

Alaeron wouldn't have gone quite that far, but Chuma the Scorpion's pleasure barge was the most opulent floating vessel he'd ever seen, that much was certain: constructed of fine wood, fittings polished to a high gleam, embellished with ornaments of gold (or at least golden paint). There were two huge, blue, long-lashed eyes drawn on the prow. Chuma's shirtless servant was, it turned out, also the barge's captain, and he led them aboard and pointed out the amenities with obvious pride, including three private staterooms, each small but well-appointed. Skiver and Jaya both agreed Alaeron should have the one with a foldout desk.

"This boat has stairs," Skiver said. "I've never even lived in a *house* with stairs." He scampered up the narrow staircase to the upper observation deck, while Jaya and Alaeron stowed their bags and then met at the prow, where four cushioned chairs were fastened to the deck. A red, tasseled awning provided shade from the sun. They sank down in their seats, Jaya groaning with pleasure, and looked at the afternoon sun glittering on the water. Without any noise, commotion, or noticeable signal, the barge began to float smoothly down the canal, toward the River Sphinx.

"Let's never leave here," Jaya said, leaning back and closing her eyes. "Let's just commandeer the ship and float up and down the river forever."

"It's a tempting thought," Alaeron said.

"Why does pleasure have to be so fleeting, but discomfort is ever in abundance?" she said. "You'd think the gods would have arranged it otherwise."

"I doubt the gods worry much about our comfort. But we should enjoy it while it lasts. Before we get to the, ah, Screaming Jungle." Might as well practice craftiness. You never knew who might be listening.

She opened one eye, looked at him, and smiled. "Now you're learning." More loudly, she said, "Ah, the Mwangi

Expanse. How I've missed it. Nothing makes you feel more alive than the constant terror of death. Though sinking into these cushions is a close second."

They floated along the canals for a long time, gradually leaving the spires and minarets of the city behind, to be replaced by green fields on all sides. "It's more lush than I'd expected," Jaya said.

"I imagine it's a ribbon of green following the river valley," Alaeron said. "And beyond that, desert. Wasteland. Ruins filled with poisonous vapors and unquiet spirits and cursed treasures." He sighed. "I wish I could explore it all. Can you imagine the secrets hidden out there?"

Skiver came along then, carrying a jug of wine and a few goblets. "No beer at all on this thing. Apparently the Scorpion doesn't drink proper alcohol, only stocks the boat with squeezings from grapes and other things. The stuff in this bottle here is made of *honey*. Can you believe it? To make spirits from something that oozes out of bugs? But a man can only stand so much water, and I daresay I've drunk worse."

He sat down and propped his feet on the rail. "Now we're traveling in style. Captain says the journey will take a while, more than a week, anyway, maybe closer to two. We're picking up some passenger at An, the City of Triangles—I guess Chuma couldn't resist the chance to make a little money, since he was sending his boat on down the river anyway." Skiver filled a glass, sniffed the contents, made a face, and passed it to Alaeron, who handed it over to Jaya before accepting a glass of his own. "Triangles!" Skiver said. "Where I'm from, we make cities out of sensible shapes. Squares, rectangles, like that. Foreigners. Who can make sense of them?"

"We're the foreigners here," Jaya said. "*They* don't have funny accents here—*you* do."

"Oh, sure, everything's relative," Skiver said. "I know it. I'm always saying that. I've said it to more guards and judges than I can count—one man's crime is another man's necessity, ain't it?" He sighed contentedly. "I'm happy to be a foreigner, if this is how they treat visitors. Give me the easy life, that's all I want."

A day into the journey, Skiver was so bored he was teaching Alaeron to knife-fight, even though Alaeron wasn't a particularly keen student. "You're not terrible," Skiver said, dancing lightly on the deck in his bare feet. "You've got decent instincts, and you're pretty quick, and you've got nimble fingers."

"I do handle acid for a living," Alaeron pointed out. "A certain amount of dexterity is—"

"But you're as subtle as a brick to the head," Skiver went on. "I can see every move you make coming ten minutes before you get around to doing it. It's best if the man you're fighting never sees where the blade is coming from. Now, ideally that's achieved by sticking the knife in his kidney while his back is turned, but if you've got no choice but to face him in a fair fight, at least try not to be totally obvious." He danced forward, his blade flashing out as his hands moved faster than Alaeron's eyes could follow, forcing the alchemist to stumble backward in retreat. "Now, if you're fighting someone who knows what they're doing, and who means to kill you, they're going to stab. Slashing is fine for making pretty scars, and if you just want to send a drunk idiot on his way without having to get rid of his body afterward, sure, slash away. But mostly in serious knife fights, it'll be a stab." He jabbed forward, three sharp thrusts in quick succession.

Alaeron wiped sweat off his forehead with the back of his hand. "All right. What do I do about that?"

"Be where the blade is not," Skiver said. "Stepping aside is better than stepping back. Faster, and puts you in a better position to take control. Watch, come at me."

Alaeron had already learned there was no point in holding back: he wasn't going to give Skiver so much as a scratch, not at his current level of incompetence. He lunged, and Skiver slid to the side, stepping closer to Alaeron, and grabbed the alchemist's wrist lightly. "Here's the bit where I break your wrist," Skiver said, letting go and stepping back. "Be aware of the line of attack, and *stay out of the way*. Watch the man. Watch his feet, and his hips, and the way he shifts his weight. You can usually tell what a man's going to do, even if he's not as bloody obvious as you. The body gives it away." Skiver sheathed his knife and held out his hand for Alaeron's. "That's enough for today."

"Let me know if you'd like to learn archery!" Jaya called from her chair, where she'd watched the lesson with amusement.

"Oh, lovely." Alaeron sat down beside her, muscles aching from too much dancing away from Skiver's leisurely demonstration strikes. The thief had moved at half speed, mostly, so Alaeron could follow his movements and try to mimic them, but it was still enough exertion to push Alaeron's endurance to its limits. "Something else I can be terrible at. You know, I don't try to teach the two of *you* how to mix mutagenic potions."

"Nor have we asked," Jaya said.

"Don't think I haven't noticed," Alaeron said.

"Do you blame us? It takes some effort to kill yourself accidentally with a bow and arrow. And while it's a bit easier with a knife, it still takes a colossal mistake. But alchemists . . ."

"You lot blow yourselves up five times before breakfast, don't you?" Skiver said. "And even if you don't blow yourselves into little bits, well, I knew an alchemist once who only had three fingers on his left hand, and that was the one he called his *good* hand. Nah, I'll stick with stabbing people for a living. Much safer."

They sat and watched the banks of the river slide by for a while. The pleasure barge was clearly not built for speed. They were regularly passed by other craft, especially small, single-sailed ones that shot by like a runner racing past a man standing still. On one of those boats, they would have been forced to sleep on deck again, though they wouldn't have needed as many nights to reach their destination. Alaeron couldn't decide if their relatively sluggish pace was a blessing or a curse. How eager *was* he to hike into the mountains that separated Osirion from the Mwangi Expanse? The idea of seeing the ruins of Kho still seemed almost like a dream to him, but its reality was growing ever closer.

Unless they were killed by hyenafolk and other monsters in the foothills, of course. Always a possibility.

A couple of days later—days spent talking, or staring at the lotus blossoms floating on the water, or watching the farmers work on the cultivated banks of the River Sphinx—they drew into sight of An, the City of Triangles.

"Huh," Skiver said, munching an apple and squinting over the railing on the ship's highest deck. "I expected more of those pointy tomb things."

"The city is named for the jagged mountains visible in the distance." Jaya pointed them out. "Though also for the pyramids in the south. This was a city to house the slaves who built those pyramids, once."

Alaeron squinted toward the peaks on the horizon. "Isn't the tomb of Kamaria the Brazen here? The mad king who worshiped the Rough Beast?"

Jaya nodded. "So I understand."

Alaeron grunted. "Plundered mightily already, I'm sure. Still, there are often hidden rooms in tombs, and I wonder what I might find there, given enough time . . ."

"Oh, well, maybe we'll stop by on our way back from the Mwangi Expanse." Skiver's voice dripped sarcasm like a snake's fang drips venom. "If we haven't had enough of crawling around ruins and having relics from the past try to kill us."

"A man knows where he stands, exploring a tomb," Alaeron said wistfully. "Undead, curses, traps. Those are things you can prepare for. In the ruins of a city that fell from the sky? There's no telling what we'll find."

"You aren't reassuring me," Jaya said. "You're supposed to be the expert in these matters."

Alaeron shrugged. "I should be able to tell a valuable artifact from a bit of broken pottery, anyway."

The barge slowed to a crawl as it approached a dock behind what was either a small government building or a large private residence, all in white stone. A man sat on the dock on a huge brown traveling pack, tendrils of smoke rising up from a pipe in his hand.

Skiver squinted. "Is that . . . ?"

"I think it is," Jaya said. "How incredible!"

Ernst, the wizard who'd saved them from the hellspawn in Absalom, stood up from his pack as the crew jumped from the barge to the dock and began tying up. He waved.

"My friends!" the wizard boomed. "Come down so I can greet you properly! Jaya! Skiver! And . . . ah . . . forgive me, I've forgotten your name, sir, but it's a pleasure to see you as well!"

"Oh, well," Alaeron said, voice flat. "A happy reunion."

# Chapter Sixteen
## Keepers of Secrets

And then a hetkoshu, a great black crocodile, took a *bite* out of the boat!" Ernst waved his arms around. "Just a single *chomp!*" He mimicked the jaws of a crocodile with his hands, snapping at Jaya's face, making her lean back and laugh. "Oh, well, yes, hilarious, but not when you're on the boat! I was sleeping, and woke up to a lot of screaming, and the deck tilting, and everything sliding down, and a beast the size of a—well, the size of great black crocodile, frankly, which is a terrible size for anything to be." Ernst shook his head.

They were all seated around a table in back of the great house, one of Chuma's many residences, beneath a white canvas pavilion. The travelers were sharing a meal while the barge was resupplied. Once they passed the cities of Tephu and Wati, chances to take on more food (and wine) would dwindle, and the crew was stocking up in preparation.

"So that's how I came to be stranded in An," Ernst said. "Boatless and bereft. Fortunately I have a gift for making friends, and I soon heard there might be a place for me on a barge heading all the way up the river, for the right price. And here I am! I had no idea I'd run into you lot, though."

"How did you escape the crocodile?" Skiver demanded. "You stopped the story at the best part, right before the bloodshed!"

Ernst waved his hand in a gesture of casual dismissal. "Oh, well, once I was awake, I had a spell or two at hand, to encourage the beast to seek an easier meal elsewhere, and to get us all ashore without becoming a meal for his brothers. My boots did get wet though, terribly. Took ages to dry. I was squelching with every step."

"And what brings you to Osirion?" Alaeron said, trying to keep his tone conversational. Skiver and Jaya were both gazing at Ernst with rapt affection, which annoyed him—didn't they find the wizard's appearance here at *all* suspicious?

Ernst beamed. "Opportunity brings me to Osirion! The Ruby Prince, in his wisdom—and, I suppose, his avarice—has thrown open his great nation to exploration. I go in search of *scrolls*, my friends, and spellbooks, and anything else the great wizard-kings of old might have left behind."

Alaeron leaned forward. "All right, but—why do you want to go all the way up the river? There's not much *there*, as I understand it. The Slave Trenches of Hakotep, I suppose, but there are unlikely to be spellbooks there. And beyond them to the north it's just . . . desolation. Shouldn't you be more interested in the Pyramid of Doom, or the Sphinx Head, or the Ruins of Tumen?"

Ernst tapped the side of his nose. "That desolation you mention. The Footprints of Rovagug, they call it here. Nothing but desert wastes. Well, and a volcano or two, and hot springs for the nobles. *Except*." He smiled. "I have it on good authority that there is a forgotten school of magic buried in those sands, between those volcanic landmarks known as Klarwa Fountain and Asulek's Mouth. I uncovered some old texts no one at my school had even *looked* at in centuries, judging by the dust. Unlike those other worthy locales you mentioned, this buried school isn't *famous*. That means I won't have to contend with a dozen other explorers. I'll have it all to myself. A school for magic. Schools have *libraries*. Oh, I can't wait." He rubbed his hands together gleefully.

"I wish we could go with you," Jaya said wistfully, and glanced at Skiver. "Do you suppose . . . ?"

He shook his head. "Our patron has other preferences."

"Then where are you three bound, if I might inquire?" Ernst asked.

"The Mwangi Expanse," Alaeron said quickly, not entirely trusting his fellows to remember the cover story. "A certain ruin in the Screaming Jungle. More than that . . . we should not say. Our patron is paying for our discretion, you see."

"Mmm." Ernst stroked his beard. "I won't press, fear not. I have often dreamed of seeing the golden streets of Osibu there, or braving the notorious ruins of Liclac, or scaling the canted towers of the Blighted Gardens."

It was apparent Ernst knew more about the Screaming Jungle than Alaeron did. He'd half assumed Skiver had just made up the name, but apparently not. "Perhaps we'll meet again when all our journeys are done," he said, "and tell you if we saw any of those places."

Ernst nodded. "But let us not speak of the parting of ways! We have a journey of many days and nights together! Happy times, my friends, happy times!"

Happy for some, Alaeron thought, watching Jaya and Skiver grin at their new companion.

The barge paused frequently in the next two days, as if reluctant to leave the comforts of civilization, making long stops at An's sister cities: Tephu in the papyrus marsh, and Wati, a city once abandoned to the dead amid a plague of madness, now increasingly given over to the living. Past Wati, they left the River Sphinx and moved into the River Crook, where there wasn't much in the way of cities apart from the great garrison at Ipeq, and precious little along the riverbanks to divert the eye, just the fields of the floodplain sliding by slowly on both sides.

Ernst settled into life on the pleasure barge like he'd been born to it. He and Skiver sparred with knives on deck, and drank wine by the barrelful (Skiver refused to admit he'd developed a taste for the stuff, but he hadn't even asked for beer when they'd stopped to resupply), and played cards and dice for no stakes but honor. Ernst and Jaya loosed arrows into the river, in competition to see who could shoot farther, and were often found leaning together, laughing, Jaya touching the bearded wizard more often in the course of half an hour than she'd touched Alaeron in their entire journey.

For his part, Alaeron's trip was an exercise in frustration. He occasionally unwrapped his artifacts and looked at them, but he didn't dare to touch them lest he activate one accidentally and reveal their whereabouts to Kormak; a pleasure barge was no place to make a stand against the Kellid. He'd started dreaming about the artifacts, and in one dream, he'd slipped the egg *inside* the red ring, and the two had fused into a new whole, but he couldn't even try that in reality.

He attempted to busy himself with his alchemical studies instead, but while his field kit was sufficient to create extracts and mutagens he'd already mastered, he wasn't well equipped to do more intense researches into new techniques, and the mystery of bestowing the power of flight upon himself eluded him. On one of the occasions while Jaya and Ernst were lounging together, he complained about his difficulties to Skiver. "If I had harpy feathers, or a bit of dragon's blood, or even a thousand crushed fireflies, I might make some progress, but as it stands—"

"Ernst can fly," Skiver said. "Heard him telling Jaya about it. He's got a spell, you know, said he'd take her flying sometime." Skiver rolled his eyes. "That's romantic, is it? Getting dragged through the air while someone holds on under your armpits? But it sure worked a trick on her, she melted like a bit of candle at the idea. Ernst has quite the line of bullshit on him."

"I don't trust him," Alaeron said, scowling.

Skiver nodded. "Well, of course not. Why would you? What with Chuma hiring him to spy on us and all."

"What?"

"Oh, I haven't heard that from Ernst's mouth, of course." Skiver poured another cup of honey wine. "But not much else makes sense. I believe the wizard came here to Osirion to plunder tombs and whatnot, sure, but what are the chances a man we'd met before—a man who'd helped us, a man we *liked*—would end up on Chuma's barge unless Chuma *put* him here? Unlikely things happen, but not *that* unlikely."

"Does Jaya know?" Alaeron said.

Skiver snorted. "Knew before I did, I bet. She's sharp as an assassin's blade, that one."

Alaeron sagged against the rail, smiling. "So *that's* why she's getting so close to him. Winning his confidence. Trying to trick him."

Skiver raised an eyebrow. "No-o," he said after a moment. "She doesn't hold his spying against him, I don't think. None of us is truly free—we all serve someone, and it's not like *we* three aren't a pack of outrageous liars. She likes the wizard. I do, too. Why don't you?"

The alchemist sucked his teeth for a moment. "Because Jaya likes him more than she likes *me*."

Skiver patted him on the back. "Ah, perfect. You just won me that beautiful knife with the silver hilt she's got. See, *she* thought it was because he can do magic just by saying some words and waving his hands around, while you've got to muck about with potions and things."

Alaeron gaped. "You made a *bet* about me?"

"What else is there to do here?" He gestured at the river. "Count the lotus blossoms floating on the water? We gotta stay entertained someways. Don't worry, we didn't say anything about it to Ernst."

"My life is one humiliation after another," Alaeron said.

"Aren't they all," Skiver said. He paused. "Well, except for mine."

Powerless. Alaeron *hated* feeling powerless. Time to seize some power. "Ernst knows how to fly, you said?"

On one of their bored afternoons, Skiver had tried to teach Alaeron the rudiments of lockpicking, using the doors of the cabins on the barge to practice with. None of the doors were equipped with particularly fearsome locks, and Alaeron had mastered the trick of popping them open in less than an hour of tinkering: he'd always had clever hands. So it was trivial for him to use one of the borrowed lockpicks to break into Ernst's cabin, though he eased the door open carefully in case there were traps, magical or otherwise.

But it appeared the wizard wasn't worried about anyone digging around in his secrets, because the door opened without any fireballs or other unpleasant surprises. Alaeron slipped in. The cabin was much like his own: small, paneled in dark wood, but cleverly made to conceal a variety of conveniences, with beds and benches and tables that all folded into the walls when not in use. Ernst's bag was empty, its contents probably moved into the sea chest at the foot of the bed. A careful examination of the chest revealed no traps—at least that Alaeron could detect—and its lock proved even flimsier than the one on the door. The alchemist lifted the lid, carefully moved aside a few of Ernst's articles of clothing, and then saw the object of his desire: a thick, leather-bound volume with hinges of gold.

Where there are wizards, there are spellbooks. And where there are spellbooks, there are things an alchemist can learn. To think Jaya had believed Alaeron considered wizards *superior*. Why, a wizard confronted with Alaeron's formula book would be able to learn *nothing*, but by studying the arcane writings in a wizard's spellbook and gathering the right components, Alaeron could duplicate almost anything a wizard could do.

Well. Assuming the spell affected the user, of course. There was no potion that would enable Alaeron to call meteors down from the heavens or make a mountain explode—an alchemist could only learn wizard spells that did things to the *wizard*. But stealing the power of flight was well within his power.

The pages of the spellbook were crowded full of arcane writing in various languages, but Alaeron knew more tongues than he had fingers and toes, and he flipped through the book's pages looking for something that seemed likely to confer the power of flight. Ah, there, a page of crabbed writing. He need only copy it down in his own formula book and he'd be able to mix up an extract to give him the same power—he was pleased to realize that most of his preparations had been on the right track, and he only needed to make a few small changes. Flight! The power of escape! And if Jaya would enjoy being carried through the clouds, well, then—

"You could have *asked*, you know," Ernst said mildly. "It's rude to snoop through another man's possessions. If there's one thing I can't abide, it's rudeness." The wizard had slipped into the cabin so silently Alaeron had to believe he'd used magic—though it was possible Alaeron had simply been so engrossed in studying the spellbook that he'd lost track of events in the world itself. Such obsessive focus was not without precedence.

Ernst sat down on his bed and frowned at Alaeron. "Stealing my spells, hmm? So you can bottle them up for yourself?"

Alaeron cleared his throat. "I apologize for the intrusion. Yes, I should have asked, and I'm sorry. Wizards, in my experience, are very possessive of their spellbooks, even though it costs them nothing to let an alchemist jot down a few lines—"

"Wizards are keepers of secrets, alchemist," Ernst said sternly. "If *anyone* can see our spellbooks, it rather devalues the contents, don't you think?"

Alaeron, who had a possessive streak of his own when it came to knowledge, could only sigh. "Yes. So. What happens now? Do we do battle? Tear the ship apart with bombs and magics? Or something more formal? A duel on the riverbank, perhaps?"

Ernst twisted a clump of his beard between his thumb and forefinger, his mud-colored eyes thoughtful. "Perhaps, if circumstances were different. The truth is, I went snooping through your possessions, too, and for even worse reasons." Ernst reached into his pocket, and Alaeron tensed, ready to snatch up a vial full of something nasty from his own pocket. The wizard came out with—

"My artifact!" Alaeron shouted. Ernst was holding the gray disc Alaeron had brought out of the Silver Mount. "By the gods, why do I even *bother* with putting wards and traps on my bag?"

"It was all the traps and wards that drew my attention, actually," Ernst said. "I thought, 'My, there's something more valuable in *that* bag than dried jerky and extra rope!' Good safeguards, by the way. Had a bear of a time getting through them, and I only dared take one of the relics you had buried in there. All that effort, though, and this little trinket doesn't do a thing as far as I can tell."

"So Skiver didn't tell you about my relics? Or Jaya?"

Ernst slowly shook his head. "No, they didn't. Though I've been trying mightily to pry any amount of information out of them. Skiver's quick with a dirty joke, and Jaya . . . ." His eyes got faraway. "She's sweet as a peach and tough as old leather all at once, isn't she? But neither one tells me anything my employer might like to know."

"Chuma," Alaeron said.

Ernst shrugged. "I assumed you knew. All of you. None of you are fools, as far as I can tell, though you don't have much else in common—cutthroat, huntress, and bottle-washer. That diversity probably makes you a better crew, truth be told. But it's not polite to talk about treachery, is it? I had an arrangement with Chuma before I even met you lot. He agreed to finance my explorations in exchange for my giving up anything interesting I found that fell outside my area of interest. But then he told me I had to get on this boat with you and try to find out where you lot were really headed, and when I objected—spying is ungentlemanly—he told me it was this, or forget about my bargain, and oh, he'd have my head lopped off, too. So here I am."

"The mighty battle mage is afraid of a merchant?" Alaeron said.

Ernst snorted. "He's rich, and he has a lot of friends. Facing him in single combat is one thing, but—actually, I take that back. I wouldn't even want to face him that way. They don't call him 'Scorpion' for nothing. He's more dangerous than he looks, and he hardly looks like a fluffy kitten."

"We all work for someone," Alaeron said. "I won't fault you for having a master. It's possible you like him even less than I like my own." He held out his hand. "My artifact, please."

"Ah. As to that. It is yours, of course—but I ask a small favor in return. Tell me where you and yours are *really* going."

"The Screaming Jungle, as we said."

"You know less about the Screaming Jungle than Skiver knows about his father, and all Skiver knows about his father is that it stands to reason he must have had one at some point." Ernst shook his head. "You didn't blink when I mentioned Liclac, or Osibu, or the Blighted Gardens, but only two of those are even real—I made the other one up. Pray tell me, which is false?"

A one in three chance. Better, if Alaeron could make an *educated* guess. "Liclac," he said, because it was one of the silliest names he'd ever heard.

"Alas, the Liclac Ruins are real, though I couldn't tell you much else beyond the fact that they exist. But 'Blighted Gardens' *does* sound plausible, doesn't it? Glad I still have the touch of invention." He held up the disc. "This is yours, for but a word of truth."

Alaeron sighed. "Fine." He wracked his brain for *some* part of the Mwangi Expanse he'd actually *heard* of. "The Red Star," he said suddenly. "The Doorway to the Red Star. That's where we're bound. Great magic there, as I'm sure you know."

"Oh, yes," Ernst said. "I've read of it. A ring of crimson stones, hovering in the air. The ruins of a cathedral to a cult so dark that, though its name is remembered, few of its tenets are. Once home of the King of Biting Ants, a sorcerer—I hate sorcerers, they never have to *work* for anything, they do magic as naturally as Skiver swears and Jaya looks beautiful. But you're lying. I can tell. There is a spell, you know, that allows those wise in the ways of magic to tell when someone is telling them a lie—the spellcaster sees worms and maggots falling from the liar's mouth, or a cloud of black and stinking smoke pouring from between the liar's lips, or a dribble of liquid offal. Do you know, my friend, that in my eyes, you are quite literally talking shit, now?"

Alaeron nodded. "I'm familiar with such spells. But last I checked, only priests and other servants of the gods could cast them. And you, my bearded friend, are neither."

Ernst narrowed his eyes. "Fine. I can tell you're lying because you're a *bad* liar. Answer me, or this trinket of yours will become so much silver dust."

Alaeron drew a vial from his pocket and uncapped it. "This is acid," he said. "A wonderful solvent, really. I've seen it eat through skymetal. Wonder what it would do to your spellbook?"

Ernst went still. "I am not entirely sure what would happen if you poured acid on a book inscribed with arcane magic."

Alaeron showed his teeth. No one could have really mistaken it for a smile. "I'm an alchemist, you know. We believe in experimentation. So how about I just pour acid on it and see what happens?"

"Stop it," Jaya said, appearing in the doorway. "You, put the acid away. You, give him back his relic. So much *posturing*."

"Jaya," Alaeron said, and "My dear," Ernst said, and then they just glared at each other until Jaya hissed and snapped her fingers.

"Stop! Ernst: we're bound for the ruins of Kho. All right? Go tell *that* to Chuma. Let him bring a mercenary army and a bunch of men with baskets and carts if he likes. It's an entire *city*, Alaeron. It's not as if we'll be able to carry all of it away on our backs, is it? Just let Chuma know he'll have to pay *me* well for the privilege of leading his men to the ruins, and that he'd better come fast, because I don't mean to delay. I have family waiting for me back in Andoran."

Ernst shook his head. "Kho? The Doorway to the Red Star was somewhat believable, but—"

"It's true," Skiver said, popping his head in. "Sorry, was eavesdropping from the hallway. Nice lockpicking, Alaeron, but you should've drugged old Ernst's wine to make sure he was sleeping while you poked around. Not a bad effort, though. You're learning. But yes, Kho. That's where we're going, and we're going to bring back treasures, oh yes."

"The lost city of the Shory Empire," Ernst said slowly.

"Yes, one of them." Alaeron capped his acid. "The oldest. The first to crash. And, more importantly, the one we have a hope in Hell of actually locating. Jaya knows the way. Or, rather, she has family in a village a stone's throw from the ruins."

"Farther than that," Jaya said. "No one would want to live that close, according to my mother."

"Why didn't you tell me earlier?" Ernst cried. "Jaya, as I held you close, as we whispered secrets—"

"We were both whispering lies," she said, but fondly. "Lies are so much more beautiful. I didn't tell you because . . . well, who knows. The habit of a lifetime of deceit? Fear that it might have dire consequences for me? Because Ralen Vadim wouldn't *like* it? Then I realized—I'm the one who knows where we're going. I'm the one who's valuable here. If Chuma wants to follow, he can pay for the—"

"Forget Chuma!" Ernst said, eyes wide. "Kho! The great city of Kho! *Shory magic!* One of the great civilizations, as old as the empire of Azlant, but far stranger! The magics they possessed, the power to lift whole cities into the air, the secret of Aeromantic Infandibulum! I will accompany you. I will lend my spells to your cause and my back to shoulder the treasures you carry out. I ask only that if we find any books, any scrolls, you *let me copy them.*" His eyes were wide and wild, and the intensity of his gaze was one Alaeron recognized. He'd seen it in his own face often enough, after all, in the mirror when he was in Numeria, desperate to plumb the depths of the Silver Mount.

And just think how well had *that* worked out.

"Fine," Alaeron said, scowling. He didn't like Ernst any better now, but he couldn't help feeling he understood him, a bit. "I don't care. Come if you like. Jaya?"

"You are most welcome," she said, but she was frowning.

"Nice of you to share your opinions," Skiver said, "but I'm chief of this little expedition, ain't I? The only word that matters is mine." He looked Ernst up and down, picked at his teeth with a long fingernail, squinted like a suspicious jeweler eyeing a suspect ring, then grinned. "The more the merrier, eh? How you planning to stop Chuma from, ah, showing his displeasure?"

Ernst bounced on the edge of the bed, turned boyish with happiness. "Oh, I'll write letters, and tell him you were indeed lying, and that you're actually going to . . . oh, who cares? Something believable. Hmm. Chuma loves money—ah! The Gembasket, yes. A valley said to be so rich in resources that precious gems litter the ground, but practically inaccessible. It's a dream of all the avaricious men from Katapesh, and Chuma is first among them. I'll say you've found a secret pass to the valley, through the mountains. And that I've weaseled and wheedled my way into your confidences, and will go with you on your journey. All right?"

Skiver twiddled his little finger around in his ear. "Katapesh. Is that the country with that wizard-king, what's his name? Nex?"

Ernst frowned. "No . . . That would be *Nex*. Named after the wizard. Who's been dead for a very long time, by the way." He paused. "Skiver, how can you know so little of the world you're presently traveling in? Katapesh is probably only about a hundred and fifty miles from us. Directly south!"

Skiver sniffed the end of his finger and made a face. "So? Who cares? You come to Almas, I'll show you five places where you can gamble, ten places where you can find a whore, and fifty places where you can find drugs and drink to erase all your pain, all within a *single* mile. *That's* knowledge, wizard—deep and narrow, not broad and shallow."

"You may have a point," Ernst said. "Certainly my teachers who urged me to specialize in a single type of magic rather than becoming a jack-of-all-trades would have agreed with you."

"And what happens when Chuma realizes you've tricked him?" Alaeron said.

Ernst shrugged. "I'll say you deceived me with tales of the Gembasket. Or some other lie. Or I'll give him some Shory relic that will make him forget all my trespasses. That's the *future*, Alaeron, we'll worry about it then. The important thing is that if he sends men, they'll be looking for us to the south, when we'll be heading to the west."

"I thought it was a whole city?" Alaeron said, looking around at them all. "More treasures than we could possibly carry out? Why not invite Chuma and his hired warriors and anyone else who can come with us? Share and share alike, strength in numbers, all that?"

They all frowned at that, and then Jaya shrugged. "Because," she said, "we want to get first *choice* of the treasures."

"Chuma's probably not too good at sharing, anyway," Skiver said. "More than likely he'd let us lead him to the ruins, then kill us, and tell Vadim we were eaten by one of those big bastard crocodiles."

"Both good points," Alaeron conceded. He sighed. "Fine. May I have my relic back now, please? Since we're all friends here?"

"Of course," Ernst said. But before Alaeron could reach out his hand to take it, Ernst flipped it toward him, sending the disc spinning through the air like the oversized coin it resembled.

The disc spun three or four times normally, then began to turn more slowly, then simply stopped, hovering in midair, emitting a faint blue light and producing a hum that made Alaeron's back teeth ache. Alaeron snatched it from the air, and it buzzed against his hand for a moment before subsiding.

He looked wide-eyed at Skiver and Jaya, and they looked back, their faces as horrified as his own doubtless was.

"What?" Ernst said. "So it hovers? What of it? That's hardly great magic. It's barely a cantrip, I don't see—"

"Surely he's still in Absalom," Jaya said. "He can't possibly track us now, can he, just from that little bit of hovering?"

"There's no way he could know we're in Osirion," Skiver said. "Right? From Absalom you can go *anywhere*, no reason to think we'd go here."

"Unless we mentioned Osirion in the Dagger and the Coin," Alaeron said. "Unless someone heard us. Unless someone told him. Did we? I can't remember."

"What are we talking about?" Ernst demanded.

"Death," Skiver said. "Fire. Pursuit. The usual."

# Chapter Seventeen
## The End of the River

They told Ernst about Kormak. "Does this make you reconsider your plans to join us?" Jaya asked him.

Ernst touched her cheek. "Pursuit by a deadly, implacable Kellid? Did you think that would discourage me from keeping company with you? Ha. I'll help you scare him away if he dares to show his face!"

"Can't hurt having a wizard on hand if he does show up," Skiver said. "But he probably won't. Right?"

"All it takes is a fast boat," Alaeron said. "Because we are on a very *slow* boat. He could catch up with us in a few days, if he followed us to Osirion. We need a faster craft."

Skiver sighed. "I knew travel on a pleasure barge was too wonderful to continue. Back to sleeping on deck again, I guess. Everyone be sure to loot candlesticks and things from your cabins so we can afford to hire another captain."

"They say the city of Ipeq was made in but a single day," Ernst said, gazing up at the airy parapets. "Constructed by an army of djinn in service to the Pharaoh of Blades, granting wish upon wish. There are many arguments against creating buildings by magic." He gestured to the soaring towers, the weirdly geometric whorled walls, the fountains of leaping water. "But this city is an argument in its favor, I would say."

"Until it all falls down," Skiver said, squinting, his expression a combination of awe and distrust. "A house built on wishes is a house built on dust. Pretty though."

Ernst slapped the barge captain on his shoulder, and the man nearly fell over. The wizard's good nature could be forceful enough to knock someone down even without his hefty backslaps, Alaeron thought. "I was instructed to take you to the river's source," the captain said, for the dozenth time. "Truly, it is my honor to serve—"

"Just take the letter back to Chuma," Ernst said. "It will explain everything." Alaeron had insisted on reading the parchment before it was sealed, wary of some treachery, but unless Chuma and Ernst had worked out a particularly elaborate code, the message was a tissue of pretty lies: it said they would take a small boat down a tiny tributary of the Crook, then an overland journey to the Gembasket, and return with riches untold.

The captain nodded reluctantly and left them on the dock. Ipeq was not the bustling metropolis that Sothis was, being mainly a military town, home to a garrison of soldiers. Supposedly the army had magical tokens that could transform into a hundred scorpion boats capable of sailing swiftly downriver to reinforce the Sothan troops in times of trouble. Alaeron's people weren't able to get their hands on such a boat—just as well, as magic boats had a tendency to vanish after a set amount of time, no matter how fast they might be—but between Ernst's insistent personality and Jaya's winning smile they convinced the captain of a felucca to take them upriver for a price that was merely extortionate instead of outright robbery.

In contrast to the pleasure barge, which had so many crewmen that Alaeron hadn't been able to learn all their names, the felucca had a crew of just three, and was powered by a large triangular sail. Light, small, and maneuverable, the boat could go far more quickly than the barge, but its comforts were considerably fewer. At least it was roomy, with space for ten or twelve passengers.

"Mashed peas and flatbread," Skiver complained over their meal, scooping up a heap of the paste with his bread. "I miss the cooking on the barge."

"Part of the joy of travel is enjoying the food of the place!" Ernst declared. "I wonder what they ate in Kho? Cloudberries? Rare birds that flew too high?"

The felucca, named the *White Heron*, bobbed gently in the water, moored to a post on the riverbank, lit only by the moon. The river grew more dangerous from here, with sandbars to be poled around and treacherous shallows, and the captain refused to sail at night, despite their offers of extra coin. The barge had stopped for the nights as well, but they hadn't been in a *hurry* then.

They ate and drank mostly in moody silence, Ernst's attempts at conversation failing to catch fire. The captain estimated that, with good winds, they'd reach the Slave Trenches of Hakotep in two more days, or on the third day at the latest. Soon their series of water voyages would be over, and it would be a hard hike over the mountains to an uncertain end. Some amount of brooding over the future was to be expected. First Jaya and then Skiver announced their plans to get some sleep, taking their blankets to the far end of the boat and stretching out on deck with the crew to slumber through the night.

Alaeron lay back and looked at the stars, Ernst leaning nearby. "You took those relics from the Silver Mount, then?" Ernst said.

Alaeron nodded.

"Then they used to be up there, among the stars, perhaps."

"The thought had occurred to me."

"If you don't mind me asking, just from professional curiosity, one scholar to another, what have you learned about the relics?"

Alaeron considered. Ernst *was* a scholar—and unlike Alaeron, who'd educated himself with stolen volumes or bought his way into the libraries of wealthy men in exchange for concocting alchemical wonders, Ernst had studied at proper schools. Perhaps he might be able to provide some insights. It was against the alchemist's nature to share too much . . . but Ernst had agreed to let Alaeron copy whatever he wanted from the wizard's spellbooks, so some courtesy in return was called for.

"When I first found the artifacts, they reacted to one another. Some have individual powers, properties I have discovered, but I believe they may actually be pieces of some sundered whole. A weapon, or an engine, or something else—who can say? If I can find a way to recombine them . . ." He shrugged. "I would be very interested to see what that whole does."

"Let's examine them, then!" Ernst said. "My expertise is more in imbuing ordinary objects with magic than in arcane technology, but I do have a good sense of how things fit together. Why not?"

Alaeron hesitated. "If we activate them, even inadvertently, Kormak may sense them. Perhaps he didn't notice the disc, or it wasn't active long enough, but to do more would be to test our luck—"

Ernst leaned forward. "Running from your problems is a sure path to sleepless nights, my friend. I do not fear some Kellid, terrible though he may be. Are we not terrible as well? Your potions and bombs, my spells, Skiver's knives, Jaya's bow—I'd call us a match for any man. And those artifacts of yours! Think of the edge *they* could give us. I say we study them, learn more of their powers, and *hope* the Kellid comes for us. Let us choose our ground, and be prepared. You say he comes armed with relics from the Silver Mount, yes? Well *so do you*. The only difference is, he knows better how to use his."

Alaeron looked at the stars. Ernst wasn't saying anything Alaeron hadn't thought himself. Truly, he was not inclined to battle, but Kormak was inclined to nothing else. When could Alaeron stop running? Not as long as the Technic League's dog hounded him. On his own, Alaeron didn't think he stood a chance against the Kellid, but with the help of his allies—especially, though he was loath to admit it, Ernst—he might be more than a match. "You may be right," he said at last. "But we should talk to Jaya and Skiver about it tomorrow. It's not a decision we can make for them."

Ernst slumped. "Of course. Caution, discretion, yes. You're right."

Alaeron spread out his blanket and slept, one hand tangled in the straps of his pack. It was true they should talk to the others. But mostly he just wanted the relics to be his and his alone for one more night.

"Sure," Skiver said over breakfast—bean cakes and hardboiled eggs. "Let's kill him. I still owe the bastard for that knife I broke off on his coat. Let's lay a trap at the end of the river and see if he wanders into it. He's a great one for striding into places and burning buildings down, but there's precious little to burn in the desert."

Jaya sighed. "I dragged you into my problems, Alaeron, so it's only fair I do my part to help you out of yours. I don't know what good my arrows will do against this man, but what strength I have is yours."

"Between my magics and Alaeron's knowledge of poisons, we may be able to improve your arrows," Ernst said. He rubbed his hands together gleefully. "So, then, Alaeron—the relics?"

They found a flat part of the deck, and Alaeron laid out the artifacts on their cloths. The short length of golden chain. The silver egg. The porcelain-and-gold top. The gray disc. The red ring, the size of a bracelet once again. The black gearwheel. "My approach was to attempt to discern their individual properties, in hopes of determining how they might fit together," Alaeron said. "The egg slows time for all but the wielder, or those he touches. The disc, as you've seen, hovers sometimes, but doesn't seem to do much else. The chain grows, adding links, and sometimes writhes like a serpent, but to no apparent purpose. The wheel sometimes turns, but it makes a terrible grinding sound. The red ring twists chance, making unlikely order from chaos. The top." He licked his lips. "The top makes . . . tornadoes. Perhaps even hurricanes."

Ernst lifted his eyebrow. "That last bit sounds useful."

"Perhaps in the desert," Alaeron said. "I never dared use it in any populated area, because the destruction it creates is considerable."

"All right." Ernst cracked his knuckles. "Let's see what fits together, shall we?"

Alaeron nodded. He hadn't tried many configurations, afraid of possible disasters—the devastation created by the top had made an impression on him—but he *was* an alchemist, and that meant he shouldn't fear to experiment. "When we stop for lunch," Alaeron said. "I wouldn't want to risk putting any of these things together on the boat. They could do more damage than a giant crocodile."

Ernst agreed, though his impatience was palpable. Skiver's initial impression had been right—Ernst was the opposite of the plodding, studious image of a wizard. Alaeron took some small pleasure in frustrating him. Hardly noble behavior—but then, Alaeron was no noble.

The time finally came, though, and after wading through a marshy expanse they sat on the riverbank (first ensuring there were no crocodiles lazing there). Skiver and Jaya elected to stay on the boat, obviously afraid Alaeron and Ernst were going to blow themselves up.

"Chains exist to bind things together," Ernst said. "Perhaps it should sort of . . ." He wiggled his fingers. "Connect the other pieces?"

"Perhaps," Alaeron said. "And gearwheels often drive chains. Perhaps the chain should wrap around the gear . . . "

They tried various configurations. Wrapping the chain around the gear did nothing. Trying to dangle the other pieces from the chain also yielded no results. Alaeron decided to focus more tightly. He made the chain his area of particular study, and learned that with the proper flick of the wrist he could make the chain extend itself greatly, going from a foot long to ten times that. The links slithered through his palm and wrapped around his wrist and halfway up his forearm, and for a moment he feared it might keep climbing to his neck and strangle him, but it stayed there. "This is a decent weapon," he grunted, slinging the chain out, letting it wrap itself around a clump of reeds, and jerking them, roots and all, from the marsh. Another flick of the wrist and the chain shortened back to a modest length swinging from his hand. "Some Technic League captain would have welded a spiked metal ball to the end and considered it a job well done."

"Look!" Ernst crowed, and held up the ruby ring with the egg inside it. The ring had tightened around the egg as it did around a finger. "Fits together beautifully!" he said.

Alaeron was annoyed. He'd dreamed about that very configuration, but hadn't gotten around to trying it. "Doesn't seem to do much, though," he said, taking the fused artifact from the wizard and turning it over in his hands.

"Somewhat resembles the top, now, doesn't it?" Ernst said. "Rounded on the ends, thicker in the middle . . ." The top was squatter, more flattened than the ring-and-egg, but there was a definite resemblance.

"The gear," Alaeron said slowly. The axis of the gear had depressions on either side, just little dimples, really . . .

"Do you think it would fit?" Ernst said.

"Let's try." Alaeron put the gear down on the cloth, and Ernst pressed the egg-and-ring against the depression in the gear's center.

The artifacts snapped together like magnets attracting. Ernst hooted.

"Still didn't do anything, though," Alaeron said.

"Put the top on the other side," Ernst suggested, turning the gearwheel over.

Alaeron lifted the top gingerly, afraid, as always, of what would happen if he accidentally set it spinning. He would never have worked this recklessly, this instinctively, on his own—his approach was methodical, careful, testing each object in isolation, then attempting to fit them together two by two until he'd tried every combination, with plans to eventually move up to permutations of three artifacts at a time . . . but what had his caution gotten him? There was a time for methodical science, but that time was perhaps not when a murderous Kellid was coming after you.

Alaeron slipped the pointed bottom of the top into the dimple on the other side of the black gear, and it snapped into place too.

They sat staring at it for a while. "Well," Ernst said. "That's disappointing."

"I don't see anywhere the disc can fit," Alaeron said, picking up the relic for a moment before placing it back down on its cloth. "Perhaps it's from another device all together, or maybe we're missing pieces of this one . . ."

"Try wrapping the chain around the teeth again. The links *are* just the right size for the gears to fit into," Ernst said. "I feel like we're close to something . . ."

Alaeron nodded, heart thumping in his chest, an exultation of impending discovery fizzing through his head. He'd felt this way when he'd discovered how to make the feral mutagen, how to create confusion bombs, and when seeing Ernst's spellbook had unlocked the secret of flight: he was on the cusp of a breakthrough.

He wound the chain around the gear. He'd fitted only three teeth through the links before the gear began to turn, and this time, there was no horrible grinding sound, just a smooth hum. The chain wrapped around the gear completely—and then the trailing end wrapped around Alaeron's arm, his wrist, down his forearm, around his elbow, to his bicep.

The gearwheel—the artifact combined—rose into the air as suddenly as a rock might plummet off a cliff, and the chain tightened and dragged Alaeron into the air after it. He squawked as his feet left the ground, and

Ernst shouted something Alaeron couldn't understand. The device rose into the sky at an angle, dragging Alaeron after it, pulling through the air, out over the river, and up and up and *up*.

Death by artifact, Alaeron thought. He should have known his life would end this way. Would the artifact stop working and drop him to his death? Or drag him up to the stars, where the device had come from originally? They said the air grew thin and hard to breathe atop high mountains. How thin would it be in the blackness of space? Surely there was *some* air up there, or else how would the sun burn? Would he fall *into* the sun?

He looked down. He saw Jaya's face, staring up at him from the felucca, growing smaller.

*I will not die*. He jerked his wrist, snapping at the chain, giving it the same flick he'd used before to shorten it.

The chain came free. The device separated into its component parts, and all tumbled down. Alaeron tumbled with them. He scrabbled desperately in his pocket as he fell, vials and tubes dropping from fumbling fingers, until he found the one he was after, a small vial with a crude drawing of a feather etched into the wax stopper.

He'd mixed the extract, which would make him as light as a falling leaf and enable him to drift gently down from a great height, as soon as he decided to study flying, because it's a fool who flies without preparing for the possibility of a fall. He gulped the contents of the vial, and suddenly felt lighter, buoyed up by wind, drifting the last few feet to land gently on the water. He touched down in the shallows, and the artifacts all gleamed there in the sand, fortunately not yet stolen by the current. Alaeron snatched them up and shoved them in his sodden pockets, along with as many of his extracts as he could recover, then splashed toward the shore. He'd traveled a hundred yards away from Ernst, but the wizard ran to him and helped him back onto dry land.

"An engine of flight," Ernst said, shaking his head. "I have *spells* for flight, you know. And you can make a potion to grant you the same power, and with a great deal more control than *that* collection of broken parts could give you."

"It wasn't just flight," Alaeron mumbled. "I think they wanted to go back to the stars."

"The stars are no place for a man," Ernst said firmly.

"And the disc," Alaeron said, brushing water from his hair. "We never found out how the disc—"

Ernst was ignoring him. "At least they're decent weapons individually, some of them. The egg, the ring, the top. Even the chain, though it *would* be better with a spiky metal ball on the end, come to think of it. A disappointment, though, that all together those artifacts from the stars don't do anything more than a decent wizard can do on his own."

Alaeron wasn't so sure. Ernst was *too* rash, too willing to jump to conclusions. He wasn't a *scientist*. But if he wanted to give up on studying the artifacts, that was fine with Alaeron. The wizard had pointed him in the right direction. Alaeron would take it the rest of the way.

The disc, he thought. Somehow, the disc must be the key. But how does it fit? He would find out. He *would*.

Skiver and Jaya arrived then, shouting, asking if he was all right, and Alaeron managed to give them a smile. "I'm fine," he said.

"So you plan to sail over Kormak and drop bombs on his head?" Skiver said. "A bit bold, but then, you always struck me as a bold one."

"When you fell, I thought you were lost." Jaya took his face in her hands and gazed into his eyes. "Do not do that again."

"Fall?" he said lightly. "Or go flying?"

She patted his cheek. "Flying is fine. Take me with you, if you like. But only after you learn how to *land*."

"All right, back on the boat, you lot," Skiver said. "The captain says all this splashing about in the shallows attracts crocodiles, and we've got problems enough without *those*."

They sailed on, the felucca flying over the water. The banks remained green, but less cultivated the farther west they traveled, and the going became harder, with many sandbars and shallows. At times they were forced to actually shove the boat over the sandy places and back into water deep enough to sail. The night after Alaeron's ill-fated experiment with combining the artifacts, there were strange roars to the north, and the captain muttered darkly in Osiriani.

"What's he saying?" Skiver asked.

Ernst shrugged. "He says this far west there are too many monsters. Lamias, basilisks. Cruel falcon-headed hieracosphinxes. Djinn and ifrits and even dragons."

"Maybe one of those will eat Kormak," Skiver said.

"The captain is threatening to abandon us soon," Ernst said. "Put us out on the bank and sail back downriver."

Skiver yawned. "He won't. He's been paid to take us all the way to the Slave Trenches."

"Nevertheless, he says his men are fearful, and he is unwilling—"

"Let me talk to him alone for a moment," Skiver said.

"But he speaks barely any Taldane—"

"I think he'll understand me," Skiver said, and sat with the captain for a few moments at the far end of the boat. Alaeron strained to hear, but Skiver didn't say much. He held up a sack of jangling coins in one hand, and pointed west. Then he held up his most vicious-looking knife, one with a curve at the end, serrated teeth on one side, and a razor gleam on the other. Using that knife, he pointed east.

After a moment, the captain nodded. That night, the adventurers took turns sleeping in shifts, with one watching guard over the others, and over the captain and his two crewmen. The next morning they ate breakfast from their own packs, too, just in case the captain decided to poison his unwelcome passengers.

"I know I said I was sick of bean cakes and pickles," Skiver said, "but what I *meant* was, I wanted biscuits and honey and butter and bacon, not strips of salted meat."

"Perhaps we can hunt in the mountains," Ernst said. "Jaya is handy enough with a bow. Fresh game would do us good." He patted his belly, which, Alaeron noted nastily, was ample enough that he could miss a few meals without doing himself any harm.

"I am a hunter of men and monsters, mostly," Jaya said. "Less often meat. But we'll see."

"Do you really think they'd poison us?" Alaeron asked. "They're boatmen. Why would they even *have* poison?"

"There are scorpions everywhere in this country," Skiver said. "A few of those crushed up in our mashed peas probably wouldn't do us much good, eh? Anyway, I've got a rule: when you make a bargain with a knife, you don't eat the loser's food."

The captain drove the ship hard, clearly eager to be rid of his passengers. Alaeron asked Skiver how much he'd promised to pay the man if he continued carrying them. "Most of what I have left," Skiver said, shrugging. "It's not like we'll have much use for money after this anyway, will we? And Ernst still has some jingling coin purses courtesy of Chuma. We'll be able to buy passage back, assuming we come out of Kho alive. I *could* have just threatened the captain, but men take these sort of things better when you offer an open hand as well as a closed fist. Just wave a knife at him, and his pride might be pricked, push him to do something rash. Offer coin, and he can tell himself he's making the sensible choice, as a businessman, and not a craven."

"You're a great deal smarter than I took you for, the first time I met you," Alaeron said.

Skiver nodded. "And you're more useful in a fight. Or at least a pirate attack. I imagine we're both fairly useless at great swaths of things, though, fear not."

The captain called out and pointed. Alaeron shaded his eyes. After days of green banks and distant dunes and the smear of mountains on the horizon, there was finally something new, ranks of dark columns stretching as far as he could see. "Is that a petrified forest?" he said.

"Obelisks," Ernst said. "The Slave Trenches of Hakotep are home to hundreds of them, perhaps thousands, most in poor repair, each said to imprison an elemental spirit. The whole area is a massive set of earthworks built by Pharaoh Hakotep I."

"Why?" Alaeron said.

Ernst shrugged. "If anyone knows, they've never told me. You're sure the pass is this way?"

"So Jaya says."

"My mother told me about this field of obelisks," Jaya said. "She traveled among them when she left her village. The pass is this way. Perhaps a week's travel from the river's source."

"A week? We have to spend a week trudging through this sort of landscape?"

"Not at all. The obelisks are quite interesting. Most of the journey will be far more dull."

"A week? That's nothing. It's a piece of piss." Skiver spat into the sand.

"You've marched through desert before?" Ernst said, amused.

Skiver shrugged. "I walked the city for Ralen Vadim, doing collections. All I did was walk, mostly, with breaks to . . . encourage people who were reluctant to pay in a timely fashion. This is nothing."

"We should walk at night," Ernst said. "It will be cooler."

"What about the lamias and giant scorpions and all that?" Skiver said.

"We're ferocious adventurers," Ernst said. "We'll chop them to pieces!"

"Then we could eat the pieces at least," Skiver said thoughtfully.

"We walk *soon*," Jaya said. "Unless you propose making camp here in the reeds, where the crocodiles might creep up on us?"

"Hmm," Ernst said. "You are as wise as you are beautiful."

The captain shooed them off his boat with swearing and cursing—or so Alaeron gathered from the general tone—but Skiver jangled the coins at the captain, and he consented to answer a few of Ernst's questions. The wizard joined them, smiling. "He says no one lives near the obelisks, but on the far side, we may find nomads or hermits or other settlers who can point us in the right direction, or even guide us into the mountains. I'm *fairly* certain he's not directing us to certain death in a snake-pit."

The Crook was essentially marsh and sandbars here, and broke off into dozens of tributaries—some small enough to step across—that snaked toward the west. "There must be a great monster of a lake in those mountains somewhere," Ernst said thoughtfully. "Waterfalls too. A river as mighty as the Crook, which flows into the even mightier Sphinx, must have a truly impressive source. It would be so interesting to find that source . . ."

Alaeron was annoyed to find that he agreed. That *would* be quite an expedition.

"Unless it's a lake of gold, it's not much use to us," Skiver said, and spat. "Best start walking. Do we try to skirt around the obelisks, or just barge on through?"

"My mother said they extend for miles in all directions," Jaya said. "We'd best try our luck and hope the elementals are bound."

"Or merely legendary," Alaeron said.

They spent the rest of that day trudging across the earthworks of the long-dead pharaoh. Great walls of rock rose and fell on all sides, curving sinuously and then turning at sharp angles, making strange geometries. The obelisks were arrayed in odd patterns, too, some in neat rows, some in circles, some standing alone. They were mostly broken, but almost all still stood taller than a man, and there were faint signs of old carvings on their sides. Alaeron wondered what the Slave Trenches would look like from above—would the ramparts and walls and obelisks form some mystic sigil? Had Hakotep I been intent on some great magic, powered by enslaved elementals? If so, its effects were indistinguishable.

It was astonishing, really, how quickly a giant esoteric building project could become just another dull part of the scenery.

Ernst paused and looked through a spyglass periodically, until finally Alaeron asked what he was looking for. "Not looking for," the wizard said. "Looking *at*. This glass is ensorcelled with a spell that detects magic, and . . . see for yourself."

Alaeron peered through the glass, at the field of obelisks to the right, and let out a long, low whistle. Each broken finger of stone pulsed with hidden light, blue and yellow and red and ochre. "The bound elementals," Ernst said. "Spirits of air, earth, fire, and water, trapped by an ancient god-king's magic, for purposes unremembered."

"I wouldn't mind some of those water elementals," Skiver said, taking advantage of the pause to remove his boots and shake out a few stones. "They'd make purer drink than this muddy warm mess in my canteen."

"Time and the weather are eroding those obelisks," Ernst said. "The ancient seals are loosening. But the god-kings made their magic to last. It may be centuries yet before the last of the protective sigils is worn away and the enslaved elementals are released." The wizard shivered. "Their fury will be terrible."

"Then we'd best move along!" Jaya called. "And leave them in peace. We'll take a week to reach the pass at this rate."

As it happened, they didn't make it out of the Slave Trenches before nightfall, and despite Ernst's halfhearted suggestion that they carry on by starlight, they were all exhausted.

"We made perhaps ten miles," Jaya said as Ernst used his magic to kindle a fire against the rapidly descending chill. "We must do better tomorrow. Perhaps it would be better if Alaeron's Kellid assassin *were* in back of us. That might encourage us to speed up."

"Are you so eager to see Kho?" Skiver said.

"To see my mother's family," Jaya said. "There are uncles and aunts and cousins I've never met. I only know their names. I wish one of you spoke the Uomoto tongue. I learned it, of course, but I've had no one to speak it with in a long time. I only hope I can make myself understood when we arrive."

"You do not speak the language with your brother?" Alaeron said.

Jaya shrugged. "He was younger, when our parents passed on. He never learned as well as I did, and doesn't enjoy trying to communicate that way. I'm sure there are those among my people who speak Taldane or Osiriani or some other language one of us can manage—they deal with adventurers from time to time, after all, some even seeking Kho. But I want to return to them as a daughter of the village, not an outsider." She sighed.

After their modest meal, Ernst studied his spellbook. Jaya checked her bowstrings. Skiver rolled dice to amuse himself. Alaeron stared up at the great clear sky and thought about his artifacts, and about the disc. Ernst eventually announced that he would take first watch, and Jaya said she would take second. Alaeron and Skiver shrugged and rolled out their bedding and went to sleep on the chill sand.

Alaeron was dreaming of an endless pit leading into the darkness when something made him snap awake. He tensed by the fading fire, expecting a desert beast—Ernst had laid wards, but who knew how effective they'd be? But instead he heard . . . soft laughter. Cooing. A gasp. Another gasp.

"They've woken you, too," Skiver whispered, his bedroll next to Alaeron's. "At least now my misery is shared. They've been at it half an hour."

"Who? What?" Alaeron whispered, though of course, he knew, both who *and* what. Ernst and Jaya had moved their blankets some distance away and behind a rock for privacy, but it was clear enough what they were doing. Alaeron gritted his teeth. He'd never been able to so much as hold her hand through a night, and now Ernst—

"We could cough," Skiver whispered. "*Loudly*. Or one of us could get up to take a piss. Except, on the one hand, I hate to deprive anyone of a bit of pleasure. But, on the other hand, if she wants me to march twenty bloody miles tomorrow, she'd best keep her and her man quiet."

*Her man.* Alaeron clenched his hands into fists. Ernst and his easy laugh. Ernst and his courage in the face of danger. Ernst and his *charm*. Alaeron had never been charming. But that didn't mean he wasn't a good *man*, or that Ernst was.

"So?" Skiver said. "Wait it out, or make a noise? But what if I go for a piss and they *don't* stop, or don't stop soon enough, and I can't pretend I don't know what they were doing, and then it's just a lot of awkwardness over breakfast? I mean, I like the chance to leer a bit, but—"

"RUNAWAY." The word was spoken as if by thunder, a great boom that came from all sides: from the stones, from the air, from the sand. Alaeron hadn't needed to piss, particularly, but that voice nearly made him wet himself anyway. Not just from being startled. Because, impossible volume aside, Alaeron *knew* the voice.

"What . . . !" Ernst shouted.

". . . in Hell . . . !" Skiver yelled.

". . . was that?" Jaya cried.

Alaeron whispered: "Kormak."

# Chapter Eighteen
## A Great Bloody Lot of Mountains

When the voice next spoke, it was less booming, but no less pervasive, seeming to come from everywhere at once.

"Alaeron. Place the relics you stole in this sack." Something fell from the sky, seemingly straight down, thrown in a high arc from who knew what direction. The sack landed at the foot of Alaeron's bedroll, glittering in the firelight: one of the warded metal bags used by the Technic League to house dangerous artifacts. "Then remove your clothes and walk east, naked and unarmed, from your camp. Do this, and I will spare the lives of your companions. You have three minutes to comply."

"What spell is this?" Ernst said. He, Skiver, and Jaya drew close around Alaeron, all peering into the darkness around them. "There are magics to make the commands of an officer heard over the din of a battlefield, but . . ." He looked through his spyglass, sweeping it in a full three-hundred-sixty-degree turn. "I don't see any magic out there, except for the obelisks, though I suppose a clever man might hide a spell among them . . ."

"Some trick of the Technic League," Alaeron said. "Not magic. Technology from the stars." He looked at his friends. Ernst seemed curious, Jaya determined, and Skiver was, unsurprisingly, grinning. "Should I give myself up? It would keep him from—"

"Stop talking garbage." Skiver said, and went loping into the darkness, a knife in each hand. Jaya ran off in a separate direction, clutching her bow, quiver on her back.

"Ha," Ernst said. "Yes, spreading out, probably a good idea. Any idea what sort of weapons he has?"

Alaeron shook his head. "Something that makes a very hot, very controlled fire. An armored coat. The League has weapons that can shatter bones inside a body, or boil metal in moments, or reduce armor to foul-smelling smoke. Kormak could have anything."

"Reassuring," Ernst said. "Time is running out. Pretend to obey him, perhaps?" And then he, too, ran off into the dark.

Alaeron cleared his throat. "My friends have deserted me!" he called. "I will do as you ask!"

"Your friends are trying to find me, but I can see them, and they cannot see me," Kormak's voice said. "You'd best hope they *don't* find me, or they won't live. The artifacts!"

Alaeron opened up his bag, hunching over it, and slipped a few items into the sack Kormak had left him: a dried old apple, a heel of bread, a hard-boiled egg, a coil of wire, a bit of frayed rope, and a bundle of leather laces. "There!" he called, hoping Kormak wouldn't know he'd lied: surely he could only track the artifacts when they were in use?

"Now your clothes," Kormak said, and as Alaeron slowly began to undress, the Kellid continued talking. "I knew you'd gone to Osirion, but I chose the wrong port, and made for Totra. When I found no sign of you there, I made my way to Sothis. A scorpion the size of a cart attacked me on the way. In Sothis I found a man named Chuma, who finally told me where you'd gone. It was the last thing he will tell *anyone*."

Oh, Alaeron thought, numb. Chuma must have died soon after dispatching Ernst to spy on them. The wizard's final letter full of lies had been unnecessary, then—Chuma would not trouble them. Alaeron should have realized that, without the artifacts, Kormak would fall back on other methods to track them—he'd proven that by burning the Dagger and the Coin to the ground after questioning the patrons. Alaeron finished unbuttoning his shirt and let it drop to the ground, shivering in the desert cold.

"I took a felucca up the river," Kormak went on. "Boats, boats, always *boats*. Boats and heat, that's what you've given me. I hate this foul country. I hail from the Realm of the Mammoth Lords, boy. Give me frozen lakes and fields of ice. But I *found* you. You never realized I could track your artifacts, fool? You've used them these past days, and the knowledge that you were so close spurred me onward. I stole one of the magic boats from the soldiers at Ipeq, and it carried me swiftly . . . until it vanished only a day after I found it."

"That's the nature of magic!" Ernst shouted from somewhere in the darkness, off to the north. "Best used only by those who understand it, not savage northmen!"

"I sank in the water," the Kellid said. "And do you know what found me there? A black lizard the size of my boat itself, with jaws so wide they could swallow a man of *your* size, my faithless apprentice. It tried to swallow me. It choked on me instead. I left its carcass in a thousand pieces in the water." The timbre of the voice roughened, though it was no less loud. "But it took my right hand. Bit it off. I will take your hands before I return you to Starfall, apprentice."

Alaeron stood up, naked except for his boots. "I'm sorry for your—"

"Boots off too!" Kormak snarled. "I'll have none of your tricks! You must—agh!"

The Kellid screamed as a bright light flared among the obelisks to the north. Alaeron spun and saw a huge figure writhing atop a ten-foot-high earthen wall, momentarily visible in a flare of light. Struck by a fireball, or some other magic of Ernst's? Whatever it was, it provided enough light for Jaya to fire a few arrows from her own position, crouched by a low wall in the east. Alaeron snatched up his pants and his coat, shrugging on the latter while hopping into the former, and ran off into the dark on his own. He hid behind a boulder and began preparing a bomb, though he was loath to throw it without knowing where exactly Ernst and Skiver were. The light from Ernst's attack had faded, and all was darkness again. He had an extract that would enable him to see in the dark, in one of his pockets, but his vials were a jumble after his ungainly flight from the camp.

"I went the wrong way," Skiver said, slipping up beside him. "Wizard and huntress get all the luck." He set off loping in Jaya's direction, and after a moment, Alaeron followed.

Light flared up on the earthworks again, a long stone's throw away. Ernst was there, standing on the wall, raising aloft his crooked walking stick, the end of which shone like a miniature sun, casting false daylight for fifty feet or so in all directions. A slumped body lay at his feet, seemingly big as a bear, head dangling down, and one arm that ended in a stump wrapped in bloody rags.

Alaeron and Skiver stopped running, and Jaya walked slowly toward them, all shading their eyes to peer up at Ernst.

Ernst prodded the body with his foot. "Dead!" he said cheerfully. "Armor is no match for fire, as many a knight has learned—you just cook inside like a chicken in a pot! Truly, Alaeron, you should have stood and faced this savage long ago. The barbarians are *terrified* of magic. I must say, I expected more." He kicked Kormak's body, and it tumbled ten feet to the ground, landing in a heap at the base of the wall. Ernst leaned out over the wall, looking down. "Ugly fellow, though, I'll give you that. More scars on his face than a privy has flies—"

"Ernst!" Alaeron shouted, but he was too slow, or the Kellid was too fast. Kormak lifted something in the one hand he had left: like the hilt of a sword, but with a round tube sticking up instead of a blade. A beam of ruby red light shone out, striking Ernst straight in the face.

The glowing walking stick fell behind the wall, light winking out, and Ernst's body tumbled down to the ground. In the darkness, it was impossible to be sure, but—

"His head," Skiver said, voice between awe and terror. "Ernst, his head, it was just *gone*."

"Burned," Kormak said, his voice no longer amplified, but carrying well enough. "*Seared*, as I had to sear the end of my wrist when my hand was taken. As I will burn off *your* hands, alchemist, and the limbs of your friends, before I take their heads, too—"

"Stay close to me," Alaeron said, and Jaya and Skiver moved in without asking questions, perhaps too stunned by Ernst's sudden death to do anything but obey. Truly powerful alchemists could create a potion to cure death, an elixir of life, but the preparation was delicate, the ingredients unspeakably costly, and

Alaeron's abilities far too meager . . . and, anyway, such a potion would be little good for someone lacking a head. He could not save Ernst.

But he might yet save his living friends.

Alaeron took the porcelain-and-gold top from his pocket, set it on the hard-baked earth of the desert, and set it spinning.

First there was dust, rising in a swirling curtain around them. Kormak approached, his hulking figure a dark shadow in the sandy mist. He hurled something toward them—a knife? a bomb? it was too dark to tell—but the object was caught in the unnatural wind. The force churned up the earth, gouging out rocks, scrub plants, and hunks of the desert floor and adding them to the expanding maelstrom. The noise became monstrous: Jaya was shouting, and Skiver was shouting back, but Alaeron just crouched over his relic in the small circle of safety, watching as Kormak's feet left the ground and he, too, began to spin.

The ring of destructive force got wider and wider as the Kellid tumbled end over end around them. Kormak was not giving in to the wind: he was trying to *swim* in the vortex, doing his best to claw his way toward Alaeron and the others. But even his ferocious dedication couldn't overcome the power of the artifact. He rose up in the wall of dust, which was now at least twenty feet high.

Skiver and Jaya were both shouting in Alaeron's ear now, but he was watching, trying to time his moment to stop the artifact and send Kormak flying—ideally back to the east, or at any rate *not* to the west, where they'd have to step over his broken body on their journey later. But the Kellid was now just one dark shape among many, spinning by faster than the eye could follow.

Jaya grabbed him by the shoulders and shook him, and Skiver screamed in his ear: "The obelisks! The elementals!"

Alaeron froze, remembering the view through Ernst's spyglass: a thousand lights, each a bound elemental, held in place by the sigils inscribed on weathered obelisks. And he was sending an expanding circle of destructive force toward those artifacts.

He slammed his hand down on the top, and it stopped spinning. Dust and rocks and unearthed plants flew out in all directions . . . along with Kormak's body, somewhere.

The earthen wall where Kormak had watched them, where Ernst had lost his head, was gone, reduced to dust and pebbles. Beyond, the forest of obelisks was damaged, half a dozen of the stone pillars shattered by the artifact's mighty wind, and things were stirring there in the darkness, huge shapes amid lights of red and blue and white.

"Runaway!" Kormak screamed and, impossibly, rose up on one knee from among the broken pillars, his form lit by the flickering illuminations of the fire and wind and water elementals waking up. The maelstrom had lifted and flung him, but he hadn't sailed miles away, instead striking the pillars, probably breaking a few of them himself on impact.

"Good try," Skiver said. "But now we run!"

Alaeron didn't run. He didn't even rise from his crouch. There was no point. Kormak had weapons they couldn't outrun.

But then something roared in the dark, and a hulking creature so large it dwarfed Kormak reached out with a stony arm and smashed the Kellid to the ground. The earth elemental turned its red gemstone eyes toward Alaeron and his companions, and *that* was spur enough to get the alchemist moving, snatching up his top and racing toward the remains of their camp, where the rest of their gear waited. He looked back and saw something like a bonfire in the shape of a snake swirl around Kormak, the Kellid's hair catching fire, and then a bearlike thing of dirty frothing water broke over him, extinguishing the flames and making the fire elemental rear back, stumbling across Kormak's legs. The Kellid didn't move, still stunned—or even dead?—from the earth elemental's initial blow.

The creatures were suddenly free from untold centuries of confinement, and they were taking their rage out on Kormak, who'd come crashing into their midst. Alaeron wanted to get himself and his friends away before the beings turned their attention to them. Jaya and Skiver had already shouldered their packs, and Skiver—ever practical—had the dead wizard's things, too. Alaeron grabbed his pack and stumbled after Jaya, into the dark and away.

They did not sleep again that night, but they couldn't run forever—at least, Skiver and Alaeron couldn't—so once it became apparent neither Kormak nor elementals were pursuing, they trudged. They soon left the earthworks of the Slave Trenches behind, and the ground became more stony as they entered the foothills of the mountain range known as the Barrier Wall, separating the Mwangi Expanse from the more or less civilized world.

They didn't speak for a long time, all too stunned or exhausted by what they'd witnessed, but when the light of dawn began to rise behind them, Jaya said, "Ernst. He died for us. To protect us."

"He was a good man," Alaeron said.

"Piss on that," Skiver said. "*I'm* not a good man, and I don't need to think he was, neither. Maybe he was, maybe he wasn't, we didn't spend that much time together, did we? But it's true enough he fought for us, and he was good company, and I'll miss him."

"He was bold," Alaeron said. "And so excited. I . . . I'm sorry I led him to this. Kormak was coming for *me*—"

"No," Jaya said. "It's my crime against Vadim that set us all on this journey. It's my fault." Her voice was steady, but Alaeron saw tears gleaming on her cheeks. She'd grown closer to the wizard than the others had in their days together, and while for Alaeron the feeling of loss was like a hollow place in his belly, he thought that for her the pain must be so much sharper.

"I'm the one who gambled away our money to that hellspawn in Absalom," Skiver said. "If I hadn't done that, we wouldn't have *met* Ernst, and Chuma wouldn't have sent him to spy on us, and he'd still be alive, so by that measure it's my fault. How far back up the chain of blame do you want to go? Piss on *that*, too. Kormak's the one who killed him, and Kormak's the one to blame. I just hope he got crushed and drowned *and* burned."

"Do you think he lived?" Jaya said. "The Kellid?"

"The elementals are mighty, and he was weak, I think," Alaeron said. "I know better than to say he's definitely dead, but I don't think you have to worry—"

"I'm not worried," she said fiercely. "I *hope* he's alive. I *hope* he comes after us. He murdered my *friend*, and I want the chance to kill him myself."

"I knew I liked you," Skiver said, and even somehow managed to grin.

That first night, after a long walk in the cruel sun, they stopped in late afternoon, exhausted from too little sleep and too much terror the night before, and slept in the lee of an enormous broken statue which might once have been a giant lion or sphinx: now only its legs remained, pocked and pitted by time. They took turns keeping watch, the others curling up in their blankets to sleep, but the night passed quietly.

The next morning they had breakfast at dawn, finishing the last of the hard-boiled eggs from the felucca. After that it was going to be all tough jerkies, hard cheeses, and the sort of brick-hard bread sailors packed for long sea voyages. "It's all up to Jaya now," Skiver said. "Vadim's reach doesn't extend beyond here. We're on our own, here in this great bloody lot of nothing."

"Another six days before we reach the pass, you think?" Alaeron asked. The mountains looked distressingly far away—and even once they reached the peaks, they still had to get *over* them.

Jaya shrugged. "Or longer. Distance is hard to judge in the desert, and I have only my mother's account of the journey, recollected many years after the fact. But at least the mountains are hard to miss. Barring sandstorms, we shouldn't get lost. Though I think we should start walking at night after this."

They stayed in the shadow of the statue, taking turns trying to sleep and keeping watch. When the sun began to sink they set off, and the following days fell into a deadening routine. They walked until they were exhausted, or until the sun tinted the horizon (the former usually came first), and camped in whatever shelter they could find. The sands were dotted with fragments of ancient structures, and they were usually able to find some kind of shelter from the sun. None of them adjusted well to the nocturnal schedule, and they were snappish and ill tempered as a whole, all of them brooding on their separate and communal troubles.

Finally, one late night, Jaya said, "I believe we will reach the pass soon. I would not care to try the passage in the dark. Shall we try to sleep, and finish our trip in the daylight?"

Alaeron agreed gratefully. He'd slept most of the day, or tried to, but there was ample exhaustion to go around in a grueling hike through the desert with only terribly uninteresting food to eat, and not much in the way of scintillating conversation. But he found it difficult to rest, energized by the prospect of reaching the pass and moving from Osirion into the great vastness of the Mwangi Expanse—and, if everything worked out and nothing ate them along the way, looking at last upon the ruins of Kho.

They were all a bit more cheerful the next morning, sensing if not the end of their journey then at least the passing of a milestone. The ground had long since gone from flat desert to steep hillsides, making all new parts of Alaeron's muscles complain.

When they were well into the mountains proper, Skiver squinted up at the jagged peaks. "There are supposed to be people—guides—near the pass, but unless they're disguised as rocks, I don't see anybody."

"I can read the shape of the land," Jaya said. "Travelers over mountains tend to follow the easiest path for as long as they can. We'll do the same."

If this was the easy path, Alaeron had no desire to experience the hard one. The slope became steeper, the path more rocky, everything barren and desolate, though there were occasional piles of stones that Jaya insisted were trail markers. Eventually, as evening approached, Jaya pointed. "Look. Smoke."

A few houses, looking like little more than piles of stone, stood on a small plateau. The hooves of innumerable goats clattered among the stones, the scrawny beasts chewing on stunted trees and scrub grass. A few people dressed in clothes gone gray with age shuffled out to greet the newcomers. They were not clearly Osiriani or Mwangi, but some mixture, as to be expected of border folk. One man, fatter than the rest, strode forward, beaming, arms outstretched.

"Travelers!" he called in Alaeron's native tongue. "I am Malako, the elder of this humble village. Do you seek guidance through the pass?" He squinted at Jaya. "Or are you a native of the villages beyond the mountains, returning home?"

"My mother came from an Uomoto village, yes," Jaya said. "My friends and I are going for a visit. But we would welcome a native willing to show us the way."

"Of course! My fourth son, Malaki, will take you, at least as far as the Vulture's Roost."

"Vultures, wonderful," Skiver muttered.

"It's an old Osirian fort," Jaya said. "Aboul-Nasar. My mother said it was abandoned, though."

"Not at all," the fat villager said. "Now it is a lodge for Pathfinders bound for the Expanse, but they trade with anyone who passes by. If you have the coin."

"Precious little," Jaya said. "But enough, I think, to pay your son—and I hope buy us a roof for the night? I love nothing more than sleeping under the stars, but my companions are accustomed to having something between themselves and the sky."

"Of course!" he said, which made Alaeron's heart rise, though it sank a bit again when the man shouted to one of his sons to chase the goats out of the old storehouse. Still, it was better than camping in the desert, and Alaeron was so weary of walking he would have agreed even if the goats *hadn't* been chased out first. Who knew he would look back so fondly on the tedium of voyaging by sea and river?

The villagers fed them stew—goat, of course—and then Jaya sat with them around a fire, practicing her mother's tongue with a few of the border folk who spoke it. Skiver and Alaeron quickly grew bored with a conversation they couldn't comprehend and sat off a little ways by themselves, sharing a skin of wine purchased at an extortionate price from one of Malako's innumerable sons.

"I thought you'd want this," Skiver said, and handed Alaeron Ernst's spellbook.

"Ah," Alaeron said, taking it, a lump in his throat. "I . . . thank you."

Skiver shrugged. "No use to me, but maybe some to you. I took his spare knife, though it's not much good. There are other things. Gold, food, the wand he took off that hellspawn, a bunch of bags and jars of powders and other things he used for his spells, I reckon. Some jewelry I thought Jaya might like, as a memento."

"She cared about him, didn't she?"

Skiver took a long pull of wine before answering. "Not at first. She came to me on the barge, asked if I thought he'd be a useful member of the party, said she thought she could tempt him over to our side. I couldn't see any harm in having a wizard with us when we got to Kho, especially with your Kellid still on our trail, so I told her to do her best. I thought her, ah, *friendliness* with Ernst all along was just an act—she's a great actor, that one—but that night by the campfire, when they woke us with their nuzzling . . . I don't believe she did that just to keep him loyal, especially since he'd thrown in with us pretty firmly by then. Sometimes you pretend to be a thing for long enough, and you *become* that thing. I know I acted the hardened killer for ages before I had the right. Maybe pretending to care about him made Jaya care about him. Or maybe it's simpler than that. Sometimes there's a spark."

"She never sparked with me," Alaeron said.

Skiver passed him the wineskin. "She's fond of you. Calls you 'her hero,' sometimes, to me. She seems to feel terrible for getting you mixed up in her problems, too. Argued with me many times to just let you go if you wanted, but I told her we were doing things Vadim's way." He clapped Alaeron on the shoulder. "The problem is, there's this guilt in her when it comes to you, and I think that keeps more pleasant feelings from getting a grip on her. It's hard to get close to a man when you feel bad about something you did to him, I'd wager. Not that I'd know, never feeling bad about anything myself, but that's how it seems to me." He took back the wineskin and sloshed it, then sighed. "I'll have to buy another of these, won't I? Could be my last chance for a good drink, unless we find a nice wine cellar in the ruins of Kho. *That* would be quite a vintage, wouldn't it? Look at me, drinking wine. I've become all sophisticated. My mother would be so ashamed of me." He went off in search of more drink.

Alaeron leafed idly through Ernst's spellbook, but with only half his attention on the contents. The rest was mulling over what Skiver had said. Perhaps he was right, and Jaya had only liked Ernst better because their relationship had no stumbling blocks in its path, apart from a certain amount of forgivable deceit and treachery. Alaeron could hardly attempt to woo Jaya now, with Ernst dead only two days, but perhaps in time, if they made it back from Kho and bought their way out of Vadim's bad graces, *then* there could be hope . . .

The alchemist slept better that night than he had in weeks. Kormak was almost certainly dead. Their destination was near. And he could hope that, someday, Jaya would go from calling him her hero to her love.

# Chapter Nineteen
## An Ancestral Home

Malako's son Malaki was a sweet boy of perhaps ten years, who offered to shoulder Ernst's pack for them. They set off at first light, walking into the shadow of the mountain along a goat track that he said was the fastest way to join up with the pass.

"Do you get many visitors?" Alaeron asked.

The boy nodded. "You are the first in two months, but there will be others. There is no other way over the mountains for long leagues in either direction, so those who wish to enter the Expanse from Osirion enter here. More come this way than come back, though." His voice was entirely too cheerful.

The slopes were punishing, making Alaeron's calves ache, and to make matters worse, Jaya and Malaki seemed entirely untroubled by the landscape, both walking as easily as Alaeron would have strolled down a street. "Just around the bend!" Malaki called as noon approached. "We will join up with a wider track, and the journey to the Vulture's Roost will be easier then."

"Good," Skiver said, limping a little—he'd been complaining of a blister on his heel all morning. "Easier is—"

They rounded the curve and came face to face with three hyenafolk.

The creatures were dressed in boiled leather and bits of chainmail, armed with spears. They were no bigger than Malaki, their doglike heads ferocious, teeth bared, necklaces of bones and fangs around their throats. The beasts made no move to attack.

"We mean no harm," Malaki said. "We only wish to pass."

The hyenafolk exchanged glances. "Meat," one of them growled. "Give us meat, or gold to buy meat, or you can *be* meat."

"Give them some food, and coin if you have it," Malaki said. "Then they will let us pass. They do not like to attack unless they have greater numbers."

"Do you have love for these dog-men?" Jaya asked, frowning.

Malaki shook his head. "They steal our goats." He paused. "Our children, sometimes. My sister, Malakelle, she would have been twelve this year . . ."

"Stealing children," Skiver said. "Huh."

"Do you know what our friend Ernst would have said about people who steal goats and children?" Jaya said to the leader of the hyenafolk.

"He would have said it's *rude*," Alaeron said. "Malaki, get behind us."

"Glad you lot came along," Skiver said, grinning at the beast-men. "We've been wanting to kill something for a couple of days now."

The leader barked, and the others raised their spears. Skiver threw a knife, which stuck harmlessly in a leather chestplate, but his next took off most of one canine ear, making its owner yap and squeal and clutch its head. Jaya backed coolly down the trail, putting distance between herself and the marauders, nocking an arrow as she went. The track was too narrow for Alaeron to risk tossing a bomb, and he considered taking a dose of feral mutagen, but then he found the golden chain in his pocket. He lashed out with it, and the chain extended, wrapping around one of the hyenafolk's spears like a constricting serpent around a throat. Alaeron yanked the chain and pulled the spear loose, then flicked his wrist to make the chain uncoil and sent the weapon clattering off the rocks. The creature growled and advanced, but then Jaya's arrow caught it in the throat, and its doglike eyes went wide. It whimpered and fell.

The other two hyenafolk growled—and then turned and ran. An arrow caught one in the back, and a throwing knife the other. Skiver picked up the spear Alaeron had torn away and methodically stabbed the fallen bandits through their necks as they tried to crawl away. "There's your meat, bastards," he said, and tossed the spear down. "You want their heads, Malaki? Mount them on sticks by your village, and they might hesitate to steal your goats and sisters again."

"Perhaps on the way back," the boy said. "I wouldn't want to carry their heads up the mountain and back down again. Did you want to loot them?" His voice was incredibly polite.

Probably terrified we'll think he's rude, Alaeron thought, coiling the chain back up. Murdering hyenafolk was a poor substitute for grieving, but it was something, and served to break a bit of the tension they'd carried since Ernst's death.

"No, have at it," Skiver said. "I doubt this lot's likely to have a magic sword or a bag of precious gems, is it?"

Malaki checked the hyenafolk, pocketing a few tarnished rings and other small items. Then he drew a knife and hacked off their tails.

"What are you doing?" Skiver asked.

"The man who runs the lodge offers a bounty for hyenafolk tails," he said, and finished his grisly work. "You killed them, so the bounty is yours."

"I think we can do without it," Skiver said. "Call it a gratuity for your services."

Malaki nodded, obviously pleased. "This way," he said, stepping over the corpses, and Alaeron and the others followed.

The Vulture's Roost was a small fort of stone and timber placed at the crest of the pass, built into the rocks with a good view of both slopes. Malaki pounded on the wooden door with his fist until it swung open. A blond half-elf in a chain shirt peered out. "What do you need, boy?"

"Tell Akfirat Zouhair I have tails for him," he said.

The half-elf shook his head. "My master's having a meal. I can pay you well enough, though, come in." He chose to take notice of the others. "Any of you lot Pathfinders?"

"Do we get a discount if we are?" Skiver said.

The half-elf rolled his eyes. "That's a no, then. Well, all adventurers are welcome; come in, take some water for the trip down, we've other provisions for sale too."

"I thought Pathfinder lodges were more exclusive than this?" Alaeron said, following the others in.

"Some are," the half-elf said. "But Zouhair will take your coin. You're not welcome upstairs, and you can't stay over—that's for Society members only—but we'll sell you salted goat meat and whetstones, fear not."

The lodge was dim, windows being a low priority in a fort, with a few long tables set up below the stone-and-timber ceiling, and a counter along one wall. Leaning against the counter was—

"What is *that*?" Skiver said, entirely too loudly.

The eight-foot-tall creature by the counter turned its head and scowled at them.

"He is derhii," Jaya said. She spoke a few words in her mother's tongue, and the derhii grunted. He looked essentially like a gorilla, but a pair of enormous vulture wings sprouted from the black fur on his back.

"Travelers," he said, in weirdly accented Taldane. "Do you need passage down the mountain?"

"That's a monkey with *wings*," Skiver whispered to Alaeron.

"Ape," Alaeron corrected automatically. "Monkeys have tails."

"Oh, that's all right then," Skiver said.

"We would appreciate your guidance," Jaya said.

"And I your coin." The derhii's voice was deep and booming, even lower than Kormak's. "I cannot carry three, however. Two, yes, but not three. My cousin is nearby, and could carry another, if you have money."

"Hold on, Jaya," Skiver said. "You want us to get carried down the mountain by a flying ape?"

"Your people carried my mother up to the pass when she left her village, before I was born," Jaya said warmly, stepping closer to the winged ape. "She spoke of the honor and kindness of your people."

The derhii grunted. "Some are honorable and kind. Others are not. Much as it is with your people. But if you can pay, in gold or armor or," he licked his lips, "wine or pesh, I will see you safely to the foot of the hills."

Skiver sighed and fished a coin purse from his pocket. Alaeron recognized it as Ernst's. "Will this do?"

"For me," the derhii said. "That much again for my cousin."

Skiver sighed. "Fine. Payment upon our safe landing, all right?"

The derhii shrugged. "I will find my cousin." He walked out of the lodge, long, powerful arms swinging.

"I never thought to see one of them," Jaya said. "My mother believed there were only a few hundred left in these mountains. They are an ancient race."

The half-elf finished paying Malaki, who left with cheerful farewells to begin the long march back down the mountain. "The derhii are trustworthy," he said, perching on a stool behind the counter. "They won't drop you and loot your corpses or anything. They know we'd warn travelers away from using their services if they started doing that." He waved his hand. "They roost among the caves in the cliffs. Mostly keep to themselves, apart from trading here and ferrying passengers from time to time. They never make any trouble, though judging by all the armor and weapons they try to get, I think they must war amongst themselves a fair bit. Won't do you any harm, though."

"How reassuring," Alaeron said, and decided he would mix up a potion of flight as soon as he had a moment. He would prefer traveling under his own power to being hauled through the sky by a flying ape, but it was too late to do anything about it now.

Skiver haggled a bit with the half-elf over supplies, buying a couple of knives to replace the ones he'd lost in the fight with Kormak. The derhii ducked back inside. "We are ready when you are," he boomed.

They went out and greeted the other derhii, a smaller female version of the one they'd originally met. "Where are you bound?" the larger derhii asked.

"My mother's village," Jaya said, and rattled off a name in the tongue of her forebears.

"We know it," the derhii grunted. "You look like those people. These don't, though."

"We're adventurers," Skiver said. "Going to seek our fortune!"

"Do you know the ruins of Kho?" Alaeron asked.

The derhii looked at one another. The big one shrugged. "There are many ruins in the Expanse. They are best avoided. Are you ready to depart?"

"Yes," Jaya said. "Best make sure your packs are secure, fellows."

The big derhii scooped up Jaya and Skiver, one in each arm, making the latter squawk. He took a few steps, huge wings beating, then lifted into the air and sailed off, flying low to the ground, cradling Jaya and Skiver like infants.

"You with me," the female derhii said. Ape's face or not, the look of amusement was obvious.

"I've never traveled this way before," Alaeron said.

"Better than walking," she said. "I don't know how you wingless ones stand plodding along in the dirt." She picked up Alaeron in her arms like a groom carrying his bride and followed her cousin into the air. She smelled strongly of sweat and musk and wet fur, and Alaeron turned his face away, but while that took him away from the odor, it presented him with the view: the mountain pass dropping away steeply, making his stomach lurch up into his throat. This wasn't as bad as being hauled skyward by his combined relics, but it was close. Below there were foothills and boulders and spires of rock, and past that, in the west . . . nothing much but an ocean of green, trees upon trees, a sea of trees, an infinity of trees. The famous Mwangi Expanse, jungles filled with beasts and terrors and ruins, threaded through with rivers so vast they made the Sphinx and the Crook seem like little more than creeks.

But Alaeron wasn't going *that* far. Their destination was closer, in some hidden valley above the foothills. The derhii flapped her wings in a steady rhythm, swooping downward, going faster and faster until Alaeron had to squeeze his eyes shut against the wind as tears streamed across his face.

He would not have believed that soaring through the air in the embrace of an ape could be boring, but it soon was—he could barely see for the wind, and the steady thrum of her wings was almost hypnotic. He even managed to doze off a bit, proving, he supposed, that anyone could grow accustomed to anything.

The trip took hours, which meant walking it would have taken days. Night was almost fallen when his derhii landed, dropping him a foot from the ground amid a stand of trees. He'd glimpsed a group of huts nearby to the north, and assumed—hoped—that was Jaya's ancestral home.

Skiver and Jaya were already settled on the ground, the assassin counting out coins for his derhii. "How do we reach you lot if we want a ride back up?" Skiver was saying.

"The villagers can call us," he said. "They have drums." Without wishing them luck or bidding them farewell, he took off again, and was soon a speck in the sky. Skiver opened his purse and turned to Alaeron's derhii, complaining that it shouldn't cost as much since she'd only carried *one* person, but the derhii just bared her teeth until Skiver finished counting out money into her palm. Then she was away, too.

"A proud and taciturn people," Jaya said.

"Greedy apes," Skiver said. "Just like most people I've met. All right then. Shall we go on? Have your happy reunion?"

Jaya swallowed, and nodded. "I hope . . . all I know are *names*, and stories, I've never met any of them . . ." She took a breath, then exhaled. "All right. Let's go."

Alaeron and Skiver followed her toward the village. *Our journey has neared its end,* Alaeron thought. *Tomorrow. Tomorrow, they would see Kho.*

*Unless something killed them first.*

"Greetings, adventurers," the Uomoto man said, leaning on a long stick at the village's edge. "Welcome to the gateway to the Mwangi Expanse, where treasures untold await those bold enough to brave its dangers. We humble villagers offer provisions and guides." He spoke Taldane with hardly any accent, and his tone was unspeakably bored.

Jaya answered him in the Uomoto tongue, and the man looked suddenly much more interested. He stepped closer, took Jaya's face in his hands, peered long into her eyes, then stepped back, laughing in delight. "You are Melima's daughter!" he said in Taldane. "Come, come!"

"Is my uncle Tamba here?" Jaya asked.

The man grew serious. "No, he is . . ." He hesitated. "Come. Your cousin Saa will tell you. Your friends are welcome too." He strode among the stone huts, chickens scattering before him, calling out in his own language. Dark-skinned people—clearly Jaya's kin to one degree or another—emerged to peer out of doorways. Small children clustered around them as they walked, tugging at their clothes, shouting and laughing, and several women stopped Jaya to clutch her hand and pat her cheeks.

"My relatives were never so happy to see me," Skiver said.

"Perhaps if they'd never met you before, they'd have been more welcoming," Alaeron said.

"Most likely," Skiver agreed.

They reached Saa's hut. Jaya's cousin was of an age with her, but taller, with hair twisted into a profusion of small braids and a face more careworn and lined than Jaya's. She welcomed them, shooed away the children, and bid the adventurers to sit with her on the stones that formed a circle around a firepit beside her hut.

Jaya said something in the fluid Uomoto tongue, and Saa said, softly, "May we speak Taldane? We all try to practice when outsiders come. Not that you are an outsider, ah . . ."

"No, no, I am, I know," Jaya said. "Cousin. I am so pleased to meet you at last. My mother told me often of your mother, her sister. Is she here?"

Saa shook her head. "No, she . . . I am the closest kin you have left, though most in the village—all the villages, here in the foothills—are related somehow. How fares your mother? We hoped she would return."

Jaya shook her head. "She passed on many years ago, when I was hardly grown. A fever. She had always hoped to come back, to bring me, but it is not an easy journey, and I'm afraid . . ." Jaya shrugged.

"You are here now, and most welcome. And your companions?"

"Alaeron, an alchemist; and Skiver, a . . ." she hesitated. "A mercenary."

"I've been called worse," the cutthroat said cheerfully. "But we're not here *just* for a happy reunion, I'm afraid."

Jaya took a breath. "It is true. A powerful man sent me. I owe him a great debt, and this is how he asks me to repay him. He wishes me to take these men to the ruins of Kho."

"Kho," Saa said, and shivered. "You must not go there. We point travelers in that direction when they ask, but they seldom return. You are a child of our people, though—we would not risk your blood. For the Uomoto, entering the city is forbidden."

"We must," Jaya said simply. "I . . . have a brother. His life depends on my success."

"Then his life is forfeit," Saa said, "and I grieve for this cousin I may never meet. For even if you go to Kho, you will not return. It has always been a place we shunned, haunted and dangerous, but of late, it is so much worse. The creatures within have spurned our ancient bargain, and are no longer content with the sacrifices we make."

"What do you mean?" Jaya said. "What's happened?"

"My mother," she said. "Our uncle. My own brother, and sister. They are gone. All taken over these past months. All stolen by some creature and carried off. It has taken half a dozen so far." She shook her head. "None have returned."

"What took them?" Jaya said.

Saa spread her hands. "We do not know. The monster comes shrouded in a cloud of darkness which no light can penetrate, and it is impossibly fast and strong. We are not without sorcerers and shamans of our own—magic is strong in the Uomoto—but they have been unable to penetrate this mystery or defend against it. The fallen city has always taken a blood price, cousin, but this is different. There are many dark creatures who dwell there, and they hunger. There is a great monolith, the Stone of Sacrifice, and oathbreakers and outlaws who must be put to death have long been bound there, left to be taken by the creatures from the ruins. Such gifts appeased them for generations, but some months ago, something in the ruins became hungrier, greedier, and it sneaks in among us at night, taking our people and leaving no sign behind but smears of blood and the smell of smoke." She lowered her voice. "There has been talk of leaving this place entirely, before we are *all* stolen away."

"Did you send out warriors?" Skiver asked. "Some of you folk look like you'd be handy with spears and bows. Have they tried to bring your people back?"

"It is forbidden," Saa said, eyes going wide. "Uomoto do not enter the ruins. It is a place of poison. Any who break that taboo, if they ever return, are bound to the Stone of Sacrifice."

"I am your kin," Jaya said. "But this is not my village. I can go where you may not. Show me the way, and if any of our family yet live there, I will bring them back to you."

"Yes," Alaeron said. "Me, too."

Skiver shrugged. "It's where I was going anyway, so why not?"

Saa stood. "I must speak to the elders, to tell them of your offer, but . . ." She shook her head. "Do not do this, cousin. You will die. You have only just returned to us."

"I must," Jaya said.

Saa bowed her head. "I am sorry I will not have the chance to know you." She hurried away.

"I'm so sorry, Jaya," Alaeron said. "If there's anything we can do, we will."

"It's motivation, though, innit?" Skiver said. "I know you didn't have much interest in seeing the ruins before, Jaya, but now you've got a *reason* to go in there. Apart from Vadim forcing you, I mean."

"Yes," Jaya said, staring at the mountains. "I do. And I mean to leave at first light." She rose and stalked off.

Skiver looked at Alaeron and shrugged. "She's still hurting from losing Ernst, and now this?" He shook his head. "I feel sorry for whatever's stealing her kin. Jaya's got a look about her that says nothing but bloody murder will soothe her."

Alaeron nodded. "I'd better prepare some extracts. I have a feeling this may be our last peaceful night for a while."

"Probably," Skiver said. "Though it might not be all that peaceful after all. This mysterious monster could come calling and haul us away to Kho." He yawned. "That might be all right. It would spare us having to walk tomorrow."

Bold talk, Alaeron thought, but I bet you'll sleep with a knife in your hand tonight.

Jaya argued with the village elders all night, and she either convinced them to trust her or wore them down. When morning came, the entire village was there to see them off, with two young warriors, slim and dark and armed with spears, to guide them as far as they could. The shaman made a blessing, and hung a necklace around each of their necks, the cords dangling pouches full of aromatic herbs, scents of flowers and crushed bark and citrus tang mingling. Alaeron wanted to ask what the herbs were, and what their properties might be—exotic ingredients from the Mwangi Expanse could make potent and rare extracts—but the sense of ceremony hardly seemed to allow it. "These charms will protect us from the foul vapors in the city," Jaya translated.

"I grew up around the corner from a tanner's yard," Skiver quipped. "I'm immune to foul vapors."

Jaya was presented with a clutch of arrows made in the Uomoto style, though Alaeron couldn't tell the difference between them and other arrows, except that the feathers on the ends were more brightly colored. They gave Skiver a knife with a bone handle and a wavy blade. Hunters and warriors were easy, apparently, but no one seemed to know quite what to give an alchemist. The shaman pressed a few small clay pots on him. Fair enough. He certainly had pockets full of bottles anyway. "Healing salves," Jaya said, and Alaeron thanked them, though he had potions of healing of his own. Unlike his concoctions, the ones given by the Uomoto would actually work for Skiver and Jaya, so he'd keep them handy.

They did not take their full traveling packs, just weapons and some basic supplies in smaller bags, though Skiver also had a bundle of sacks rolled up tight to carry off any loot he might find—something he didn't mention to the villagers. The Uomoto mostly seemed to believe Jaya's party had come to deliver them from whatever evil stalked them in the night, with Jaya a long-lost daughter of the village returned in their hour of need with her brave companions to set things right. Probably guided by prophetic dreams, Alaeron didn't doubt. No reason to let them know they were here for plunder first, and rescue only coincidentally.

The warriors led them up a steep and winding path, and then off the path entirely, stepping carefully between the trunks of great trees, moving slowly and watchfully while the others followed. Jaya had said her village was a half-day's journey from the ruins, but the cloud-hidden sun was not yet at its zenith when the silent Uomoto warriors led them out of the trees. Alaeron's sense of direction was not fantastic, but he could tell they'd maneuvered to approach the mountains from the west, and were now facing east. Mountains rose up on either side, but there was a high cleft valley before them, sheltered by the spires of the barrier mountains. "Follow us carefully now," one of the guides said. "For we enter the Fields of Glass, and the safe paths are few and known only to us."

"Glass?" Alaeron said. He saw nothing before them but a valley of trees and meadows, its far reaches shrouded by mist. "I don't see any—"

The clouds moved, revealing the sun, and Alaeron gasped and averted his eyes as a thousand thousand fires bloomed in the valley. No, not fires, but flashes of reflected light, twinkling from countless—what? Crystalline formations? Pools of water? Or actual shards of literal *glass*? Jaya had mentioned this place, but the tale hadn't compared to the reality.

"The city fell screaming," one of the guides said. "And stars fell with it, and shattered, and when the sun shines down, the broken stars throw their brightness back into the sky. Join hands now, and tread carefully, for the way is sharp, and those who look too closely will be dazzled. Mark the way we go closely, for if you return this way, you will make the crossing alone."

They all linked hands, eyes squeezed almost shut, as they entered the valley. Sparkles glittered on all sides, filling the width of the valley entirely, but when the sun went behind a cloud again, making the sparkles fade, Alaeron asked them to pause. He knelt by a shard of blue-tinted crystal and prodded it. The shard didn't move, embedded firmly in the ground. Glass from some ancient tower shattered by the city's fall, or a natural formation? He couldn't be sure. Perhaps this was all a folly, and these weren't the ruins of Kho at all. Perhaps there were monsters here that had nothing to do with the legendary flying city of the Shory.

"Alaeron, time is burning," Jaya said sharply.

"Of course, I'm sorry." He rejoined the human chain as the guides led them on a winding path among the shards. Some chunks of crystal were as large as wagon wheels, others no bigger than a fingernail, but he could see how walking through this place could be deadly. Many of the shards poked up from the ground like spikes, and to stumble through here in full sunlight, dazzled by brightness, would be an invitation to stumble and fall and be cut to ribbons.

Beyond the fields of glass waited a forest shrouded in mist. The fragrance of sweet flowers was heady, intoxicating, almost overwhelming. Alaeron knew flowers—many extracts depended on them—and he smelled orchid and plumeria, but there were countless other scents, most far more alien. Perhaps there were flowers here that grew nowhere else on earth. What powers might they possess?

"This is as far as we can go," one guide said apologetically. "There is the Stone of Sacrifice. The ruins wait beyond these trees, but we may not look upon them. Go. Come back safe. Return our lost ones."

The guides made their way back through the Fields of Glass, leaving the adventurers to contemplate the stone. It was the size of a house, squarish, black and oddly shiny, stained with blood, and a profusion of iron manacles dangled from its face, enough to bind half a dozen people. "This is no natural stone," Alaeron said, squinting. "It is a made thing. Did the villagers attach the irons, or . . ."

"No, they have always been there," she said.

Alaeron ran his finger over the stone, frowning. "There are marks here, very old ones, in the stone . . ." He closed his eyes, feeling the shape of the markings until a picture of them formed in his head. He whistled, opening his eyes. "These . . . these marks are in the Shory language. I can't *read* that language, I don't think anyone can, but examples of it survive, and the shapes of the letters are very distinctive. Whoever scratched these marks into the rock long ago was *Shory*. I think this rock might have been part of a dungeon in Kho, a chunk of wall flung to this spot when the city fell, or was smashed from the sky by the Tarrasque, depending on which story you believe. The Soaring City *is* here. Six thousand years ago it fell, and this is *where* it fell. I . . . I don't think I really believed it, before now."

"We'd best go on in, then," Skiver said, "before you're paralyzed by believing." He set off around the Stone of Sacrifice, moving silently, followed by Jaya. Alaeron came after them, every clank and clink of his many bottles and vials making him wince. He wasn't made for stealth. Perhaps there was an extract for that—surely there was a spell in Ernst's book that allowed one to move silently . . .

A great flap of wings came from above, and a derhii landed in a clearing before them. He was bigger even than the derhii who'd carried Jaya and Skiver down, armored, and armed with a javelin.

"Humans," he growled, crouching before them. "You look like an Uomoto, woman. Why do you venture into taboo lands?"

"My family comes from the village, but I am from the wider world," Jaya said.

"Hmm." The derhii looked them over impassively. "You would do well to turn back. This valley is death for those who cannot fly above the dangers as my people do."

"Flying does us no good," Skiver said. "How are we meant to snatch up treasures if we *fly*?"

The derhii laughed. "You seek treasure, then. Of course. Men always do. But where there are treasures, there are those who hoard them, and protect them. Any treasures you might find already belong to someone *else*, and they will not willingly part with them. You may enter as treasure hunters, but you can succeed only as thieves."

"Thieving works," Skiver said. "Care to tell us what we can expect?"

The derhii shrugged. "I have many tasks before me this day. I cannot afford to spend time pouring words into the ears of men who will be dead soon."

"I hear you lot like arms and armor," Skiver said. He drew a pair of glittering knives. "These were forged in Andoran. Blades weighted for throwing. They fit sweet in the hand and slip into flesh neat as you please. I'll trade you blades for words."

"I could just wait," the derhii said. "Fly above you, and swoop down to strip your corpses when you are killed." He shrugged. "But I will trade. Words cost me nothing. The valley runs north and south. You approach near the middle of its length. Beyond these trees you will find the river, which follows the line of the valley, running from the source in the north to trickle out in the south. When you enter the valley, look south to see the Sunset Towers, once called the Towers of the Sun, before they fell. Creatures of the deep earth dwell within them, beasts made of living glass. Sometimes they wander the surface, and their touch is slow death to all things that live, causing live flesh to transform into living crystal. Beware them. To the north, the river is spanned by the Obelisk Bridge, but the crossing is treacherous for those who have no wings to save them when the ground collapses. There are other crossings, even more dangerous. Beyond the river, Shadow Hill is home to deadly shades, and there is no treasure there, only darkness and death. The broken Domes of the Polymatum lie on the far side of the river as well, in the center of the valley, and you will find the rat-people called Hadi nearby. They may trade with you—if you want treasure without bloodshed, they may accommodate you, if you survive to reach them. But they are vicious bargainers, and you may leave poorer than you entered." The derhii glanced skyward. "I would not enter the Domes themselves. They are home to daemons, the ones who take the sacrifices your kinsmen leave bound to the Stone."

"Are these daemons the ones raiding my family's village?" Jaya demanded.

The derhii frowned. "They do not venture out. They send their minions to the Stone, but the daemons seldom stir from the Domes, let alone from the valley itself."

"Do you know who or what *is* preying on my people?"

The derhii looked up again, clearly eager to be flying. "I . . . cannot say. But there is a place. The Pit of Endless Night, it is called. Look for a broken dome, and at the center, a great hole, a tower thrust into the earth like a knife into a heart. That place is full of pale monstrous creatures, things that might have been humans like you once, long ago. They are degenerate creatures now, ravening and mad. And there are other things that still resemble men, dressed in rags and ancient jewels, but scrabbling hard lives in the caves. There are rumors the dwellers in the dark have a new leader—some say a new god. I do not know what manner of creature he may be, but some say he hungers for sacrifice even more than the daemons in the Domes. This new god may take you, too, if you venture too close to the Pit." The derhii snatched the knives from Skiver's hands and lumbered into the sky, soaring above the mist and out of sight.

"The names he had for things," Alaeron said thoughtfully. "Pit of Endless Night, all right, that's merely descriptive, and Obelisk Bridge likewise, but the Domes of the Polymatum? The Sunset Towers, which were once the Towers of the Sun? That's not something savages and monsters would name a place. I've heard the Shory had servants, a race of winged creatures who did their bidding . . . could they have been derhii? Could their descendants *remember* things about the city, stories passed down, all these thousands of years later?"

"You were listening to the names?" Skiver said. "I was only listening when he said 'treasure.' I say we find these ratfolk and see what we can get off them. Even lesser relics could satisfy Vadim if they've got some of that Shory writing you were talking about scratched on them."

"Barter for your treasures if you must," Jaya said. "I am bound for the Pit of Endless Night. If the stealer of my kin lives there, then I will face him, and bring out any of my family who live."

Skiver sighed. "All right. The Pit of Endless Night, too, then. I could wish it had a more cheerful name, though."

# Chapter Twenty
## Rats

Keen to heed the derhii's warnings, they moved through the trees carefully. There was no mistaking the Sunset Towers, off in the distance to the south, though they no longer actually *towered*—they looked like a massive tangle of driftwood, once-mighty spires that had been sheared off their bases when the city crashed, and were now tumbled together. Some were entirely horizontal, others merely painfully diagonal, and it was a wonder they'd maintained their tubular shapes: the Shory built their towers strong. Beneath the greenery, the towers glittered, as if they had been carved from gems instead of ordinary stone—and perhaps they had. Who knew what wonders the great empire of the sky had created? Alaeron counted five structures in the heap, but it was hard to tell, as they were so heavily overgrown with leaves and vines it was difficult to be sure where one tower left off and another began.

"Reckon we could get in there?" Skiver said. "Find a window, climb inside? They look like they were mighty fine towers, once, and people keep precious things in towers."

"Creatures made of glass, who carry a petrifying plague," Alaeron said. "Remember?"

"There's dangers everywhere," Skiver muttered. "For all we know, the derhii just made that stuff up to scare us away from the *really* prime treasure, did you ever think about—"

Something glittered near the base of the tower, tall as a man but shining like crystal—and it *moved*, not toward them, but off to the north, away from the tower, disappearing behind a heap of rubble.

"Look at that thing," Skiver murmured. "Guess the ape wasn't lying entirely. You reckon that thing is made of diamonds? We could creep up and kill it, break it into jewels we could carry . . ."

"If the derhii was telling the truth, it could poison us with a touch, and I suspect knives and arrows would bounce right off it," Jaya said. "I'd just as soon avoid starting fights for no particular reason."

Skiver cast a last glance at the tower, sighed, and began walking on east toward the mist. The ground sloped upward, and they threaded their way through trees before cresting a low rise and emerging from the mists to see the ruins of Kho spread out before them.

Alaeron was staggered. He'd seen ruins before. Collapsed temples, ancient fortresses, even the remains of the mountain-sized ship in Numeria. But he'd never seen anything like this.

"It's like someone picked up Absalom in his hands and threw it down on the ground," Skiver said, voice as close to reverent as Alaeron had ever heard it. "Dropping a whole city like a plate, so it shatters into pieces."

"This is what happens when a city falls from the sky," Jaya murmured. "Truly, it was madness to lift their cities so high."

Alaeron bit back a reply. He thought it was *wondrous*. The fact that the city had crashed was a tragedy, but not necessarily an argument against the whole notion of cities in the sky. The power and art necessary to achieve such a feat . . . truly, the world had fallen as far as the city of Kho itself when such wonders were lost to deep history.

The ruined city was too much to take in with a single glance. The most striking elements were the sections that seemed almost intact: a cluster of square buildings there on a low hill, wreathed in unnatural shadows. Crystal towers that leaned against the steep sides of the cliff walls penning in the valley, standing almost upright, their thousand windows reduced to empty holes, some with fires flickering within. Great tilted obelisks that might have been civic art or part of a magical propulsion system or monuments to heroes fallen seven thousand years before. A river that started as a waterfall at one end of the valley snaked a winding course through the ruins, spanned here and there by fallen towers: once homes to high adepts or Shory royals, their spires were now reduced to mere bridges for the convenience of whatever creatures made these ruins home. Everything in this lower city was alive with vegetation, and hundreds of flowers bobbed in the breeze, sending their mingled scents of sweetness, sharpness, and strange poisons aloft.

A cluster of domes dominated the center of the valley, gleaming structures of silver metal and black glass, cracked but still fundamentally intact, each one larger than the Golden Cathedral in Almas. "The Domes of the Polymatum?" Alaeron said, pointing. "I wonder what it was meant for. That name . . . it could have been an arcane college, I suppose. A polymath is someone counted an expert in multiple fields of study."

"Ernst would have wanted to explore it," Jaya said.

"Maybe we'll do it for him, then," Skiver said. "Derhii warnings be damned. I *still* say the winged apes might just be trying to keep us away from the choicest pickings."

The far northern end of the valley was misty, making details difficult to discern, but there seemed to be another intact portion of the city there, whole blocks of buildings standing more or less upright, though canted enough that one trying to walk the cracked and buckled streets would stumble like a drunkard. A dozen streams cascaded down the white stone and crystal shimmers to join the river on the valley floor, and black towers stood tilted and leaning around the upper city like poisonous mushrooms sprouting up among stones.

"I don't even know where to begin," Alaeron said.

"Well, think quick," Skiver said. "Just a reminder that we're not here to map the place or do a complete inventory, all right? We're here to fill our sacks with Shory relics, enough to make even a grasping old man like Vadim happy, and then bugger off home." He glanced at Jaya. "And to rescue her family and kill off whatever's taking 'em, of course, but let's not forget the *original* point of this exercise. So, Alaeron, you're our expert on ruins and such: what's the likeliest bit?"

"The domes," Alaeron said. "Even if the derhii hadn't said we might find traders there, I'd say the domes. They're the nearest intact structure we can reach, apart from those buildings wreathed in shadow, and I don't like the look of those. So let's make our way over the river."

"I must find my family," Jaya said.

"True enough," Skiver said, "but I'd say we all stand a better chance of surviving here if we keep ourselves together. How about we snatch up some relics first, and then we can move on to the rescue mission? Who knows, we might even find something that can help us get your people back."

Jaya frowned, and for a moment Alaeron thought she would insist on striking off on her own, but then she nodded. "First the domes," she said. "And after that, the Pit." She gazed down into the valley floor. Alaeron followed her line of sight and saw it: a ring of jagged black glass, all that remained of some smashed dome, and at its center, a smooth hole leading down into darkness. Water from the river's tributaries swirled down the rounded chasm like it was a drain.

"Right, the Pit," Skiver said, and gave a shudder. "I ever tell you lot I grew up in the sewers, mainly? I love a dank hole in the ground, oh my, yes I do, never doubt it."

They began working their way down the slope, Jaya in the lead with her bow drawn, moving carefully and low to the ground, stepping over chunks of masonry and fused lumps of metal. Alaeron came along in the middle, hands in his pockets where his relics and bombs and extracts (many freshly prepared the night before) awaited him, his fingers dancing over them, planning for contingencies. Skiver was in the rear, because, as he said, "Who better to watch out for backstabbers than a backstabber like me?"

They crept along among husks of buildings, peaked or rounded roofs torn free of their walls and left scattered at strange angles. The valley was far from silent: the wind whistled through broken towers, birds chittered and chirped, and there were constant distant groans, shiftings, and the pattering of falling stones as well. The ruin was still settling, still collapsing, still falling further apart under the beatings of weather and the slow devastation of vegetation, even after thousands of years. A ruined city, but ruin is also a verb, Alaeron thought. *This city is still in the process of being ruined.*

"Ho ho, what's this?" Skiver paused by a larger-than-usual chunk of polished black stone. "I see a *door*."

Alaeron and Jaya joined him in the shadow of the ruin. Twice as tall as a man, and equally as wide, the structure seemed to be a cube tilted up on one corner, half embedded in the earth. There was indeed a door-shaped rectangle of paler stone on one face, only partially buried, and Skiver ran the point of a dagger around the cracks, chiseling out ancient dirt. "What do you think? Some dead Shory noble's treasure-room?"

"Or a prison cell holding a terrible monster," Jaya said.

Skiver sniffed. "Anything kept in a box six thousand years is dead, like as not, but maybe it had some precious possessions. Trading with rat-people is all well and good, but we don't have all that much to trade *with*. Some of Alaeron's bottles and vials and precious ingredients? I know he won't part with his pretty relics, and who can blame him. My knives? Jaya's arrows? Or coins? I have some left, but will they want those? There aren't a lot of shops around here."

"Ernst had magic items," Alaeron said. "A spyglass, other things."

"I know, and I brought them. They might be worth something, right enough. But it's better to *take* than to *trade*, am I right?" Skiver knelt and began chopping at the earth covering the bottom (or top?) portion of the door with a knife almost as big as a short sword, and Jaya sighed and knelt to help him, unfolding the small spade they'd used to bury their waste during their travels across the desert. In a few minutes they'd cleared away enough dirt to reveal the whole door.

Skiver whistled as he peered at the cracks, occasionally probing the space with the tip of a knife. "No traps that I can see," he said after a moment, satisfied. He drew a length of stiff metal from his coat and slipped it into the crack, ready to try and lever the door open.

"Wait!' Alaeron said. "I'm sure you excel at finding the sort of traps rich merchants use to defend their treasure rooms, Skiver, but these ancients may have more esoteric methods. May I?"

Skiver snorted. "He'll be telling you how to string a bow next, Jaya, you watch."

"He only wants to feel as if he's helping," she said in a tone that mixed condescension and affection, with the former in rather greater proportion than Alaeron would have liked.

"I've broken into a lot of barrows and vaults over the years. I'm not exactly new at this." Alaeron pressed his ear against the door to listen for wires humming under tension of the shifting of great weights, sniffed at the crack around the door for noxious vapors, knocked his knuckles against the stone in search of hollow compartments, and, mostly, trusted his instincts. He stepped back. "All right. It could be full of poison gas or ravenous monsters, but there's no danger I can detect."

Skiver grinned. "Well, isn't *that* reassuring?" He set his pry bar in the crack and pulled. Alaeron was reminded uncomfortably of the way he'd heaved on a similar bar in his feral form, just before Zernebeth died.

The seal on the door broke with a hiss, and Skiver stumbled backward. "Let's plunder, then!" he said, recovering his footing and hauling the door open. The cube's interior was dark, but Alaeron had alchemical lights, cold-burning, that he'd threaded through lengths of string so they could be worn as necklaces.

He handed one each to his companions, and lifted another high before him as he stepped inside. Skiver didn't argue that he should have the honor of first entry, of course. Honor didn't mean much to him, Alaeron figured, and it was always safer to go last.

They entered a small corridor, canted sideways like the cube itself, so there were doors at an angle above them and doors similarly tilted below. The interior of the cube was divided into several rooms, it seemed, the inner doors all hanging half off their hinges. They seemed, amazingly, made of wood—the cube must have been sealed perfectly against the elements.

"I'll check this room, you lot do those." Skiver gestured to the doors on the floor. "If we find anything good in those, we can climb up into the rooms above us and check those too."

Alaeron almost spoke out against them splitting up, but they wouldn't be more than ten feet apart, separate rooms aside. He contented himself with saying, "Just look well before you climb down, all right? If the rooms are too deep to get out of easily, don't go in." Amazing what a little change of orientation could do, he thought. Turn a box sideways, and what were rooms became pits. Jaya and Skiver nodded, then crouched to peer into their holes while Alaeron looked into his, the one farthest from the door. The contents of the room were a jumble, but there were intriguing gleams, so he clambered in, sliding down toward the lower corner where things had gathered. He stood ankle-deep in refuse, sorting through bits of shattered pottery and broken pieces of metal, but didn't find anything of particular interest. "I think this was just a storage room!" he shouted. "The sort of attic where you put the ugly antiques you don't want to look at anymore!"

"Antiques can be valuable!" Skiver called back, his voice muffled. "There's bugger-all in this room, though. I'm going to check another." There followed a series of thumps and scrabblings, presumably the noise of Skiver climbing out.

Alaeron spent a few more moments picking through the wreckage. Even a pot from Shory could be valuable, if it were whole, or interestingly decorated, but Vadim wouldn't be content with broken fragments, and there was nothing here worth the trouble of carrying out again. He jumped up to the doorway, grabbed the edge, and hauled himself out, puffing as he dragged himself from the hole. Jaya climbed out of her pit a moment later, rather more gracefully, clutching something in her hand. "Is this anything?" she asked, handing it over.

Alaeron squinted. It was tarnished brass, some sort of musical instrument, obviously, but no longer than his index finger. "A child's whistle, perhaps?" he said. "You can give it a blow if you want. Probably the first Shory music that's been heard here in millennia. We can take it—it's certainly very old, and doesn't weigh much." Jaya smiled and tucked the pipe away, but Alaeron thought it was an inauspicious beginning to their search. Vadim wouldn't be satisfied with children's toys. He wanted items of self-evident worth, Alaeron knew—or hidden power. "Did you have any luck, Skiver?" he called.

The man didn't answer. Alaeron ducked his head into the two other doorways on the floor, but neither held Skiver. He squinted at the ceiling, where doors sagged down like broken limbs. "Are you up there?" he called.

Jaya shouted for him from beyond the entryway. Alaeron hurried out, nearly plunging into one of the bottommost rooms as he went, and found Jaya crouched outside. "Look," she said.

The bone-handled knife Skiver had been given by the Uomoto villagers lay on the ground. Skiver was hardly the sort of person to drop a knife accidentally. "And there." She pointed. Skiver's alchemical light was on the ground, the thread he'd used for a necklace broken. "Very little sign of struggle," Jaya said. "And not much indication of where he might have gone, since the ground is so rough and stony here. But I think it's safe to say . . . he was taken."

Alaeron closed his eyes, but only for a moment, because this was a bad place to give up any of his senses. "We should have stayed together."

"That's a lesson for next time," Jaya said sharply. "Not something to dwell on now. There's no blood here, no body. He may not be dead. What do we *do*?"

"We can search for him—it's possible that whatever took your family took him as well," Alaeron said.

Jaya cocked her head. "You're staying then?"

He frowned. "What do you mean?"

"Skiver was the only leash Vadim had on you," she said. "But he's gone, so you can . . . fly free, if you like. I wouldn't blame you. I wouldn't want to be in this haunted place, if I had a choice, but Vadim has other leverage over me."

The idea of flight hadn't even occurred to him, and considering it now, he found little about it that appealed to him. "But, I—no, Jaya. I wouldn't leave you." He shook his head. "Why would you think that? Over this long journey . . . I've grown fond of you. Of course I'll stay, and help. I couldn't live with myself otherwise."

Jaya rose up on tiptoe, kissed him on the lips, and wrapped her arms around his shoulders. "Oh, Alaeron, thank you. You can be so preoccupied, so faraway, I know you're just thinking about your artifacts and your great truths, but it was hard to tell if you . . . if you cared, at all."

"Being sent on this journey has been wonderful," he said. "If I'd stayed in Almas, Kormak would have dragged me back to Numeria. I would never have learned how to combine my artifacts, or seen the legendary ruins of Kho . . . I'd never have met *you*, and my life would be poorer for it."

"Mine as well," she whispered in his ear, then stepped back. "I suppose we *must* try to rescue Skiver, though. Vadim won't be happy if we return without our keeper."

"I've grown fond of Skiver, too," Alaeron said. "Although, I admit, not in quite the same way I have for you."

She nodded. "For a treacherous thief and degenerate gambler and grasping plunderer, he's not a bad sort. I do hope he's all right."

"Skiver is good at taking care of himself," Alaeron said. "We should be worried for the health and well-being of whoever *took* him."

Jaya laughed at that, but not much, and not for long. They both knew there were things in Kho far more dangerous than Skiver. "Do you have any potions to find lost thieves?"

"Would that I did . . ." He considered. The feral mutagen might help. In that beastly form his senses were vastly heightened, especially the sense of smell, and they had Skiver's bag, which might provide enough of a scent for Alaeron to track its owner. He reached into his coat pocket, lifting out a cloth-wrapped artifact to get to the vials that had slipped underneath it during his clambering—

The cloth. It was too light by far. All the relics were weighty, heavier than it seemed they should be based on their mass alone. This cloth, checked in red and white, held the red ring, or at least, it was *supposed* to. Alaeron swore and unwrapped it.

"What's that?" Jaya said.

Alaeron held it up. A wooden ring, crudely whittled, plain and unpainted. "Skiver," he said. "He *stole* my *relic!*"

"For, what, the third time?" Jaya shook her head. "He wanted it to gamble with, remember? Maybe he thought one of the villagers would be willing to play dice with him." She sighed. "May it bring him some luck, then, wherever he was taken."

Alaeron hurriedly unwrapped the other relics, to make sure Skiver hadn't stolen them as well. If he'd taken the golden chain, or the spinning top, or the egg . . . But they were all there, nestled in their individual cloths. "Well, that's something—" he began, but stopped talking when the relics began to move. They didn't buzz and click and hover, they just shifted, moving slightly toward the northeast, like flecks of iron pulled toward a lodestone. Alaeron moved the disc back away from the others, and it slid forward again.

The alchemist looked up at Jaya and grinned. "They're *attracted!*" he said. "I should have known. The first time I saw the relics, they were trying to pull themselves together, to form a whole, and they *still* want to be together, influencing one another, *pulling*. I never noticed before, because I kept them all close together anyway, but now that one piece is far away, they're moving visibly toward their missing mate."

"What does that mean?"

"Practically speaking," Alaeron said, "it means we have a compass, only instead of pointing north, it points at *Skiver*."

Alaeron hung the disc on a string and let it dangle from his wrist. It exerted a steady, gentle tug toward the northeast. "The domes are that way," Alaeron said. "I wish I could believe he just abandoned us to explore on his own."

"Skiver likes company," Jaya said. "He told me once that he prided himself on choosing friends who were slower than he was." Alaeron gave her a quizzical look. "That way he doesn't have to outrun whatever's chasing them," she explained. "He can just outrun his slower friends, and let the monsters occupy themselves killing the ones left behind."

"I don't think he's as hard a man as he pretends to be," Alaeron said.

"I think he's cut a lot of throats, and not lost much sleep over it," Jaya said. "I've known lots of men like him. I don't know that he'd be in such a hurry to rescue *you*, if you'd been taken. But, no, perhaps not as bad as he pretends to be. People are complicated. Almost no one is entirely a hero or a villain."

Alaeron grunted. "Not even Kormak?"

"I will kill the Kellid if the elementals didn't, if I ever have the chance," Jaya said. "But by his own lights, he's just fulfilling a mission for his employers, bringing back a faithless apprentice and a thief. When he tells the story, he's the hero, I bet, and you're the crafty villain, forever eluding him."

"Perspective is all," Alaeron muttered. They reached the edge of the river, which ran surprisingly strong, wide, and clear.

"We need to find a crossing," Jaya said. "We could try to ford it, but it looks deep in the middle, and it could be treacherous."

"There's no shortage of fallen towers spanning the water," Alaeron said, gesturing both upstream and down. "Take your pick." While Jaya puzzled over which of the nearest towers might provide the most solid crossing, Alaeron gazed at the domes. They were towering, and remarkably clear of vegetation compared to the rest of the ruins. He looked to the north, where the river began, and saw the mist had burned off, letting in sunlight that made the leaning towers glitter. Dark specks moved in the sky there. Birds? If so, they must be enormous. Or maybe derhii? If they were the descendants of the slaves or servants of the Shory, they might make their homes in those high towers.

"This will do," Jaya called, and Alaeron trotted over. While some mighty towers spanned the river, she'd chosen something altogether less impressive, a fallen pillar only about as wide as Alaeron was across the shoulders, half-submerged in the river, and not quite extending all the way across—they'd have to get their feet wet at the end, or leap for the far shore. He frowned and pointed to another pillar a bit farther along the river. "Why not that one? It's twice as wide, and reaches all the way across."

She rolled her eyes. "Do I tell you how to . . . to wash your bottles or mix your herbs? The pillar you like is smooth, and slimy with moss for half its length. The one I picked is rough and pockmarked to provide good footing, and only has a patch or two of moss, easily stepped over. Unless you're an acrobat, you'll slip on yours, fall in, and drown. But if you like, I can try to cross on mine, and you on yours, and we'll make a race of it."

Despite their dire circumstances, Alaeron couldn't help smiling. "You're usually so tolerant and mild! I meant no offense. I just question . . . well, everything. It's how I've always been, since I was a boy."

"Just remember, I'm the one with experience hunting and tracking in wild places—and in places reclaimed by the wild. I'll leave the bomb-throwing to you, and you leave the trail breaking to me." She set off across the column, walking as casually as if the narrow pillar were a sidewalk. Alaeron followed, moving considerably more slowly, but she was right: his boots gripped the rough surface of the stone, and there was hardly any moss to trip them up. The river was not so terribly deep, but he didn't want to fall in. A river that ran through a ruined city of ancient magic, populated by daemons and creatures afflicted with crystalline plagues? There was no telling what arcane contaminants might have gotten into the water. Or what shat into it upstream.

He jumped for the sandy shore and made it, tottering only a little when he landed. The disc at his wrist tugged, pulling him more directly north now that they were on the far side of the water. "Shall we make for the domes?" Jaya said.

"It's as good a place to search as any," he answered.

She led the way, bow at ready, as the great black domes rose up before them. Like bubbles of gleaming tar, Alaeron thought. Like blisters in rotting skin. Probably that was unfair. In the right light, in a different setting, they'd be very pretty. But here . . . it was hard to remember there was a world of whole, unbroken things beyond the ruins of Kho.

"Movement," Jaya said. "Spread out." She ducked behind a shattered column, and Alaeron scurried toward some shelter of his own, a boulder with an eye carved into the side. He peered around the edge at the approaching creature.

*Rat-people*, the derhii had said. Alaeron had expected people who were somewhat ratlike, or at worst wererats, but these . . . these were rats, moving like people. Huge rats, almost three feet long, but waddling about on their rear legs, wearing pieces of overlarge armor held together with bits of wire. Clearly they were not ordinary beasts of sewer and dungeon, but possessed of some intelligence, perhaps as a result of the strange emanations and magical residues in the ruins. The derhii said they might be willing to trade, so . . . He stood up, cleared his throat, and said, "Hello?"

They hissed and scampered backward, gabbling in a language Alaeron had never heard before. He should have mixed an extract to help him understand foreign tongues, but he hadn't anticipated the need to treat with rats in armor. One turned and called out, and a larger creature emerged from the shadow of one of the domes: dressed in studded leather armor, terribly hairy, big as a tall child or a small man, with a pointy face. Rats with a wererat master? That seemed natural enough. "Humans," the wererat called in Taldane.

"We've heard you might be willing to trade?" Alaeron said.

The wererat cocked his head. "We trade with the derhii. We must. They are death from above. But you . . . you are not death. You are lost."

"Ah, no," Alaeron said, "we're looking for a friend who's lost, though—"

"You. Are. *Lost*." The creature pointed a sharp-nailed finger at him, almost accusingly.

A dozen more armored rats boiled forth from the shadows of the dome, bearing knives and spears and axes, jabbering in their peculiar language, yellow fangs glinting.

# Chapter Twenty-One
## The Pit of Endless Night

Jaya's first arrow took the wererat in the throat. He fell screaming, clawing at his throat, his body twisting and shifting as he tried to transform. Werecreatures were not so easily killed, Alaeron knew, but a sharp arrowhead and a length of wood through the neck must hurt regardless. Alaeron wasn't pleased with their chances against a dozen filthy disease-carrying vermin, especially when the vermin were armed and armored, so he grasped the silver egg in his pocket and activated it, praying it wouldn't shatter into pretty shell-like fragments when he did. The time egg's surface was more cracks than not at this point, but it worked for him once more, and everything around him stilled and turned faintly blue.

Jaya has loosed an arrow, and its velocity was such that it still moved now, albeit in slow motion, reminding Alaeron of an old riddle: how could an arrow get anywhere at all, when at any instant in time, the arrow must inhabit a single finite quantity of space? During that moment, it was occupying space, not moving, and since it was not moving, what carried it forward? All things are motionless in an instant, and time is nothing but a succession of instants, so therefore, motion is impossible.

It made a certain amount of sense in theory, but the arrow and the murderous rats were moving anyway, in defiance of all thought experiments to the contrary, so Alaeron had best move, too. He eschewed artifacts now in favor of his more direct weapons, the bombs he'd mastered during his time with the Technic League. A bomb of fire; a bomb of ice; a bomb of splashing acid. He did not throw them, but walked toward the unmoving bevy of rats and placed the bombs before his enemies at strategic locations. When the bombs left his hands—or the range of his aura?—they hung unmoving in the air, and would not finish falling until the egg's effects ended. He hurried to Jaya and pressed her hand against the egg, making her gasp as she caught up with his timestream.

"You cheat," she said, squeezing his hand. "I *like* that. Shall we take up a position behind them, where I can loose arrows? Once the little ones are dead, we can interrogate the big one to see if he knows where we can find Skiver. I think I have a silver knife. The prospect of permanent death might encourage him to open up."

"Yes, but let's hurry. The egg won't slow time forever." They carried their gear around the crowd of rats, with Jaya pausing to kick away the wererat captain's blades. A pile of rubble by the eastern curve of the dome seemed a good spot for sniping, so they made their way toward it and climbed up the tumbled rocks to the top.

Where they found someone else already stationed, crouching, frozen in the timeless moment. He was belly-down on top of the rock, with a long silver tube in his hands, pointed toward the place where Alaeron and Jaya had been. His clothes were torn rags, except for a clean dark coat of good cut. His face was a snarling mask of cuts and welts and bruises, and his hair was singed and burned half off his head.

Kormak. And as Jaya gasped and Alaeron gaped at him, the egg's charge ran out, and they rejoined the forceful flow of time.

The Kellid's eyes widened when he saw them, less than a foot from his face, but he'd already been in the act of triggering his device, and a wave of unspeakable heat flowed from the end of his silvery tube, just past Alaeron's face; it was like putting his cheek an inch from a red-hot stove. The bombs he'd placed went off at the same moment, the flame bomb with an explosive whump, and the rats began screaming. Alaeron grabbed the first vial his hands touched and slammed it into Kormak's face. The Kellid turned his head away, but not far enough—the vial broke across his brow and nose, driving sharp fragments of glass into his left eye. Alaeron recognized the pungent scent of the fluid that sprayed across Kormak's face. No corrosive acid or vile poison, alas, but a potion that allowed the drinker to see in the dark; the most dangerous thing in *that* was finely ground bits of carrot. Still, having it smashed into an eye blinded by glass wouldn't feel good.

This was the second man from Numeria Alaeron had blinded. It was becoming a habit.

Kormak rolled over, writhing and clutching his face, and Alaeron reached out to grab the weapon—the one he'd used to burn Alaeron's workshop, and the Dagger and the Coin, and Ernst himself, and who knew what else. But the silver metal was so hot he pulled back his hand before touching it, afraid he'd lose all the flesh off his hands.

Jaya tugged at him, yelling, and they slid back down the boulder. Alaeron glanced back at the host of rats:

some were on fire, some frozen solid, some twisting on the ground with grievous injuries. The stench of burning rat hair was monstrous. Kormak's beam had incinerated the column Jaya had been hiding behind. "Come *on*," Jaya shouted as a dozen more armored rats boiled up from the shadows at the base of the domes, and they raced off north, hoping they could escape in all the confusion.

The eastern wall of the valley was close by, covered in crawling vines and bobbing flowers in red and green and yellow and purple. It would have been beautiful, even idyllic, if not for the screams of rats and the stench of battle. Maybe Kormak and the rats would kill one another, but Alaeron wasn't hopeful. Nothing seemed to stop the Kellid. Alaeron just hoped he hadn't burned Jaya's village to ashes in his quest to find his quarry.

They took shelter beside a cracked fountain, in the shadow of a huge headless statue of a noble figure pointing skyward—though because of the tilt, the statue was actually pointing at the mountains to the east. "We have to find Skiver," Alaeron said. "And get out of here."

Jaya shook her head. Her face was smeared with dirt and glistening with perspiration. She'd never looked more beautiful. "We have to kill Kormak. Not just in revenge for the way he murdered Ernst—to keep him from murdering *us*. He'll dog our heels forever, follow us back to Andoran . . . we have to make an end to him. Skiver told me you were gifted at setting traps. Do you think you could set some here?"

Alaeron looked around. "That tower," he said, nodding to an eighty-foot spire that leaned against the cliff wall. "It looks like it could collapse at any moment." He thought for a moment, then held up a vial. "Could you hit a target this size from, say, fifty yards?"

She snorted. "As easily as you can lace up your boots, alchemist."

"Then this could work," he said.

"Alaeron!" Kormak called, and the alchemist flinched to hear the Kellid using his given name. It seemed so much more personal than being called "runaway" or "thief."

Alaeron and Jaya were in the ruins of the tower, watching. The Kellid limped, blood running down his face, but he came on, implacable despite his wounds. "Did you think taking my eye would stop me? The Technic League will give me a new eye, one better than I was born with, as they did my old friend Gannix. I'm half machine already, boy. I have steel bones in my legs. They fixed up my heart after it got nicked by a knife—I should have bled to death, but now my heart is *armored*. I do not just bear their weapons—I *am* one of their weapons."

They made his body a machine, Alaeron thought. For some reason, that made him think of the skeletal remains he'd seen in the Silver Mount, with bits of metal fused to the bones, a similar melding of biology and technology—

That was it. Despite the enemy approaching, Alaeron smiled. The gray disc, the seemingly useless part of the machine—perhaps it was not meant to connect to the other relics directly, but to connect those relics to the wielder's *body*, just as some weapons and armor had been integrated into Kormak's body. What if the disc could act as a linkage that would bind Alaeron's body into the machine, make his own muscles and bones and mind a part of the engine? Could it work?

He wasn't willing to have the disc surgically implanted into his body just to test the theory, and merely holding it in his hand was clearly not sufficient, as he had discovered, but perhaps there was another way, something less invasive. Unfortunately, Skiver had one of the relics necessary to test his theory.

There was no time anyway—there was work to be done now. Jaya fired an arrow at the Kellid. It bounced harmlessly off his long, armored coat, but he turned and started walking toward the crumbling tower where they were hidden. Jaya and Alaeron hurried off their broken ledge, hopped down to ground level, and raced out the back of the tower. Jaya chose her spot, half-hidden by the soot-stained fragment of a marble staircase, and drew her arrow.

"Wait," Alaeron whispered. "Wait until he's there . . ." They could see Kormak moving on the other side of the tower, through the glassless windows, coming closer. Alaeron was terrified the Kellid would swoop out in a curve to try and flank them, but he came on straight, either too tired or too impatient for anything but the direct approach.

When the shadow of the tower fell upon Kormak, Alaeron whispered, "Now."

Jaya loosed. Her arrow struck one of the bombs Alaeron had planted around the tower. It was a delayed bomb, one Alaeron had set to go off in a few minutes, but shattering the vial would set it off, too.

The vial broke, exploding outward in a blast of concussive force that triggered half a dozen other bombs. Their explosions set off others in a carefully constructed cascade. Every bomb Alaeron had prepared, his entire arsenal, was arrayed in a half-moon around the spot where Kormak stood. He was hit from all sides by shrapnel, fire, acid, frost, madness, stink—the full complement of Alaeron's abilities. Kormak didn't even have time to scream.

And, as the alchemist had hoped, the bombs secreted around the base of the tower served to further destabilize the ruin. Tons of stone, crystal, and metal seemed to sigh, and then collapsed, burying Kormak beneath the rubble. The noise was immense, and great clouds of dust rolled forth from the devastation. The heap of shattered stone was twice as tall as Alaeron.

Jaya stood up, waving dust clouds away, and scowled at the rubble. "I won't believe he's dead until I see his body, preferably headless. He survived an assault by elementals, after all."

Alaeron nodded. "I understand. Though I suspect the elementals soon began squabbling amongst themselves. Still, I don't much want to dig through the rubble just to look for proof of life, do you? We'd need shovels, picks, and many days. Even if he's not dead, he's entombed, and we'll be gone long before he can dig his way out, metal bones or not."

Jaya sighed. "I will never stop having nightmares about him. Even when I'm safe in bed somewhere thousands of miles away, if I hear a noise downstairs, I'll fear it's him."

Alaeron put a hand on her shoulder. "Unless you're sharing a bed with me, I don't think you'll need to worry."

Jaya raised one eyebrow. "That's not the way to tempt a woman into your bed, alchemist." She rose. "Come. Let's find Skiver. Is he in those domes?"

"Ah." Alaeron blinked at her, then looked at the disc tugging at his wrist. "Huh. No. He's north of here, actually."

"Good. I don't want to see where those rats make their warren. And we'd better leave before they come to investigate the sound of that tower falling."

"The Pit of Endless Night." Alaeron peered at the vast hole in the earth before them. The disc on its string around his wrist tugged steadily forward and downward, urging them to descend. "How did I know it would be the Pit of Endless Night? Why not the Pit of Pleasant Afternoons?"

"Could be full of treasures," Jaya said doubtfully. "Buried treasures."

"Probably just monsters," Alaeron said.

"Some monsters collect treasure."

"You are ever the optimist." Alaeron paced around a small section of the pit, stopping at one of the many rivulets of water that poured down inside, split off from the river. The hole was easily fifty feet across, a drain that would never be filled, ringed by a circle of jagged black glass—presumably a dome like those of the Polymatum, but utterly shattered. "This was a tower," he said. "Look how smooth the sides of the pit are. It's a tower that was jammed down deep into the earth, a tower that goes *down* instead of *up*. Like an icepick jammed into body. Must have happened when the city fell." He knelt on the edge, though he was unwilling to lean too far forward to look down. There was nothing but darkness down there, but it was an echoey sort of darkness, the sound of falling water a loud and constant rush. Shame he'd smashed his potion to improve night vision into Kormak's face, though who knew if even that would have penetrated such profound gloom? "The tower must have broken through into some natural cavern or system of caves on impact. There's no telling what's down there."

"Other than Skiver," she said.

"And, presumably, whatever took him," Alaeron agreed. "How do we get down there?"

"Ropes and grapnels," Jaya said, sighing. "Assuming we have enough rope."

Jaya opened her pack, then froze. A strange, high-pitched tittering sort of laugh emerged from the cave.

Alaeron went still as well, both of them staring down at the dark. The laughter was human, and distant, but distressingly manic and gleeful, the sound of something so far around the bend of insanity that it couldn't even see mere garden-variety lunacy from its vantage point. The roaring of some monster, or even the screams of the tortured, would have been preferable to the sound of that mad good humor floating up from the dark. After a few moments, it trailed off, and silence reigned again, broken only by the distant rushing of the river and the whistles of birds.

"I wonder what's so funny?" Jaya said at last.

Alaeron hefted a coil of rope. "I'm afraid we'll soon find out."

# Chapter Twenty-Two
## A Noble Son of Shory

They opted not to use alchemical lights, afraid the illumination might attract unwanted attention from the laughter or some other denizen of the dark. No reason to make themselves glowing targets, after all. The downside was that they couldn't see anything much at all, except for a gradually shrinking perfect circle of blue sky above them. Alaeron had read once that if you looked up at the sky from the bottom of a well, you would see stars, even in bright daylight, but he now had experimental proof that such was not the case. Though to be fair, he wasn't at the *bottom* of this well.

He wasn't convinced this well even had a bottom, though it seemed logical that it must, somewhere. They couldn't even talk properly because of the roar of falling water, so much louder now that they were in the echo chamber of the pit. Alaeron began doing mental sums. So many gallons of water, presumably falling into this pit for thousands of years, and it wasn't filled up, which meant . . . well, nothing, really. Perhaps there was a subterranean river at the bottom. Or perhaps a thirsty creature, maybe some immense subterranean spawn of

Rovagug, was drinking up every drop and pissing it out somewhere leagues away, creating a warm yellow sea. There was no way to tell, because there was nothing to see but blackness, and nothing to hear but *noise*. They'd reach the end of the ropes with nothing but infinity below them and a brutally long climb above—

His feet touched solid ground.

Alaeron grunted and felt around with his foot, probing the ledge beneath him, and determined it was solid enough to hold his weight. The wall before him sloped away inward, which suggested this might be a cave or at least a depression in the wall. Instead of pulling straight down, the disc on his wrist began to tug him slightly forward. Jaya's voice spoke, right in his ear: "I think there are caverns ahead."

"No use groping in the dark," he said, and took a tube of green fluid from his pocket. He shook the vial vigorously, and it began to glow as the chemicals inside mixed, producing light enough to push back the gloom a bit. They'd found one of the embedded tower's windows, an upside-down arch, but instead of opening onto bedrock, it led to the mouth of a seemingly man-made tunnel that sloped sharply downward and beyond the range of sight. Jaya hammered spikes into the tunnel wall and securely looped their climbing ropes around it. It wouldn't do to get stranded in here. Alaeron had mixed his elixir of flight, but he wouldn't want to trust his life to the effects of an extract he'd never tested. He could always assemble the arcane engine and let it lift them out—except, no. Skiver had stolen one of the components. Ah, well. All the more reason to find him.

Jaya shook up her own alchemical light, dangling on a string around her neck. "I wish we had Ernst and his sun-on-a-stick," she said, sighing.

"His ability to hurl fireballs would be useful, too. Shall we?"

She grunted. "Lead on. You have the Skiver-compass."

Alaeron started along the tunnel, which spiraled down into the rock, offering a new blind curve every few feet. It would be trivial for someone to ambush them, and these lights advertised their location, but any creatures who lived down here were probably used to fighting in the dark, so Jaya and Alaeron needed to be able to see. And yet, as they walked down, down, down, nothing set upon them—no giant spiders, no subterranean underdwellers, no hideous oozes, no enormous fanged worms, none of the things Alaeron had encountered during his many previous delves into dark parts of the earth.

"Light ahead," Jaya said, pointing, and Alaeron nodded and tucked his own lamp away under his coat. Jaya did likewise, and they crept down the tunnel, rounding a curve. They found a high-ceilinged cavern, lit by torches on the walls. Half a dozen tunnels branched from the room—some leading up, some down, some more or less level. The sound of metal clashing on metal emerged from one, but there was a regularity to the noise that suggested weapons practice rather than a pitched battle. Alaeron sniffed at another tunnel and frowned. "Someone's cooking down there. Since when do monsters that live in caves cook? I smell *spices*."

"Look." Jaya beckoned, leading him to a short tunnel that led to a long, low, rectangular room hacked out of the rock. The room was a jumble of corpses, some pinned to the walls with spears: giant spiders, pale eyeless lizards, huge centipedes with mandibles like scimitars, and all manner of underground vermin. "Someone has been cleaning out these caverns," she whispered. "I wouldn't expect any creatures in this place to be that organized."

"There are people down here," Alaeron said, frowning. "And by 'people' I mean 'creatures with some vestige of civilization.' The derhii we met beyond the Stone of Sacrifice mentioned humans living below, and said they had a new leader. I think they took Skiver." He gestured toward one of the caverns—which, naturally, sloped downward. Of course. "The disc likes this direction."

They left the puddle of brightness created by the torches, but soon found walls covered in bioluminescent fungus, creating a bluish-green illumination that wasn't as good as real light but was much better than pitch blackness. The low tunnel sloped gently down, and the disc at Alaeron's wrist began pulling more sharply. The other artifacts in his pockets began to jostle, too, trying to reach their mate. "I think we're close," Alaeron said.

A sudden gust of wind blew down the tunnel, and Jaya looked at him, eyes wide. "There's an opening to the surface somewhere here," she whispered.

"Yes," said a voice beyond the end of the tunnel. "I wanted more air, good air, yes, so my people went to dig dig dig. Many died, yes, but sweet air down below now." The voice was male, and spoke Taldane with an accent that didn't sound remotely like any Alaeron had encountered in all his travels, all mushy vowels and clunking consonants. "Come! Come!"

"So much for the element of surprise," Alaeron said. Jaya got her weapons ready, and Alaeron led them toward the end of the tunnel.

The cavern they entered was like the throne room of a mad subterranean king. The space was dominated by a chair big enough to pass for a bed, dark wood carved all over with strange winged beasts. A man sat on that throne, his skin as black as the spaces between stars, far darker even than Jaya's deep brown coloration. His eyes were bright, wide, and piercingly blue, his head absolutely bare, and he wore tattered robes of purple chased with gold.

Immense banners hung on the stone walls behind him, also a rich purple in hue, decorated with a golden symbol: something like a crown, topped with wavy lines that might have been meant to represent wind, or water. Boxes and crates were stacked along the walls, some filled with the soft gleam of jewels, some with the glitter of gold, and one holding small carvings: winged lions in jade, a black onyx tower on a base shaped like a cloud, a golden derhii holding a spear aloft. Torches flamed on all the walls, smoke rising up to the chimney this strange man had caused to be cut into the rock.

"Welcome!" the man on the throne called. "Your friend has been saying you would come, yes, how glad I am to meet you all!"

"Our friend?" Alaeron said.

"That would be me." Skiver's gloomy voice emerged from nowhere. "He knocked me over the head and dragged me down here."

The stranger leapt up from the throne—he was smaller than Jaya, but nimble and quick—and pulled one of the banners aside, revealing an alcove cut into the rock. The alcove held a black iron cage. The cage held Skiver.

The rogue waved. "This mad bugger locked me up. I picked the lock twice, but when I try to escape, he just grabs me again and puts me back. He's faster than he looks."

"Excuse me . . . sir . . ." Alaeron said. "But why have you taken our friend?"

"For glory!" the man cried, looking up to the narrow chimney. "He will make my great city fly again!"

Alaeron glanced at Jaya. He cleared his throat. "Your city? You claim to be Shory, then?"

"A noble son of Shory." The man sat back down on the throne, shaking his head, then bobbing it, then shaking it again. "The empire is in disarray, yes? But I, I was born and reared to lead, and we will soar again, oh yes. Kho, the greatest of cities—it will rise again."

"The Shory have been dead for thousands of years," Alaeron said.

The noble shook his head and clucked his tongue. "No, not dead, only sleeping. These are the banners of Kho on my wall, and they will wave in the sky again. This was the chair of my father!" He smacked his hand down on the arm of his throne.

"Cloth and wood from Kho would have disintegrated millennia ago," Alaeron said. "And, forgive me, so would *men*."

"Oh no, no. I was *sleeping*. In my room, with this chair, and these banners, and chests of gems and gold, in a *special* room. My father made it, you see, so that we could be safe, if ever the city began to fall." The noble's left eye started to twitch. "The room protected me: wrapped in force, wrapped in time, to wait for rescue, to keep me safe until someone could *find* me. But no one ever did."

"Stasis?" Alaeron murmured. He'd heard of such things—there were rumors of stasis rooms in the Silver Mount, places where time did not hold sway, where all the contents waited, frozen. Could this man truly be a Shory noble, sealed for millennia in a bubble of arcane magic? "How did you get out?"

"One of the *beasts* in the ground cracked the seal," he said. "A crystalline thing, its flesh was glass, oh yes, and it turned my *walls* to glass, it woke me up, tried to turn me to glass. But I am a noble son of Shory. I cannot be killed by *beasts*."

"Son of a dead empire," Alaeron murmured. "You could teach us so much! You're the last of—"

"No, not the last!" The noble gripped the chair's arms and leaned forward. "There are sons and daughters of Kho in these caverns. Survivors of the Fall, who bred and lived in the dark, forgetting their pasts. Many generations lost, yes, and they are savages, but they are *strong*, good warriors, fighting forever in the dark, and they are learning now to fight together, stand together, to sing Shory songs of war. When I make Kho rise again, they will rise with me!" He giggled, and the laugh was terribly familiar, the same cackle they'd heard up above, carried by strange currents of air to the surface. "But you. You are outsiders. You are not Shory. So you will be *fuel*."

Skiver suddenly lunged out of the cage, throwing a knife. It stuck in the Shory noble's arm. He glanced at the blade, plucked it free—he didn't even bleed—and dropped it on the floor. "I am *noble*," he said slowly, as if talking to an idiot. "A favored son of Kho. Blades do not cut me."

The rogue sighed and slouched over to join Jaya and Alaeron. "That's the third time I've stabbed him," he complained. "The first time he just laughed at me, sounded like an asylum full of mad children. I keep thinking he might have a weak spot. But he doesn't, as far as I can tell. Except his *mind*."

"What do you mean, we will be fuel?" Jaya said.

"Surely Aeromantic Infandibulum was not based on human sacrifice?" Alaeron said, only belated realizing he should have tried to sound more horrified and less intrigued.

The Shory gnawed on his fingertips for a moment—the nails were so cracked it made Alaeron shudder just to look at them. "I . . . I do not know how the city *used* to fly. I am *noble*, I was not a pilot, not an engineer. I did not tend the arcane engines, there were people to do that for me."

Of course, Alaeron thought in disgust. The only surviving voice of an ancient empire is a privileged rich man with no practical knowledge.

"But I have a new way to make the city fly," the Shory noble said. "I will feed you to the astradaemons in the Domes, and they will give me fiendish magic to raise the ruins high!"

"Astradaemons," Skiver said. "He keeps talking about those. What are they? Something to do with, ah . . . asses?"

"They eat souls," Alaeron said softly. "And you know . . . a place like Kho should be bursting with the spirits of the unquiet dead, but we haven't seen a single ghost. If there are astradaemons here . . . they could have *eaten* all the ghosts. They must be the creatures that take the criminals your people sacrifice, Jaya. But now this lunatic is out procuring for them."

"It is sad," the Shory noble said matter-of-factly. "She is very pretty, this one with the bow and arrow, and your friend, he is funny, so funny, always with another knife, ha ha! You I am sure are very nice also, man who talks and talks. Now, now, in the cage, all in the cage, I will take you to the Domes when night falls, then you go into another cage. The lesser daemons will prepare you. It takes time, I'm told, they like to season you with suffering and plagues, but soon the astradaemons will have a feast. A hundred more souls or so, they say, and Kho will rise—"

"What Kho?" Alaeron shouted. "There's no city up there—you've seen it! Just rocks and broken stone jumbled in a valley. It's like saying a dismembered body will get up and dance again, like saying you'll drink from a cup that's been shattered and crushed into dust. Kho is less than a ruin."

The Shory went very still. "It can be fixed," he whispered. "They have promised me, the daemons promised—"

"Oh, well, a daemon promised," Alaeron said. "Making deals with daemons, that always works out well, they're quite reliable."

"The Shory will rise again!" the noble shouted, standing up. "Do not tell lies, no lies, or I will tear off your arms and legs, yes, your soul does not live in those, you can go to the daemons without them—"

"You don't need daemons," Alaeron said. "You need science. Skiver, do you still have Ernst's things?"

"In my bag." He inclined his head to one corner of the cavern, where his things were jumbled. "This mad bastard dumped everything out on the ground."

"I was looking for candied cloudberries," the Shory noble said, almost contrite. "I haven't tasted them in . . . " He giggled. "Five thousand years!"

"I am a scientist," Alaeron said. "An arcanist, and an engineer. All the things you need. May I show you something?"

The noble frowned and shrugged. "You can do better than the daemons can?"

Alaeron sniffed. "Of course. Making a city fly? A trivial matter. Why, Kho used to be in the sky—it remembers flying. That makes it so much simpler, you know. And I won't require any souls. One of those boxes of jewels you mentioned, perhaps, as a consideration for my time . . . but we can talk terms later." As he spoke he began putting Skiver's possessions back in the bag, then lifted out the object he'd been looking for.

"You lie," the Shory said, disgusted.

"No," Skiver said. "Alaeron's the real thing, right enough. He's been inside the Silver Mount, that great mountain ship of a thing that fell from the sky? Oh, wait, that's after your time—"

"Perhaps not," Alaeron said, rising. "No one is sure when the Silver Mount fell, and history becomes muddy when you're talking about timescales on the order of thousands of years, but it may have been before the fall of the Shory Empire."

"The great silver mountain," the noble said, frowning. "In the north? It came down in the Rain of Stars, yes, long ago, we looked down on it once, flying above, but we did not fly too close, oh no, it's full of poison, that place. You have been?"

"Been inside," Alaeron said. "Found its secrets. Came back out."

"Then you . . . perhaps you . . ." the noble said.

"Yes," Alaeron said kindly. "Could you come closer?"

The noble stepped toward him, eyes wide. Utterly mad, Alaeron thought. But so hopeful. The man was almost sad. Except for the kidnapping, and the human sacrifice. "Now what I have here," Alaeron said. "Is not actually *science* . . ." He raised the wand Ernst had taken off the hellspawn gambler in Absalom, what seemed like a hundred years ago. The end sparkled. Alaeron waved it at the noble.

The Shory's eyes rolled back in his head, and he collapsed unconscious on the uneven stone floor.

"And what if he'd been just as immune to magic as he is to knives?" Skiver demanded.

Alaeron shrugged. "He was in stasis for six thousand years. It didn't seem likely he was immune to magical sleep. But if so . . . I would have kept bluffing about being able to make his city fly again, I suppose, and waited for some other opportunity. Should we tie him up?"

"He's strong," Skiver said. He stepped around the noble and pulled the banners down from the wall, rolling them up and stuffing them in his recovered bag. "Must be on account of being a noble, eh? He carried me under one arm like a bundle of sticks. Unless you've got a hundredweight of chain hidden in your bag, I wouldn't bother with bindings. Let's just grab some of these lovely Shory trinkets and leg it." He scooped up a handful of jewels, but mostly concentrated on the carvings: Vadim would want *unique* items, after all, things that could only have come from Kho, never seen elsewhere.

Alaeron thought about the golden chain from the Silver Mount—it could wrap around things so tightly it would never let go unless you knew the trick of loosening it—but he didn't want to leave that down here, so they'd have to hope the mad noble stayed unconscious for a while. But thinking of the chain reminded him. "My artifact, please?"

Skiver winced. "Noticed that, did you? Here you are." He pulled the red ring off his thumb and dropped it into Alaeron's palm. "Didn't do me a bit of good anyway."

"Well, you're such a mess, it's quite a challenge even for a relic from beyond the stars to impose order on *you*."

"I am happy to have Skiver back, too," Jaya said. "But I think we should *go*."

"So how do we get out of here, then?" Skiver peered upward toward the circle of bright sky. "Climb up those ropes you two came down?" He spat. "That's not my idea of fun. Climbing up a rope's a bastard of a lot harder than climbing down one, too. You know how the Shory noble came down here? He *jumped*, with me in his arms, the lunatic, and just landed here on this ledge. I nearly shit myself. I should have. Would have served him right."

I could fly, Alaeron thought, but besides being untested, he wasn't sure his extract of flight would allow him to lift two people—it was his first attempt, and might not be that strong. But . . . "I may have a better way," he said. "May I try something?"

"If it spares me dragging myself up a rope, go ahead," Skiver said.

"If it's *fast*," Jaya said. "Who knows how long the noble will be sleeping? Or how often his people patrol these tunnels?"

Alaeron swiftly removed the artifacts from his pockets and began to assemble them, combining them as he and Ernst had on the riverbank. When he had all the pieces put together and the golden chain wrapped around the gear, he pulled the disc off the string on his wrist and held it in his palm. Could this possibly be the solution? Taking the disc into himself?

"Wish me luck," he said. The disc was too large to swallow, but if his theory was right, perhaps merely holding it inside his body would be sufficient to create a link between engine and flesh. He slipped the disc into his mouth.

The moment it touched his tongue, a jolt went through him. The golden chain slithered up his wrist, his arm, and on around his chest, then looped around and around, pulling the rest of the artifacts with it. The gearwheel pressed against his chest like an exceedingly uncomfortable breastplate as the chain crisscrossed further, looping around his waist, arms, and legs, binding the machine to him and armoring him in links of gold.

I am the machine, he thought. The machine is me.

Suddenly, everything made sense. He felt his body rise up into the air, hovering over the ground, but he didn't go sailing off helplessly upward into space. Why would he? The disc gave him control, *conscious* control. The engine without the disc was like Zernebeth's arcane walker without a driver: full of power, and grace, and speed, but with no *direction*.

But this device did so much more than grant the power of flight. He could *see* that now. That creature in the Silver Mount had been a pilot, or a navigator, or an arcane shipwright, or all three. Alaeron rose a little higher (distantly aware of Skiver gasping, but he was so small compared to the world Alaeron could see now, the alchemist barely noticed him). With a thought, Alaeron slowed down time, because sometimes things happened quickly, and more time was always useful to consider options. He looked around not with his *eyes*, he had so much more than *eyes* now. He peered up through the layers of rock above them, and he saw how the ruins of Kho *fit*, how order had been turned into disorder, and how it could be repaired. The ruin was an error, and he was capable of correcting errors. With the order-creating power of the ring, combined with the colossal kinetic energy of the spinning top, he could create a whirlwind that picked up broken things and put them down again *whole*. He could fix what politics, or the Tarrasque, or simple decadence had torn asunder.

Somewhere, something hurt. Not in his body, exactly, but not entirely in his mind. His vision turned from blue to red. There were too many pieces missing from the

city, too many things broken, stolen, and shattered—
too much entropy to overcome. Order had no chance
here. The city couldn't be reassembled; there were
holes in space, punctures connected to other *planes*,
magic gone that couldn't be regained, and worst of all,
he was trying to reach out with limbs he didn't *have*,
to use tools he didn't possess—parts of the Silver
Mount, perhaps, or psychic powers possessed by the
ship's pilot/navigator/repairman that Alaeron lacked.
He couldn't do it, couldn't fix this, couldn't make
this disaster and wreckage, this collection of broken
junk, into a city that flew. *No one* could. Someone was
screaming at him and shouting a word. What word?
Was it a name—

He got dizzy, and he fell, the disc dropping out of his
mouth to hit the ground. The rest of the engine started
to lift him up in the air, once more a driverless coach
racing as fast as it could, and Alaeron desperately clawed
at the device on his chest, tearing the egg free from
the ring. The artifacts fell into their component parts,
dropping him on the ground, the chain shortening and
going limp. He rolled over and vomited.

"You're bleeding from your nose, one of your ears—
there's blood in your *eye*," Jaya said, horrified. "What
did you do?"

"Trifled with things man was not meant to know?"
Alaeron said, rolling over and wiping at his mouth.
His head pounded like it had been used as a drum.
"I always hated that expression. There's nothing man
was not *meant* to know. Only what he knows, or doesn't
know *yet*. But I may be willing to grant there are things
man is better off *not* knowing."

He tried to stand up, failed, slumped down. "That
artifact is more powerful than I'd imagined. It really

*could* make Kho fly again, if the place weren't shattered into a thousand pieces. This engine . . . I won't say it makes its user into a god. Nowhere near that. But perhaps gods have creatures who do their washing-up, who mend their broken pots or fix their shattered wheels? Laborers who carry out great works under their direction, like the slaves in Osirion who built those pyramids? This engine might give you the power of a god's slave. But it's no good to me. A man like me using it is like a child trying to wield a giant's battle-axe. I can't even lift it. At best I'd kill myself trying. I might be able to use the engine to *fly*, that much might be safe, but there are easier ways to take flight." He wiped at his nostrils, leaving a red smear across the back of his hand. "Ones that are less bloody."

"Maybe stick with those," Skiver said. "Being a god's a shit job anyway, and being a god's handyman sounds worse. Not worth bleeding out your eyeballs over anyway."

"The pursuit of truth is nothing if not perilous," Alaeron croaked. He tried to sit up, groaning and holding his head. "Funny. I thought just understanding the devices—the *device*—would be enough for me, that truth was its own reward. But I find myself entirely outraged that I can't *use* the thing properly, now that I've figured it out. I could feel the machine trying to force my body and my mind into the right shape to use it, but it just didn't work. Like a kraken trying to put on a pair of pants. Too many limbs and not enough fabric."

"So," Skiver said after a moment, looking up toward the surface. "Ropes, then?"

"Ropes," Alaeron rasped. And then he vomited again.

# Chapter Twenty-Three
## Aeromancer

After they lay around the edge of the Pit panting for a while following their climb, Skiver sat up. "Back to the village for a bite to eat, then a derhii ride to the Vulture's Roost? We didn't quite fill our sacks with loot, but the things I snatched from that pisspot of a throne room will make Vadim happy enough, I think. And I know the way to get here now, so I can draw him a map, and he can send an *army* if he wants the rest."

"I'm going to the domes," Jaya said, standing up and shouldering her supplies. "You heard the noble. He says the sacrifices are being 'seasoned.' My people may yet live."

"Seasoned with *disease*," Skiver pointed out. "So they're likely as good as dead anyway, right?"

"Diseases can be healed," she said, scowling. "My people are great healers. And even if they die, better they die free, than in some cage lorded over by creatures from the Outer Planes."

"Or you could take back a plague that wipes out your whole village," Skiver said, then sighed. "Fine, all right, suit yourself. But you know, strictly speaking, I don't *need* you anymore, and neither does Vadim."

She shrugged. "See that he frees my brother when you return. I wish you safe travels."

Alaeron struggled to his feet. The climb had been harder on him than on either of the others—Skiver was an experienced second-story man, after all, and Jaya could probably climb ropes all day for fun, but alchemists weren't built for that kind of exertion. "Jaya, wait—I'll go with you. I might be able to help."

"I won't turn you down," she said, smiling. "Your assistance is most welcome."

"Damn it," Skiver said. "Why did you lot have to come rescue me anyway? Why not leave me to die? Now I feel *obligated* to return the favor." He kicked at the ground, then looked up, a gleam in his eye. "Daemons, though. I can stab them all I like and nobody will try to arrest me, right? And are they very rich, do you think?"

As they walked back to the Domes, Alaeron filled Skiver in on what he'd missed, chiefly the reappearance of Kormak, though the armored rats also rated a mention, as did their wererat leader. "Probably not a *real* leader," Skiver opined. "Don't get me wrong, I've got nothing against wererats—worked with one once, wonderful smuggler—but they aren't usually good for anything above sergeant or so. I imagine the wererats are just to keep the little rats in line, and someone's pulling *their* strings, likely those daemons of yours."

"They're not mine," Alaeron said. "We'd better hope stealth works for us. I don't like our chances facing off against astradaemons. I don't know much about them, just what I've read in books, but from what I understand . . . I wouldn't recommend stabbing them, Skiver. They can rip the soul out of any creature that possesses one."

"Huh. And what happens if you lose your soul?"

"You die," Jaya said. "No soul, no life."

"Huh," Skiver said. "And here I am alive and well. Just goes to show all those people who said I had no soul were talking nonsense. Fine, we'll be dainty and stealthy, see if we can find the prisoners and slip out unnoticed. First, though, let's stop by and see this tower you dropped on our Kellid friend. I made myself a little promise that I'd piss on his grave if I got the opportunity."

"Raise your hand if you're surprised." Skiver nudged the heap of rubble while Alaeron and Jaya groaned. "I knew he wouldn't stay buried."

"There's a broken pickaxe here," Alaeron said, pointing. "Someone dug him out. Who? Why?" He knelt to examine the rubble.

"Alaeron," Jaya said from behind him.

"It's not as if he has allies here," Alaeron muttered.

"Alaeron," Skiver said.

"The man's luck is ridiculous, it's like—ha, I wonder if he *does* have an artifact that tilts probability in his favor, that would make a certain amount of sense, I—"

"*Alaeron!*" his companions shouted, and he finally turned around.

"The rats heard me shouting," Kormak said mildly. He had Jaya by the hair, a knife held to her throat. His was no ordinary knife: the blade was glass, a shade of blue unseen in nature, and looking at the weapon made Alaeron's eyes tear up. The Kellid had a boot on the back of Skiver's neck, and when Skiver tried to move, Kormak shifted his weight slightly, and Skiver squawked and went still, sprawled on the ground.

Alaeron stared at him. The Kellid's hair—what bits hadn't been burned off—were gray with rock dust, his ruined eye now an empty black socket, his clothes so shredded that he wore little but rags and boots beneath his impeccable coat. He bled from dozens of abrasions. How far would this pursuit go? How far would Alaeron *let* it go?

"Fine!" the alchemist said. "You've pursued me to the ends of the world, or at least one of the darkest corners. I bow to your invincibility! Take the relics. Take me, if you must. But spare my companions. They have nothing to do with our problem."

"This one shot arrows at me," Kormak said. "This one tried to stab me in the kidneys, and would have done worse, given the opportunity. No, you'll all share the same fate. They wanted me to bring you back to Starfall, so that you could face the justice of the Technic League. But they will be content with the end I have authored for you."

"And what end is that?" Alaeron was suddenly bone-weary. This had been the longest day in a journey full of long days. He just wanted some ending. It didn't have to be a happy one. It just needed to be an end.

"Despite all the rock you dropped on me, the rats still heard my cries," Kormak said. Apart from his mouth moving, he might have been a statue, and Jaya and Skiver were just as still, she to avoid having her throat cut, him to avoid having his neck broken. "You know I can be very loud when need be. The rats came and dug me out, and dragged me before their masters. That's where they would have taken *you*, fools, if you hadn't attacked them and run away."

"Their masters," Alaeron said. "The astradaemons."

Kormak shrugged. "There are those in the domes, too, I'm told, somewhere up above. But I was below the domes. I spoke to the leukodaemons."

Alaeron frowned. "They are daemons of . . . what, disease?"

"They are devoted to Apollyon, the Horseman of Pestilence, from the daemon realm of Abaddon," Kormak said. "Quite reasonable creatures. They will make any deal at all as long as it helps to spread disease. They're archers, too." He tightened his grip on Jaya. "Their arrows are poisoned with noxious plagues, and their quivers are inexhaustible. They could march forth and destroy the world—but they prefer a slower course. Time for their infections to simmer and spread. Perhaps they eat suffering. I do not know. They've poisoned this whole place, you know. Treasure hunters." Kormak spat. "Here the only treasure is death. The leukodaemons are like your employers. Like your Vadim, and your Chuma. They are traders in relics. The rats, and perhaps even the ape-men, they trade relics looted from Kho, pretending they come from some other ruin in the Mwangi Expanse, and every relic is tainted, spreading strange fevers far and wide, their true source impossible to trace." He chuckled harshly. "I could have let you take your treasures. Followed and watched you succumb to sickness. But you, alchemist, I fear you might have a healer's touch."

Alaeron had never made a particularly deep study of healing potions, though he had some basic ones, but decided it wasn't prudent to argue the point. He was happy with the outcome, after all. This information from Kormak had very likely saved their lives and kept them from falling victim to horrible plagues. Of course, now Kormak was probably going to kill them anyway.

Kormak went on. "So I made an agreement with the leukodaemons. They will spare me. And they will put you and your friends in the cages below the domes, along with the humans stolen from and sacrificed by the savages in these valleys. They will test their new plagues on you, and your suffering will be long, and as you approach death . . ." He snapped his teeth savagely, like a wild dog. "*Then* the astradaemons will descend from their place high in the domes and eat your souls, preventing you from finding rest or peace in the hereafter." He grinned. "This is your reward for leading me such a fine chase."

"What . . . what do *they* get out of this?" Alaeron managed. "The daemons. How do you know they aren't tricking you?"

"There are many interesting things in the Silver Mount, boy," Kormak said. "You know of the strange fluids that give men visions—you made bombs from them, and drove the crew of my ship mad, you may remember. But there are other substances. Bizarre molds and fungi. Spores from beyond the stars. Exotic poisons. Slimes that crawl, and ichors that make limbs turn green, and stink, and burst, revealing bones covered in alien growths. The leukodaemons are very interested in these things. I will take some of their rats back with me to Numeria, and send them home with samples. Everyone is happy. Except for those of you who will suffer and die, of course."

A crowd of rats emerged from behind tumbled ruins, creeping forward with weapons clutched in their forelimbs. Jaya stared at Alaeron, and her eyes were not pleading: it seemed to Alaeron that they were urging him to run. Or was that just some streak of cowardice and wishful thinking?

"Time to stop running," Kormak said, as if reading his mind. Alaeron hoped he didn't have *that* power.

Suddenly, darkness descended, as if a black curtain had been drawn over the sun. Alaeron stumbled back, thinking he'd been struck blind, but Kormak roared, "No more tricks! Darkness cannot hide you. Rats love the dark!"

Whatever the cause of the unnatural darkness, Alaeron could use it to escape and try to plan a rescue attempt later . . . if he could figure out where to run *to*. He chose a direction at random, took three steps, and slammed into someone who wrapped him in an embrace.

"Arcanist," the mad Shory noble whispered in his ear. "I have come to *save* you." He tittered, and Alaeron was lifted off his feet and squeezed by arms that were wiry but impossibly strong.

Kormak roared and bellowed, doubtless trying to find Alaeron, but he had to cope with the magical darkness the noble had conjured while also trying to maintain control of Skiver and Jaya. The noble began to run, carrying Alaeron as easily as the alchemist himself might carry a sack of grain, and the darkness moved with them. The Kellid's roar grew fainter, lost behind them. Alaeron tried to speak, to say, *Wait, my friends, I can't leave my friends*, but the noble's grip was so tight he couldn't draw breath. Ribbons of deeper black seemed to flicker in his vision, and then points of light burst like exploding stars. *Can't breathe. Suffocating. Going to—*

Something prodded Alaeron in the cheek, and he groaned and rolled over. Then he remembered his circumstances, and bolted upright.

The Shory noble stopped poking him with his gnarled wooden staff and leaned back in his throne. Alaeron was on the floor, unbound—not that it mattered. His coat was gone, and his belt with the loops for his vials, and his pack with its weapons and treasures . . . and Ernst's stolen wand.

"Squeezed you too hard, I see, squeezed you right to sleep, ha, but sleep is wonderful, yes? I had not slept since my chamber was breached," the noble said. "It had been *months*. I think I was afraid to sleep, truly, after so long, afraid I wouldn't wake up again. I should thank you, many thanks, yes, I am so *rested*, of course. I think I was going mad, a bit mad, yes yes. But I am not mad now. Also not angry. Never never angry."

Alaeron tried to take a personal inventory. His head didn't ache, which suggested the Shory hadn't hit him on the skull to knock him out, but his tongue felt thick and his brain was not moving as swiftly as it might have. "My friends," he said.

"Yes!" the noble said, nodding. "Friends! I remember friends. Mine are dust, all dust. I looked for other chambers, other safe rooms, but they were all cracked, full of mold and ooze and monsters, no life. Perhaps their children's children's children are in my army now? But I remember. I threatened your friends. That is why you put me to sleep, yes? To save them?"

"That's right," Alaeron said carefully. At least he wasn't actually being murdered. Talk was much better than violence, anyway.

"Yes. But you saved them. Good saving! Until the big man took them. Oh well. Big men do that, don't they, they *take*. He was mighty, he gave chase, he wielded a burning light that cut through my darkness and *nearly* singed my flesh." The Shory grinned. "I made clouds of darkness cling to his face, ha, like leeches feeding on his eyes, and we escaped. You! And I! Now. You will do what you said. You will lift me up high. You will make my city *fly*. You will do this thing."

"Ah. But . . . my friends? Did they escape Kormak— the big man—as well? Are they in a cage here somewhere?"

"Alas! They are with the rats. The big man chased me, but the rats *know* better, they chased your friends instead, much safer, ha. They must be down below the domes now, in the cages. To be tested. There is one plague, I saw, it makes black spots on your skin, and the black spots grow wider and wider, and split open, and inside: little mouths! With little teeth! They bite at others who come near and spread the infection through those bites! Ha. So clever, yes. Not a plague, they said. A parasite? But like a plague. Good. Good for enemies."

"But not good for my friends." Alaeron stood up, only wobbling a little. "And I need them, they're my apprentices, my associates, I need them to help me make your city fly—"

"Proof," the Shory noble said, shrugging. "I can bring your friends back. Not by bargains—I stole you from the daemons, they will not like that, we are enemies now, but I do not fear them. I have an army, bigger than theirs, and I am a *noble*, disease does not touch me, and my soul is protected, wrapped up in wards. But it will cost me many of my people to bring back your friends. I will not pay that price without proof that you can do what you say."

"Fine," Alaeron said. "I can't start with the whole city anyway. But . . . is there a safe place on the surface, where we can work?"

"I am safe everywhere," the noble said blithely. "And when you are with me, so are you. Yes. Safe from everything *except* me. So. Show me. Make my heart glad."

Alaeron had no idea what the arcane engine's lifting capacity was, but when he'd felt his senses expand with the disc in his mouth, he'd been confident that he could move mountains if the need arose. So a ruined chunk of masonry should, logically, provide no difficulty. He was still worried as he looped the golden chain around the twisted metal bars protruding from the floor of the chunk of stone the Shory noble had named his "flying throne room." The throne room was in fact a relatively intact balcony, fallen long ago from some tower, but it had the advantage of actually possessing a railing on one side, which would be a great comfort to Alaeron if they actually managed to get airborne . . . even if the other side of the balcony, which had once been attached to a tower, had no such safety measures in place.

The noble had insisted on dragging his ridiculous chair to the surface, too—or, rather, having his followers do it, hauling it to the surface on ropes. They'd hauled Alaeron up that way, too. The Shory noble couldn't fly, but he climbed walls like a spider, and he'd clambered up from the Pit of Endless Night and shouted encouragement at the workers below. The members of the noble's army were hunched and twisted from a lifetime underground, but they still seemed human, and apparently had a few words of the genuine Shory language mixed in with their patois—or so the noble proudly claimed. They stared at Alaeron with open fascination, though whether it was because he was an outsider or because the noble had decided he was their savior was unclear.

"This is just to show you what I can do," Alaeron said, putting together the pieces of the engine. "I'll need my assistants to do anything on a larger scale." He hadn't figured out how exactly he would follow through on the claim that he could restore Kho to its old magnificence—or, more accurately, how he would wriggle out of the responsibility. But getting Jaya—and even Skiver—back safely was the first priority.

"Yes, yes, let's fly!" The noble sat down in his throne, which his followers had fixed to the ten-foot-wide stone platform by the simple expedient of driving huge spikes through the legs; the antique-lover in Alaeron cried out in silent anguish. "Up, pilot! You shall have a great place in the new empire, yes, great for a commoner. You shall be, hmm . . . helmsman. No, *aeromancer*! That's it, that's better, yes."

Alchemist, arcanist, artificer, and aeromancer, Alaeron thought. Well, why not? He finished connecting the pieces of his arcane engine. "Hold on, ah, my lord?"

"I am an emperor now," the noble said. "You may call me Your Soaring Highness."

"Yes. Of course. Hold tight." Alaeron made sure the golden chain was secure, the engine connected to the platform, and then slipped the disc into his mouth, maintaining a grip on the chain with one hand.

His previous experience had prepared him, but it didn't make things any easier. His consciousness expanded, his body and mind strained for tools he didn't possess . . . but he tried to focus on something simple. *Rise*.

The engine hummed, the gearwheel turned, the golden chain tightened . . . and the ten-foot-wide balcony rose smoothly into the air, dragged along after the engine, which now floated at the end of the taut chain like a kite on a string. That level of levitation barely required any effort at all—like lifting a teacup with your hand, perhaps. Of course, even holding up a teacup would get exhausting given enough time, but Alaeron didn't plan to do this for that long.

The noble pounded his fists on the arms of his throne and cheered as they rose up, five feet, ten feet, fifteen, twenty. The debased Shory followers on the ground hooted and waved their spears in the air.

"Higher!" the noble screamed. "Higher!"

Instead, Alaeron went lower. The noble shrieked in outrage as the balcony settled back to the ground. As the enraged Shory emperor stood up from his throne, Alaeron gave the golden chain a practiced tug and tore it loose from the gearwheel, shutting down the whole engine. He spat the disc out of his mouth. It was speckled with blood, and his nose was trickling a bit too, but his ears and eyes seemed fine. Marvelous. Using the arcane engine at this level would kill him relatively slowly.

"Take me back *up*!" the noble screamed

"Rescue my assistants," Alaeron said.

"I could kill you," the noble said.

"My death won't give you wings," Alaeron replied. His voice was mild. He was too tired to scream and shout and make speeches. So he just shrugged.

Until the noble lifted his arm, and Alaeron realized the lunatic *might* kill him anyway, and then he spoke very quickly: "Why content yourself with just a throne room when the whole city could fly? Save my assistants, and with their help, I will make great things happen!"

The noble lowered his hand. "All right. Yes, a flying chair is fine, a flying city is better." He turned to his followers. "Gather our forces. We strike the Domes at dusk."

"I'm going with you," Alaeron said. If possible, he would get Skiver and Jaya and flee this lunatic.

The noble smiled. "Yes. Because *I* am going, and where I go, you go, Aeromancer."

The domes glittered black and silver under the moon, which seemed bigger and brighter here than it ever had in Andoran, or even Numeria. And the stars! Arrayed in such profusion, each one lighting up unknown worlds. Alaeron felt a stab of sadness. If only he had the resources to use the arcane engine to its fullest capacity, he could see all those worlds. Perhaps if he traveled to Absalom and underwent the test of the Starstone, and succeeded and became a god, he could join Desna as the god of the stars, and leave the cares of this world behind.

Perhaps.

But for now, he had to concentrate on not dying.

The army of the Shory Empire was a ragtag bunch, perhaps a hundred soldiers armed with weapons that ranged from spears tipped with bits of broken metal to ancient ceremonial swords encrusted with gold and gems. They had crept through hidden tunnels, emerging quite close to the Domes of the Polymatum, and now they massed behind their leader . . . which meant, unfortunately, massing behind Alaeron, too. He would have much preferred to be at the rear.

"The daemons have deceived us!" the noble shouted, loud enough to make Alaeron wince. "We have given them souls and slaves, and they promised us the skies, but what have they given us? Empty wind, empty words. But the gods are good. They have brought us aeromancers, yes, three of them, but two are trapped below. We will free them. We will slay!"

Alaeron couldn't tell whether the noble's people even understood him, but they seemed eager enough to fight—to live in the tunnels in the Pit of Endless Night, they must have been accustomed to fighting.

"Now!" the noble shouted, and raced toward the domes, gripping Alaeron by one wrist and dragging him along like a child's doll. The debased Shory descendants followed, eerily silent. Alaeron had never been in a charge before, but he'd expected more whooping—then again, battle cries would rather give away their tenuous element of surprise.

They reached a narrow hole at the base of one dome, no wider than two men going abreast, and Alaeron prayed there wouldn't be guards posted there. He knew little of military strategy, but even he'd heard enough songs and poems to know that a small force could hold a narrow pass for a long time against massed attackers. The fact that the noble leapt into the pit without hesitation suggested that, in addition to his total ignorance of Aeromantic Infandibulum, he also had a profound lack of knowledge about military matters. What exactly *did* Shory nobles know, then? Little of value, it seemed, which might explain why Kho had fallen. Alaeron was Andoren: he knew all about the evils of decadent, useless aristocracy.

No denying the fellow was *brave*, though. Wielding only a ridiculous ornamental sword, he slew the two sleepy rats guarding the tunnel, not even letting go of Alaeron in the process. The alchemist nearly tripped on one of the corpses, though fortunately he kept his feet—otherwise the press of bodies following would have trampled him. Yes, the rear would definitely have been Alaeron's preference, had his wishes been taken into account. Better the trampler than the trampled.

The noble spoke a word and a flurry of floating lights swirled into life, like a swarm of orange fireflies, casting enough light to see by. These tunnels were of soft earth rather than the bedrock of those in the Pit, and the passages had been made for smaller creatures, so Alaeron had to duck his head frequently to dodge away from roots and protruding rocks. There were numerous side-tunnels and branchings, but the noble never hesitated over which direction to choose. He'd been here before, clearly, doubtless to make his arrangements with the daemons. Alaeron wished he'd asked a few more questions about what to expect—

They burst into a huge torchlit chamber, a little piece of Abaddon under the earth. The noble let go of Alaeron and ran, shrieking, toward a group of enormous creatures in the center of the cavern. The alchemist moved aside, pressing his back against the stone wall to the left of the tunnel, making way for the massed Shory warriors, who followed their master.

Alaeron had never seen a leukodaemon. Numeria was not so terribly far from the Worldwound, and monstrous creatures sometimes strayed over the border, so he'd seen the corpses of terrible creatures, all tentacles and teeth and tongues. But these leukodaemons . . . there were four moving about the cavern, each twice the height of a man or more, a sickly greenish aura clinging to them, and all surrounded by clouds of stinking flies. The mist of vermin and poison made it hard to make out their exact shapes, but they were spindly-limbed, and where their heads should have been, they had only the bleached bone skulls of horses—except one, which seemed to bear the skull of one of the monstrous lizards said to hunt deeper in the Mwangi Expanse. Were the skulls somehow their *heads*, or did they merely wear skulls as helmets or decorations, or—

"Help us!" someone shouted, and Alaeron shook himself out of his numb shock. The Shory noble laid about him with his sword, slashing at the daemons, to no apparent effect. One of the leukodaemons swung its ponderous head toward him, and the noble suddenly vanished. At first, Alaeron thought he'd been killed, but then he realized the madman had simply wreathed himself in darkness again, along with many of his followers. Shory descendants were fighting with armored rats and wererats, kicking over piles of jewels and statues and all manner of relics and treasures. Kormak had said the leukodaemons poisoned the relics here, to spread strange plagues throughout the world—this must be where that poisoning happened.

Alaeron shuddered. If they *did* bring Vadim treasures, they would kill him, and perhaps many other people in Almas. This expedition was doomed to failure, but worrying about Vadim's wrath was a problem for another day. He looked around for the source of the cry for help, but everything was chaos and smoke and flies and the clash of metal. The leukodaemons were loosing arrows, fired from enormous bows made of animal bones, killing debased Shory and their own rat-people indiscriminately.

Alaeron climbed up on a heap of boulders and looked around the cavern. There—on the other side of the battle, of course—were stacks of cages made of metal and wood, holding all manner of creatures: apes, pigs, goats, hyenafolk, jungle cats . . . and humans. "Help us!" someone within shouted, and Alaeron began to work his way around the edge of the cavern, sticking close to the wall, trying to avoid the fighting. One of the leukodaemon arrows struck the wall beside him, and where it impacted, writhing worms and greenish slime showered down. After that he ran, making straight for the cage. A dozen humans were inside, Jaya and Skiver among them, the rest presumably kidnapped villagers and sacrificial victims. Two or three were on the cage floor, moaning, glistening with sweat, obviously ill. Skiver grinned and reached through the bars of the cage to clasp Alaeron's hand. "Glad you could make it. Care to let us out?"

Alaeron looked at the cage door. There was no lock, and when he rattled it, the door seemed welded shut. He pulled, but it didn't give. Alaeron sighed. "Just a moment."

The feral mutagen. He'd considered taking it before the battle, but it made him savage—made him *want* to fight—and he didn't want to give up his wits in these circumstances. But now he had little choice. He had no bombs to blow apart the door, and didn't have time to let acid eat the bars. He needed strength. Alaeron tossed back the mutagen, grunted as it hit his system, then shuddered as claws tore from his hands, muscles bulged throughout his body, and teeth lengthened in his mouth. Skiver drew back in alarm, and Alaeron gripped the cage door and strained. He snarled and growled as he pulled, muscles burning and straining, until the door popped free, its hinges squealing under his onslaught. Alaeron hurled the cage door at a pair of giant rats, then waded into the nearest node of the battle, opening rats with his claws, snarling at a wererat in a spiked helmet. He was about to charge a leukodaemon when Jaya screamed in his ear: "Alaeron, let's *go!*"

The battle frenzy began to fade as he asserted his conscious mind over the bestial fury, and he shook himself, snarled in agreement, and followed her toward the tunnels. Some of the escapees were carrying their wounded, and with his feral senses, Alaeron could smell the stink of disease on them. He hoped the Uomoto healers were up to the task of saving them.

The way out of the tunnels was easier: they just kept moving *up*. They met no resistance, and when they reached fresh air, some of the rescued Uomoto began to weep. "Hurry home," Jaya said, kissing a gray-haired man—perhaps her uncle?—on the cheek. A few of the villagers spoke to Alaeron in their own language, presumably thanking him, and he tried to be gracious even as the fangs crowding his mouth began to recede.

"Let's go while we can," Skiver said. "I don't know who's going to survive that fight down there, but I don't want to hang about to congratulate either side on their victory."

"Yes," Alaeron said. "Let's—"

"Let's *fly*!" the noble crowed, leaping up from the hole at the base of the Domes, shadows trailing from his shoulders like a cloak. The villagers shrieked and ran from him—as well they might, since he'd stolen most of them from their homes. Jaya and Skiver stepped back, but didn't run, and Alaeron just raised his hands. "Yes, of course." He glanced at his companions. "I told him how you're my assistants. That I had to save you before we could make his city fly again."

"Of course," Skiver said. "We're what you'd call *essential*."

"Did your people win?" Alaeron said, inclining his head toward the pit.

The noble frowned. "What? They're fighting leukodaemons. Deacons of disease. Handpicked— handmade?—followers of the Horseman of Pestilence. No, my people will all be slaughtered. It's sad, so sad, but that is the price of the sky!"

Alaeron closed his eyes. Saving his friends had meant consigning those poor mad people to death. They'd chosen to follow the noble, true, but *Alaeron* had been the one to pit them against foes they couldn't possibly defeat. And their new emperor obviously cared nothing for the value of their lives.

"Come, come," the noble said. "We go fast, must be fast, much to do, so much work, oh yes."

Alaeron looked behind him. The freed Uomoto were all gone, back home, into the dark. That was something, at least.

The noble hurried swiftly along, and Alaeron and the others went after him, moving as quickly as they could across the broken ground. The noble skipped like a child on his way to a party. "Hurry hurry, fast fast, while the daemons are still busy, yes, before they come looking for me—"

The earth rumbled, and they all stopped and looked back at the domes. Something was moving at the base of one dome, wriggling out of the earth, and a cloud of buzzing black flies rose up before it.

"Too late for that," Skiver said. He drew a knife, then looked at it, and snorted. "I might as well try to fight a bear with a spoon."

"Boring, so *boring*," the noble said, as a leukodaemon slithered up out of the hole and stood. "I want to *fly*, not play with daemons!"

As if in response to his words, the daemon spread terrible black wings, its horse-skull head or helmet swinging back and forth, scanning the night. The creature beat its wings and lifted a few feet off the ground, trying to get a better vantage.

"Stupid daemon!" the noble shouted. "Why should *it* get to fly! Not fair not fair not *fair*!"

That man was their only hope to fight off this demon. The man who'd just called the demon's *attention* by shouting at it. Alaeron didn't like those odds. "Jaya," he said. "Do you still have that sling?"

She handed the sling over wordlessly, her eyes fixed on the daemon and its bow. The daemon drifted back to the earth, then started loping toward them.

Alaeron had a few bottles on his person that contained substances so unique that he was loath to ever use them, because then he wouldn't *have* them any more. One bottle was made of magically treated glass, and contained a substance that Zernebeth had found deep in the Silver Mount, oozing from a shattered bank of machinery. She had insisted that the pink slime was alive, and that it responded to organic matter violently and unpleasantly. She hypothesized that the slime was a scavenger that destroyed organic waste for the denizens of the Mount, though she admitted it might be a weapon, instead. She'd only recovered a small quantity, and an even smaller quantity had found its way into Alaeron's possession. He hadn't studied it thoroughly, being distracted by his relics . . . but perhaps it was time to use it anyway.

Alaeron carefully removed the bottle—the slime inside sensed his warmth and surged toward his hand, making the bottle shift. The thing inside ate through most materials. It had taken Zernebeth ages to develop skymetal-infused glass that could resist its corrosive qualities.

The glass would still shatter with a hard enough impact, though.

Alaeron put the bottle in the sling, whirled it around and around, and slung the pink slime at the onrushing leukodaemon. The glass shattered, but the monster didn't slow. Jaya loosed arrows, and Skiver threw knives, and the Shory noble hurled insults—too annoyed to think of actually *fighting*, it seemed—but nothing had any effect.

Alaeron dropped the sling and grabbed the two flasks he had nearest to hand—just alchemical fire, not even magical, but fire *was* good at burning out disease, so maybe . . . He hurled the flasks just as the leukodaemon leapt into the air again, vast wings stretching out over them, blotting out the moon.

The flasks of fire struck and burned merrily in the creature's wings, limning it in flame. The horse's skull on top seemed to be smiling. The daemon beat its wings, the flame barely an inconvenience, flies buzzing around it like an aura of foulness. The daemon drew its bow.

And then dropped it. The bow fell from suddenly spasming claws, and the daemon tumbled after it, falling to the earth where it crouched, shuddering.

Its skull fell off, bouncing all the way to Alaeron's feet. The bone itself was smoking, and had far more holes than eyes and nostrils could account for. There were smears of pink slime around the new openings.

The daemon writhed, clawing at the place where its neck should have been. The slime had certainly hurt it, or at any rate distracted it, but Alaeron had no illusions that such a creature would die easily. "Run!" he shouted, and immediately led by example.

Skiver and Jaya caught up with him, and the noble ran alongside, as easily as if taking an evening stroll. "Nice, nice, very nice," he cackled. "You will be my Minister of Artillery, too, perhaps, Aeromancer. We will raise the city high, and cast the daemons down, yes, we will!" The noble gestured behind him, and darkness streamed from his fingers like smoke from a fire, a cloud of impenetrable night billowing out to cover their escape. The noble might have done something like that *earlier*, Alaeron thought sourly. He was unlikely to get his hands on something as exotic as that pink slime again.

Not that it mattered, really. Alaeron was by no means certain he would even survive the night. But at least he hadn't been captured and caged by a leukodaemon.

One should celebrate whatever victories one could, he supposed.

"Our destiny is upon us!" the noble shouted from his throne. "We'll shake the daemons from the domes, the shadows from their hill, the marids from the Cistern Major, the flying apes from their towers, yes! The Shory will rise again! And we will rain devastation down upon the upstart empires, yes, the ones who've risen from the ruins we left behind, they will burn. You will make bombs for me, Aeromancer, and we will turn all their cities into ashes."

Alaeron paused in his assembly of the arcane engine. He'd planned to give the Shory possession of the device, to tell him the rest of the city was beyond saving, and hope the madman might be satisfied with a mere flying platform . . . but even that was too great a weapon to give him. The engine could lift huge weights, Alaeron was sure. What if the noble added on to his platform? Enslaved others to build for him? Lashed the engine to some great temple or castle? What if someday he *did* manage, if not a flying city, at least a lethal airship, a flying citadel? A madman who owned the skies . . . Alaeron had led innocents to their deaths today. Could he unleash the Shory noble on the world as well?

"Let me consult with my associates for a moment," Alaeron said, beckoning Jaya and Skiver close. The moon was so bright he could see their faces clearly, which was too bad: Jaya looked terrified, and even Skiver was worried. "Trust me," he said. "I will take the noble away. He . . . won't trouble us again. I'll return if I can, but if I can't . . . This has certainly been a memorable experience. I've learned a lot."

Jaya seized him and kissed him, a kiss more passionate than Alaeron had ever received, and when she released him and stepped back, he just stood, dazed—until Skiver planted a kiss on his mouth, too. He was far less sparing with his tongue than Jaya had been, and his chin far more stubbly. "There," he said, patting Alaeron on the cheek. "For luck, eh? Don't read anything into it."

Alaeron wiped his mouth on the back of his hand—Skiver was a sloppy kisser, and the matter of his breath was best left unconsidered. "Be well," he whispered, then turned toward the noble, who was babbling about finding the other Shory ruins and looking for more stasis chambers, more sleeping nobility. Just what the world needed.

"Majesty!" Alaeron called. "My associates will coordinate matters on the ground. You and I will ascend, and when we have a proper vantage point on the city as a whole, we will begin the great assembly."

"Up!" the noble shouted.

Alaeron lashed the engine to the center of the platform with the golden chain. "If I may, majesty, we are going much higher this time. I had best secure you as well, to make sure the royal personage is safe."

The noble gestured impatiently. "Yes, yes, Aeromancer, do what you think best, only take us up!"

Alaeron stretched out the trailing end of the golden chain and looped it around the noble's ankle, cinching it tight, then extended it farther, looping the chain around the fluted bars of the railing, chaining the engine and the noble alike to this little fragment of the city of the fallen sky.

When he was sure the engine was securely bound, Alaeron touched the chain and slipped the disc into his mouth. He took the platform up as his senses expanded—and when they expanded, he noticed the fifth person in the ruins, crouched atop the crumbling tower beside them. Kormak, of course.

As the platform reached the top of that tower, the Kellid leapt for it, making the whole balcony rock. Alaeron, his body hooked into the engine's workings, remained level as a spinning top, but the Shory noble had to cling to his throne to keep from losing his seat. "Interloper!" he shouted, and stood up.

Finally, Alaeron thought distantly. Someone who can actually kill Kormak.

But the noble took one step and fell on his face. He sat up and began clawing at the chain wrapped around his ankle, but of course it wouldn't come free. The chain was reluctant to unwind at the best of times, unless you knew the trick of it, and Alaeron had bound him well. The noble began to curse rapidly in his own language.

"Treacherous apprentice," Kormak said, crouched on the swaying platform before Alaeron. "Did you think I would let you fly away, little bird? Some of the rats saw you rising up on this balcony earlier today. I thought you might come back here, so I waited. It pleases me to see blood pouring from your nose and your eyes, but you still draw breath, and that offends me. How would you like to die? I can hurl you to your death. But, no, I want to see the light go out of your eyes, I think."

Alaeron was part of the engine now. It was hard to believe the Kellid had been so threatening before, because viewed from this perspective, he was insignificant: an unwieldy blend of fragile flesh, forced into concert with inappropriate pieces of technology, some of which seemed achingly half-familiar to Alaeron in this state.

That technology didn't belong inside Kormak. It was disorderly, it was *wrong*, and with a flick of his wrist, Alaeron used the power of the engine to remove it.

The steel bones in the Kellid's legs tore through his flesh. The Kellid gasped, dropping to the floor of the platform, and Alaeron expected him to slide off and fall. Instead, the man grunted, reached out with his hands, and began to drag himself toward Alaeron.

Even deep in the workings of the engine, some part of Alaeron's mind and body knew fear. As his attention wavered, the platform shifted, and the noble squawked, furious. The movement of the platform worked in Kormak's favor, and the Kellid slid a foot closer. He grinned, blood frothing in his mouth, and wrapped a hand around Alaeron's ankle. The strength in his grip was astonishing, and with a sudden sinking feeling the alchemist knew he would be pulled down. The whole platform would fall from the sky like a dropped stone. They would all die—but Kormak clearly didn't care. "Caught you," the Kellid whispered.

The disc in Alaeron's mouth tingled, and he brought his full focus to bear, making time slow to a trickle while he examined Kormak. There was more metal in him, but it was just a shell of dumb material around his heart, armor he wore on the inside, rendering him immune to heart-strikes from blades. But his heart *itself*, beneath the shell . . .

Alaeron could not speak because of the disc in his mouth, but if he could have, he would have told Kormak: *The heart is an engine too*. Just a pump for taking blood in and forcing blood out under pressure. The heart was a machine of flesh, its actions purely mechanical, and while the armor might stop a blade, it did nothing to improve the function of the engine it protected.

With a thought, Alaeron stopped the Kellid's heart from beating.

Kormak stopped trying to drag himself up Alaeron's body. He looked merely puzzled at first, then enraged . . . and then his face went slack as his body's vital fluids stopped circulating. His grip on the alchemist's leg released.

To stop a heart with a thought. The power of this artifact was intoxicating and monstrous. Alaeron tilted the platform, the movement prompting another dismayed shout from the Shory noble and sending Kormak sliding down and off the edge, tumbling away out of sight.

Alaeron wondered if the Kellid's soul had taken flight when he fell, on its way to whatever afterlife they imagined in the Realm of the Mammoth Lords, or if the astradaemons in the Domes would snag Kormak's eternal essence from the air and devour it.

Alaeron looked up at the moon, a beautiful silver circle in the sky. His vision began to blur. He couldn't do this for much longer. The Shory noble had regained his seat, and he was clapping, shouting, "Yes, Aeromancer, we will tear out *all* their bones, all the upstarts, you will be my engine of war!"

The alchemist looked over the edge of the platform. The ruins of Kho were down there, somewhere, though all he saw was darkness and a handful of tiny points of light that might been bonfires in the villages of the Uomoto. Just a few lights. So many fewer than the stars in the sky.

Alaeron spat the disc out of his mouth, over the edge of the balcony, letting it fall away. His abrupt separation from the engine was jarring, and he fell to the stone balcony, realizing he'd been levitating a few inches without even knowing it. He scrabbled, grabbing hold of the railing and pulling himself up to his knees. The arcane engine whirred louder and they began to rise even faster, straight up. The Shory noble howled with glee as their rate of ascension increased, his plans to reconstitute the city apparently forgotten in the joy of flight.

The air was getting thin, and terribly cold, biting through Alaeron's coat and making his ears and nose go numb. He reached into his pocket with shaking fingers and took out a vial, uncapped it, and swallowed the contents.

Shame I never had a chance to test this one, he thought. I hope it works.

"Your Soaring Majesty," Alaeron said. "Enjoy the stars."

"The stars?" the last emperor of the Shory said, frowning, just before Alaeron stood and let himself fall off the edge of the platform.

He fell, face toward the sky, and watched the platform ascend, briefly blotting out the moon before it began to shrink, diminished by distance. Alaeron's body twisted and turned over, and then he was falling with the wind blowing into his face so hard he had to squeeze his eyes shut, tears streaming across his temples and into his ears.

He tried to fly, though he wasn't sure how exactly one went about that. However it was done, he wasn't doing it properly, that was for sure. He'd used the spell from Ernst's book as the basis for a formula to give him the power of flight, but he hadn't been able to find all the right ingredients. Unable to acquire an eagle's feather, he'd made do with ground batwing, doubtless intended for some necromancer's ritual. The substitution had seemed reasonable enough, in a theoretical sense, but in practice . . . bats were not eagles. And falling was not flight. He'd used the last potion capable of slowing his fall the day Ernst and he figured out how to make the engine fly, and nothing else in his pockets would do him any good now.

Alaeron wondered how long it would be before he hit the ground. Death on impact from such a height would be quick and painless, at least. And he'd get to find out what the afterlife was like, that was something any seeker after knowledge should relish. Though come to think of it, if he landed in Kho, the astradaemons would eat his soul. Shame his last kiss had been with Skiver. Jaya's had been more to his liking. He—

By the gods, he was uncomfortable. Falling wasn't so bad, it was almost pleasant, but why was his *coat* so tight, it didn't fit at all, it was binding up his—his—

Alaeron twisted frantically, tearing the coat off his body and flinging it away, where it caught an updraft and floated off into the dark. It was a wonderful coat, its many pockets full of wonderful things . . .

But it had been binding up his *wings*.

Alaeron laughed as the wings unfolded from his back. They'd torn through his shirt, which was half rags anyway, but his coat had been woven of tougher stuff. He banked and soared and sailed, gliding in slow descending circles, shouting with joy—*this* was flying, not sitting in some chair on a floating balcony, but *this*, swooping on great leathery membranous wings, and he flew around one of the high towers of Kho, startling a few derhii who stared and pointed. "Hello!" he shouted at them, and laughed. He was alive. Kormak was dead. The would-be Shory emperor was chained to a rock well on its way to the spaces between the stars. Why *not* laugh?

Though come to think of it, he had no idea how long this flight spell would last. He arrowed downward, using the moonlight gleaming off the Domes of the Polymatum to orient himself. Jaya and Skiver were still where he'd left them, though now they were standing over a ruined corpse. They squawked in alarm as

Alaeron landed beside them in a crouch, folding his wings instinctively against his body. The wings—the result of his wonderful mutagen—were awkward and unwieldy now that he was on the ground, throwing off his balance terribly.

"Are those *bat's* wings?" Skiver said. Jaya just stared at him, eyes shining in the moonlight.

"No," Alaeron said. "They're no bat's. They're mine." But he grunted in pain as the heavy wings suddenly drooped and then tore loose from his back, falling to the ground and withering like fallen leaves. He reached back and touched his shoulder, and his hand came away wet with blood, but the wounds felt shallow, like he'd torn off two huge scabs. The mutagen could use some refinement, then. But it had gotten him to the ground in one piece.

Jaya threw her arms around him, squeezing him tight, which hurt his fresh wounds, but he wasn't about to complain.

"I was just cutting your Kellid's throat," Skiver said, tucking a knife away and gesturing at what remained of Kormak.

"I told him that the man's *legs* are missing," Jaya said, releasing Alaeron. She never held him for long enough. But maybe, after they got back home . . . "He won't be getting up again. But Skiver said 'better safe.'"

"Can't hurt," Alaeron said. Then he frowned. "Where did you get a knife? Didn't the rat-people disarm you?"

"Took our weapons, our coin, and everything in our packs," Skiver said cheerfully. "Little plundering bastards. But they didn't take my coat, probably because it looks like such shit. Here, you can have it, you look cold." He took off the ragged garment and handed it to Alaeron.

The alchemist took the coat, but almost dropped it, as it weighed far more than he'd expected. "What's in here?"

"I cut a hole so I can slip stuff into the lining," Skiver said, winking. "Basic thief trick, that is."

"So what have you stolen this time?"

"A knife or two. A handful of jewels we took from his Shory majesty's cave. And a few of his other trinkets. I imagine they're the only treasures in this whole place that aren't tainted with some horrible disease or another, what with being sealed in a magic room for six thousand years. They'll have to be enough to satisfy Vadim, though I bet they *won't*." He sighed.

"Well, as to that . . ." Alaeron knelt by Kormak's corpse. He didn't want to look at the body—the Kellid had been a monstrous unstoppable killer, yes, but he was still a man, and Alaeron had seen enough dead men today. He opened the dead man's coat and found the weapons hanging at Kormak's belt, and on a strap across his chest: the tube that belched fire, a slim silver rod tipped with a copper ball, a lens attached to a handle, a six-fingered gauntlet with claws of black metal. "These are relics," Alaeron said. "Not from Kho . . . but it's not as if Vadim will know that. They're unique, unlike anything he's seen before, and if anything, they're even older than the ruins here. And they're not poisoned, which is a point in their favor. Mixed in with those genuine Shory relics, these should serve."

"Good enough for me," Skiver said. "I'm taking the bastard's coat for my own, though. I could use a coat you can't stab, or crush, or set on fire. Never needs cleaning either. Save me loads on my laundry bill." He wrestled the coat off the dead man and shrugged it on. Though Kormak was far taller than Skiver, the coat didn't drag on the ground when Skiver donned it, the hem shortening to just brush the tops of his boots, as it had on the Kellid. Magical—or technological— garments were so useful.

A few derhii came spiraling down, two smaller, one huge with silver fur down his back. "You flew," the silverback said, pointing at Alaeron.

He nodded. "I did."

The derhii sniffed the air. "There are fires beneath the domes of Polymatum. Did you light those?"

Alaeron shrugged. "Indirectly, yes."

"And the madman who said he was a Shory emperor," the derhii said. "The one who came shouting at the bases of our towers, telling us we must be his slaves as we were in ancient times, threatening to kill our young. He has fallen into the sky, chained to a rock, screaming. Was that your doing?"

"I do bear responsibility for that," Alaeron said.

The derhii looked at one another. Then the silverback began to laugh. "You are a hero of the derhii, hairless one! We owe you a debt."

"Good," Skiver said. "How about flying us out of here before the daemons and rats your hero *didn't* kill come after us?"

# Chapter Twenty-Four
## Final Dispositions

The derhii returned them to the village just as the escapees were arriving, and Alaeron and his companions entered along with the others. The entire village woke, and it became an impromptu festival as goats were slaughtered, disgusting fermented fruit drinks poured, and singing, dancing, and chanting bursting out around every fire. The village shamans clucked over the sick and took them away to work their healing arts, and one slathered a cooling goop over Alaeron's shoulder wounds, though she either didn't understand or pretended not to when he asked what the ingredients were.

There were some oathbreakers and criminals among those who'd returned, people chained to the Stone of Sacrifice, but upon hearing of the horrors that befell those so sacrificed, the village elders agreed they would be merely exiled instead, and they were permitted to spend the night and take part in the feast.

"Hell of a homecoming, that," Skiver said, shaking his head and sipping something that smelled of goat milk and alcohol. "Poor bastards."

"Better than being experimented on by leukodae-mons," Alaeron said, watching Jaya talk with her uncle, aunt, and cousins who'd been rescued from the cages in the fleshpit. "Do you think the monsters will try to take revenge on this village?"

Skiver shrugged. "They've been there who knows how many centuries, and never come out before. I think they like to lurk in secret. Daemons like that have masters, don't they, just like everyone else? They serve Apple-John, or something, the Shory noble said. I imagine they'll get a stern talking-to for letting some of their prisoners escape. And with the Shory army stuck down there, they'll have plenty of victims to keep them busy, lots of souls to eat and that."

Alaeron shuddered. "Don't remind me. Those people died because of me—"

"Stop that shit talk," Skiver said. "They pledged their service to a lunatic, and they got what you get when you do that. You put an end to his reign, didn't you, and saved all these people in Jaya's village. How many would he have taken? He could have emptied these foothills in his quest for the sky. Now he won't. It's not a clean win, I'll grant you, but nothing in this world's clean, is it?"

"I suppose you're right," Alaeron said.

"Shame you lost all your relics," Skiver said.

Alaeron nodded. "Yes. But I figured out what they were first. Frankly, they became a lot less interesting for me after that. And anyway, on the trip back, I'll be busy figuring out how to disable those weapons we took from Kormak. I'll let Vadim have them as interesting relics, but not as working weapons. That kind of power in criminal hands . . . no offense."

Skiver shrugged. "Vadim's a bastard. I don't blame you. He could have paid off my debts quick as that." He snapped his fingers. "Took it out of my wages, even. I could have stayed at home. But he thought I'd learn a lesson about gambling beyond my means if I had to flee the city just ahead of the leg-breakers. I learned some lessons, all right. Still, when I get you lot home with a sack of plunder, he'll make things square with the ones I owe. It'll be nice to get back home. I've had my fill of foreign parts. I need *ale*."

Alaeron frowned. "How are we *getting* back?"

"Coat full of jewels," Skiver reminded him. "And I took a fat purse off Kormak, too—he came well-provisioned for hunting you. We'll travel back to Almas in great style. The derhii say they can carry us north into Thuvia, and we can get a riverboat to the ocean and a ship to Absalom from there. And from Absalom, it's easy. We'll give Vadim his treasures and . . ." He shrugged. "See what happens. I bet you and Jaya might get a bit closer, eh?"

"One can hope," Alaeron said, and grinned almost as widely as his friend usually did.

They spent three days in the village. Jaya wanted to make sure there would be no retribution from Kho, and to spend time with her family. But finally, following a last night of feasting and celebration, the villagers played their drums and called down the derhii, who told them there was fresh war in the ruins. Sensing the weakness of the rat-people and the daemons, the strange crystalline creatures and the debased humanoids from beneath the earth were attacking, and the other denizens of the valley were lending their support to one side or another, or attempting to profit from the disarray.

"Look at you," Skiver said, punching Alaeron in the shoulder. "Increasing chaos wherever you go."

The flying apes carried them north to the river city of Lamasara. Once they hit the coast, they found a ship heading northwest and Skiver paid the captain enough to convince him to head northeast instead. Alaeron had hoped Jaya would want to share a cabin with him, but she took her own quarters, saying she knew he needed space to work on disabling the artifacts stolen from Kormak, and she didn't want to get in his way. Whenever he tried to kiss her, she would just talk about how eager she was to see her brother again. *Once we're home,* Alaeron thought, *and she knows he's all right, when she sees everything is fine, then . . .*

"Well," Vadim said, holding up a golden statue of a derhii to the light. "I must say. I expected you all to die. Maybe not Skiver," he amended. "But the alchemist, definitely, and I thought the girl-thief would be killed trying to escape at some point. And instead, you bring me . . . this. A statue of an ape with wings. I had expected rather less, I admit. But I'd been hoping for rather *more.*"

"My brother," Jaya said. "Free him." She was gripping Alaeron's hand so tightly it made his fingers cramp.

Vadim leaned back in his chair, drumming his fingertips on the desk and gazing at the two sitting in hard wooden chairs across from him. Shelves behind him held relics from all over Golarion . . . but nothing from Kho. Or from the Silver Mount, for that matter.

"One statue," Vadim said flatly. "Gold, yes, lovely gold, but do you know what I invested to send you on this trip? What it cost me, arranging for your travel, supplying Skiver with coin? And you bring me *one statue*? I will *kill* your brother, Jaya, I—"

"You don't want to do that, boss," Skiver said, scraping delicately at his nails with the blade of a thin silver knife. He was still wearing Kormak's coat, and looked quite menacing in it. "Why, kill her brother, and these two might not deliver the rest of the things they found in Kho. A cask of jewels. A little carving of a tower on a cloud. Some other statues. Oh, and lots of strange relics made of . . . what's it called, alchemist?"

"Skymetal," Alaeron said levelly. "It's not surprising the Shory had such things—they were *masters* of the sky."

"And where are these treasures?" Vadim said softly.

"They thought it would be better to put them in a safe place," Skiver said, "until Jaya got her brother back, and Alaeron got your word you wouldn't trouble him any further."

"If they trusted my *word*," Vadim said, "they wouldn't need to resort to such measures."

"I never said it was logical," Skiver said. "But they said they wanted to take measures, and these are the measures they took."

"And you just allowed this?" Vadim's voice was disturbingly calm.

Skiver shrugged. "They saved my life. More than once. Rescued me when a lunatic who lived in the tunnels under Kho wanted to feed me to a daemon."

"So you feel you owe them a debt of honor," Vadim said.

"It's more about wanting to make sure you honor all *your* debts," Skiver said.

Vadim stared, eyes hard, and the two guards behind him shifted. For a moment, Alaeron thought it would turn to violence, but then Vadim snorted. "You're a shifty shit, Skiver, but it's not like I didn't know that going in. Guess you'll want proof I paid off your debts, too, won't you?"

"It would set my mind at ease," Skiver said.

"Ha. I did it before you left town—what, did you think I'd just sit around watching the interest build up? I didn't doubt *you'd* return. I'll get you a receipt.

But you, Skiver—*you*, personally, on pain of the kind of pain you know I can bring down on you—you will give me your guarantee that the relics they brought back are worth canceling their debts?"

Skiver just nodded. "You'll have the only absolutely guaranteed relics from the ruins of Kho. That should be worth more than all three of us combined."

Vadim stroked his beard, then shrugged. "I hate a square deal, but sometimes that's the only deal in town. You, archer, had better piss off out of my city, though, and if I ever hear of you dealing in relics again—fake *or* real—it'll be the end of you. Understood?"

"Yes, sir," Jaya said, lowering her eyelids demurely. "I understand, and once again, I am sorry my desperate circumstances led me to deceive you." As always, Alaeron was amazed at her acting ability: as if she hadn't been cursing Vadim's name just the day before, as if she were genuinely contrite. She should give up being a thief and hunter and take up life on stage.

"Take her to her brother, Skiver," Vadim said. "And then see them both to the edge of the city. You, alchemist, are welcome to stay in Almas. And I trust you'll stay out of my affairs in future?"

"I will, of course," Alaeron said, squeezing Jaya's hand. "But I think I'll go where Jaya does."

Vadim rolled his eyes. "Young love," he said. "Doesn't it sicken you, Skiver?"

"More than anything, sir," Skiver said.

They'd taken her brother out of the cage in the basement and put him in a small ground-floor room that held nothing but a bed, a table, a washbasin, and a chamber pot. When Skiver opened the door, the prisoner was doing push-ups with his shirt off, his dark skin glistening with sweat. "Doesn't he look delicious," Skiver said, and the man looked up, then sprang to his feet with the sort of natural athleticism Alaeron had always felt he, himself, was unfortunate in lacking.

"Do you know, I don't even know his name," Alaeron began, but then Jaya shouted "Letsego!" and flung herself at him.

Letsego swept her up, embracing her, and she wrapped her legs around his waist and kissed him, fiercely, tangling her fingers in his hair.

"Ah," Alaeron said, blinking. "You two must be . . . very close."

Letsego lowered Jaya to the ground, then frowned. "Well, yes, of course we're close, we're—"

Jaya cleared her throat. "He thinks we're brother and sister, Letso."

The man widened his eyes. "You kept up that charade all this time?"

Alaeron swallowed, but it still felt like he had a stone in this throat.

Jaya shrugged, looking embarrassed—but what did it matter how she *looked*? She gave away nothing she didn't mean to, Alaeron realized now. "It just never seemed like the right time to tell them," she said, and then put her arm around the man. "Skiver. Alaeron. I'd like you to meet Letsego. My husband."

Alaeron didn't answer. Skiver let out a long, low whistle. "Well, well," he said, and bent at the waist. "As far as liars go, let me bow to the master."

On the ride to the outskirts of Almas, Jaya sat beside Alaeron in the back of the cart, speaking insistently into his ear. "I'm sorry, it's just, Letso and I have often found that it's better for me to be seen as . . . *available*, potentially. It's nothing *personal*, I wasn't lying to you specifically, it's just one of the things we do, we pose as brother and sister. It's not nice, I know, but it's hard to make a living, and when no one knows I'm married, it gives me certain . . . options, do you understand? I admit, at first, I wanted to string you along, too, to make sure you'd come help me, but I *did* grow fond of you, truly, and I *would* have told you the truth, but I didn't want you to be angry with me, and on the way home, there was never the right *time*—"

She's much more talkative when she isn't lying, Alaeron thought numbly. "What about Ernst? Were you . . . *fond* . . . of him, too?"

"We needed a wizard," she said, drawing away from him. "I wanted to ensure his loyalty. I didn't think that sort of . . . encouragement . . . was *necessary* with you."

"Oh, no," Alaeron said numbly. "I'm loyal even in the absence of encouragement. Devoted, even. To a fault."

"I never lied to you," she said. "Well, apart from the big lie, about Letso being my brother, but I never promised you anything else, you know, about *us*, about what we might be."

"But you *looked* at me," he said. "You touched my hand. You touched my cheek. And that kiss—"

"I thought you were going to die, idiot," she said. "And Skiver kissed you, too, did you think that meant you had a future together?" She sighed. "I know I used you. And I'm sorry. Truly."

The cart slowed. "Everyone out!" Skiver shouted. "Walk east and stay out of Almas, all right? I just know Vadim would send me to kill you if you ever came back, Jaya, and that would be awkward for both of us."

Jaya reached out to touch Alaeron, but he shied away, not looking at her face. She sighed. "Be well, alchemist," she said, and jumped down. Alaeron heard her making her farewells to Skiver—the man didn't seem to hold her long deception against her, but why would he?—and then Letsego's head popped over the side of the cart.

"I wanted to thank you," he said. "For helping my Jaya. And for bringing her back safe."

His head is such a pretty target, Alaeron thought. And me without any bombs. "Take care of her," he said.

"Oh, she can take care of herself," Letsego said, and winked.

After they were gone, Skiver climbed into the back of the cart. He sat down beside Alaeron, but didn't say anything.

Finally the alchemist sighed. "Well," he said. "I wish I knew where to go from here."

"Oh, that's an easy one," Skiver said. "We go *drinking*."

Skiver had either held on to some of the jewels from Kho or Vadim had paid him well for his services. Either way, he took Alaeron to a rather fine tavern and paid for a curtained alcove so they could sit on cushions and drink in seclusion. Before long Alaeron was deep in his cups, lamenting Jaya's betrayal, cursing himself for a fool, and shrugging off Skiver's attempts at consolation and filthy jokes alike. He stared glumly into a small glass of brown liquid and said, "Heartbreak aside, there are practical considerations here. I was hoping to leave with her. She's cunning, and well-traveled, and knows the world. I thought she could help me disappear. I can't stay here. What if the Technic League sends someone else after me? They aren't the forgiving sort. What do I do *then*?"

"I was thinking about that," Skiver said. "How about we send them a message explaining that their man

Kormak was murdered by one Ralen Vadim, who now has in his hands a great lot of Technic League weaponry, which he's planning to sell?"

Alaeron raised his head, blinking. "What?"

"And you tell them you'll be happy to give them details of Vadim's security arrangements, and the layout of his house, and where he's probably storing their artifacts, and when he's likely to be out and about and not very well guarded, and all that, in exchange for them forgiving your misbehavior?"

"You would betray Vadim that way?" Alaeron said.

"Vadim? He's like a father to me, Alaeron. Wait, I didn't have a father, just my mother's boyfriend, and he used to beat me with a strap and call me a bastard and kick me up and down the street." He grinned. "The man's getting too old, anyway. I think I could do a better job running his enterprises in Almas than *he* can, and I've got all the right connections, both locally and overseas—or did you think all that time I spent wandering around Absalom was used making crooked bar bets? The only thing standing in my way is Vadim himself. Did you see how he let Jaya's brother go? And didn't even chop off your hands or anything? Clear sign he's getting too old and soft."

"It's worth a try," Alaeron said slowly. "But the Technic League is treacherous. They might pretend to an agreement, and then try to kill me anyway. They're *not* soft."

"Oh, if they want to do it the hard way, we can make some provisions for that, too." He reached into Kormak's coat and removed a squarish object, moon-silver, and set it on the table. Then he drew out an impossibly long rod, like a black metal spear, topped with a flower of razor-sharp petals, and laid that on the table, too. "Did you ever wonder," he said, removing a silver chain topped with a spiked golden ball, "how the Kellid bastard carried around so much artillery?" As he spoke, he continued to remove objects—orbs that flickered with rainbow colors, a coiled whip that slithered of its own accord, a teardrop-shaped crystal that pulsed with bloody red light, a multi-legged thing like a cockroach the size of a rat that waved its antenna, and more besides. "He kept a few things on his belt, close to hand, but there's much more hidden in the coat. He was a walking armory, that one. This coat's not just stab-proof. The pockets in here are *deep*."

"Extradimensional space," Alaeron said, eyes widening as Skiver continued to pile up tools of the Technic League on the scarred wooden table. "A coat whose pockets are bigger on the inside than the outside!"

"Now, I don't know how to use any of these things," Skiver said. "But, you know . . . I bet you can figure them out. So if the League does try to betray you, we can make them regret it. What do you say? Want to join my new organization? We'll get you all set up in a new lab, get you a pretty assistant to wash your bottles for you, and so forth. Eh?"

"These artifacts," Alaeron said breathlessly, picking up one of the rainbow-orbs. It flashed more quickly when he touched it, lights flickering in concert with his pulse. "What could they all do? What could they all *be*? It could take me *years* to unlock all their mysteries!"

"I'll order us another round," Skiver said, clapping him on the back. "We should celebrate. After all, you look like a man in love."

# About the Author

Tim Pratt's stories have appeared in *The Best American Short Stories*, *The Year's Best Fantasy and Horror*, and other nice places. He is the author of two story collections, most recently *Hart & Boot & Other Stories*, as well as a poetry collection. He has also written several novels, including the contemporary fantasies *The Strange Adventures of Rangergirl* and *Briarpatch*; the Forgotten Realms novel *Venom in Her Veins*; and, as T. A. Pratt, seven books in the urban fantasy series about ass-kicking sorcerer Marla Mason: *Blood Engines*, *Poison Sleep*, *Dead Reign*, *Spell Games*, *Broken Mirrors*, *Grim Tides*, and the prequel *Bone Shop*. He edited the anthology *Sympathy for the Devil*, and will co-edit the forthcoming *Rags & Bones* anthology with Melissa Marr.

Tim has won a Hugo Award for best short story, a Rhysling Award for best speculative poetry, and an Emperor Norton Award for best San Francisco Bay Area-related novel. His books and stories have been nominated for Nebula, Mythopoeic, World Fantasy, and Stoker Awards, among others, and have been translated into French, Czech, Dutch, Russian, Greek, Korean, Spanish, German, and a few other languages.

He lives in Berkeley California with his wife Heather Shaw and son River, and works as a senior editor and occasional book reviewer at *Locus*, the Magazine of the Science Fiction and Fantasy Field. He blogs intermittently at **www.timpratt.org**.

# Acknowledgments

Though no book is written without a lot of hours spent sitting alone and mumbling to oneself, I wouldn't be able to carve out those hours without help from others. My thanks first to my wife Heather Shaw, who is unfailingly supportive; to my young son River, who sometimes lets me sit on a bench and write in between games of tag and hide-and-go-seek at the park; to my agent Ginger Clark, for making the deal happen; to my editor James Sutter for being so enthusiastic about and supportive of my weird ideas; and to my co-workers at *Locus*, for general awesomeness and flexibility.

# Glossary

All Pathfinder Tales novels are set in the rich and vibrant world of the Pathfinder campaign setting. Below are explanations of several key terms used in this book. For more information on the world of Golarion and the strange monsters, people, and deities that make it their home, see the *Pathfinder Roleplaying Game Core Rulebook*, the *Inner Sea World Guide*, or the *Pathfinder Roleplaying Game Beginner Box*, or visit **paizo.com**.

For further reading on the history of Kho and the strange creatures living in its ruins, as well as tips and rules for incorporating it into your roleplaying game, see *Pathfinder Campaign Setting: Lost Cities of Golarion*.

**Abaddon:** Evil plane devoted to destruction and home to daemons.

**Absalom:** Largest city in the Inner Sea region.

**Aeromantic Infandibulum:** Ancient magic which powered the flying cities of the Shory Empire, and which modern spellcasters have been unable to replicate.

**Alchemist:** A spellcaster whose magic takes the form of potions, explosives, and strange mutagens that modify his own physiology.

**Almas:** Capital city of Andoran.

**Andoran:** Democratic and freedom-loving nation north of the Inner Sea.

**Andoren:** Of or pertaining to Andoran; someone from Andoran.

**Apollyon:** Horseman of Pestilence. One of the four lords of all daemons.

**Arcane:** Type of magic that does not come from a deity.

**Astradaemon:** Extremely powerful evil fiend that consumes mortal souls.

**Azlant:** The first human empire, which sank beneath the waves long ago.

**Barrier Wall:** Mountain range that separates the deserts of northern Garund from the jungles of the Mwangi Expanse.

**Black Sovereign:** The ruler of Numeria—once a mighty barbarian warrior, but now hopelessly addicted to alien drugs supplied by the Technic League.

**Chelaxian:** Someone from Cheliax.

**Cheliax:** Devil-worshiping nation.

**Chelish:** Of or relating to the nation of Cheliax.

**Coins:** Mercantile district in Absalom.

**Daemons:** Evil denizens of Abaddon who exist to devour mortal souls.

**Derhii:** Intelligent flying apes.

**Desna:** Good-natured goddess of dreams, stars, travelers, and luck.

**Dwarves:** Short, stocky humanoids who excel at physical labor, mining, and craftsmanship. Stalwart enemies of the orcs and other evil subterranean monsters.

**Eagle Knights:** Military order in Andoran devoted to spreading the virtues of justice, equality, and freedom.

**Elves:** Long-lived, beautiful humanoids who abandoned Golarion millennia ago and have only recently returned. Identifiable by their pointed ears, lithe bodies, and pupils so large their eyes appear to be one color.

**Eye of Abendego:** Enormous permanent hurricane west of Garund.

**Garund:** Continent south of the Inner Sea, renowned for its deserts and jungles.

**Gearsmen:** Powerful metal automatons retrieved from the Silver Mount, which obey the commands of the Technic League—at least, most of the time.

**Gembasket:** Legendary location in Katapesh, said to be bursting with precious jewels.

**Gnomes:** Race of fey humanoids known for their small size, quick wit, and bizarre obsessions.

**Golarion:** The planet containing the Inner Sea region and the primary focus of the Pathfinder campaign setting.

**Hadi:** Strange society of intelligent, oversized rats found only in the ruins of Kho.

**Half-Elves:** The children of unions between elves and humans. Taller, longer-lived, and generally more graceful and attractive than the average human, yet not nearly so much so as their full elven kin.

**Halflings:** Race of humanoids known for their tiny stature, deft hands, and mischievous personalities.

**Half-Orcs:** Bred from humans and orcs, members of this race have green or gray skin, brutish appearances, and short tempers, and are mistrusted by many societies.

**Harrow Deck:** Deck of illustrated cards sometimes used to divine the future. Favored by Varisians.

**Hellspawn:** A human whose family line includes a fiendish taint, often displayed by horns, hooves, or other devilish features. Rarely popular in civilized society.

**Hyenafolk:** Bestial and savage race of hyena-headed humanoids.

**Inner Sea Region:** The heart of the Pathfinder campaign setting, centered around the eponymous inland sea. Includes the continents of Avistan and Garund, as well as the seas and other nearby lands.

**Irrisen:** A realm of permanent winter north of Varisia, claimed by Baba Yaga and ruled by her daughters. Currently controlled by Queen Elvanna and her bloodline, the jadwiga Elvanna.

**Katapesh:** Mighty trade nation on the eastern coast of Garund.

**Keleshite:** Of or related to the Empire of Kelesh, far to the east of the Inner Sea region.

**Kellid:** Traditionally uncivilized and violent human ethnicity from the far north.

**Kho:** Legendary flying city of the ancient Shory Empire, which crashed thousands of years ago for unknown reasons, landing in the jungles of the Barrier Wall Mountains, just north of the Mwangi Expanse.

**Leukodaemon:** Evil fiend that harvests mortal souls via disease and pestilence.

**Mana Wastes:** Region in Garund where an ancient magical war renders spells unreliable.

**Mwangi Expanse:** The massive jungle region spanning a huge portion of Garund.

**Mwangi:** Of or pertaining to the hot, southern jungle region known as the Mwangi Expanse; someone from that region.

**Nex:** Nation in Garund formerly ruled by a powerful wizard of the same name.

**Numeria:** Land of barbarians and strange alien technology harvested from a crashed starship near the nation's capital.

**Orcs:** A bestial, warlike race of humanoids originally hailing from deep underground, who now roam the surface in barbaric bands. Universally hated by more civilized races.

**Osirian:** Of or relating to the region of Osirion, or a resident of Osirion.

**Osiriani:** The native language of Osirion.

**Osirion:** Desert kingdom ruled by pharaohs in northeastern Garund.

**Outer Planes:** The various realms of the afterlife, where most gods reside.

**Pathfinder Lodge:** Meeting house where members of the Pathfinder Society can buy provisions and swap stories.

**Pathfinder Society:** Organization of traveling scholars and adventurers who seek to document the world's wonders. Based out of Absalom and run by a mysterious and masked group called the Decemvirate.

**Pathfinder:** A member of the Pathfinder Society.

**River Sphinx:** The main river running through Osirion.

**Rovagug:** The Rough Beast; the evil god of wrath, disaster, and destruction. Imprisoned deep beneath the earth by the other deities.

**Ruby Prince:** Khemet III, the Forthbringer, current ruler of Osirion.

**Screaming Jungle:** Dangerous jungle south of the Mwangi Expanse.

**Sellen River:** Major river that borders Andoran and leads from the Inner Sea up to Numeria.

**Shory:** Ancient empire, now long since fallen to obscurity, which was most famed for its flying cities.

**Silver Mount:** A great vessel from another world that crashed down from the sky long ago and landed in Numeria, forming a huge metal mountain that leaks strange ichors. Explorers sometimes breach its inner chambers and retrieve strange technological artifacts, most of which are subsequently controlled by the Technic League.

**Skymetal:** Metal that falls to Golarion as meteorites and has exceptional (and sometimes magical) qualities.

**Slave Trenches of Hakotep:** Ancient Osirian monument in which potentially thousands of stone pillars stand arranged in strange patterns, each one containing the spirit of a bound elemental. Its purpose remains unknown.

**Sorcerer:** Spellcaster who draws power from a supernatural ancestor or other mysterious source, and does not need to study to cast spells.

**Sothis:** Capital of Osirion.

**Starfall:** The capital of Numeria, located near the base of the Silver Mount.

**Starstone:** Stone that fell from the sky ten thousand years ago, creating an enormous dust cloud that blotted out the sun and began the Age of Darkness, wiping out most preexisting civilizations. Eventually raised up from the ocean by Aroden and housed in the Cathedral of the Starstone in Absalom, where those who can pass its mysterious and deadly tests can ascend to godhood.

**Taldan:** Of or from Taldor; a citizen of Taldor.

**Taldane:** The common trade language of Golarion's Inner Sea region.

**Taldor:** Former empire in the Inner Sea region, now mostly fallen into decadence.

**Tarrasque:** One of the Spawn of Rovagug, a legendary monster said to be nearly unstoppable.

**Technic League:** Corrupt society of researchers who comb through the wreckage of the Silver Mount looking for strange technology that they can exploit for personal gain.

**Test of the Starstone:** Deadly trial in which mortals attempt to pass through magical traps surrounding the Starstone and actually touch its surface, thus being transformed into gods. Rarely passed.

**Thuvia:** Desert nation on the Inner Sea, famous for the production of the magical sun orchid elixir.

**Towers:** Gambling game using a harrow deck.

**Ulunat:** One of the Spawn of Rovagug, a great beetle whose shell still stands in Osirion and provides shelter to the mansions of the city's most wealthy.

**Uomoto:** Tribe of Mwangi people living closest to the ruins of Kho.

**Varisia:** A frontier region northwest of the Inner Sea.

**Varisian:** Something from Varisia, or else a member of the often maligned Varisian ethnic group, which is known for its music, dance, and traveling caravans.

**Vudrani:** Someone or something from the exotic continent of Vudra, far to the east of the Inner Sea.

**Wererat:** Rodent lycanthrope; someone who can change from a humanoid to a rat and back again.

**Wizard:** Someone who casts magical spells through research of arcane secrets and the constant study of spells, which he or she records in a spellbook.

**Worldwound:** Constantly expanding region overrun by demons a century ago. Held at bay by the efforts of the Mendevian crusaders.

I n a village of the frozen north, a child is born possessed by
a strange and alien spirit, only to be cast out by her tribe
and taken in by the mysterious winter witches of Irrisen, a
land locked in permanent magical winter. Farther south, a
young mapmaker with a penchant for forgery discovers that
his sham treasure maps have begun striking gold.

This is the story of Ellasif, a barbarian shield maiden who
will stop at nothing to recover her missing sister, and Declan,
the ne'er-do-well young spellcaster-turned-forger who wants
only to prove himself to the woman he loves. Together they'll
face monsters, magic, and the fury of Ellasif's own cold-hearted
warriors in their quest to rescue the lost child. Yet when they
finally reach the ice-walled city of Whitethrone, where trolls
hold court and wolves roam the streets in human guise, will
it be too late to save the girl from the forces of darkness?

From *New York Times* best-selling author Elaine
Cunningham comes a fantastic new adventure of swords and
sorcery, set in the award-winning world of the Pathfinder
Roleplaying Game.

***Winter Witch*** print edition: $9.99
ISBN: 978-1-60125-286-9

***Winter Witch*** ebook edition:
ISBN: 978-1-60125-332-3

# Winter Witch

## Elaine Cunningham

# PATHFINDER®

## · TALES ™ ·

The race is on to free Lord Stelan from the grip of a wasting curse, and only his old mercenary companion, the Forsaken elf Elyana, has the wisdom—and the swordcraft—to uncover the identity of his tormenter and free her old friend before the illness takes its course.

When the villain turns out to be another of their former companions, Elyana sets out with a team of adventurers including Stelan's own son on a dangerous expedition across the revolution-wracked nation of Galt and the treacherous Five Kings Mountains. There, pursued by a bloodthirsty militia and beset by terrible nightmare beasts, they discover the key to Stelan's salvation in a lost valley warped by weird magical energies. Will they be able to retrieve the artifact the dying lord so desperately needs? Or will the shadowy face of betrayal rise up from within their own ranks?

From Howard Andrew Jones, managing editor of the acclaimed sword and sorcery magazine *Black Gate*, comes a classic quest of loyalty and magic set in the award-winning world of the Pathfinder Roleplaying Game.

***Plague of Shadows*** print edition: $9.99
ISBN: 978-1-60125-291-3

***Plague of Shadows*** ebook edition:
ISBN: 978-1-60125-333-0

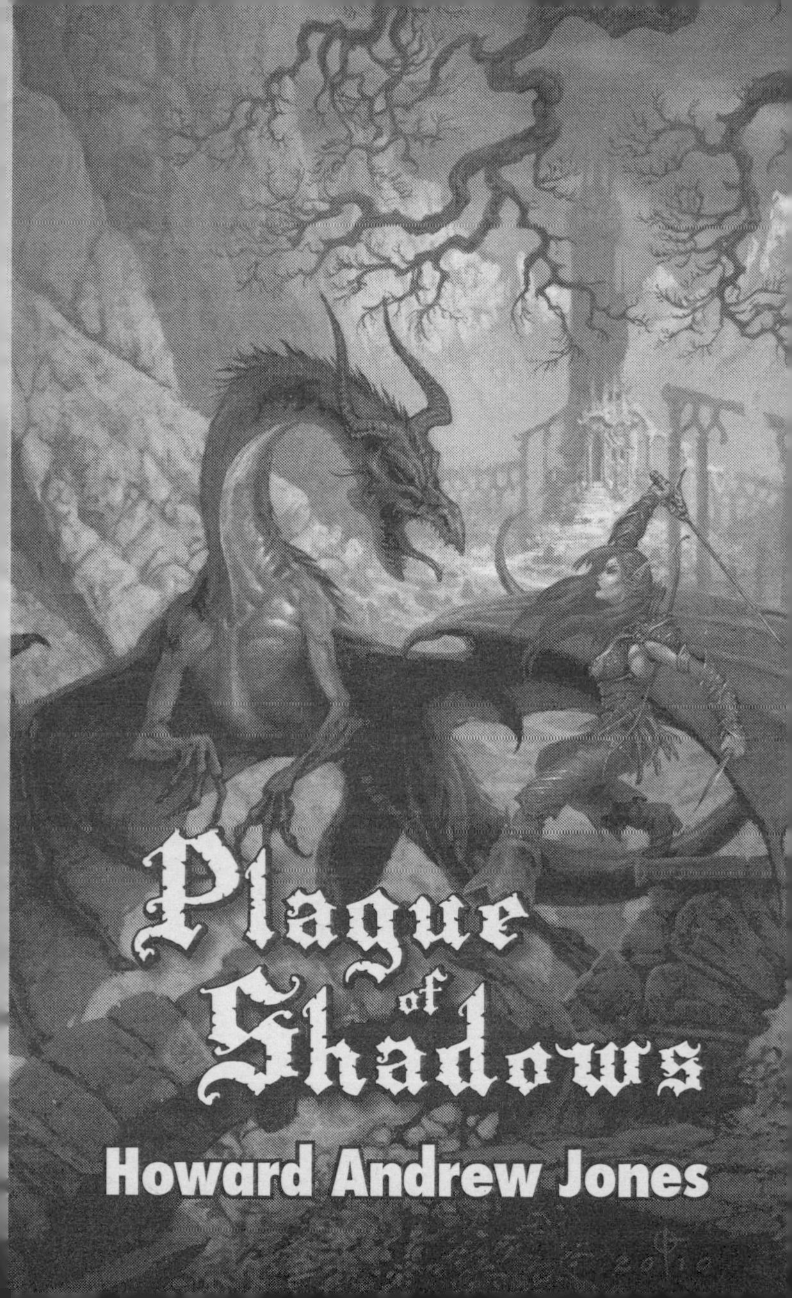
Plague of Shadows
Howard Andrew Jones

In the foreboding north, the demonic hordes of the magic-twisted hellscape known as the Worldwound encroach upon the southern kingdoms of Golarion. Their latest escalation embroils a preternaturally handsome and coolly charismatic swindler named Gad, who decides to assemble a team of thieves, cutthroats, and con men to take the fight into the demon lands and strike directly at the fiendish leader responsible for the latest raids—the demon Yath, the Shimmering Putrescence. Can Gad hold his team together long enough to pull off the ultimate con, or will trouble from within his own organization lead to an untimely end for them all?

From gaming legend and popular fantasy author Robin D. Laws comes a fantastic new adventure of swords and sorcery, set in the award-winning world of the Pathfinder Roleplaying Game.

*The Worldwound Gambit* print edition: $9.99
ISBN: 978-1-60125-327-9

*The Worldwound Gambit* ebook edition:
ISBN: 978-1-60125-334-7

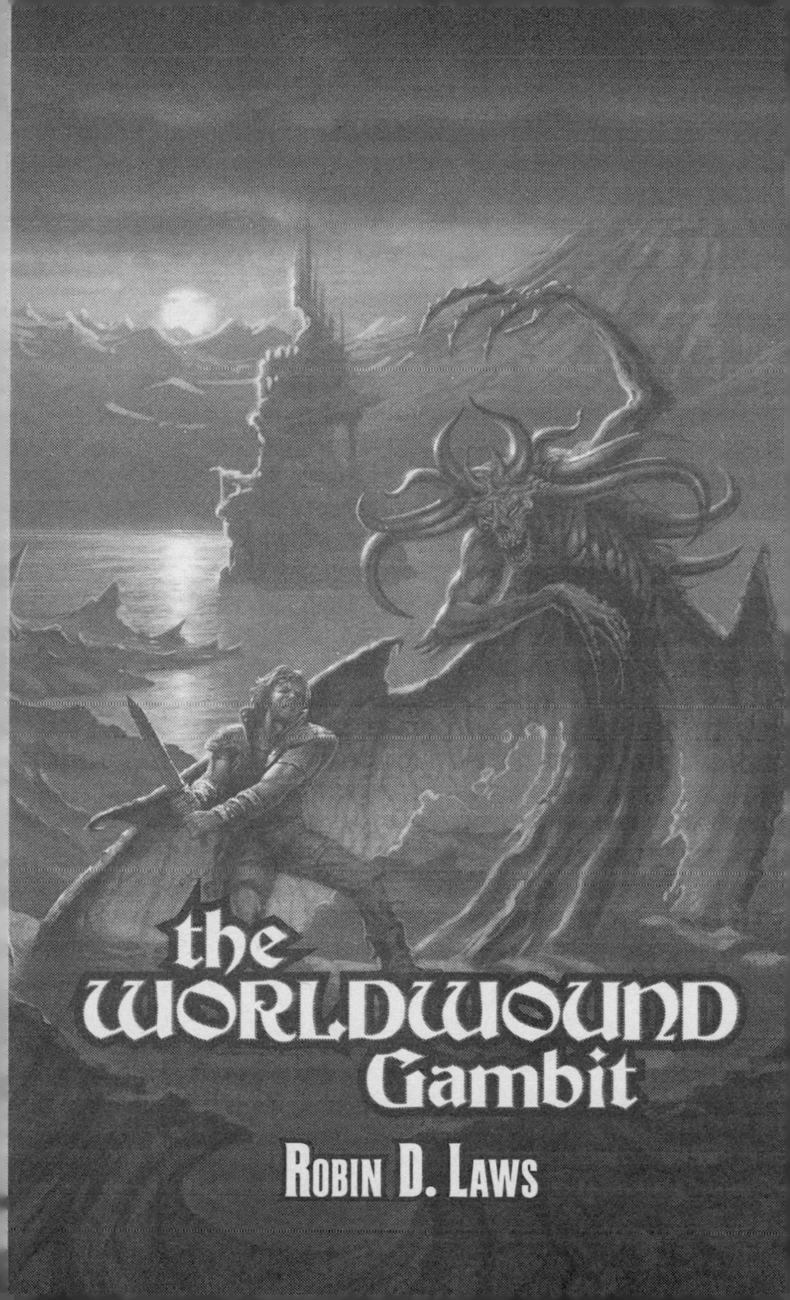
the
WORLDWOUND
Gambit
Robin D. Laws

**O**n a mysterious errand for the Pathfinder Society, Count Varian Jeggare and his hellspawn bodyguard Radovan journey to the distant land of Tian Xia. When disaster forces him to take shelter in a warrior monastery, "Brother" Jeggare finds himself competing with the disciples of the Dragon Temple as he unravels a royal mystery. Meanwhile, Radovan—trapped in the body of a devil and held hostage by the legendary Quivering Palm attack— must serve a twisted master by defeating the land's deadliest champions and learning the secret of slaying an immortal foe. Together with an unlikely army of beasts and spirits, the two companions must take the lead in an ancient conflict that will carry them through an exotic land all the way to the Gates of Heaven and Hell and a final confrontation with the nefarious Master of Devils.

From Dave Gross, author of *Prince of Wolves*, comes a new fantastical adventure set in the award-winning world of the Pathfinder Roleplaying Game.

*Master of Devils* print edition: $9.99
ISBN: 978-1-60125-357-6

*Master of Devils* ebook edition:
ISBN: 978-1-60125-358-3

# Master
## of
# Devils

## Dave Gross

A warrior haunted by his past, Salim Ghadafar serves as a problem-solver for a church he hates, bound by the goddess of death to hunt down those who would rob her of her due. Such is the case in the desert nation of Thuvia, where a powerful merchant about to achieve eternal youth via a magical elixir is mysteriously murdered and his soul kidnapped. The only clue is a ransom note, offering to trade the merchant's soul for his dose of the fabled potion.

Enter Salim, whose keen mind and contacts throughout the multiverse would make solving this mystery a cinch, if it weren't for the merchant's stubborn daughter who insists on going with him. Together, the two must unravel a web of intrigue that will lead them far from the blistering sands of Thuvia on a grand tour of the Outer Planes, where devils and angels rub shoulders with fey lords and mechanical men, and nothing is as it seems . . .

From noted game designer and author James L. Sutter comes an epic mystery of murder and immortality, set in the award-winning world of the Pathfinder Roleplaying Game.

***Death's Heretic*** print edition: $9.99
ISBN: 978-1-60125-369-9

***Death's Heretic*** ebook edition:
ISBN: 978-1-60125-370-5

# Death's

# Heretic

## James L. Sutter

# PATHFINDER
## TALES

To an experienced thief like Krunzle the Quick, the merchant nation of Druma is full of treasures just waiting to be liberated. Yet when the fast-talking scoundrel gets caught stealing from one of the most powerful prophets of Kalistrade, the only option is to undertake a dangerous mission to recover the merchant-lord's runaway daughter—and the magical artifact she took with her. Armed with an arsenal of decidedly unhelpful magical items and chaperoned by an intelligent snake necklace happy to choke him into submission, Krunzle must venture far from the cities of the capitalist utopia and into a series of adventures that will make him a rich man—or a corpse.

From veteran author Hugh Matthews comes a rollicking tale of captive trolls, dwarven revolutionaries, and serpentine magic, set in the award-winning world of the Pathfinder Roleplaying Game.

***Song of the Serpent*** print edition: $9.99
ISBN: 978-1-60125-388-0

***Song of the Serpent*** ebook edition:
ISBN: 978-1-60125-389-7

# Song of the Serpent

## Hugh Matthews

In the grim nation of Nidal, carefully chosen children are trained to practice dark magic, summoning forth creatures of horror and shadow for the greater glory of the Midnight Lord. Isiem is one such student, a promising young shadowcaster whose budding powers are the envy of his peers. Upon coming of age, he's dispatched on a diplomatic mission to the mountains of Devil's Perch, where he's meant to assist the armies of devil-worshiping Cheliax in clearing out a tribe of monstrous winged humanoids. Yet as the body count rises and Isiem comes face to face with the people he's exterminating, lines begin to blur, and the shadowcaster must ask himself who the real monsters are . . .

From Liane Merciel, critically acclaimed author of *The River King's Road* and *Heaven's Needle*, comes a tale of darkness and redemption set in the award-winning world of the Pathfinder Roleplaying Game.

***Nightglass*** print edition: $9.99
ISBN: 978-1-60125-441-2

***Nightglass*** ebook edition:
ISBN: 978-1-60125-441-2

# Nightglass

## Liane Merciel

You've delved into the Pathfinder campaign setting with Pathfinder Tales novels—now take your adventures even further! *The Inner Sea World Guide* is a full-color, 320-page hardback guide featuring everything you need to know about the exciting world of Pathfinder: overviews of every major nation, religion, race, and adventure location around the Inner Sea, plus a giant poster map! Read it as a travelogue, or use it to flesh out your roleplaying game—it's your world now!

# EXPLORE YOUR WORLD!

**paizo.com**

## NOVELS!

Tired of carting around a bag full of books? Take your ebook reader or smart phone over to **paizo.com** to download all the Pathfinder Tales novels from authors like Dave Gross and *New York Times* best seller Elaine Cunningham in both ePub and PDF formats, thus saving valuable bookshelf space—and 30% off the cover price!

## PATHFINDER'S JOURNALS!

Love the fiction in the Adventure Paths, but don't want to haul six books with you on the subway? Download compiled versions of each fully illustrated journal and read it on whatever device you choose!

## FREE WEB FICTION!

Tired of paying for fiction at all? Drop by **paizo.com** every week for your next installment of free weekly web fiction as Paizo serializes new Pathfinder short stories from your favorite high-profile fantasy authors. Read 'em for free, or download 'em for cheap and read them anytime, anywhere!

## ALL AVAILABLE NOW AT
## PAIZO.COM!